TAMPA BURN

TAMPA BURN

RANDY

WAYNE

WHITE

G. P. PUTNAM'S SONS

NEW YORK

G. P. Putnam's Sons
Publishers Since 1838
a member of
Penguin Group (USA) Inc.
375 Hudson Street
New York, NY 10014

Grateful acknowledgment is made for permission
to quote from the following:

"A Horse with No Name" by Dewey Bunnell © 1971
Warner Bros. Music Limited. Copyright renewed. All rights
for the Western Hemisphere controlled by WB Music Corp.
All rights reserved. Used by permission. Warner Bros.
Publications U.S. Inc., Miami, FL 33014

"Tin Man" by Dewey Bunnell © 1974 WB Music Corp.
Copyright renewed. All rights reserved. Used by permission.
Warner Bros. Publications U.S. Inc., Miami, FL 33014

Library of Congress Cataloging-in-Publication Data

White, Randy Wayne.
Tampa burn / Randy Wayne White.
p.   cm.
ISBN 0-399-15181-8
1. Ford, Doc (Fictitious character)—Fiction.   2. Tampa (Fla.)—Fiction.
3. Marine biologists—Fiction.   4. Florida—Fiction.   I. Title
PS3573.H47473T36   2004   2003069023
813'.54—dc22

Printed in the United States of America
10 9 8 7 6 5 4 3 2 1

This book is printed on acid-free paper. ♾

BOOK DESIGN BY MEIGHAN CAVANAUGH

THIS BOOK IS

FOR NEIL NYREN,

WHO GOT ME

OFF THE BOAT.

———————————

AUTHOR'S NOTE

The islands of Sanibel and Captiva are real, and, I hope, faithfully described, but they are used fictitiously in this novel.

The same is true of certain businesses, marinas, bars, and other places frequented by Doc Ford, Tomlinson, and pals. When you spend as much time cruising around in a boat as I do, it's hard not to mention people whom I've met and like, and find interesting.

In all other respects, however, this novel is a work of fiction. Names, characters, places, and incidents are either the product of the author's imagination or are used fictitiously. Any resemblance to actual persons, living or dead, or to actual events or locales is entirely coincidental.

This book demanded extensive research in several fields, and I am grateful to the experts who took the time to advise me. I'd like to thank Dr. Thaddeus Kostrubala, a brilliant psychopharmacologist, for his friendship, and for his cheerful willingness over the years to provide me with detailed behavioral profiles on some truly nasty fictional characters. Much of the detail in this book regarding shock therapy was provided by Dr. Kostrubala, including his touching recollections of administering the treatments as a resident in training. His e-mails, and our discussions, concerning Praxcedes Lourdes were also immensely helpful.

Captain Tobias Rose of the Tampa Pilots' Association also provided me with great assistance, including detailed information of the responsibilities of port pilots, as well as touring me around Tampa Bay as we plotted Doc Ford's night route.

Long-time carnival operator Darrell Boyd, known as DB, provided invaluable insights into the lives of sideshow operators and the town of Gibsonton, as did Chuck Osak, owner and operator of the Showtime Restaurant.

John Dunn, director of communications at Tampa General Hospital, was generous with his time, as was the staff at the Tampa Burn Center— one of the great medical facilities in the country. Joe Guidry was also a great help.

The tarpon spawning project Doc Ford references is an actual project. It began in the mind of Craig A. Watson, director of Aquaculture Lab at the University of Florida, and the first attempt took place at my home and dock at Pineland, Florida. I'd like to thank Craig, Doug Colle, Jeff Hill, Scott Graves, John Baldwin, and Dan Conklin for allowing me to play a small role. Running home from Boca Grande Pass at night in my skiff during a full-moon eclipse, with scientists and my youngest son, Rogan, aboard—along with a live 100-pound anesthetized tarpon—will never be forgotten. The same is true about the night several unnamed fish guides sunk a police boat.

Something else I'll never forget is the first time I saw America in concert. It was in San Diego. I was on a book signing tour. I seldom go out; avoid crowds like the plague. But being back in Southern California, listening to them nail hit after hit, was one of the truly great nights.

Gerry Beckley and Dewey Bunnell are two of our finest composers. For them to allow Tomlinson to work as a roadie, and for them and Warner Brothers Records also to allow me to use their lyrics in this novel, is a great honor. I would like to thank Dewey, Gerry, Willie Leacox, Michael Woods, Rich Campbell, Pete Leonardo, and Bill Crook for their generous hospitality while on the road. America's road manager, Erin Edwards, deserves special thanks. She is a great and gifted lady.

Also providing valuable aid or information were Tom Taylor, Dr. David Melzer, Major Robert Macomber, Captain Kerry Griner, and Sergeant Jim Brown of the Lee County Sheriff's Department, and Carol Wirth, who contributed information on anesthesiology.

AUTHOR'S NOTE

My close pals Dr. Brian Hummel, Kristin Hummel, Gary Terwilliger, Donna Terwilliger, Bill Spaceman Lee, Genny Amsler, Sue Williams, Roberta Petish, Debbie, Pete, and Maggie Flynn all deserve thanks, as do Rob and Phyllis Wells for letting me hide out and write in the boathouse.

These people all provided valuable guidance and/or information. All errors, exaggerations, omissions, or fictionalizations are entirely the fault, and the responsibility, of the author.

It has become my habit, during the last weeks of work on a novel, to disappear to some remote place so that the common, daily interruptions don't impose. For this book, I chose Anse Chastanet (Ons Chas-ta-nee) on St. Lucia in the Windward Islands. Anse Chastanet is a five-star tropical wilderness resort; six hundred acres of coastal mountain rainforest and beach. In a lifetime spent traveling, I have never stayed at a more beautiful place.

I'd like to thank my new friends there, and hope we meet again soon: Nick Troubetzkoy, a new addition to my list of Mad Russian pals; Karolin Troubetzkoy; Michael and Karyn Allard; Dr. John Wassel; Luci New; Gillian Hurtig; Ike Ononye; and Sharon Brown-Horton.

Finally, I would like to thank dear, dear Debra Jane Objartle White for her kindness, friendship, guidance, and support over many years, and Lee and Rogan White, once again, for helping me finish a book.

Humanity has a limited biological capacity for change, but an unlimited capacity for spiritual change. The only human institution incapable of evolving spiritually is a cemetery.

—S. M. TOMLINSON
One Fathom Above Sea Level

God, why'd you send me down here with a trigger finger and a tallywhacker, if you didn't expect me to use 'em?

—TUCKER GATRELL

CIUDAD DE MASAGUA
REPUBLIC OF MASAGUA
CENTRAL AMERICA
APRIL

Several hours before Praxcedes Lourdes abducted Marion Ford's son, he was sitting in a smoky cantina with his getaway driver, bragging about his new fame.

In Spanish, he said, "'The visitor who burns men alive.' It's what the poor assholes in Nicaragua call me. The peasants. And in Guatemala. The 'night visitor.' They use my name to scare hell out of children. To make brats behave when they disobey. Understand? At a certain age, kids stop believing in Santa Claus. Even some of the saints. But they'll never stop believing in me."

Prax was smoking a Cohiba cigar. He inhaled, perhaps smiling, though it was impossible to tell because he wore a mask made of thin wire mesh. Guerrilla fighters wore identical masks during Nicaragua's Contra war to hide their identities. Eyebrows and pink cheek flush were painted on the outside—a clownish touch.

Lourdes *liked* that.

The man always kept his face covered. When he traveled or went out at night, he wore surgical gauze, the kind that protects from germs. Because of certain Asian viruses, it was no longer an oddity.

At other times, he wore a bandana or a bandage wrap, plus sunglasses—except for now, in this dark bar. The Contra mask, though, was his favorite because he could smoke and drink, and also because it provided him with a face when he looked in the mirror.

The driver watched smoke sieve through the mesh. He averted his eyes.

"Not long after General Balserio paid me to come to Masagua, your people started calling me *Incendiario*. Using only the one word. That's a better name, don't you think? It sounds like a rock singer in the United States. It's got star appeal. *Sexy*—not that you coffee peons know anything about show business."

Prax made a card-fan with his hands, as if creating a marquee above the table, and said with flair, "The great *Incendiario*. Like I'm star of this half-assed revolution, more famous than your generals. Which I am. In the mountains, when people say my name, they *whisper*. You know why?"

The driver was staring at the table, aware the man was not speaking to him; an answer wasn't expected. He was bragging to please himself. Even so, the driver replied, "It's because the people of Masagua are superstitious. They don't believe that you are—" He paused. He'd almost said "human." "That you really exist."

Lourdes leaned forward slightly. His Spanish was unusually accented—French Canadian with a dose of Florida cracker. The accent was amplified when he grew strident, and he became strident now.

"No. It's because Masaguans are stupid turds, like most people. No smarter than a bunch of sheep, including your genius generals. What I had to teach them was, if you kill a couple thousand enemy, nothing changes. But if you scare *two hundred thousand* of them shitless—make their families afraid to leave the house at night—*that's* when a war starts going your way."

The mask seemed to bob oddly. Another smile?

"But not you, Reynaldo. I don't scare you. Do I?"

The driver reached to take a drink of his rum, but stopped because he realized his hand would shake if he lifted the glass. He said, "Why should

I be scared? In my village, we speak well of you. We hear the rumors"—
he shrugged as if unconcerned, but his laughter was strained—"crazy stories. Lies. But we fight for the same cause, so we know you're a good man."

In reply to Lourdes' dubious gesture—the way he tilted his head—the
driver spoke a little too loudly when he added, "It's *true*. We teach our
children that you are a great revolutionary. That they have no reason to
fear you."

"No reason to fear me?"

"As God is my witness! That is what we teach children."

Signaling the waitress for another drink, Praxcedes said softly, "Talking
to God like he's your pal. That's brave. They send a hero like you to drive
the car."

Sarcasm? Reynaldo couldn't be sure.

He was glad when Prax changed the subject, saying, "The boy and his
mother live in what used to be a nunnery, *Claustro la Concepción*. It's across
from the presidential palace, next to the market."

He was back discussing the kidnapping.

Reynaldo nodded. "I know the market. We sold vegetables at the *Mercado
Central* every Sunday. I know the city as well as any man."

"Um-huh. Brave and a genius, too."

That inflection again.

"If you know the city, then you know about the tunnel that connects
the convent with the park."

Reynaldo answered, "A tunnel? A tunnel runs beneath the street from
the convent?"

Praxcedes blew a stream of smoke into the older man's face. "There's
something you don't know? Then keep your mouth closed while I explain."

The driver sat motionless, silent, as Prax told him that the convent,
where the boy lived, had been built in the 1500s. The tunnel had been
built in the 1600s, during the Inquisition.

He said, "The nuns dug the tunnel to save dumb Indios, just like you,
who were sentenced to death. I was telling you about my fame? History,
that's how it started.

"During the Inquisition, Spaniards burned Indians at the stake if they wouldn't turn Catholic. Thousands of them. When the Indios screamed, if they called out to God—like for mercy?—the priests wrote their words on paper. To those assholes, that was a form of *conversion*. It's what they *wanted*.

"I've got a laptop computer with a wireless connection," Lourdes said. "I'm not like the rest of you ignorant hicks. I do research. All the time, I'm learning. The Catholic thing, burning men alive to win a war. When I read it, I thought, *Perfect*. Even though it was years after what the soldiers did to me."

Lourdes stopped and stared at his driver. "You've probably heard all kinds of stories. About why I look the way I look."

Reynaldo dipped his head twice, slowly. *Yes.*

"Later, when we've got the boy, if you don't screw up, maybe I'll tell you what really happened. The details. Would you like that?"

He watched the driver think about it for several seconds.

"Yes."

"Then you'll *understand*. The church, the government, they're both the same. Big shots trying to screw you if they can."

With a whistle of scorn, Prax took a kitchen match, struck it, and leaned close to refire his cigar.

Reynaldo looked long enough to see, floating above the flame, one sleepy gray eye and one lidless blue eye leering out at him from the mask. Prax wore a hooded brown monk's smock that was common in Central America. The hood was back, so Reynaldo could also see the damage that fire had done to the man's scalp. The top of his head appeared to be a human skull over which gray skin had been stretched too tight, torn, then patched with melted wax. There were tufts of blond hair growing out of white bone.

When Prax spoke certain words, he lisped, which suggested that his lips and face were also scarred.

When Reynaldo had first received the assignment to drive *Incendiario*, he'd been excited. He'd hoped, in a perverse way, that he would be among the few to see the great man's face.

After only a few hours, though, Reynaldo regretted his decision to drive the car.

Prax didn't behave like a great man. His Spanish was a Yankee's Spanish, rude and profane. He talked incessantly, always about himself, and he wore his monk's robe and mask like a costume—even his hand gestures were theatrical.

The exaggerated mannerisms reminded him of something; something he'd seen as a child. At a circus, perhaps?

Reynaldo couldn't bring the memory to the front of his brain.

In the light of a flaming match, the driver looked at the eyes inside the mask. He was glad the mask separated them.

IN THE morning darkness, Praxcedes said to Reynaldo, "The entrance to this thing, this tunnel, it's too small. My shoulders won't fit. I can't believe the stupid bastards didn't warn me about this!"

Straining, beginning to sweat, Prax whispered to himself in English, "Jesus Christ, you'd have to be a freak show con-tort to squeeze through this bastard."

"Con-tort" was carnival slang for contortionist. Prax, whose name had once been Jimmie Gauer, remembered lots of slang. As a child, his family had worked carnivals all summer, then wintered in Florida. They had a trailer there in a tiny carney town.

Sweating, now beginning to panic, Lourdes added, "I get down there, what if it caves in? Then what?"

Reynaldo said, "Well, the General will still pay you your money. If we can find you."

Lourdes thought, *You'll suffer for that, smart-ass.*

It was dark in the park at 2:30 A.M., shadows of trees above. Beyond, the lighted windows of the presidential palace created a citreous checkerboard against a loft of mountain peaks and stars.

They'd found the Mayan stele that marked the entrance, then strained together to lift the stone. Now, stuck in the tunnel's mouth, *Incendiario* was balking.

Reynaldo said carefully, "Some people are not comfortable in narrow places. There's a word for it that I can't remember. Shall I crawl through and get the boy while you wait here? There is no shame in being frightened."

Lourdes snapped, "You're calling me a coward? *Screw* you. You'll regret that mouth of yours one day."

He took a deep breath as if about to submerge, exhaled, and forced his body through the entrance.

Underground, he had to pull his elbows against his ribs and wiggle to turn. He rushed to find his micro light. The tunnel was walled with brick, and smelled of mold and water. The floor was brick and broken stone that was etched with Mayan hieroglyphics a thousand years old: grotesque faces; birds clutching snakes.

Crawling, Prax stopped several times, panting, so much sweat dripping off his face that he removed the mask. He felt as if his lungs might implode.

Finally, he saw frail bands of light ahead. Then he came to a grate that moved easily in his big hands. Prax rolled out into a hallway, stood, and fitted the mask, feeling his lungs expand to normal.

The convent was built of stone, ceilings twenty feet high, religious murals on walls that were poorly illuminated by bare bulbs where torches had once burned. He'd been briefed on the convent, what to avoid. They'd told him that the boy's room was on the second floor near the staircase. He'd also been told that the guard normally stationed there would leave after midnight, claiming to be ill.

Even so, Prax moved quietly up the steps. His smock was belted at the waist, hood up. He fished his hand into a pocket and removed a knife. He snapped the blade open, then stopped at the top of the stairs.

To his left was a hallway that ended at a set of wooden doors. The boy's mother, Pilar Fuentes, would be inside, asleep at this hour. A famous lady, and drop-dead gorgeous, too—he'd seen her photo in newspapers. A social hotshit even though she looked pure Mayan, and probably a snob. Even in Central America, the rich always were.

Prax considered paying the snob a quick visit. Was tempted to see for himself if she was as beautiful in the flesh. Or perhaps—this idea flashed behind his eyes—perhaps abduct the boy *and* the mother.

For a moment, that excited him, and he began to think about it; how it might play out.

Why not? He'd soon need a woman. A test subject. Someone to try things with that he'd never been able to pay or force a prostitute to do. Not with his face. Not this old face, anyway.

But a *new* face . . . ?

For years, he'd wondered what it would be like. Now it was happening. Happening because he was making it happen. When he wasn't planning, he was on the internet, researching. Thinking about it so much, that lately it was hard to think about anything else. *Dreamt* about it.

Pilar Fuentes. Yeah. Take the famous beauty. Surprise the society snob in bed. He could abduct her along with the boy, and then . . . and then . . .

But wait . . .

As the idea unraveled, his excitement drained.

It wasn't workable—even though it would be a sweet way to screw over the jerk who was the woman's ex-husband, Jorge Balserio.

Prax despised authority, felt it in his belly, and General Balserio was as arrogant as anyone he'd ever met. The man was his employer—which was another good reason to snatch her, because Balserio still paid him like he was some Indio peon heel, even though the government was *this* close to falling.

Incendiario deserved a fair chunk of the credit for that.

Taking the kid was supposed to be the final straw.

So it was tempting to take her, keep her all for himself.

But sometimes, Prax knew, it just wasn't smart to screw with the locals.

TO THE right of the stairs was a second set of doors. On the doors were tacked clippings from magazines: baseball stars, a map of the moon, and a photograph of a great white shark. The shark was leaping out of the water toward a skin diver perched on the skid of a helicopter.

There was also a plastic sign in Spanish that read, NO GIRLS! TRESPASSERS WILL BE VIOLATED!

The boy's room.

Smart-ass rich punk.

Lourdes wondered how smart-assed the kid would be once his arms and mouth were taped.

He touched the wrought-iron latch. It was locked, which was no surprise. The guard had told them that there was only one key.

"He's methodical," the guard had said. "So organized. He's more like a grown man."

From a pocket, Prax took a miniature blowtorch nozzle and threaded it to a 7-ounce propane tank. Assembled, it was the shape and size of a handgun. He opened the valve, lighted the torch, enjoying it, that *sound,* the pressurized hiss.

He lowered his black glasses and adjusted the flame until it was orange-blue, shaped like a scalpel. Then he moved the flame over the deadbolt, up and down, for less than a minute before the bolt gave way.

Prax pushed the door open and stepped into the boy's room.

It was a large room, with windows that opened onto a courtyard and fountains below. The room was illuminated with bluish light that came from a half-dozen glass aquaria that held coral and fish.

The largest tank was in the center. Clown-colored fish swam among aerator bubbles, while beneath them, what Prax recognized as a moray eel watched open-mouthed, its eyes reptilian. The moray was big, as thick as his wrist.

The boy was in bed beneath the open windows. He appeared as a charcoal shape.

The blowtorch hissing, Prax walked toward the bed, but stopped when he heard the boy ask in Spanish, "Hey—who are you? What's burning?"

It was an adolescent voice, but deep.

Prax had spent lots of private time in front of a mirror. He had the hood pulled over his head, mask fixed, looking just the way he wanted—spooky. He answered, "Shut your fucking mouth. Don't say another word, or I'll set your bed on fire."

That was something he'd learned: Scare them fast. When you take down a mark, shock them quick, let them know who's boss.

But the kid didn't scare easy. He was sitting, rubbing his eyes with his fists. "Hey—*you* get the hell out of my room. If I call the guards, they'll shoot. That's if you're *lucky*."

The boy's self-confidence, his calm, were infuriating.

Prax hissed back, "You little punk, you're leaving with me," as he lifted the torch so that the kid could see his mask. He stood there letting the boy look at him, feeling the boy's eyes and the heat of the flame on his face. Then slowly, very slowly, he pulled the mask down just low enough so that the burn scars on his forehead and his lidless eyes were visible.

He heard the boy's quick intake of breath. Heard the boy whisper, "Jesus Christ, it's . . . You're *real?*"

Prax answered, "Oh, yeah. Every fucking story you've ever heard. I'm real."

Oh, man, he liked that. Loved the timing of it, the kid's reaction, and the way he'd listened, frozen, as Prax spoke his best line, laid out the words just right. Now, readjusting his mask, he motioned with the blow-torch. "Get your clothes on. Do what I say, you won't get hurt. *Move.*"

When the boy didn't budge, he turned, walked across to the aquarium, and plunged the nozzle into the water. A portable torch burns at more than 2,000 degrees Fahrenheit, and within seconds, the fish and large moray began to contort in the super-heated bubbles.

"Stop! Quit it."

"Your voice. Too loud."

"You're *killing* them."

"I'll stop when you move."

"Go to hell. I won't."

Stubborn little son-of-a-bitch.

Looking at the kid, trying to read him, Prax said, "You do what I tell you to do, or . . . my partners are in your mother's room right now. I'll call them, they'll bring her in here, and I'll use this on your mother. How'd you like that? I'll burn her fucking face right off."

"You leave my mother alone!"

That did it. Prax Lourdes could hear it in the boy's voice. From now on, anything he wanted, *anything,* all he had to do was threaten to have some-one harm the woman.

The torch was still in the water. He watch the moray writhe on the bottom. Then the clown-colored fish began to explode into fleshy clouds as their air bladders ruptured.

"Get your clothes on. You'd better hurry."

The boy leaped out of bed and found the reading lamp: Big kid with blond hair, shoulders like they were built from planks, square jaw, and pale eyes. He wore boxer underwear, his abdominal muscles symmetrical.

"I'm hurrying. *Enough.*"

He didn't sound so self-assured now.

Prax lifted the torch from the tank and closed the valve as he watched the boy dress. He was already dreading the trip back through the tunnel, having to squeeze through that darkness.

To take his mind off it, he settled his attention on the boy, concentrating on the boy's face, the way it was constructed. Along with all his internet research on plastic surgery, it was something else he'd been doing lately: studying the facial makeup of other men—particularly young men.

There were interesting, subtle differences.

Staring at the boy, Prax was startled to realize that the kid was handsome; had a face that was nicely proportioned. Maybe even *beautifully* proportioned. Which shouldn't have been a surprise, considering his famous mother.

Jesus, to have that face, his soft skin.

Prax Lourdes was torn.

The most innovative reconstructive surgeon in America was Dr. Valerie Santos. She wasn't like that strung-out Mexican quack he'd been using.

Yeah, Dr. Valerie. That's what the press called her. Cool lady who went by her first name. All those awards, her photo in *People,* and a great web page where someone answered e-mails from potential patients who had questions.

He'd already received several detailed replies.

Fake profiles, that's the way he was playing the internet con. His most ingenious was posing as a teenage South American burn victim who was working on a film script.

Dr. Santos and Prax were destined. He knew it the instant he read about her, because of where she did her magic: Tampa General Burn Unit, right across the bay from the little carney trailer park where he still remembered spending winters as a boy.

Lourdes loved the idea of cornering the big-shot lady doctor, referencing one of her e-mails, then pointing to the kid's face and telling her, "Harvest *that*."

There was something else, however, he'd been coveting: the chance to light the boy's clothes on fire.

What a rush that would be, watching this pretty child run.

ONE

THE morning that Pilar Santana Fuentes arrived at Dinkin's Bay and told me that our son had been kidnapped, I was in waist-deep water, a couple hundred yards down the mangrove shore from my rickety stilt house, wrestling with a sixty-pound tarpon.

I heard a woman's voice calling in Spanish, "Marion? Marion! I thought you were *expecting* me."

She sounded irritated. Demanding. Which didn't fit with my image of who Pilar is, or *was* in terms of her normal behavior, but I let it go.

She'd telephoned from Central America. So, yes, I'd been expecting her. Even so, I was unprepared for the thumping heart and twittering, nervous jolt I got when I saw her. Nervous, because I believed her to be my long-lost love.

I like interesting-looking women, and women who are interesting. I have zero interest in the Hollywood concept of beauty unless humor, character, and intellect are added to the mix. Those are the sexiest of qualities. I try to maintain those standards, all the while understanding that I am not the most attractive of men at first glance. Maybe not even at third or fourth glance.

I like women as people. That is a grounding common denominator.

Pilar undoubtedly has all the feminine qualities that attract males of our species. Her body is so achingly, obviously female that the first time I saw her, I felt an actual sensation of physical pain. At the time, she was married. I suspect I felt pain because I believed that I had no chance of winning her as a lover.

Wrong.

Later, after we became lovers, I felt the same radiating ache at the thought of losing her. I thought I never would.

Wrong again.

Now, seeing her for the first time in years, my reaction was familiar though unexpected, and so was the powerful lancet of pain.

I had my right hand clamped on the tarpon's lower jaw, the fish's body cradled in my left arm. Tomlinson was in the water with me. Tomlinson, my storklike friend with his blond and gray hippie hair braided into samurai shocks. He was shirtless and had one of his old sarongs tied Gandhi-style between his legs, like baggy shorts or diapers.

Wearing his hair like a samurai was his new thing. He'd taken to wearing samurai robes on his boat, too, and around my house when he visited. Something to do with his decision to re-enter this life as "a spiritual warrior."

Whatever that meant.

That was the kind of question I asked only when I had a lot of time—and a lot of his favorite rum on stock, which is El Dorado, a superb but little-known rum from Guyana. Tomlinson had found El Dorado on a recent South American "rum quest" and was never without the stuff.

He was holding a clear plastic water-gun. In the squirt gun, I'd diluted several milligrams of metomidate. Metomidate is a potent, effective tranquilizer. Tomlinson's job was to squirt the mixture through the tarpon's mouth very, very slowly, irrigating its gills until the fish began to show signs of light sedation.

After that, I would steer the tarpon back to my lab and into the big galvanized holding tank I'd stationed there just for this project.

Working with biologists from the University of Florida, we were trying to be the first to spawn and hatch tarpon in captivity. Interesting work.

To get an idea of what a tarpon looks like, imagine a giant, prehistoric herring. With its chromium scales and massive tail, it's one of the world's great game fish. For Florida, the tarpon is a swimming, breathing precious metals industry—pure silver. Same with much of the Caribbean.

Sportsmen travel from around the world just for the chance of a hookup. The fish brings millions of tourism dollars annually into the state.

Yet, few seem to appreciate the animal's economic worth.

Over the last few decades, loss of habitat and deteriorating water quality have impacted the tarpon population. Fishing guides from the islands, Key West to Cedar Key, have been saying for years what we biologists have been slow to prove: Each year, there are fewer fish.

So this was a worthwhile project, entirely the idea of the first-rate scientists at the U-of-F, and I was delighted to play a small role.

When Pilar called to us, Tomlinson looked up briefly, then looked again. He whistled softly, and said to me in a low voice, "Wowie-zowie, she hasn't changed, amigo. She's still easy on the eyes. Even from this distance, I can tell."

He'd met Pilar years ago in Central America. It was not long after the lady had ended our love affair, and before I knew that she was pregnant with our child. I'd been badly wounded when Tomlinson and I were there; nearly killed. The two of them had spent some time together in a makeshift hospital, nursing me.

Or so I heard later—I was delirious most of the time.

Tomlinson took another quick glance. "That sort of woman, you don't often see. It's almost like her body puts off an odor. Pure sex mixed with . . . something, man, *something*. She's different from most people you meet."

His tone had an unusual quality. Did he want me to pursue the subject?

But then he returned his attention to the fish, saying, "We don't want this guy to go through any more trauma than we have to. Can Pilar give us a few minutes? She's in a hurry, I can tell. Ask her if she can wait until we have him in the pen."

I smiled, for a couple of reasons. For one thing, Tomlinson, the unrepentant hipster, was telling me—me, the supposedly competent biologist—the proper way to deal with this fish. Another reason was because I find my various frailties and stupidities just so damn funny.

Which means I have no shortage of things to smile about.

Here I was, a grown man, reacting with all the emotional and intellectual maturity of some love-besotted adolescent. My heart was pounding, my thighs actually felt watery—that's how nervous I was at the prospect of seeing Pilar again face to face.

I didn't want to worry about the tarpon. What I wanted was to dump the fish, run to shore, and take the lady into my arms. I wanted to sit her down and listen to her voice. I wanted to hear why she'd traveled from Masagua to Sanibel Island, Florida, to meet privately with me. What was so important? Why all the secrecy on the phone?

I have been madly, passionately, irresponsibly in love with only one woman in my life. Now here she was.

So that's why I was wearing the wry, silly smile. It was because I knew that I was reacting like a simple, silly-ass teenager. Even when I *was* a teenager, I wasn't the emotional teenage type. Which is why, on a deeper level of awareness, the way I was feeling also tickled at my intellectual gag reflex.

Knock it off, Ford. She's keying a chemical response in the lower region of the brain. Never confuse love with the effects of serotonin.

In a rational world, emotion is an indulgence. Usually, it is an untidy one.

So, as I walked with the tarpon, I tried to establish a different kind of grounding by stepping back and reminding myself what had happened, and how it had happened.

WHEN we'd had our affair, Pilar was married to a political aristocrat and egomaniacal thug named Balserio. I'd been in Masagua working as a biologist under the auspices of the American embassy. Actually, I was doing deep-cover intelligence assignments, working with an Aussie SAS partner. He was a crazed surfer/oceanographer named Thackery.

Thackery had infiltrated some ultra-left-wing environmental group that was helping to finance the rebels. It was through him that I met Pilar in a remote Pacific village, where she was setting up a trade school for teens.

The physical attraction I felt caused me physically to shake when I was near her. The emotional attraction was just as strong. I'd never felt anything like it before or since.

For a time, I think she may have felt the same. At least, she behaved as if she did.

It was an impossible situation that became untenable when Pilar became pregnant with our son.

Not that I knew. She never told me until long after I'd fled the country, escaping from her bedroom via some long-forgotten tunnel that ran from a Masaguan convent into a park. I left with a bounty on my head.

Her husband swore he'd have me killed—or do the job himself. That's all she told me.

Several months later, when I read that he'd been assassinated, I was one of many who did not mourn. Anyone who did mourn for Jorge Balserio wasted his tears.

But Balserio resurfaced, alive and well, a year later. He'd staged his own death to give himself an opportunity to escape his many enemies.

Pilar contacted me the moment she heard. "You can never come back here," she told me. "He still despises you."

His soon-to-be ex-wife had given birth to a chubby baby boy. A *blond, blue-eyed* baby boy.

Aside from Thackery, the crazy surfer, I was the only gringo around. And I was the one who'd had an affair with Pilar.

Which is all the Latin general needed to know.

SQUIRTING a stream of fluid into the fish's mouth, Tomlinson asked, "What are you watching for? How can you tell the drug's kicking in?"

I still had the tarpon cradled in my arms, feeling the slickness of it, smelling the good, sweet tarpon odor that is unique to the fish.

I answered, "I'm watching its gills. The color. But more than that, too.

In the first stages of sedation, there's a slight loss of reactivity to external stimuli. And a decrease in the opercula rate."

Tomlinson touched his finger to the side of the fish's head. "The operculum is the gill covering, right?"

"Yep. That's what I'm doing now, counting how many times the gills are beating per minute. In deep sedation, there's a total loss of reactivity, even equilibrium—which we want to avoid. We want something in between."

Tomlinson said, "Real-l-l-ly. That sounds very interesting, though, man. Very heavy. A complete loss of reactivity. What's it called, metomidate? I may try a few hits of this stuff myself. Take a couple of squirts down the ol' hatch."

Then he added quickly, "But strictly as an experiment, of course. Nothing recreational, because I know you wouldn't be cool with that. I am a social scientist, don't forget."

Looking from the fish to Pilar, who was still standing on the shoreline, I said, "Don't even joke about it. Metomidate—if it's anything like a sedative we use called quinaldine—can cause corneal damage in fish *and* people. Which is why we need to get this right. So no more screwing around, O.K.?"

After another minute or two, I could feel the fish begin to go limp in my arms, its big, truncated tail now fanning the water like a slow, slow metronome.

"He's ready," I said. "Let's walk him to the tank and see how he reacts."

"It's what you expected so far? The reaction?"

I told him so far, yes. But reminded him that this was just a trial run. Which is why I was using a male tarpon instead of a female. I didn't want to risk attempting to anesthetize a female until I knew for certain how much of the drug was needed, and how a sedated tarpon would react if confined in a holding tank for an hour or more. A sexually mature female can produce more than twelve million eggs in a single spawning season. If I screwed up and killed a fish, I didn't want it to be a member of the brood stock.

A valid point Darwin didn't make but could have made: In most dimorphic species, males are interchangeable, and so expendable. Perhaps that's why only primate males seem to inherit the war gene.

As I waded toward the marina, steering the tarpon along, I called to Pilar, "I'll meet you at the house. The boardwalk's to your left through the mangroves. Doors are open, there's mosquito spray on the railing, and there're drinks in the fridge. So make yourself at home."

Because I spoke to her in English, she replied in English. It was lightly accented, her tone more formal because the language was less familiar. "I've always been interested to see how a man like you lives, Marion. It's been a long time."

Emotional indulgence or not, silly or not, that made my heart pound even harder.

NOT all fish have scales, but all fish produce slime—a glyco-protein called mucin, actually—and the mucin produced by tarpon has all the adhesive charm of super glue mixed with axle grease.

I'd been wrestling with the fish. Tomlinson had not. So, while he played host inside, I stood outside, showering, sluicing off the slime and mud and salt. The southwest coast of Florida had been having some spectacular lightning squalls during our tropical-bright afternoons. So the rainwater pouring out of the cistern was fresh and warm.

Florida has two seasons—the winter dry and the summer wet. It was a Tuesday, the sixth of May, the very front edge of the rainy. So I lathered and rinsed over and over, using all the water I wanted. It was an extravagance not to be enjoyed come fall.

As I washed, my brain bounced back and forth from topic to topic. I seldom have trouble concentrating. Just the opposite. Friends accuse me of tunnel vision. Of being hermitlike in my work habits to the point of excluding the realities—and the conveniences—of a modern world.

Things *they* see as conveniences, anyway. Such as television, and VCRs. Add to the list: cellular phones, shopping memberships, Palm Pilots, DVDs, internet dating services, all varieties of cable and satellite interconnectings, and magic pills that cure ancient ills.

I was having trouble focusing now, though. My attention kept shifting from the sedated tarpon to Pilar. The tarpon was in its tank on the bottom deck of my house, which is built on stilts in the shallow water of Dinkin's Bay. Before my shower, midway through it, and while I was still drying off, I jogged down the steps, towel around hips, to reconfirm that the fish was still holding itself upright, gills working slowly but steadily in its metomidate-laced pen.

More than once, I also paused to listen to the bell tones of Pilar's voice and occasional laughter coming from inside. An individual's voice is as distinctive as a pheromone signature. It caused me to think of the way it had been with her. The emotional and physical intimacy. The way it had been when we were alone, clothed or naked, our bodies and our minds coupled.

In her e-mail, and then on the phone, she hadn't told me what she wanted to discuss. Just that it was personal and important.

Because she'd assured me it had nothing to do with our son, I didn't feel any great anxiety. Anticipation—that better describes it.

As I showered, I tried not to admit to myself what it was that I secretly hoped, because, once again, it was silly and out of character. Still, the feelings were there. Truth was, I hoped that she'd come to tell me that she wanted to give us a try. That she was tired of living without the father of her son, and there was no longer any reason for us to be apart.

Which generated in me a nagging guilt. Guilt because I was now in a full-time relationship with a great lady by the name of Dewey Nye. More than just a relationship, really. It's the closest I've come to what Tomlinson calls "instinctual testicular disobedience."

By that, he means domestication, plus sexual exclusivity—a combination he has successfully avoided over the years.

Dewey and I'd been splitting our nights between my stilt house and her home on Captiva Island—a sacrifice on her part. I have an outdoor shower and a propane cooking stove. In her designer home, she has a bathtub the size of a swimming pool and a gourmet kitchen.

Even so, I think she was enjoying the change. I was, too—a surprise to many, including me. But true.

Every morning, I'd make breakfast before sending her off to her new job teaching golf and tennis at South Seas Plantation, a classy Captiva resort.

In the afternoons, we'd work out, then take turns cooking dinner. We'd even discussed opening a joint bank account to pay household expenses.

Something else that I had accepted with surprising calm: The lady had hinted more than once that she'd give marriage serious consideration if asked, because she wanted to start a family before she hit her late thirties.

"If I can just get enough beer into a certain thick-head, half-blind nerd to get him to pop the question," she once whispered in my ear.

So, yes. I was in more than just a relationship. I had a partner and a mate. A spectacular one, at that. Infidelity has as much to do with the brain as the body, so my guilt was not misplaced.

Tomlinson has pointed out on more than one occasion that I maintain such tight control over my emotions that it has stunted me spiritually— not that I much care about spirituality.

I knew now, though, how wrong he was. When it came to Pilar, I seemed to have no control at all.

"MARION. You look good. Healthy. But you've lost weight. Too much."

I was walking toward her as she spoke, arms outstretched, but she surprised me by giving me the briefest of hugs and pulling away. Then she seemed to study me for a moment before adding, "It's been so long since I've seen you, I realize that maybe I'd always imagined it. Our son. That I could see him so clearly in your face."

There may have been a touch of nostalgia in her voice. But there also seemed to be an undertone of cool reserve. Or was I imagining it?

Even so, I didn't trust myself to speak. I felt too big and clumsy and inarticulate to have someone like her even briefly in my arms. Like I might stumble, fall, and break one of her ribs or something.

I said, "I've been working out a lot. Swimming and running," and realized, as I spoke, what a stupid, inane thing to say after so much time apart.

I tried to rally. "You remember Tomlinson? He's the friend who was with me in Central America when I got the concussion."

Idiotic. Of course she remembered. They'd not only spent a couple of days together, they'd been here the last twenty minutes talking while I showered.

Pilar seemed not to notice what a bumbling fool I'd become. She stepped farther away from me, as if requiring distance, her eyes a liquid sheen; eyes that seemed aloof and wise and penetrating.

Her clothing was crisp; her hammered silver bracelet and jade necklace simple, elegant. She wore beige slacks and a white blouse. The starched collar provided a classic pedestal for her classic face. Pilar's is the face of the pure Indio, though she is not pure Indian. It is the face of royalty you see carved into the pyramid walls and stone stelae of Mexico, Guatemala, and Peru. High cheeks, black eyes, and black Mayan hair. But her hair was cut and styled so that she looked like a successful, modern business executive. Or a high-level politician—which she'd once been.

In the time I knew her, she'd always worn her combed hair long. It had added a softness to her appearance that wasn't now evident.

Except for some additional wrinkles at the corners of her eyes, though, and delicate sun lines on her forehead, she hadn't otherwise changed. She stood there looking up into my face, not smiling. She seemed a stranger. A person whom I'd once known, but no longer knew.

"Remember when I used to call you Señor Feo? Mister Ugly. That was before him."

I said, "Before Lake."

Meaning our son, Marino Laken Fuentes. It was a name that, like the boy's mother, had both Spanish and Mayan roots.

"I'm wondering if he's grown at all to look like you. A little, perhaps, but not a lot. The eyes, maybe. The jaw?" She seemed to be thinking about it, comparing.

"So now you think I'm handsome, I suppose." I grinned, hoping to make her laugh.

She didn't.

"He's such a fine young man. There's nothing ugly in goodness, and he's a good person. Kind and decent. The same qualities I saw in you when we first met."

I wondered if she'd switched tense accidentally, or if it was because she no longer believed that I possessed those qualities.

I asked, "Is he with you? I'd love to see him."

She shook her head quickly and then, for no apparent reason, rushed to me on tiptoes and squeezed my arm briefly. It was spontaneous, emotional—an involuntary action linked to the boy we'd made together. The temptation was to hold her there, to kiss her, and then carry her off to some private place.

I might have tried, but just as quickly, she backed away and put her face in her hands. It took me a moment to realize that she was crying.

Tomlinson cleared his throat—a rare moment of awkwardness for a man who is at home in the most bizarre situations—and said, "Wish I could stick around, but I've got to get back to my . . . to my gardening."

Staring dumbly at Pilar—I've never known how to behave when a woman begins to cry—I asked him, "Gardening? What're you talking about? You live on a sailboat, for God's sake."

His expression told me, *I'm just trying to help,* which I should have realized.

As I finally moved to put my hands on Pilar's shoulders, I listened to him use words to blanket the sound of her crying. He was using them to provide her with a private space. "Hey, man, I've been growing chili peppers for years, you know that. Plus, I've been planting some very special flora on islands near here. The magic herb, if you *must* know, though it's always been my impression mum's the word, far as you're concerned."

Seeming to speak to Pilar, he added, "I've been target-farming deserted islands, the few with enough high ground to cultivate. Small Indian shell middens are the best. They seem to add a spiritual kick to my special crop."

Pilar had allowed me to hold her for a moment, but now she disentangled herself, crossed the room, and found a tissue in her purse. "I'm sorry. It's not like me to lose control like that. Marion will tell you."

Not quite true. I'd seen her explode into rages a couple of times. Not often, but her temper could get out of control. And in bed, she had zero control—happily. Her abandon was unforgettable. That was especially true when she'd been through situations of intense stress. Get a couple of glasses of wine in Pilar, and sex became a vent without taboo. With some women, sex is more of a physical event than a coupling. Pilar was one of those.

Tomlinson replied, "Doc can tell you just as honestly that I am almost never in control. So rest easy. You're among friends."

That earned a tiny smile. "You really weren't talking about hot peppers, were you? *Ajís,* that's what they're called in my language."

Tomlinson nodded at her perceptiveness. "No, my dear, I am not talking about peppers. I think you know exactly what I'm talking about. One of the nights we were together in Central America, the night Doc was feverish, still unconscious. Didn't we—?" He hesitated, unsure if he should continue.

Pilar wasn't uncomfortable with the subject. "Yes. Yes, we did. It was very relaxing, and we laughed."

Tomlinson smiled, tugging at his hair, his expression saying, *I thought so.* "If you're still interested, I have plenty of flora to share. Our friend here does not partake."

I was surprised, even shocked, when she replied, "I know. In the years I knew him, I never even offered."

My Pilar?

He said, "You gotta love the big palooka anyway, though, huh?" The two of them simpatico, him standing shirtless at my galley stove in his diaper-style sarong, stork legs sticking out, his skeletal frame visible beneath black sailor's skin, muscle and tendons traced with veins, one shock of samurai hair arcing unicornlike from the top of his head.

"The moment we started talking," he continued, "I knew that, spiritually, you were an interesting soul. You got lots of stuff going on inside there, don't you, my dear lady?"

He eyed her intensely for a moment. I found his tone and manner unusual when he added, "Some people live at the top of a whole pyramid of *shishos.* I had an instant . . . *awareness* of who you are, what you are. Same the first time we met in Masagua. You've got a complicated chemistry going on. You're what we in the mojo business call a *complicated* spirit. Still evolving."

She said slowly, "I have the same strong feeling about you, Tomlinson."

I didn't interpret what he said as much of a compliment. Even so, he placed his hands together palm-to-palm in front of his face, and bowed slightly at the waist.

Her expression focused, she turned to me. "Marion, do you trust this man?"

"Are you serious?"

"Yes. It's important."

"I've known him for a long time. I trust him with anything but my female friends. When he's sober, anyway."

"I can tell you're joking."

I was joking. Kind of.

I listened to her say, "I *like* him. There's a quality about him. I get a sense of goodness and strength. I remember how kind he was to you when you were in the jungle, so badly injured."

Turning her attention once again to Tomlinson, she added, "I made a decision while we were talking. It surprised me. I didn't expect it to happen. I came here to tell Marion something important. I need his help. Perhaps you can help, too."

Tomlinson said, "I'm trying to imagine how any man on earth could refuse to do anything you asked. Seriously—has anyone ever tried?"

Again this was said with an odd, insightful tone.

Pilar didn't smile when she answered, "You may regret agreeing before you've heard what it is I'm asking. Let me tell you about it first. Then decide."

Tomlinson said, "O.K., I'll listen. But I already know what my answer's going to be."

TWO

PILAR said, "They've taken our son, Marion. He's been kidnapped."

Her words seemed to bang around, echoing inside my auditory canal. I had to wait for a moment until my brain translated the noise.

"*Kidnapped.* When?"

"Five days ago. Slightly less."

"*Who?* Who did it?'

"Balserio."

As Tomlinson said, "Oh God," I banged my fist on my thigh and said, "Why didn't you tell me right away? On the phone."

"I'll explain why. Now's not the time to second-guess my decisions. Please."

I said, "Wherever he is, we'll find him. Don't worry. *I'll* find him." My head snapped around. "Do you think they hurt him? Do you have any information at all?"

I watched her battle to hold the tears in check. "That's the worst. I think they may *have* hurt him, but I don't know how badly. Laken is so strong-willed. In his room, there was a struggle. Some furniture was broken. Some glass. Plus"—she paused for another moment—"plus, when you hear about the man who took him. Who did the kidnapping. He's . . . he's horrible. Sick. A monster. Everyone in Masagua is afraid of him."

When I began to press for details—Who was the man? Had federal investigators been assigned to the case?—she shushed me with a warning finger. "I'll explain it all. We don't have enough time to waste it by rushing."

From her reaction, though, I got the strong impression that it disturbed her to linger on the subject of Lake's abductor. It scared me, her reaction. Gave me a chill.

The three of us were outside, sitting in cane-backed bar stools on the northeastern side of my porch. It's the portion of porch that hangs over my shark pen and looks out over the bay.

On the teak table between Pilar and myself were Ball jars filled with iced tea. Tomlinson held a tumbler of dark Guyana rum cloaked in his big bony hands, as if trying to warm it. Unseen below us, beneath dark water, two bull sharks and a smaller, 70-pound hammerhead shark circled. Like ocean currents, sharks are always moving.

It was a little before eight P.M. on a Tuesday night so humid that the air had a steam-bath weight. I could feel water molecules settling upon my skin. It was ten minutes or so until sunset, and a couple hours past low tide, so the tidal lake that is Dinkin's Bay was refilling.

I rose from my chair and began to pace.

Pilar said, "It happened Wednesday night or early Thursday morning. We live in a place you'll remember—the *Claustro la Concepción*. The old nunnery right across from the presidential palace."

Yes, I remembered. Stone walls, high ceilings, lots of wood and shadow. It smelled of canvas and heavy furniture, like a museum. In the city, it had been the only safe meeting place for Pilar and me, our one refuge. A convent where lovers rendezvoused. Ironic.

"Safety," she said. "That's why Laken and I lived there. When I was involved with the government, Masagua had a period of stability. Brief stability—*I'm* not taking credit, understand. The first in its history, but that's changed. It's become a political nightmare again."

From news reports on my shortwave radio, that was true. I knew generalities, not the details.

Masagua is the smallest country in Central America. It's on the Pacific Coast, between Costa Rica and Nicaragua. It's made up of rural islands, mountains, active volcanoes, and rainforest. It's also the poorest country in the region. Unemployment and infant mortality rates are high, the median income low.

Nothing catalyzes political unrest like a failed economy. I knew there were two rebel armies vying to take control. Jorge Balserio was the head of the most powerful rebel force—the F.L.N., or National Liberation Front. I'd heard he'd formed a government in exile based somewhere in Florida. Miami, probably.

The fact that he'd faked his assassination—killing some of his own men in the process—just to save his own skin had apparently been forgotten.

"Our rooms," Pilar said, "are on the second floor of the convent. Laken's room is down the hall from mine. Because I still work as a government consultant, the military provides armed guards. See? I thought we were safe."

I interrupted. "Is General Rivera still the head of the military?"

Juan Rivera was an old political enemy but also my old friend. He's a baseball freak—a left-handed pitcher who carried his fantasy of playing pro ball into middle age. Picture Fidel Castro: the fatigues, the beard, but bigger and without the psychosis.

"No, the general's been gone for more than a year. After he lost his command, he disappeared—to avoid a firing squad, some say. Which was a terrible loss for me. Juan was one of the few people in the government I could still trust.

"That's something you need to know. Our government's close to collapse. There are so many traitors and rebel insiders now, there's almost no one—I'm not exaggerating—*no one* that I can speak to in confidence. I trusted Juan, but almost no one else. No longer. That's why I couldn't speak openly on the telephone.

"The armed guards I mentioned? I thought our son's personal guard, Gilberto, was devoted. But the night of the kidnapping, Gilberto went home, saying he was sick. I've been told he's joined the rebels."

Because I hoped it would nudge her into telling us more about the kidnapper, I asked, "What makes you think Balserio's involved?"

"Because they delivered a video and he's mentioned in a way that implicates him. I brought it so you can see for yourself. The man who abducted Laken"—she stopped, visibly pained—"I can't call him a man. I *won't.* Jorge Balserio, he's responsible for what's happened, and he'll burn in hell for what he's done. Bringing that terrible person into Masagua."

It took Tomlinson's gentle questioning to get the story out of her. Less than three years before, Balserio's rebel army had been so ineffective that it had become the butt of jokes. No respect from the general population meant no support. Desperate for power, Balserio had taken desperate military risks—one was a stab at psychological warfare.

Using political connections and bribes, he bought the freedom of a hundred or so of the most dangerous criminals in Nicaragua and Colombia. In exchange for their freedom and other perks, the criminals agreed to fight for Balserio as mercenaries.

I was explaining to Tomlinson that such bartering wasn't uncommon among guerrilla armies, when Pilar interrupted. "Letting men out of prison, that's one thing. I've heard of that. But Jorge, he took inmates from asylums, too. *Insane* asylums. And animals who *should* have been in insane asylums. He wanted the sickest kind of men. Men who'd do things so brutal that people would support him out of fear.

"It worked," she added. "He's winning the war. People are afraid to leave their homes at night. They're flying his flag, and they'll vote for his party because they don't want one of his monsters to come knocking on their door."

I clubbed my thigh with my fist again as I listened to her describe how frantic she'd been when she found the door to the boy's room forced open, his bed empty, plus this odd discovery: All the fish in his main aquarium were dead.

I said, "Dead? How?"

She shrugged. "It was as if they'd exploded."

That made no sense. My brain started to consider the possibilities, but then swung back to task. I had to ask again, "What makes you think they hurt Lake?"

Pilar had brought a simple straw purse. It was the type they sell in the open markets of Central America, and that are used by peasant women. From the purse she took a CD.

"Judge for yourself. On Thursday morning, a brown paper package was found outside the compound gate. It makes me nauseous to watch it. Do you have a computer that plays DVDs?"

I didn't, but Tomlinson did.

"My laptop's in the marina office," he said. "I'll be right back."

ASIDE from exchanging e-mail photos, I hadn't seen my son in nearly four years. Now here he was on a computer screen, his pale eyes staring out into mine, looking so lost and alone that his fear seemed directly proportional to the dread I now felt.

He was lying on a bare mattress in a poorly lighted room. They'd used duct tape. His wrists and mouth were taped, and a section of rope tied around his waist suggested they'd used it to pull him along, leading him to this dingy-looking place.

There was a window, Venetian blinds drawn, pale light leaking through, and a floor lamp. A moth was beating itself against the lamp's nicotine shade. It could have been a cheap motel. It could have been a cabin in the woods.

The video began with a close-up of the boy's face, his eyes blinking into the lens. There is something heartbreakingly vulnerable about people who have been bound and gagged. The physical debasement is implicit. It is something that might be done to animals before they are thrown over the hoods of hunting vehicles.

Looking at my son's face, I wondered how long he would be scarred by this violation. I wondered if he would live long enough to suffer through it and heal.

My son.

Those two words had once seemed a foreign combination. But I'd come to like the sound.

Maybe we're all trapped, to a degree, by our own self-image. I'm an anti-gizmo snob. I'd once had internet service because I'd needed it for research, but canceled it when I was done. Bringing another computer into the lab had taken some convoluted rationalizing.

Tomlinson hadn't helped matters when he told me, "Buy it, man. Hell, I just got a cellular phone *and* a beeper. So my Zen students—when they're panicked, or in trouble with the cops—I'm just ten digits away. I'm thinking about getting one of those infrared laser pointers, too. From my boat, I can screw with the guides at night. Hell, I'm a Buddhist monk, but I've come to the conclusion we're all destined to be microchip whores."

I bought the desk PC anyway, and so it was through the internet that I got to know Lake. In the last year or so, we'd been e-mailing almost daily. Sometimes we wrote in Spanish, sometimes in English. The early letters had been strained, but they'd gotten to be friendly and often funny. They'd certainly become far more familiar. He'd started out addressing me as "Father," then as "Dad" when he wrote in English. He seemed most comfortable, though, calling me "Doc"—two friendly equals exchanging thoughts and news—and that's the way it had stayed.

Fact was, I'd been fretting about why I hadn't heard from him in nearly a week.

Now I knew.

He was a smart kid; loved natural history. He knew his birds, reptiles, and plants. He asked a lot of questions about my work in the marine sciences. Lately, he'd been setting up several of his own saltwater aquaria. I'd been helping.

I saved his letters. Sometimes, alone at night, I'd reread my favorites.

Science is its own language. Lake already knew that. Science was the language we shared.

So credit the internet for changing the way I felt about my boy. He went from being the child I'd fathered, to an individual. He became the articulate young man whose sense of humor and intellect exceeded my own. I began to think of him not just as our son, but as *my* son. Laken Fuentes—the name "Laken" taken from some obscure Mayan legend. He didn't seem to mind when I shortened the name to Lake.

I liked that. People who get pissy about their names being shortened make me uneasy.

MY house is actually two small wooden houses built under a single tin roof. The houses are separated by a breezeway, or what used to be called a "dog trot."

I live in one of the houses. The other is a small but well-equipped laboratory from which I run my company, Sanibel Biological Supply. Collecting marine specimens to sell to schools and research labs around the country is not a booming enterprise, but it's what I do, and I do it to the best of my abilities.

We were in the lab now. In the center of the room, I've installed a university-style science work station: an island of oaken drawers and cupboards beneath a black epoxy table, complete with a sink, faucets, electrical outlets, and double gas cocks for attaching Bunsen burners.

We were standing at the work station. Tomlinson's white Apple laptop was open before us. To my right, beneath the east windows, on a similar table, was a row of working aquaria, octopi and fish therein. There were additional glass aquaria above on shelves.

To my left, along the east wall near the door, were more tanks filled with fish and crabs and eels. My lab always smells of fish, formaldehyde, disinfectant, books, old planking, and barnacles that grow at water level on pilings below the pine slab flooring.

Tomlinson touched the computer's Play button. As the DVD began to spin, aerators charged the air with ozone and provided a pleasant, bubbling backdrop for a video that was anything but pleasant.

When Lake's face filled the screen, mouth taped, I felt Pilar place her hand on my arm for support. Or perhaps to support me. It was the first time I'd felt any emotional or physical connection from her since her arrival.

At first, the audio was garbled. But then, off camera, I heard a man's smoky voice say in Spanish, "Grunt so that your mother can hear you. One grunt for yes, two for no. Have we hurt you?"

The man had a distinctive lisp. I also noted that he had an equally unusual accent. The dominant inflection was the cracker-American that is poor white Southern. But there was something else mixed in there, too. French? Close but not quite right.

The man waited before he said again, "Make some noise, kid. Have we hurt you?"

The tone was threatening. Even so, there was another long pause before the boy grunted twice. *No.*

Pilar whispered, "I know him too well to believe that. He's injured. They've done something to him."

The man asked, "Have we treated you all right?"

Once again, the long hesitation said more than the boy's single grunt. *Yes.*

During that space of silence, the cry of a bird could be heard from outside. It was a muted, two-toned whistle.

The man: "Do you think we'll kill you if your mother doesn't cooperate?"

This time, the boy grunted instantly. *Yes.*

Now the shot widened so that much of the room was visible. I could see that Lake was barefooted and wore blue jeans without a belt—he'd dressed in a hurry. I pressed my glasses to my face and leaned closer, trying to focus on detail.

There appeared to be a raised ribbon of welt that ran the length of the boy's right forearm. It might have been a burn were it not so narrow. Flames are seldom projected like water from a hose or, say, from a Bunsen burner. Something else I noticed: His feet seemed to be stained with something. Blood?

Possibly.

He wore a dark blue T-shirt, only a portion of an insignia visible: An M and a T overlaid.

The boy was a Minnesota Twins fan. He liked the Cubs, the Red Sox, and the Mets, too. Some combination.

That'd earned him an internet introduction to Tomlinson, which is why they were now e-mail pals, too.

I remembered Lake writing to explain. He liked the Twins because they had one of the lowest payrolls in baseball, but still produced winning teams. He liked the Cubs, the Mets, and the Red Sox because they were perennial underachievers, plus the brilliant and quirky Bill "Spaceman" Lee had pitched for the Sox. Tomlinson loved him for that.

An advocate of the underdog. It was a characteristic I credited to his mother.

As the shot widened, the camera jolted, then the aperture became fixed. A person then moved into the frame—a large man who was oddly dressed, I realized.

When he appeared, Pilar's fingers squeezed my arm.

At first, the man's face wasn't visible because he wore the kind of hooded cloak that I associate with cloistered monks. The hood was pulled over his head.

Also, he was holding a *Miami Herald* up to the camera. It was the Latin American edition, printed in Spanish. He held the paper long enough so the day and the date could be read. He had a big Caucasian left hand, and hairless fingers that were thick and badly burn-scarred. I noticed that he didn't wear a wristwatch.

The paper had been published on Thursday, five days before.

I wasn't prepared for what I saw when the man lowered the paper.

Perhaps I should have been. There are certain varieties of bank robbers, kidnappers, and other career criminals who use disguise as an excuse for wearing bizarre clothing. It's a kind of fetish. Part of the psychological profile.

This guy was certainly dressed bizarrely. He wore black sunglasses over a mask that had painted eyebrows and rouged cheeks. The mask may have been more than a fetish, though, because there was enough of his forehead showing to see that, like his hand, his face had been scarred by fire. A tuft of blond hair protruded from a waxen area of skull that was visible from within the cloak.

The mask keyed some long-gone memory. Where had I seen one similar? The Maya of Central America are big on masks. They use them in all kinds of festivals and ceremonies. In the States, it's Halloween only. In Maya country, though, masks are part of the culture.

Guatemala?

No...

Then I remembered. It was during the civil war in Nicaragua. I'd been traveling the country doing marine research, but I was also imbedded, doing government service.

That's where I'd seen a similar mask. Several, actually. Members of guerrilla death squads wore them to hide their identities. The masks were light, made of wire mesh, like mosquito screening, so they were cool in the jungle heat. I'd been told they were modeled after some old Mayan mask that had been used in sacrificial ceremonies.

The Indios relish their blood traditions.

The cosmetic touches—painted eyebrows, pink cheeks—seemed satirically feminine.

I watched the mask move on the man's face as he said, "The kid can't really talk right now, so I'll have to talk for him. That's because he's all tied up!" Then the three of us listened to him make an oddly high-pitched clucking sound that became a staccato barking—laughter.

It could have been the parody of some inane comic, but the tactlessness wasn't intentional. Even in Spanish, there was a clumsy white-trash stupidity about the way he hammered the punch line.

He's all tied up!

It was a bully's joke, a bully's laughter.

I wanted to jump through the screen, grab him by the throat, and squeeze until his eyes bulged. People who've been scarred or disfigured are usually eager to spare others pain because they've endured the worst that life and human nature have to offer.

Not this one. His scars seemed tailored to his personality. He seemed right at home with a face that he preferred to keep hidden.

Still chuckling, he said, "So, hello, hello, hello, to the beautiful and famous Pilar Fuentes Balserio. I've got a message for you from your husband, Jorge. When I lead him back to the presidential palace, me and the General and the rest of his army expect you to be in the bedroom, with your clothes off, waiting to . . ."

He then launched into a sexually graphic tirade so angry that it was more like an assault, a scenario with details designed to shock.

After enduring less than a minute, Tomlinson said, "My Spanish isn't the best, but this guy's a freak, man. A serious wack job."

I said, *"Listen,"* as Masked Man continued the rant. It went on for another half-minute before his mood seemed to darken and he abruptly shifted subjects.

"But enough about me!" he said—that heavy comedic punch again. "The point is, we've got your kid. He's alive. If you want him to stay alive, and if you want to get him back, you're going to do exactly what we tell you to do. If you don't, the General says I can have him. *Me.* That's an honor. For *you,* I mean. So here's what we want you to do—"

Not looking away from the screen, I asked Pilar, "Should I get some paper? Or have you already made a transcript?"

She was no longer touching my arm. She had, in fact, moved closer to Tomlinson. "I have every word on paper, even the sick parts. There's only about another minute left. Watch first, then read the transcript."

The demands he made seemed to be the first of a long list. They weren't random. They'd been thought out. He knew exactly what he wanted—or what he was supposed to say. One of those demands was that Pilar go as soon as she possibly could to Miami, where, he said, she would receive further instructions.

Balserio's government-in-exile was in Florida, I remembered.

When the video ended, I said to Tomlinson, "There are parts of this I'd like to see again. Can you use the computer to freeze-frame and zoom in?"

Tomlinson was tugging at his samurai horn nervously. "You name it. Modern times, man. Whatever you want."

THREE

ALONG with the DVD, Pilar told us, the package also contained an Iridium satellite phone receiver. The kidnappers could contact her, but it couldn't be used to call out.

Though I didn't mention it, I knew that the phone could probably also be used as a tracking device. Global Positioning System trackers are neither expensive nor difficult to acquire. For a few hundred bucks, a suspicious hubby or wife can hide a GPS transmitter in the family car and follow every movement.

As she told us about the phone, I read the transcript once again, reviewing the list of demands made by Masked Man:

She had to leave for Miami within forty-eight hours. She couldn't contact law enforcement. If she'd already contacted police, she must now stop cooperating. Along with the phone, she was to either carry a portable computer or find a way to check her e-mail at least twice a day while traveling.

Masked Man said they would contact her via satellite phone or internet and tell her how next to proceed. As long as she continued to cooperate, they would continue to provide proof that Laken was alive.

In the video, he used the royal "we." Excessively, it seemed.

"Before you leave for Miami," he said, "collect half a million dollars in cash, U.S. Don't ask us how. The Masaguan treasury has plenty. You've got pull and connections. Find a way. Pack it in the kind of briefcase photographers use to protect their stuff. The kind that seals tight without locking. Then have the briefcase delivered by diplomatic pouch to the Masaguan consul general's office in Miami no later than Wednesday morning. Don't wire the money, don't transfer it from a foreign bank. Do it just the way we say.

"Once you're in the States, we'll call and tell you when to go to the consul general's office and get it. Don't do it until we tell you. Or check your e-mail. Check it a lot. The half-million is for starters. Just to show us you really care about your kid. We'll want more than that. This is all about politics. Political change. Jobs and better pay. Schools, health care, all the standard stuff. And quit fucking over the Indios"—the staccato laughter again—"I bet you Spaniard bastards regret that you ever burned a single Indian at the stake *now*. Especially since they let yours truly back out on the street. Paybacks are a bitch, huh?"

That's how the video ended. With Masked Man walking toward the camera, his chest blackening the screen.

A COUPLE of details interested me. Things that I thought might give us information the kidnappers didn't expect us to have, or want us to know.

As Tomlinson futzed with the computer, I asked Pilar, "Has anyone else studied this? I'd be interested in hearing what your experts had to say."

She said, "The first thing I did when I found Laken's room empty, I called the head of our national police. The same when the video was delivered. Two investigators were with me when I watched it for the first time. But you heard the demands. They said I had to stop cooperating, so I did. The police wanted to stay on the case, but I said absolutely not, leave me alone."

"Just because you're not cooperating doesn't mean they've dropped it," I said.

She shrugged. "I don't know. As I told you, I can't trust anyone in the government. You hear one thing, but something else is really happening."

"Did your treasury department come up with the money? A half-million's a lot of money. If you're not cooperating, why would they provide the ransom?"

"I didn't ask the treasury. I would have had to explain why I needed the money. People gossip, and the wrong people could find out. I wasn't going to put Laken at greater risk."

Pilar explained that, instead, she'd gone to an old and trusted friend for help, her country's wealthiest jeweler. Like Colombia, Masagua is famous for its emeralds. Pilar had inherited stones from her family estate, and she'd also collected emeralds since childhood. She'd asked her friend to spend the weekend liquidating her collection on the international market.

"It's all the savings I have, and I loved those stones. I mean, I really loved some of them. But what choice did I have? I hate those bastards for putting me in this position!"

She was furious.

Trying to calm her, Tomlinson told her that money, jewels, and other such things were nothing more than symbolism.

"They're trophy collections," he said. "But when someone you love is in danger"—he made a *poof* noise with his lips—"the trophies, your collection, it becomes meaningless."

Nodding as if agreeing, she said, "Yes, but I had so many superb stones . . . I just hope there's enough."

I said, "You're not alone in this. I'll put up at least half. I can get the cash in—" My main account is on Grand Cayman Island. I took a moment to calculate how long it would take to transfer money to my bank on Sanibel . . . how much I could borrow, and how quickly my broker could sell off most . . . probably all of my stock portfolio. "By tomorrow afternoon late. Or I'll just reimburse you. That'll be easiest."

I live so simply, have so little interest in the things money buys, that I've saved quite a bit over the years. Emeralds I'd taken from Masagua had contributed to my pile.

"No," she said, "you don't have to do that."

Her tone told me more. It said to accept my offer equated to indebtedness, and she preferred not to be indebted to me. She didn't want my help.

I said, "I insist."

Pilar made a noncommittal gesture that dismissed the subject, then told us that her friend was going to pack the money in a heavy-duty photographer's briefcase addressed to her. He'd make certain it got into the consul general's diplomatic pouch and on a flight in time so that it was in Miami by tomorrow morning, Wednesday.

Clever. It's illegal to bring more than ten thousand dollars cash in or out of the U.S. without declaring it, so it would have been idiotic to try and sneak a half-million through Miami customs. Diplomatic pouch—which, by international law, could *not* be searched—was the only safe, legal way to get that amount of money into the country.

I asked, "Before you told the two feds to drop the case, did they happen to make any comments about the video?"

Pilar hesitated. "They did. But what I'd prefer first is for you to tell me what *you* think. Maybe you saw something they didn't. I don't want to bias your thinking. Does that seem reasonable?"

It seemed more than reasonable. So Tomlinson and I batted it back and forth.

For starters, I'd gotten the impression that Masked Man may have spent many years in Central America, but he wasn't a member of the two most common ethnic groups. He was neither Mayan nor of Spanish descent.

It wasn't just the accent, either. His sentence rhythms had a white-trash crudeness. Same with his tasteless, honky-tonk comedian shtick. There are degrees of inappropriate behavior that raise hackles on the back of the neck, and Masked Man exceeded the limits. His pornographic rant, the mood shifts, his showy behavior, all pointed to either a personal viciousness or pathology. The line is sometimes fine, and difficult to decipher.

Tomlinson said, "Just from the few scars that were visible, his face has gotta be a mess, man. Normally, I'd feel sympathy for someone like that. But I've got a very strong vibe that this one's got snakes crawling around up there where his brain should be. He was all messed up on the inside long before he got those scars on the outside. That's my read."

Tomlinson and I were sitting on lab stools, the laptop between us. Pilar stood listening, letting us talk even though our words hurt her—her expression was not difficult to interpret.

Something else we agreed on was that only two people were in the room. Just Lake and Masked Man, although for some reason he wanted us to think there were more. The way he consistently referred to "we" or "us." It seemed intentional.

"Maybe it's a power trip," Tomlinson guessed. "The more people he's got behind him, the more power he has. He wants us to see him that way. He's in control, man. A *force*. But it's bogus.

"The same with his political tirade. The pro-Indian stuff. More schools, jobs, and hospitals. He didn't mean any of it; complete bullshit. I agree with the whole power-to-the-people philosophy, but that's not where that dude's head was at. The vicious ones, the really bad dogs, they manufacture excuses for revenge. Politics, injustice to the Indians. I think that's *his* excuse."

I'd been watching Pilar's reactions. Now I said to her, "You know a lot more about this guy than you've told us. I'd like to hear it."

Years ago, when Pilar was nervous or upset, she couldn't stand still. In that way, at least, she hadn't changed.

I watched her move across the lab and pause by a tank that held snappers, then cross to another that held octopi. She stopped and stared at octopi that were peeking out from their rocky ambush holes, focusing on her with golden, glowing cat eyes.

Without turning, she said, "You two are good together. Maybe it's the combination, one of you analytical, the other intuitive. You're right on most points. Maybe *all* points. I don't know enough about him to say. What I do know is, out of all the mercenaries that Balserio brought into the country, the criminal you just saw is the worst.

"Our federal police identified him right away. Everyone in Masagua knows him by reputation. *Not* by his name. His reputation. His real name's Praxcedes Lourdes. He's a Nicaraguan. During their revolution, he was a death squad assassin. But when the war ended, he kept on killing. The police tried to catch him, but they never did, so the courts tried him in absentia. They found him guilty and sentenced him to time in a psychiatric prison. When that didn't bring him in, they finally sentenced him to death by firing squad."

But they still failed to catch him.

"He'd become famous the way certain serial killers become famous. The peasants in Nicaragua called him 'the Man-Burner.' Some variation of that. He terrorized that country. Then Jorge paid cash or maybe political favors to get Nicaragua to drop the charges against him, and Lourdes came to Masagua and terrorized our country."

I said, "Praxcedes. That sounds like an Arawak name. An Indian name."

"Yes. He's from the Moskito Coast. Moskito Indio country, but he behaves more like a Carib Indian. The crazy violence."

"You heard his accent. He's not Nicaraguan, and he's no Indian. Where do you think he's from originally?"

The woman shook her head. "A padded cell. Or hell, as far as I'm concerned. That's where he's taken me."

I had to ask: "His nickname, 'the Man-Burner.' Does he really—?"

She was already moving her head in affirmation, still looking at the octopi, her expression numb. "There are so many stories . . . I *won't* tell you. They say he enjoys it. He's the reason our people are afraid to leave their homes at night. The psychological effect of what he does, always at night . . . incredible. That one sick person can change the political momentum of a country is incredible . . ."

She let the sentence trail off into silence. Tomlinson gave her several seconds to finish before he asked, "But why would Balserio have someone like that kidnap Lake? You're well known and well liked in your country. A popular figure. Your son has to be just as well known. I'd think the public would be outraged. It'd be political suicide to be associated with something like that."

Pilar turned to him, her expression soft, private; an expression that seemed to share uncertainty. Once upon a time, she'd exchanged such looks with me.

"I agree," she said. "But I can't think straight. Since I found Laken's bed empty, I've been in shock. So I'm trusting in *you* to help me understand this. Jorge is shrewd, that much I can tell you. He wouldn't have chosen Lourdes to abduct Laken if he didn't have a plan."

She hesitated, seemed to wince with distaste before she added, "Our police dug out a little more information on him." She leaned and, from her purse, she took a manila envelope, then handed it to me.

"In the files, they found old photos taken of Lourdes when he was a teen. They were part of his medical records when he was in the burn ward of the indigents' hospital in Managua. They're the only known photos of him without a mask or a scarf over his face. I can't stand to look at them again. Even be in the same room when they're out, so I'll go outside for some air while you look."

WHEN the screen door had closed behind Pilar, I removed two glossy black-and-white photos and handed one to Tomlinson. One was a close-up of Prax Lourdes' face. The other was a wider head-and-shoulders shot.

He had suffered second- and third-degree burns over most of his face. In medical terms, a third-degree burn is called a "full-thickness" burn because the outer layer of skin is destroyed along with the entire layer beneath. Often, there is also damage to subcutaneous tissue, muscle, and bone. Lourdes had been burned to the bone on the right cheek area, much of his chin, and on the top of his head. The man's mouth was a wedge of skeletal teeth that suggested a dental schematic—something to be used in medical schools, like a cadaver.

Tomlinson whistled softly and said, "I guess I should feel sorry for him. But I get such a bad vibe, man . . ."

I said, "Pilar said the Nicaraguan authorities had a warrant out for this guy's arrest, but never caught him. How can you not find someone with a face like this?"

I looked at Tomlinson. "Does that make any sense to you? He was sentenced to time in an insane asylum, then to die by firing squad, yet he somehow manages to blend in with the general population? *How?*"

Tomlinson shrugged.

I slid the photograph I was holding back into the envelope. "At least now I understand why he wears the mask."

"FAST forward. I'll tell you when to stop," I said.

Several short sections of the video interested me. The first was the silence that was punctuated by the bird's call: a hushed, two-toned whistle that was distinctive.

Pilar had returned. We listened to it several times before I turned to her. "Do you recognize the bird?"

At first, she seemed puzzled, but now her expression brightened. "Nine or ten times I've watched this nightmare, and I completely missed it. A quetzal bird. It's singing in the background. Maybe it's because I've forgotten how rare they are in other countries."

To Tomlinson, I said, "The quetzal is a really beautiful green bird with a long tail. You find it in the high mountains, the cloud forests—only in Central America."

He said, "I know, I know, I saw one once. A bird with, like, these emerald crystals for feathers. I love the way your brain is working today, Dr. Ford. A little bird *could* tell us something. It's already telling us they're still in the mountains. And it might tell us more."

I said, "Some birds are time specific."

"The time of the day or night when they sing, you mean?"

"Exactly. Let me check my library. While I do, find the section where the camera gets a clear shot at the lamp beside the bed. There's a moth on the lampshade. See if you can freeze it and zoom in."

I returned a few minutes later with my *Field Guide to the Birds of Mexico and Central America,* along with Daniel Janzen's *Costa Rican Natural History*—an excellent primer on the flora and fauna of the region.

I read silently from both books before saying, "The male quetzal begins a round of territorial calling just before dawn. He usually calls until a couple of hours after dawn, then goes silent during the day. So there you go. It *does* tell us something. It suggests this video was shot in the morning. Probably very early morning, because the window blinds don't seem to be that bright. Not much light at all."

To Pilar, I said, "Lake was abducted late Wednesday night or early Thursday morning of last week."

"Yes."

"What time did they find the package outside the convent gate?"

Sounding eager, as if a bulb had just gone on in her brain, she replied, "I see where you're going with this. It was around ten A.M. on Thursday. The same day the newspaper he was holding was published."

"Do you have any idea what time the Latin edition of the *Miami Herald* arrives in Masagua City?"

"It comes on the first direct from Miami. A LACSA flight that arrives at the international airport at seven-twenty A.M. I've flown it enough, I should know."

"This time of year, sunrise in Florida is around six-forty. In Central America—"

"We're an hour earlier. We don't use daylight savings time. But sunrise is nearly an hour later because of the volcanic peaks to the east."

I said, "I remember it being about a forty-minute drive from the airport to downtown Masagua City. I'm talking about how long it took the kidnappers to drive from the airport to the convent, and deliver the package after shooting the video."

She replied, "About forty-five minutes if it's early in the morning, because the traffic's light, yes. Sometimes an hour."

"Your people found the package around ten, but it could have been dropped off an hour or even two hours before."

Pilar nodded.

Looking at the screen, Tomlinson interrupted, saying, "O.K., here's the moth." Then he turned his blue, weary prophet's eyes on me. "A very savvy piece of reasoning, Doc. I certainly wouldn't have caught it. Mind if I try to nail it to the wall? To make sure I'm thinking independently and not just following your lead?"

"Go right ahead."

"O.K. First, let me verify something before I try to distill this little gem into a couple of sentences. Pilar, am I correct in assuming that Masagua City is high enough in the cloud forest that you might hear quetzal birds?"

"We hear them often. It's the only capital city in Central America where the bird is found."

"Do you know of any other airports that are at an elevation high enough to find quetzals?"

"No. None."

"Are there any other major cities at a similar elevation where the *Herald* is delivered early in the morning?"

Pilar said, "All the major cities in Central America get the *Miami Herald,* but only Masagua is high enough."

Tomlinson was twisting a frazzled end of his hair, concentrating. "Then here's what we know: This video was shot within a few minutes' walking or driving distance of the international airport in Masagua. The room *has* to be nearby because the time window is so damn narrow. They buy the paper in or near the airport, return to the room, and start the camera going while it's still early enough for a quetzal to be calling. Unless the bird's behaving unusually—which birds sometimes do. Even so, it seems a reasonable conclusion."

I said, "That's the way I read it. I think the data's strong enough to hold up. I think we can say with some certainty that slightly more than four days ago, Lake was being held in a building that was within a few minutes of the international airport in Masagua."

Tomlinson added, "They also have to be in a structure near trees, don't forget. Almost certainly tall trees. A cloud forest bird? A combination like that—all near an airport?" He sighed, pained by what we'd discovered. "Even stoned out of my gourd, if I'd had half an hour, even I coulda found him."

OUTWARDLY, I was calm. Inside, though, I was seething. The Masaguan feds had seen this same video on Thursday morning, shortly after the CD was delivered. If they'd realized the importance of the bird call, figured out the significance, they could have sealed off all the likely housing around the airport, sent in a hostage rescue team, and my son might be safe right now.

In any hostage situation, abductors are at their most vulnerable in the earliest stages, before they've had time to calm down, reassess, and reorganize.

It would have been an ideal time to hit them.

I know because I've become a reluctant amateur expert not only on kidnapping, but kidnappings that take place in Latin America. I've been forced to learn because of events in my life, and because I've spent so much time living near equatorial lines.

Latin America is the most dangerous place in the world when it comes to that particular crime. More than six thousand people are abducted annually. In Colombia, it's a tax-free, $200-million-a-year business. In Mexico, there are as many as two thousand kidnappings a year, with ransom demands ranging from five thousand dollars for common citizens up into the multimillions for bankers and businessmen.

Foreign executives who work in the oil and energy industries are favorite targets. Insurance agencies such as Chubb, Fireman's Fund, and Lloyd's of London now offer policies that underwrite ransom payments, medical treatment, and interpreters, and even continue to pay the salaries of the missing.

Premiums are not inexpensive.

Business? Kidnapping has become an international industry.

It was in Guatemala that kidnappers started a chilling, profitable trend. They began to abduct and ransom the children of wealthy locals and foreign workers. Payoffs became bigger, negotiations easier. The practice spread through Ecuador and Venezuela, where each country suffers about two hundred kidnappings a year.

Pilar's country, Masagua soon followed.

I'd heard and read so much about it and become concerned enough, slightly more than a year ago, to warn Lake in an e-mail. I told him why he was an obvious, high-risk target. Of far more value—now, at least, it seemed—I'd also included advice on how best to survive an abduction.

The tips had been assembled for him by a friend of mine, a hostage negotiator who works for the State Department.

I'd sent the paper along with a note from me that read:

During these screwy times, everyone in the world should be prepared,
and they should damn well know that:

- During a hijacking or hostage assault, the most dangerous phases
  are the first few minutes and—if there is a rescue attempt—the
  final few minutes. Anticipate what you should do before it happens
  so that you won't panic if it happens.
- In the first minutes, terrorists are adrenaline-fogged and prone to
  irrational overreaction. This is when most hostages die. Remain
  calm. Avoid eye contact. No sudden, threatening movements.
- Do not struggle or try to escape unless success or your own death
  are certain.
- Aspire to be inconspicuous. Do *not* give your captors the impression that you are memorizing their facial features or keeping note
  of their actions.
- Talk normally. Don't complain, don't show anger. Follow all orders
  and instructions.
- If questioned, keep your answers short. Don't stand out.
- If involved in a lengthy hostage situation, the opposite becomes
  true. It's easier to kill an object than a human being. Make sure
  your captors know your name, the names of your family members. Establish a rapport.
- Remember that you are a valuable commodity to your captors. It's
  important to them to keep you alive and well. Find a way to survive. Others have. You can, too.

All good advice. The kind that can save a life or lives.

Trouble was, I knew there was a possibility that Lake hadn't even read
the damn thing. He'd certainly never made any specific references to the
data in a reply e-mail.

Boys his age are bulletproof. Or think they are.

But maybe, just maybe, it'd helped him.

Even so, I was immensely thankful that I'd made the effort. Thankful because it took a bit of the sting out of the overwhelming guilt I felt. It was guilt that any parent would have experienced.

My child had been taken. Even though I'd anticipated the possibility, I wasn't there to protect him when it happened.

Unforgivable.

It's guilt that destroys us—one of Tomlinson's favorite sayings.

Pilar felt the guilt, too. Of that, I was certain. And for good reason.

When I'd sent my warnings to Lake, I'd sent the same warnings to her. Our son was an obvious, high-risk target. Serious measures needed to be taken.

She'd never responded.

I'd yet to mention that to her.

I never would.

OH YEAH, she was feeling it.

Pilar pressed a blinding hand over her eyes, moaned softly, and then I listened to her say, "I'm so sorry, Marion. It never crossed my mind that a noise in the background could be important."

The bird call. She was still punishing herself for not zeroing in on the quetzal.

She added, "That morning, while I was watching this awful thing, Laken was just a few miles away? We could have sent in soldiers and saved him. Oh dear God. I feel terrible I didn't understand . . ."

Tomlinson reached and put his big hand to her shoulder, communicating with touch—*Don't blame yourself. Victims should never blame themselves*—but stuck to business, saying, "O.K., O.K. We're done with the subject. There's nothing more to learn from background noise. Let's discuss other elements in the video."

He watched me nod before saying, "So far, we both agree that Lourdes videoed this by himself. But I'm still thinking he had to have one or more accomplices."

"Why do you say that?"

"Because the way Pilar describes it, your son was kidnapped from a place that's downtown in a busy city. And from a building that was guarded. There almost had to be a driver. Don't you think? Or a chopper maybe. Someone waiting to get away fast."

I said, "O.K, I'll go along with that."

He turned to Pilar. "Do private planes fly in and out of the international airport?"

"Yes. Of course."

I was looking at the moth on the screen, comparing it with photos in the book. The insect's wingspan was massive—more than six inches. Finally, I found it: *Ascalapha odorata*, the Bruja Negra or Black Witch moth. An insect common to Central America—further confirmation that the video had been shot in the region.

I said, "That's what I'm asking myself. Why would someone kidnap the son of a popular political figure, then head straight for a hideout close to the airport?"

Tomlinson was now allowing the video to play in slow motion—an eerie thing to watch—as he asked, "Does your ex-husband have enough political juice in neighboring countries to get passports for Lourdes and your son? Visas, I.D.s? I'm talking about credentials good enough so they could hop on a private plane and take refuge in another country. No way you can fly a kidnapped child out on a commercial plane, so that leaves military or private."

I leaned close to study my son's haunted eyes staring back at me, then focused upon the red welt that snaked up his arm. I'd dismissed the possibility of it being a burn. Now, though, I reconsidered.

As Pilar replied, "Yes, documents, passports, Balserio could get anything he wanted," I looked across my laboratory sink at the Bunsen burner. I pictured the scalpel-blue flame it produced, then reviewed variations of propane torches.

A portable welder's torch came to mind. They were cheap, easy to use, readily available even in Third World countries, and intimidating if used as a weapon—something that would appeal to a sociopath who liked fire.

I remembered Pilar saying that the fish in Lake's main aquarium had been killed. Stick a welder's torch in an aquarium, and the swim bladders of fish would soon explode, expanding in the super-heated water.

Son-of-a-bitch.

Lake *had* been burned. The wound seemed a defensive variety. People under attack throw their forearms up to protect their face.

It told me something that I couldn't share with Pilar, and would not share with Tomlinson. That brand of assault is indicative. If Praxcedes Lourdes had already burned Lake, then he planned to kill him. That seemed probable to me.

What was the statistic I'd read? It had been compiled by some government agency in Britain. In kidnapping cases worldwide, only about forty percent of the victims are recovered alive even *after* the ransom is paid in full. If the victim has been seriously abused or mistreated—severed ears or pinkie fingers are common examples—then chances of the abductee surviving drops to nearly zero.

Paying Lake's ransom, following his kidnapper's orders, made sense only in that it might buy us a little time.

I jumped, startled that anyone could speak calmly when Tomlinson said, "As long as we have the computer out, maybe you should check your e-mail. They said you should check it often."

Pilar still sounded despondent. "You're probably right. I tried from my hotel last night, then again this morning. So far, nothing. I need to buy a laptop while I'm here. I don't have one."

I pointed to my desk model on the far side of the room. "You can use mine, or we can hook Tomlinson's up to the phone. His'll be faster."

We did. She checked.

She had an e-mail from the kidnappers. There was also a note from our son.

Sitting at the computer, nervously regarding what she was about to read, Pilar said, "When Jorge Balserio is back in the presidential palace— and he probably *will* be, unfortunately—he'll owe that animal a debt more than favors and money. I wonder how he'll deal with his famous monster then?"

She was talking, once again, about the possibility that Balserio had provided passports and a private plane. She was also talking about the man who'd abducted our son.

I was picturing the burn scar on Lake's arm, my child's terrified eyes staring back into mine, and I was thinking: *If Balserio's smart, he'll kill Lourdes.*

But I was also thinking: *If I get to Lourdes first, he'll never have the chance.*

FOUR

THE night he kidnapped the boy, Prax Lourdes told his driver, Reynaldo, "Drive fast, but not so damn crazy that you bring the *federales* down. I got us this far, don't screw it up now."

He was sitting in the back of a dented Toyota Camry, his hood down, still wearing the mask. Engine running, the car sat in the shadows of a park that separated the presidential palace from the convent, and a line of colonial buildings—columns, plazas, balconies—built in the 1700s.

Through the tinted windows, Prax could see shadowed ficus trees and royal palms in the park, homeless adults and children sleeping on benches, and a horse grazing near the ornate marble band shelter. The horse was all head and ribs.

Lourdes wasn't hot, yet he couldn't stop sweating. Returning through the tunnel, goading the boy along ahead of him, he'd felt that same shitty fear, like drowning. The tunnel walls, the darkness, seemed to crush at the muscles in his heart.

But he'd endured it. The boy was in the trunk now, mouth, hands, legs all taped.

He'd not come easily. A surprise. The kid wasn't just a smart-ass, he had some balls, too. He'd even taken a swing at him back in the room. Big kid for his age, with muscles. Quick, too. But still just a kid.

Prax had thrown him down by the hair, and scorched his arm with a quick shot of the blowtorch. He'd screamed out, but only briefly and not loud. But then he became real cooperative when Prax told him, "You try that shit again, I'm going straight to your mother's room and set her hair on fire. Or I'll have my pals do it. How'd you like to hear your mother scream?"

Yeah, that was the key to this kid. Threaten the mother with make-believe hacks, and he'd do absolutely anything. Prax got no more trouble from the little bastard after that.

Lourdes knew he couldn't linger, but he still took the time to go through the kid's drawers. The kid had lied when he said he didn't have any cash hidden away. Stashed among baseball cards and a bunch of beetles pinned to a board, he found slightly more than five hundred dollars in Masaguan córdobas, and a thousand in U.S. currency: ten crisp $100 bills.

Clipped to the bills was a business card that read: SANIBEL BIOLOGICAL SUPPLY/MARION FORD, and signed, *Happy Birthday, Lake!* There was also a photograph that showed a studious-looking man with glasses.

When Prax flashed the photo at the kid and said, "Who's the creep who sent you the money?" the kid had replied in a very odd tone, "He's a man I hope you get a chance to meet real soon, mister."

The way the kid said it, it was like the creep was supposed to be scary or something.

THEY'D left the boy in a rental cabin, still taped, and also handcuffed to the bed. Now Reynaldo parked the Toyota a few blocks away from the cabin at the edge of a smoldering industrial dump, behind a corrugated building next to the airport, as he'd been ordered to do. He sat shivering in the morning darkness, lights off, Lourdes beside him, waiting for some early flight to arrive. Reynaldo didn't know why.

He continued to shiver as Lourdes said, "I said I'd tell you how it happened. About what the soldiers did to me. You said you wanted to know."

Lourdes' voice was smoky deep. He spoke softly, but because of his harsh American accent, he sounded loud.

Uneasy, Reynaldo replied, "Only if you want to discuss it. Another time, if you like. It doesn't have to be now."

There was a hint of irony in Lourdes' voice when he said, "Oh yeah? I think you're wrong. I think it's now or never."

There was a meanness in there, too.

"But first, tell me what you've heard. I always enjoy hearing the bullshit going around about me. Being lied about comes with being famous."

Prax watched the driver take a gulp from the bottle of *aguadiente* he now held between his legs, and saw that his hand shook. Lourdes got a kick out of that.

"I've heard what most have heard," the driver began. "That you were adopted by a tribe of Indians on the Moskito Coast of Nicaragua. As a young teenager. That your parents must have been killed in a shipwreck, because they found you starving, wandering the beach."

"The Suma tribe," Prax said. "Moskito Indians. They took me in. They named me. I became one of them. My adopted father was the village leader."

Reynaldo said, "Yes, your father was the leader, and so soldiers came to kill him. That they burned your house, your whole family. Only you survived. After that, you dedicated your life to revenge—"

"To the Revolution. Anything against the government whores."

"—that you dedicated your life to the Revolution. That is what I heard."

"Yeah," Prax said. "The same old stuff. But since we're working together, since we've become such close buddies, you and me, I'll tell you the details. Things almost no one knows. Then you can go back to your village, brag about it, and act like a big important man."

Reynaldo smiled for the first time, saying, "Yes, I'd like that."

He meant it.

LOURDES said, "Before I tell you, let me ask you a couple of questions first. Nothing too personal. Just some stuff I want to know. I heard you and General Balserio are tight. At least, I hear the General trusts you. That you guys go way back together."

"I have served the General over many years, and in many ways," Reynaldo said modestly. "When he has special needs, special assignments such as this, he calls on me. It is an honor."

Then, because he could sense Lourdes was driving at something, maybe trying to extract confidential information, the driver added, "But we are not friends as neighbors are friends. I only do what he tells me to do, and he only tells me what I need to know."

Prax said, "For this job, he told me he would send an amount of cash to cover expenses, plus my fee. He said that someone—you, I'm thinking—would deliver the money to me. And that this same person would arrange for a plane to take me and the kid to one of the General's hideouts in Nicaragua. Do you have the money?"

Because Reynaldo had been ordered to give Lourdes the money—but only when he was safely on the General's plane—he felt he could answer truthfully. "Yes. It's in a briefcase. I will give it to you soon."

"And the plane?"

"Yes. Everything's arranged."

Lourdes asked, "After the kid and I get to the General's camp, do you know what his plan is after that? How's it going to work?"

"I have no knowledge of anything once you get on the plane," the driver said.

Prax Lourdes adjusted his mask and nodded. He believed that the man knew nothing else. But he was pretty sure of what General Balserio had planned. The entire population of Masagua was terrified of *Incendiario*. News that he'd kidnapped the son of Pilar Fuentes, the General's former wife—and perhaps the mother of the General's son, some still whispered—would make Lourdes the focus of a united, national hatred.

"I will then rescue the boy," Balserio had told him. "It will be something to be done for cameras. But you will escape, Praxcedes. That I promise you! You will escape, and I will become an even more popular national hero. And you, of course, will be rich with the additional money I'll pay you in my gratitude."

That last part, Prax didn't believe. What he believed was, Balserio planned to murder him during the boy's rescue. Get that on film, and the people of Masagua wouldn't just make him president, they'd make him king.

Lourdes used his big hand to pat the driver on the shoulder. Felt him shrink away as he said, "Tell you what: Show me the cash. Let me count it first—you're going to give it to me in a couple of hours anyway. Then I'll tell you what almost no one else knows about me. What the soldiers did, and what I've done to a bunch of those bastards since. All the juicy little details. Deal?"

THE money was right there in the car. Reynaldo had it hidden in space where the spare tire had been kept. He watched Lourdes count it—a little less than seventy-five thousand dollars—before they got back into the car.

Prax didn't tell Reynaldo the whole deal. He'd never told anyone the entire truth. He just told him about the soldiers, and the hospital, and about how he'd dedicated his life to taking revenge for all the poor peasants.

Same old bullshit.

Just as he didn't tell him he was going to double-cross that pompous asshole, Jorge Balserio. That he was going to steal the money *and* the kid, then split.

He had everything all set: A guy he'd bullied at the national library to do the internet stuff for him, because he would need to have e-mails forwarded once he and the kid were in hiding. Plus, his own chartered plane, not Balserio's. And a ship. An old freighter, but with an infirmary that was going to be very specially equipped once he got his hands on that money.

So he was tempted to tell the General's little stooge that he was going to burn Balserio—but burn him in a different kind of way. It would've fed Lourdes' ego to let an insider know that he was outsmarting the famous man.

But he didn't. Didn't say a word, even though he'd already decided that the driver would never get the chance to tell anyone.

FIVE

THE olfactory memory has no linkage in time, so reading e-mail over Pilar's shoulder, our bodies so close, her familiar odor reconnected us across years. I might, once again, have been with the woman whom I believed to be my love.

The temptation was to rest my hand on her shoulder. But she no longer invited that kind of familiarity.

She read the kidnapper's e-mail aloud, first in Spanish, then made a quick translation into English for Tomlinson's benefit, her voice animated:

"On Wednesday, May seventh, at two in the afternoon, be at the Cacique Restaurant on West Flagler near Northwest Miami Court. It's across from the Dade County courthouse in downtown Miami. You'll hear from us. Don't bring the money. If you contact the police, if you're followed, your brat dies. Answer this so we know you got it."

The e-mail was unsigned, the subject line blank. It came from an internet address that seemed to be a random series of letters and numbers: *xyxq37.*

Because she was a mother, though, and because it was the human thing to do, she'd opened Lake's e-mail first—which is why it was so difficult to control the emotion in her voice as she read aloud.

His note—if he'd actually written it—was distressing:

Mother,

Do what they say. I want to come home. Please help me. I'm afraid. He says if you cooperate, he'll let me write to you again.

That Lake switched in reference from "they" to "he," I noted, was suggestive.

Seeing his e-mail name, *Chamaeleo@Nicarado,* at the bottom of the note produced an unexpected surge of emotion in me.

Chamaeleo.

It was an unusual name chosen by an unusual boy. It'd taken some thought. *Chamaeleon* is the genus of wise-cracking lizards once used in popular beer commercials. Kinda funny.

Over time, though, I learned the name had more complex meanings. *Chamaeleon* is also the genus of certain sea iguanas similar to those found in the Galapagos Islands. Charles Darwin drew important inferences from the iguanas while aboard the HMS *Beagle* touring South America, making notes that led to his theory of natural selection.

Lake had finally told me that.

Impressive.

I'd added my own third interpretation: Chameleons adapt and change appearance fast—something that would appeal to a boy his age.

I think most parents come to learn what I was slow to realize: It is the unwise adult who assumes that youth automatically equates to an absence of depth and wisdom. Children are *complicated.*

Reading over Pilar's shoulder, smelling the good odor of hair and skin, I said, "They want you to respond. What are you going to say?"

"I'll write that I'm going to do exactly what they tell me to do. I don't want them to hurt Laken. What do you expect?"

"I think you should add something like . . . well, that you aren't cooperating with authorities, but you *are* bringing a male friend to Miami. Because I'm going with you. Big cities can be dangerous. Write something like that. Even if you aren't carrying the money, you need protection. Say there're no cops involved, but you have to watch out for your own safety."

"And what if they write back and tell me to come alone?"

"Pretend like you didn't get the e-mail. Don't acknowledge it."

Because she was shaking her head, not buying it, I added, "Look, Pilar, there's something very basic you need to keep in mind here. You're a target. What some might consider an easy target. Stop shaking your head and listen.

"You're the one who told us there are people in the Masaguan government who know you're picking up a half-million in cash from the consul general's office. Two feds saw the DVD, heard the demands. So now maybe their entire office knows. Or staff members in dozens of offices. You can't trust them. *Your* words.

"Then there're the kidnappers. They know you're here, which means that everyone associated with them knows. What's to stop one or more of them from trying to intercept you? Cut you out and steal the money for themselves? That's what makes you a target. Day or night, from the moment you pick up the briefcase at the consul, you're a target. It puts you right in the middle."

I puzzled over something for a few seconds before it came to me. "American Indians used to form two lines and make prisoners run between them; hit them with stick and clubs and stuff—*gauntlet,* that's the word. Running the gauntlet. With that much cash involved, you could be attacked from either side at any time. So I'm going with you to Miami."

Tomlinson said, "Doc's right. You can count me in, too."

"When you write back, there's something else you should add," I told her. "Lake's next message needs to contain something personal. That only you or I would know. Something that tells us the e-mails are really from him."

My meaning had implications so dark that she didn't comment. Just nodded.

NOW we were on the bottom deck of my house, Pilar standing, watching Tomlinson and me preparing to return the sedated tarpon from its holding tank into the bay. The fish had been in the tank for nearly an hour. Gill coloring and opercula rate were both fine. So far, this first step in what would be a long and complicated series of procedures had gone well.

Like everything else in my life lately, my luck had been good.

Until now.

I am forever and alternately amused then pissed off at how blindly I stumble through life. How is it that I keep forgetting one of the most powerful laws of physics? It is the law of "momentum conservation." The law states that momentum lost by any collision or impact is equal to the opposite momentum gained.

The law applies to our own day-to-day lives because, during good times or bad, we need to remind ourselves that just when it seems life can't get any better—or worse—things inevitably change.

And my life had been going very, very well. Lucky in life. Lucky in health. Lucky in love.

I'd been running, swimming, and lifting weights daily with Dewey, who was not just my lover but my all-time favorite, kick-butt workout buddy. With her drill sergeant goading, I'd started eating better, watching my diet.

Something else: A while back, I'd given up alcohol. Had to. I'd gotten into the dangerous habit of drinking myself to sleep every night. So I quit. I piled all the bottles of booze into a box, marched them down to the dock, and left them buried in the marina ice machine for some thirsty soul to discover.

Many months later, when I mentioned to Dewey that I missed having a beer or two at sunset with the rest of the marina family, she offered a suggestion that was as appealing as it was simple. She said, "Do you remember when we first met? Weeknights, you never let yourself drink more than three beers. Ever. Weekends, you'd cut it a little looser, but you never broke your weekday rule. Even for parties. Why not go back and do that?"

Which is exactly what I did. No more than three drinks a night. Ever.

So I was in the best shape I'd been in the last ten years or so. I was enjoying the slow and lazy existence that is life at a small marina on the west coast of Florida. I had tropical blue mornings, glassy slick days on the bay, and Gulf Stream sunsets with cold beer in hand.

For work, I was involved with this new research project. I had a chance to play a role in being among the first scientists to devise a way to strip tarpon of fresh sperm, called *milt*, use it to fertilize eggs in captivity, and then raise the hatchlings until they were mature enough to release.

Life had never been better. Which is why I should have known my luck was due to change. But why did the Fates have to choose my son? The world always seems at its cruelest when it selects a child as an instrument of misfortune.

Holding the tarpon's lower jaw, my right arm cradling its belly, I lifted the fish from the tank, then carried him along the boardwalk, taking quick, short steps because of his weight and slickness. His tail made a heavy, drug-dulled fanning thud against my inner bicep.

Once on the mangrove bank, I waded into waist-deep water, immersing the fish, walking him, forcing clean bay water through his gills. It would be a while before he recovered and I could release him.

Tomlinson was beside me, still shirtless, bony ribs showing, baggy Gandhi shorts dragging in the water. He said, "I'm sorry, Doc. What a soul downer. Because of my ex-love, the Nipponese mummy—her and her beef jerky heart—I can't see my daughter. The girl's been poisoned against me. But the thought of someone snatching Nichola makes me want to cry. I *could*, too. Right now. Bawl like a baby. I know how you must feel."

I said, "Something like this happens, it's like a light goes on. Why the hell didn't I spend more time with him? Why not get off my dead ass, grab a plane, and make the occasional visit? I'm the one who should have taught him how to fish, play ball. That sort of thing. Instead, we just traded e-mails. Now look what's happened."

"Don't do that, man. Don't do the punishment gig. Besides, we both know why you couldn't go visit. It's because of *her*."

Tomlinson swung his head toward my stilt house. "It's because of the woman, Pilar. You think you're still in love with her, man."

I said, "It's that obvious?"

"Oh yeah. You look at her like she's a combination religious shrine and delicious morsel. Every time you'da went to Masagua to visit, it woulda been like having your heart winched out through the bunghole. No way, man. That's why you didn't go. You *couldn't* go."

After a moment, he added, "In my opinion, it was for the best."

Looking at the fish, but concentrating on something else, I said, "T.M.?

You've got good instincts. Probably the best of any person I've ever met. The way Pilar reacted to me . . . well, what's your impression?"

He said, "She's not an easy one to read, man. A monster grabs her child, and she can still keep the emotional shields in place. How many women would be as calm as her under these circumstances? But, yeah, I definitely tuned right in on the vibes about you—weird that she'd let them show when she's so good at the stoicism bit. You're not going to like what I have to say."

"That's O.K. Tell me the truth."

"For starters, she was more than chilly, *compadre*. She was distant, with a little touch of distaste thrown in. That was my strong impression. It may have seemed like she loved you once, but not now. She doesn't even appear to like you much—which doesn't mesh with the relationship you apparently once had. Did you ever notice her behaving oddly before?" His question seemed to have broader implications.

"No, not really. What do you mean by that?"

"Nothing . . . Did you do something to offend her? Piss her off?"

"I don't know. I've thought about it and thought about it. A few years back, we spent a couple of great weeks together down in Panama. It was like we'd never been apart. Then, nearly two years or so ago, she began to cool. Finally, she dropped right off the radar screen. The only time she contacts me is with a card at Christmas, a photo of Lake enclosed. Not even a note from her. And when I telephone, she's never in."

"Did you ever ask your son about it?"

The tarpon's tail was beginning to flag more strongly now. "No. I wouldn't impose on a child with a question like that. You wouldn't either."

"Then my advice, Doc? After you release the fish, take her aside and ask her. Get it out on the table. What you've got to deal with now is too important to have any problems communicating. Which is why I'm going to leave you two alone."

He was already slogging away when I called, "How about a beer later?"

Over his shoulder, he replied, "You betcha. After you talk to her, raise me on the VHF. Or my brand-new cellular phone. I can't wait to hear how my pal screwed up this time."

PILAR was visibly uneasy now that Tomlinson was gone, the two of us alone near the big wooden fish tank on the lowest deck of my stilt house. Though she was within arm's reach, her uneasiness created a distance that seemed an insular vacuum. It made a wall of those few feet.

Communication is as rare as conversation is routine. She manufactured conversation to make the wall between us less evident. For a wall to exist, we had to have once been intimate. That was something she seemed unwilling to acknowledge.

Tomlinson was apparently a comfortable subject. She spoke of how unusual it was for her to like and trust a man so quickly. She'd liked him immediately when she met him in Masagua. She liked him even more now, she said.

When she asked, "Does he have family?" I got the impression that she was actually asking if he had a wife or lover.

Maybe that's why I replied with several harsh truths that I seldom share. "He has a daughter, Nichola, who refuses to see him. He has a brother who's a heroin addict—Rangoon, if he's still alive. His father's gone native somewhere in the Amazon basin. He was a paleontologist. A brilliant one before he disappeared."

That jolted her. "So strange. So tragic."

I nodded. "A century or so back, his family accumulated a fortune on a couple of patents. Something to do with a synchronizing device that allowed airplanes to fire machine guns through spinning propellers. It made the killing ratios huge. The First World War alone, it had to account for thousands of dead. Some fortunes, I guess it's heirs that pay the price."

"I'm surprised a man like Tomlinson would accept blood money."

For some reason, her elevated opinion of my friend, even though accurate, continued to irk me. I am often asked how Tomlinson makes a living. I always evade. It's something never discussed around the marina. This time, though, I answered with another harsh truth.

"He *doesn't* accept family money. Hasn't since he was a teenager and found out the source. By then, though, he'd spent a bundle, so he still feels like he's stained for life. When he told you about the crop he was growing on the islands? That's how he's made his living ever since. Smuggling dope. Selling drugs. Sails to the Yucatán, sails back. Or sometimes as far south as Guyana. He's gone into the rum business, too. Something legal, finally."

I paused, startled by the perverse pleasure I took in telling her that. Yet it didn't trouble her. Even though the illegal drug trade has made chaos of Latin America's economy, she seemed to approve. I could see it in her expression, just as I could also see that I'd been diminished in her eyes by my small betrayal.

That's exactly what I'd done, too—betrayed the confidence of my best friend.

In an idiotic effort to redeem myself, I added quickly, "Not that he needs to do that anymore. It's a long story, but he also has a huge following as a Zen teacher—people who're devoted. He could probably double his great-grandfather's fortune within a few years, they're so many. If he pushed the money thing. Which he'd never do. The man's motives are pure. No one doubts that."

Talking once again like I was Tomlinson's friend.

Pilar said, "He's a religious leader?"

"Through his writings, his teachings. You really have no idea. He's always been that way, but then word about him began to spread on the internet."

"I guess I should find that surprising," my former lover said, musing. "But I don't. There's something very powerful about the man. Spiritual. When I met him in Central America, I felt it."

I told her, "Oh, there is, there is. Everyone says the same," as I walked to the wooden fish tank. I put my hands on the rim and stared down into a world that I have always preferred because of the precise interlinkings, and clarity.

I HAD the skimmer net now, cleaning out the detritus of shrimp husks and bits of fish scale, while snappers, immature grouper, and tarpon spooked below, their dense muscularity crackling.

I pretended to concentrate, perplexed by my reaction.

It was summer dusk, and mosquitoes were moving over the water out of mangrove shadows. Light in the western sky beyond the mangroves, beyond the marina, had an oyster sheen. High clouds to the east still reflected a rusty, mango band of sunset upon cumulus canyons.

Eastward, if viewed from that high vantage point, was central Florida, cattle pasture, citrus, and saw grass. A hundred miles beyond were the condominium reefs of Palm Beach, Lauderdale, Miami.

Different beaches. Different light. Different molecular makeup, in scent and feel, to the sea wind. Visible from the cumulus towers was an entirely different species of Florida.

Tomorrow, we would be there.

I asked the lady, "Hungry?" eager to change the subject.

She shook her head. "I haven't wanted food since I went into his room and found him missing. I don't need to eat. I have a room at Sundial Resort on . . . is it Middle Gulf Drive? I think I'll go there now. I'm exhausted."

I said, "I can see that. Tired because of the trip? Or maybe it's the company."

She refused to be drawn into that discussion. "I'll call you in the morning. We can talk about what time we should leave for Miami. Do you know your way around the downtown area?"

I replied, "I don't know my way around the downtown area of any city in the world."

She didn't smile. "In that case, we'd probably better leave early. It may take us a while to find the restaurant where we're supposed to be."

I agreed and told her that I'd walk her to her rental car. I put down the skimmer net and turned her easily by touching her elbow. I guided her instantly shoreward, along the boardwalk toward the mangroves, by touching her elbow a second time. Suddenly, I knew how people with communicable diseases feel.

I wanted to ask her, *Why?* Why was she reacting this way? She wasn't just cool, she was icy. Tomlinson was right. There was more than just a touch of distaste. What the hell had I done to offend her?

I wanted to press it, but the timing didn't seem right. Instead, I stuck to the subject. I told her what we had to focus on now was finding Lake, staying smart and negotiating his freedom. So the first thing we had to do, I told her, was make a decision. Was she absolutely certain she didn't want any kind of official help? I added, "Professional help, I'm talking about."

Walking, still maintaining a measured distance between us, she said, "I don't see how it's possible. The American FBI, Florida law enforcement agencies, they certainly have no jurisdiction over a kidnapping committed in Masagua. Even if they did, I wouldn't risk getting my son killed."

Her tone seemed unnecessarily sharp, and I matched it when I replied, "He's my son, too, remember. That's why I want to consider all the options. Review all the assets to make sure we bring him home safely."

"Biologically, you have taken the role of his father. Of course. I'm also aware that in the last two years or so, you and Laken have developed a . . . well, at least a friendship through your correspondence. But let's be clear about one thing, Marion. When it comes to Laken's well-being, *I* make the decisions. *¿Claro?* I welcome your advice, your input. But I have final say."

She'd stopped in the mangroves where the boardwalk exits onto the edge of the gravel parking area near the gate to the marina. Mosquitoes had been trailing us in an orbiting veil, and now they began to vector, flea-hopping off clothing, seeking skin.

I took half a step toward her. I watched her take a full step back as I said, "I'm well aware that the FBI has no jurisdiction in Central America. That's not what I meant by professional help. There may be other options. I know people who are military types—covert extraction experts— who might be willing and able to help us find and free Lake."

She said, "You don't think I'm already aware that you know those kind of people? Apparently you never realized that I'm not stupid. Why do you think I came to you looking for help? It's not because you're his *father.* And it's certainly not because I think you're a *nice* person."

Her tone was so bitter, so accusatory, that I was momentarily speechless. She'd never spoken to me like that. I'd never heard her speak to anyone like that.

"What in the hell is wrong with you, lady? You're furious at me, and for no reason. You've been treating me like I'm poison. *Why?*"

When she tried to turn, I caught her arm and pulled her to me, my face looking down into hers. "I'm not going to let you run away. If I've done something, if I've said something to hurt you, get it out. Let's talk about it. But no more of your passive-aggressive crap. You're too good for it, and so am I. Plus, you're the one who said it—we don't have time."

Her face was shadowed in the mangrove dusk. She looked into my face, then looked at her arm until I took my hand away, freeing her. I watched her straighten her blouse, her slow, deliberate gestures telling me that I should feel like a bullying ass because I'd stopped her.

In a voice that was maddeningly aloof, she said, "All right. Maybe I should have told you months ago. When I first found out."

I didn't like the sound of that. I could feel my pulse in my neck and the side of my head.

"Found out what?"

"About *you*. Who you really are. What kind of man you are. In Masagua, when we met, when . . . when I began to have feelings for you, *thought* I fell in love, it was with a man who I believed was a marine biologist. A scientist. A good and decent man, a researcher dedicated to his profession—"

I said, "I was. I still am."

She held up a palm—*quiet*. "I knew there was also a possibility that you were working for the American State Department. Or military. I'd heard the rumors. I'm not stupid. But most such agents are simply abroad to gather data, to make quantitative analysis. They're observers. I had no problem with that. But you did more, Marion. That's what I discovered. Far more."

I stood silently, breath shallow, fists clenched as I listened to her add, "A person brought me the files. Someone showed me the photos. A person who became interested in your background and did the research. I couldn't believe what I read. What I *saw*. I didn't *want* to believe.

"You did illegal things in my country. And in Nicaragua, too. Unthinkable things. The worst, though, was what you did to a man named Don Blas Diego." Her voice became harsh, emotional and accusatory, as she added, "You knew. You *had* to know who that kind and decent man was. You knew that Don Blas was my—"

I interrupted. I had to interrupt because I couldn't allow her to finish.

"At the time," I said, "I *didn't* know who he was. And for a long time afterward. I swear it. I truly didn't know, not until much later."

I did not add that Don Blas Diego had been neither a kind man nor a decent man. What good would it serve now, telling her the truth? To challenge her family memories?

On one level, I was pained that Pilar had been hurt. On another, I was shocked that those documents still existed. Supposedly, there had been only one file maintained on my activities: a book-sized dossier that, not so long ago, I had tossed into a driftwood fire after making an exchange with a friend on a deserted beach. I'd watched the pages burn and curl, feeling the first suggestion of freedom from a past that had consumed me. That such a file still existed in Masagua seem illustrative of the chaos that was now crippling it.

Something else: Clearly, someone had chosen me as a personal project. Or a target. Had singled me out as the focus of a lot of deep digging and single-minded research. More troubling, that person necessarily had a first-rate intellect. They'd had to correctly reassemble a lot of convoluted links to find those files, and then unscramble or decode them.

Who?

Why?

Trying to maintain emotional composure, keeping my expression blank, I watched her draw a deep breath, struggling to get herself back under control. But then I winced as she said, "You're not the good man I thought I cared for. How could you have done those things?"

In a whisper, I replied, "There was a war going on."

"Yes, but it was *our* war. Not yours. Do you know what concerns me the most since I found out? That he calls you 'Father.' If he believes your blood runs in his veins, will he try to emulate you? Already, he's becoming more and more like you. At night, I go to sleep worrying about it. Will that part of you be in him? That gene, that kind of . . . of evil? Is there a killer inside of my child, waiting?"

I said, "There's a difference between evil and carrying out orders."

"So you tell yourself. It's a way of rationalizing. You can't see that? Or maybe you simply can't admit it."

"I've admitted more than most."

"And you can still live with yourself?"

I said, "It was touch and go there for a while. Just because you don't see the scars doesn't mean they're not there."

I thought the honesty of that would leach some of the anger out of her. It didn't.

"To open that folder, to see what was inside . . . I was in total shock."

"Don't be so sure that all the things you were told, the files you saw, were true."

"Photographs don't lie, Marion."

"Oh, they can. Believe me, they can."

Completely out of character, she then put her hands on hips, leaned toward me, and in a shrill whisper that became a whispered shriek, yelled, "I hope to God everything I read about you *is* true. I hope it's *all* true. Because I need someone smart and ruthless to help me get my child back. I hope you are a vicious son-of-a-bitch and you find the people who've taken my son!"

Trauma changes us; fear can transform us. In that instant, I realized something. I realized that I no longer knew this person. Heartbreaking.

Staying composed, hoping my calm would help to calm her, I said, "At least now I know why you've come back to me. Now, at least, I know the truth."

"Did you expect something more?"

There was still a filament of hysteria in her voice.

I don't know why I said it. Maybe I wanted to hurt her because she'd hurt me. She'd certainly done that more than once over the years. Or maybe I really meant it when I replied, "I don't know what I expected. But I can tell you what I hoped. I hoped you'd come to tell me that you wanted me back. Because I love you. I've always loved you. You can hate me, loathe me, whatever you want. But nothing is going to change the fact that I still think of you often. I'm not an overly emotional person. But that's the way it's been, Pilar, from the day we first met."

When I stepped toward her now, she did not retreat. Her body went slack when I took her into my arms and pulled her face to my chest. She neither responded nor struggled to free herself as I squeezed her close and continued, "No matter what you've read or heard, I'm still the man you were in love with. I'm the same person. So you must still feel *something* for me."

I felt her shudder—a prelude to tears, perhaps?—as I turned her face upward and pressed my mouth to hers. For several long seconds, she simply hung there, lips against mine, as if she were asleep, or numb. But then gradually, very gradually, her lips seemed to soften as her legs found a base beneath her. Then I felt her mouth move and open slightly as her hips lifted against mine . . . her arms tightening gradually around me, squeezing, losing herself in the moment. . . .

More so than any woman I've met, Pilar is made up of two distinct and different physical, emotional beings. One is public. The other, she keeps locked away, caged deep—the sexual Pilar. To know the first, you would never, ever guess the existence of the second.

The sexual Pilar can emerge voluntarily or involuntarily, but when that woman appears, it's like a creature set loose. The transformation may be gradual, but it is total, and there are no boundaries, no taboos. Once the transformation passes a certain point, there is no stopping her body, because Pilar's body takes total, sensory control.

For a few powerful seconds, I sensed the creature trying to slip from its cage, its body seeking mine . . . but not for long. Her muscles seemed to spasm in sudden realization . . . then she stopped, frozen, before Pilar turned her face away and pushed me backward.

"No. I can't. I *won't*." Her voice was husky.

Her body, at least, remembered the way it had been between us.

I said, "I'm not perfect. But I'm no monster. You know that. And you still love me. That won't change between us."

Did I really believe that? Probably not. It was another way to repay the hurt she'd caused me.

I expected to hear Pilar reply. Instead, I was shocked to hear a second woman's voice answer from nearby mangroves at the edge of the parking lot. It was a familiar voice, deeper, with a pure Midwestern accent. The woman was obviously, and for good reason, furious.

"What a sweet little scene for me to interrupt," said the second woman. "Doc Ford with another woman. What an asshole thing for you to do, Ford—you were my *best friend*, damn you! This is the kind of trailer-trash bullshit I never would have expected."

I looked up and got a glimpse of Dewey Nye—long legs, white tennis shorts and blouse, blond hair glimmering from beneath a dark sun visor.

I said, *"Dewey?"*

"Yeah, that's right. It's me, ol' buddy. Surprise, surprise."

"Dewey . . . whoa, wait, hold on. Something happened—"

She didn't give me a chance to finish. Raising her voice to drown mine, she told Pilar, "A monster is just about *exactly* what he is, lady. Which shocks the hell out of me. He's a damn Jekyll and Hyde, which, thanks to you, I just found out. So you can have him. Forever you can have him. I'm outta here for good."

I got another quick glimpse of long legs and blond ponytail swinging before I heard her car door slam.

She'd sold her 'Vette and bought a new two-seater Lexus. I can never remember the model. The roadster showed impressive stability as she spun it around in the parking lot, kicking a wake of shells and dust as she accelerated away.

The encounter had sobered Pilar, and my hands were shaking as I combed fingers through hair in momentary shock, whispering to myself, *"Oh . . . that poor, dear girl."*

After a long, long silence, mosquitoes screaming in my ears, Pilar said, "I'm sorry that happened. I truly am. Is she someone you care about?"

"Yeah. She is, very much. We've been together for a while."

"I've seen her before. That time in Panama. I remember now. Very athletic and beautiful. Dewey? I've forgotten her last name."

"That's her."

"I can never let you kiss me again, Marion. Ever. Or hold me. I'll explain that to her if you want. That it meant nothing to me. I'll tell her that, too, if you like."

Looking closely at Pilar, I said, "Even if that's true, I don't think she'd believe it."

SIX

I WENT back to the house, took the keys to my old Chevy pickup truck off the hook over the front door, and went looking for Dewey. I'm not the most compassionate of people, but anyone who hurts a friend and does not swiftly try to make amends ranks, in my book, among the lowest of the low.

There was a second, more selfish consideration. I realized something: I didn't want to lose the lady. Not like this. Not because of something I said—words I was now already fairly certain I didn't mean.

I drove toward Captiva Island on SanCap Road, past Sanibel Gardens, past the Sanibel Rum Bar & Grille at the intersection of Rabbit Road—Tomlinson's new favorite hangout. Then past the elementary school where the ball diamond lights were on, a couple of the beer-league soft-ball teams tinging away with aluminum bats.

It looked like Nave Electric was playing the Timber's staff. I drove faster than normal, windows open, one hand on the wheel, the Gulf of Mexico off to my left, the bay beyond, houses and tree fringe to my right.

A Campeche wind was blowing off the Gulf, stirring the tops of palms. It leached a cumulative heat from the island's sand face, weighted with the odor of sea grape, palmetto, oak leaves, prickly pear. My truck's lights cre-ated a tunneled, pearl conduit, stars above, vegetation gathered close on this part of the road, traffic sparse.

I looked at my plastic watch: 9:07 P.M.

Dewey had sold her beachfront home because it was impossible to refuse the small fortune a software magnate had offered her. Besides, as she said, the house was never much more than a hotel to her anyway, she'd traveled so much during her years as a tennis pro. There was no vested emotion. In fact, the place had personal baggage and some bad memories.

So she'd banked half the money, and used the rest to buy and remodel a luxury bungalow, bayside, hidden in a coconut grove between Mango Court and Dickey Lane, just past Twin Palms Marina and the Sunshine Café on Captiva Island.

At Mango Court, I turned right down the sand drive, her property isolated by high ficus hedges and security warning signs, expecting to see her Lexus parked beneath the open, roofed carport.

It wasn't.

She hadn't run home with her tail between her legs, as might have been expected.

Why was I surprised? Dewey almost always does the unexpected. It's one of the reasons I value her. She is five-ten, 155 pounds or so of pure nonconformist female, highly competitive, though secretly super sensitive despite the fact that her vocabulary has a consistently salty, seagoing flair.

Dewey is *different*. Maybe it's because her life has been so different from the lives of most women. Her family is from somewhere in the Midwest— Iowa or Kansas or Ohio, I think. But because her father was a tyrant and a bully, she grew up attending the Nick Bollettieri Tennis Academy in Bradenton, Florida. She got used to living in a dorm, adjusting to a communal society and life on the road because she never got the chance to experience anything else. For a while, she was ranked one of the top twenty tennis players in the world. But then there was an elbow operation, and a knee operation, and she decided to concentrate on golf, a game she loves.

Something else Dewey concentrated on for a time was Walda Bzantovski, the Romanian tennis great and her long-time lover. But things hadn't worked out.

Which is why she was now living on the islands, splitting her time between this classy, plush bungalow on Captiva, and my spartan stilt house on Sanibel.

Until tonight.

SO where do female ex-jocks go when they're furious? Or when their hearts are broken?

Probably the same place men go, I decided. To seek comfort and counsel in a best friend. Or in a friendly bartender.

I was her best friend. At least, I *had* been. Which left option number two. So I drove from place to place, checking the parking lots of bars.

I looked for her car at the Mucky Duck, R. C. Otters, 'Tween Waters, and the Green Flash without results. Back on Sanibel Island, though, I got lucky. I drove through the lot of the Sanibel Rum Bar & Grille, and her Lexus was there, hood cool to the touch.

I'd driven right past the place on the way to her home.

The Rum Bar is built into a little strip mall that it shares with a health club and a couple of other island businesses. But it's still got a tropical feel, the way it's decorated; plus, it attracts all the fishing guides and service industry locals as well as tourists on their way to and from Captiva Island.

I didn't see many familiar faces on this Tuesday night, though. The bar was packed, two or three deep, ceiling fans swirling overhead, flags and nautical charts from Central America and the Bahamas on the walls, a local band, the Trouble Starters, singing about what they were gonna do when the volcano blew as I walked through the doors.

Dewey was there. She was in the corner of the room next to the Cuban refugee boat that the owner had salvaged in the Florida Keys and had converted into a table. She was playing a game called Ringmaster: Swing the brass ring accurately and it will arc on its string and lock itself onto a hook six feet away.

Dewey wasn't alone. Not a surprise. Women as attractive as Dewey spend few lonely moments in bars. She was with a group of five men, the central focus of their attention. The men were drinking mixed drinks. They wore bright Hawaiian shirts or polos, a couple of middle-age bellies showing, and neatly pressed khakis on an island where almost everyone wears cargo shorts in May.

So they were tourists, probably down here fishing or golfing or attending some kind of convention. They had the look of money, with their styled hair sprayed in place, waxed Docksiders, and heavy gold watch bracelets and rings. So I made another guess: maybe corporate executives, or attorneys, or members of the same investment team on Sanibel for a meeting, cutting loose a little, showing off for the tall blonde with the bawdy vocabulary.

Dewey saw me the instant I walked in. Without pausing, her eyes swept through me and away as if I were invisible.

For a moment, I thought she might throw an arm over the shoulder of one of her new buddies; do something to try and instigate jealousy. But, no, she was too classy for that. Instead, she shoved one of the men roughly, tossed her head back, laughing, and took her turn with the ring. First, though, she placed her chalice-sized margarita on the refugee boat—Dewey, a woman who seldom drank alcohol.

I thought to myself: *Uh-oh. Trouble.*

There was that potential.

AT THE BAR, I paid for a Bud Light, told Mark, the bartender, that Tomlinson—a Rum Bar regular—would probably be in later, and strolled over to the little circle of men clustered around Dewey. They greeted me with cool glances, their body language screening me out, telling me it was their little party, go away.

But I didn't go away. I stood there watching for a quarter of an hour, listening to the kibitzing, trying to assess, evaluate, hoping Dewey would excuse herself and give me a chance to explain.

Her new friends were salesmen from a national sporting goods chain based outside Chicago. There were four underlings, judging from their ingratiating manner, and there was the big boss, Corporate Vice-President in charge of something.

I never heard what.

Corporate V-P was authoritative, but in the chummy way that head coaches use. He wasn't overtly arrogant, but he did have a CEO's knack for assuming center stage. He was shorter than I but much broader, with dense black hair and the layered, geometric facial structure that women seem to find attractive.

There were a couple of more details I noted: His underlings were working hard for him, through deference and flattery, helping him make a play for Dewey.

Something else: There was a wedding-band width of sunburned skin on the ring finger of his left hand.

Salesmen get an unfair rap. Their profession is a favorite target of derision, when in fact I know it to be among the most demanding of occupations. I know because, when it comes right down to it, I'm a salesman. I sell marine specimens—and I'm not the world's best.

If you're gunning to be a top salesman, you'd better possess all the social skills, and nearly every intellectual gift. The field's about as competitive as it gets. But there was something about this little group I disliked. Maybe it was the missing wedding band. Maybe it was the way the pack was trying to herd the female stranger into the arms of its alpha male. Or maybe I was deluding myself—I do it regularly—by trying to intellectualize my jealousy.

Whatever the reason, there was no doubt that I overreacted when Corporate V-P caught me staring at Dewey. He glared at me for a moment, and when I refused to break eye contact, he said, "This is a private party, champ. Or maybe you're just lost and mistook us for friends. Well, we're not."

Which received nervous laughter from everyone but Dewey until I replied, "The only thing lost seems to be your wedding ring. I'm willing to make a guess. The ring's back in your hotel room. Probably hidden under the condoms you bought at the airport."

Groaning, rolling her eyes, Dewey said, "Smooth, Ford. Jesus. Mister Congeniality," as Corporate V-P stepped toward me, his underlings moving aside, creating room for us and thus a small stage.

"*What* did you just say to me?"

I repeated what I'd said, not budging as he advanced toward me, still looking into his eyes, which made him uneasy, I could tell. But he was committed to it, his employees watching, and he couldn't back down. Not without confronting me first, establishing for them that he held a higher rung on the machismo ladder, anyway.

He stopped, his nose close to my own, intentionally invading my personal space. "Do you know this guy, Dewey?"

"Yeah, Hal. Unfortunately. He's one of the local island playboys. A real lady killer."

"He's got a big mouth."

"Not usually. Which is why you should just let it go. Doc's not the physical type. He likes to look through his telescope. It'd be like taking a poke at your high school principal."

To Dewey, I said, "Thanks, friend," as Corporate V-P told her, "I'm tempted to knock those glasses right off his ugly face."

Now Dewey threw her arm down between us like a toll gate and said, "Stop it. I want both you boys to do me a favor. Quit acting like jerks or I'll run you both outside, then spank your asses, O.K.? So knock it off!"

Which gave him his out. He grinned, then began to laugh. His underlings laughed along with him, but I noted what may have been an edge of disappointment. They'd wanted it to happen.

"O.K., gorgeous. For you, if he's a friend of yours. I'll let it go this time." Corporate V-P used his index finger to warn me. "But no more smart-ass remarks. *Capisc'*?"

Before I could answer, though, he made a serious error. He threw his right arm around Dewey, pulled her roughly to him, and kissed her on the side of her mouth—a kidding sort of roughhousing move that was also markedly territorial. Some women endure that behavior with mild, passive smiles. But it's not the sort of thing Dewey has ever tolerated, or ever will.

"Hey . . . what the hell do you think you're doing, you *jerk*. Get your hands off me!"

I was already moving toward him as Dewey knocked his arm free, then shoved him hard in the chest. She's a big, strong woman. I've spotted her when she's bench-pressed 160 pounds, sets of ten.

Hal, the Corporate V-P, went backpedaling through his covey of underlings, who, surprisingly, did not catch him. The refugee boat is hip-high. He somersaulted over it backward, knocking off all the drinks that were on it.

From the bar, seeing it, a couple of women whooped, and the band, who'd been playing right along, stopped now, except for the drummer—his unplanned solo creating a hollow, galloping sound as others called, "*Whoa, fight. Hey, a fight!*"

The bartender, Mark, was immediately there as Hal got to his feet, fists clenched, humiliated, furious. Because he knew us, Mark asked me, "What the hell's going on here? I'm not going to tolerate any trouble. You know that. Doc, you of all people!"

Dewey was gulping down the rest of her margarita, talking as she did. "Don't worry about it, Markie. My ex-boyfriend, Professor Dumbass, and I are hitting the bricks. Especially him."

I could see that Hal and his friends didn't like it at all when she added to Mark, "If any our local girls come in here, warn them about this group of short-tails. They're just slimy types on the make. O.K.?"

HAL, the Corporate V-P, couldn't let it go. He had to follow us into the parking lot.

"Whoa, whoa, hold on you two. You think I'm going to let you say that kinda crap and get away with it?" Hal's tone saying he had no choice—he had to stand tall for his team.

All I wanted was to be alone with Dewey, to try and explain why I'd said what I'd said. Not that I was even sure myself. The shock of it all had rattled me. It'd dredged up old feelings and long-gone memories. But Dewey was an integral part of my present. I hoped we were close enough friends that I could tell her about it, and that she'd understand. If she'd just give me a chance.

Which she wasn't willing to do. Not here, not now.

Car door open, she turned to me and said, "Look, pal, it shouldn't be such a big deal. You got caught screwin' around. It happens to people all the time."

I said, "Not to us, it doesn't. Dewey, something's happened I just found out about. I'll follow you home and explain."

She was getting in the car. "Yeah, I know, I know. The only woman you'll ever love is on Sanibel. I heard. So go back to your love shack and tell it to her, Romeo."

I realized she was feeling the margaritas.

When I touched her elbow, she yanked her arm away . . . and that's when Hal, the Corporate V-P, came striding across the parking lot.

Saying, "Stay in the car until I get rid of this guy," I turned and walked toward Hal to put some distance between him and Dewey. Which, as I should have known, guaranteed that she'd get out of the car.

Hal was saying, "Lady, I think an apology is in order."

I was holding both hands out—*Stop right there*—as I said, "She's not going to apologize to you or anyone else, so just drop it. What you should do, Hal, you and your buddies, is march yourselves back into the bar and have a drink. Because I'm really not in the mood to put up with you and your self-important bullshit."

Behind me, I heard Dewey say, "Jesus, Ford, you really are in a mood tonight," as Hal's voice changed, all pretense of control gone: "Fuck you, *champ*. Who the fuck do you think you are? You don't even know who I *am*. Do you have a clue who you're talking to?"

Dewey was right. I was in an unusual mood. Whatever it was, I'd had enough. I walked toward Corporate V-P, saying, "I'm the guy who's going to knock you on your ass in front of all your little playmates if you don't turn around and leave us alone right now. Go. Get out of here. Leave!"

Which he couldn't do. Not now. I'd left him no wiggle room, no honorable egress—a stupid choice on my part. So he took two fast steps toward me and tried to take me out with a single, mighty, overhand right fist. I stepped in close, absorbed most of the impact with my shoulder. Then I locked my left arm under his right elbow as I dug the fingers of my right hand into the delicate area behind his jawbone, just below the neck. I tilted his face back toward the stars as I applied pressure to his elbow—already furious with myself that I'd allowed the situation to escalate to this point and eager for a way out.

As I held him, I said, "I'm going to give you one more chance to walk away. The lady's right. I'm no fighter. You win . . . *O.K.?* So let's stop it now. You go back to the bar, we'll get in our cars and leave."

Behind me, I heard Dewey call to him, "He's wearing *glasses,* for Christ's sake! You think that's fair?"

Talking about me like I was handicapped, yelling to protect me.

Maybe Corporate V-P found encouragement in that, because, despite the hold I had on him, he began to kick wildly, trying to knee me in the groin.

I blocked most of them with my hip, but he got in one shot that nearly connected. Came close enough to make me woof and my lungs spasm.

That did it. He'd had his chance, and I'd had enough. I released his jaw, squatted slightly, then drove my open palm hard up under his chin. I used my thighs to create torque, twisting at the hips.

The blow cracked his teeth together—a sickening sound—and lifted him momentarily off the ground. I caught him in both arms, controlling his body, then pinched the thumb and middle fingers of my left hand around his throat. With my right, I slapped his face once . . . twice, and then I swung in behind him, threading my forearms under his armpits.

His voiced was an octave higher now: "You son-of-a-bitch. I'll *kill* you for this."

There was enough light in the parking lot to see that his mouth was frothing blood.

Breathing heavily, wrestling him, applying more pressure now, I said into his ear, "No more threats. You're just making it worse."

Then I leveraged my arms up through his, locked both hands together, and forced my palms against the back of his head—a dangerous pressure hold called a full nelson.

I was aware that Corporate V-P's four men were not standing idly by while I humiliated their leader. They were the vocal type, at first calling out encouragement and instruction. Then commanding me to stop, to let him go, or they were going to call the cops or kick my ass. The threats varied. I thought I was keeping careful peripheral track of them—they were banded together off to my left.

But not all of them.

My hands locked behind his head, I walked Corporate V-P toward my truck and slammed his body hard against the fender, then slammed him hard a second time. I increased the pressure on the back of his head as I said, "It's time for you to go home, Hal. What do you think?"

The pain he was in changed his voice, and his attitude. "Yeah, O.K., O.K., Jesus Christ, that's enough. It was a misunderstanding. Seriously, no hard feelings . . . goddamn it! You're breaking my neck!"

So I let V-P stand, releasing pressure, unthreading my fingers—which is when one of his sales crew jumped me from behind. The guy had a strong arm around my throat, but I got my fingers around his wrists and snapped his hands free without much trouble. Then I ducked under, pivoted, got behind him, and drove his arm up into the middle of his back. Drove it with such force that it certainly dislocated his shoulder, and maybe broke it.

Along with his scream of pain, I heard, "Doc, watch it!"

I turned to see Dewey intercept another of the salesmen—Hawaiian shirt, beer gut—who was charging toward me. She stopped him with a stiff-arm, then dropped him with a single overhand right to his nose. The punch had all the speed and accuracy of her once much-feared tennis serve.

That was the end of it. Hal's underlings had risked enough for their Corporate V-P. He'd lost, so had they, and I knew they'd never look at him or behave the same around him again.

Something else I knew: Back at corporate headquarters in Chicago, the story about Hal, the fight, and how it started would spread quickly. Either Hal would soon be gone, or he would muster sufficient political muscle to oust his underlings. But there was no way his career could endure them hanging around, because he'd been exposed for what he really was, and they'd witnessed it. Authentic leaders are sustained by the strength of their own character. Sham leaders succeed only because they are passable character actors.

Hal had been unmasked.

The hierarchy of corporations is as complicated—and no less primal— than the hierarchies of pack animals. In such packs—wolves or lions or chimps, for instance—alpha males rise to power, then survive or are banished by jockeying underlings.

I didn't feel the least bit sorry for the guy.

At her Lexus, rubbing her already swelling knuckles, Dewey told me, "And I tried to help you beg out of it because of your glasses. All these years, I didn't have a clue. What were you back in school, some kinda hot-shit wrestling champion or something?"

Opening the door for her, I said, "Something like that."

SHE didn't want me to follow her home, but I did. Her bungalow has a Spanish tile roof and conch-pink siding. The house is built on low stilts a couple feet above a quarter-acre of bare limestone gravel, the property landscaped for minimum maintenance.

The moon was three days before full, high overhead—its mountainous polar regions visible where the temperature was 300 degrees below zero out there in space. In the moon's cold light, I could see papaya and palms planted in ornamental clusters, and a banana thicket, too. The papaya and sugar bananas were good. Some mornings for breakfast, Dewey and I would eat them chilled, fresh lime juice squirted on.

Seeing the fruit trees in moon shadow caused me to realize something. Caused me to realize that I might not awake in bed with her ever again, the two of us lounging around, talking during breakfast, laughing at silly things, sharing small secrets. The end of something was in those shadows. I felt a quaking sense of loss.

I knocked. She refused to allow me in. Finally, though, she came out onto the porch. She had ice in a plastic bag, holding it on the knuckles of her right hand.

Standing in the moonlight, I told her about Lake. What had happened to my son. Her reaction—horror, revulsion—was genuine. She'd had some bad things happen in her life. She knew tragedy and grief.

I had to admire her core toughness when she added, "But that doesn't change what I heard tonight. The words you said to the boy's mother. I *know* you. The way your voice sounded. What I heard really, really hurt because I know you meant everything you said. Didn't you?"

There was no anger in her tone now. Just pain and grief. I shook my head and made a sound of exasperation. "I have too much respect for you, our friendship, to do anything but tell you the truth. Truth is, I *don't* know. It was a shock seeing her. Then finding out about the kidnapping. Hell . . . the only thing I'm sure of is that it scares me, thinking that I might lose you. Lose us. I don't want that to happen."

I put my hands on her shoulders. Listened to her try and repress a sniffle—Jesus, now I'd made her cry.

I said, "Can I come in? I leave for Miami in the morning. I don't know how long it'll take for me to find my son. If I *can* find him. This may be our only night together for a while."

But she remained steadfast. "Doc, look . . . what you need to understand is, this not a small deal. If you really are in love with someone else, I've got to make some important decisions fast. We're beyond the dating part. The kid games part. At least, I *thought* we were."

There was an intentional, underlying meaning there that I didn't grasp.

She removed my hands from her shoulders, touched her fingers briefly to my face, her blue eyes gray in the moonlight, as wide and sad as I had ever seen them. "I'm not telling this to hurt you. I know you don't need any more pressure—not with what's happened to your son. I've got to say it, though. You know how we've talked about maybe getting married, maybe one day having kids?"

I nodded.

"Well, pal . . . I'm more than six weeks late. My period, it's way late. After work, I stopped at Bailey's General Store and got one of those little test kits. The kind where you pee on the strip. It changes color if you're pregnant. I went to your place thinking we could have a little ceremony. We could find out together.

"But there you were with a woman. A woman who's already been through it. She's already the mother of your son. I get out of the car kinda mixed up, but with all those hopes about us, marriage and a baby, and that's when I hear you say those words to her, *I'll always love you.* That's exactly what you said. And *meant* it.

"You see what I mean? Why something like that would hurt so bad? So I'm not ready to talk about it. Not tonight. Not this week. Probably not for a long while."

I said, "Oh Jesus . . . I am so, so sorry . . ."

She touched her fingers to my cheek again. "I know you are, you big idiot." Then: "Go on home, pal. I'll get in touch with you when I'm ready. We'll talk. Just give me some space."

I covered her hand with mine. "But, Dew, I want to know. Get the test kit. Go to the bathroom now and find out. You really think you might be pregnant? It's . . . that's kind of *exciting.*"

Did I mean that? *Maybe.* Maybe I did.

But she shook her head.

No.

"Please."

"Uh-uh, no, I can't. Because *I* don't want to know. Not now. I need to get my emotions under control first. After that, we have to have a serious talk. When it's time.

"I don't want the fact that I am or am not pregnant to have any influence. That way, when I find out, we'll both know how things stand between us. The decision will already have been made about us being together. Do you see why I have to do it this way?"

Yeah, I did. A smart lady.

She let me hug her close to my chest and hold her for a moment before she went inside and locked the door.

SEVEN

SEEN from the I-95 overpass, downtown Miami is an island of ascending spires, silicon on steel, beneath a sky that is incandescent with Gulf Stream colors—lime, corals, blues.

We were on the Interstate now, Tomlinson, Pilar, and I. We were cloverleafing our way down into the city, jockeying among six fast lanes blurred with cars operated by Haitians, Jamaicans, Dominicans, and other tropical immigrants whose donkey-cart driving skills were superb at five miles an hour, but lethal at eighty.

Thrown into the mix were Winnebago Buckeyes, German tourists, and Friendly Sam New Yorkers, plus Cuban Americans who actually knew their away around the badly marked highways, and so used horn and accelerator as weapons of intimidation.

Driving in Miami, even midmorning on a Wednesday, is not for the faint of heart.

Because my old truck doesn't have air-conditioning, and because Tomlinson's Volkswagen Thing is only slightly safer and faster than four slabs of drywall bolted around a toy engine, Pilar asked us to drive her rental Ford.

Lucky me.

I'm at home in a boat under the worst of circumstances. The same is not true of cars. Waves, squalls, and sea bottom are relatively predictable. Miami drivers are not. Which makes me edgy. So I drove with hands at ten-and-two, concentrating mightily on the idiotic maneuverings and macho posturing of other lanes, while Tomlinson maintained a running dialogue with Pilar, the two of them already fast friends.

"Miami, my sister. Behold the great Concrete Mango—South America's northernmost nation. Miami and I, we've got a kinda love–who-cares relationship going. I love her, but I just don't draw enough water for Miami to care about me. Not many dudes do.

"See that building, the tallest building, the one that looks like it's a geode crystal with a broken point? The way it's sheared off at the top? That's the Wachovia Center. A cop banged my head into a wall there a couple times during an antiwar protest way, *way* back. That thing's built *solid,* believe me.

"Then see the Miami Deco-looking high-rise, the one that looks like it's a chunk of chrome off an old Cadillac? That's the Bank of America Tower. I dated one of the top execs there for a while. She was something, man. We'd go across to the Hyatt, Japengos, for appetizers and margaritas. Or eat on the eleventh-floor terrace, the whole city spreading out, then head back to her office. Spend the afternoon with the intercom turned off, making bunny-love magic—which is all I'm going to say about *that.*"

I interrupted. "Thanks for sparing us the details. What might be nice for a change is to hear some silence. Or maybe we could just listen to the radio."

Still talking to Pilar, he said, "Mister Grumpy. It's because of the driving stress. You can drop this guy into any jungle or island on earth, and he's right at home. Put him on a freeway, though, and his knuckles turn white."

"I'm trying to concentrate," I said. "Something wrong with that? All these lunatic drivers . . . my God—did you see the stunt the idiot in that Explorer just pulled? And besides, you're supposed to be helping me look for, what is it, the Second Street exit?"

"Northeast Second Avenue. That's our exit. But first we jump on the I-Three-ninety-five. So we've got a little time."

Pilar said to me, "I enjoy listening to Tomlinson. He's very sweet, and he's made me laugh for the first time since it happened. I don't see why you should object to the two of us talking."

I thought: *Perfect. Now she's bonding with my best friend.*

I concentrated on driving, yet couldn't help but listen as Tomlinson launched into his monologue about the evils of gas-guzzling SUVs such as the crazed Explorer, muscle cars, pickup trucks—a shot at me, there—and the petroleum industry's scheme to control the world economy.

I find it amazing that someone of his intelligence and insight is a predictable dupe for every left-wing conspiracy theory that comes along. But an individual's politics, like religion, I have learned, is not a reliable or fair gauge of intellect or humanitarian intent. I know intelligent people who embrace equally ridiculous right-wing absurdities. So I try to judge people individually, which is what reasonable people do.

Not that he didn't have a good point about squandering the Earth's fossil fuels. It is a commodity of finite measure, and a consistent agent of hypocrisy: Many Americans abhor the prospect of drilling for oil in our own boundary lands and oceans, yet we all live eager, modern, petroleum-based lives. I can certainly be counted among the hypocrites.

But at Dinkin's Bay Marina, we'd become so tired of hearing Tomlinson's anti-SUV lecturing, his save-the-Earth posturing, that Mack, Jeth, Felix, and a couple of the other fishing guides came up with an idea. A way to play a joke on Tomlinson.

Tomlinson's Volkswagen is several decades old and looks like a German staff car. It's a rusted antique with an 8-gallon fuel tank and a tiny engine that gets thirty-plus miles per gallon—a fact that he's also hammered us over the head with.

So a couple months back, the guides began to slip into the parking lot at night and funnel gas *into* his car's tank, topping it off each and every time Tomlinson used the vehicle.

Every day he got in to use the Volkswagen, he found that the tank was full.

He drove twenty-five miles to Terry Park in Fort Myers to play Roy Hobbs baseball. He drove a hundred miles to Siesta Key Beach to lead the Sunday night drum circle. He drove across the state to visit his boat bum pals at Bahia Mar Marina in Lauderdale. He drove to Stan's Chickee Bar in

Goodland and did the Buzzard Lope. He drove to Placida and took the ferry across to Palm Island to teach meditation and lead seminars on Tomlinsonism—his own brand of Buddhism that has so grown in popularity that the man now bundles his hair under a fedora and wears Hollywood sunglasses when he leaves the marina.

I hadn't exaggerated when I told Pilar that, thanks to the internet, his followers seek him out from around the world.

Our reluctant prophet put hundreds of miles on the Volkswagen, and his gas tank remained full.

At first, he bragged piously about his car. While we drove around in our oil suckers, destroying a fragile planet, he was meeting all transportation needs while leaving only the tiniest of environmental footprints.

"Real men don't have to drive a big car," he told us. "It's like the bumper stickers you see. Ask yourselves this: What kinda car would Jesus have driven?"

While Mack wondered aloud, "Hummm . . . something amphibious?" Jeth, the stuttering fishing guide, replied, "There's a NASCAR driver named Hay-zus. If that's the one you mean, he runs a 340 big block Dodge V-8, 750 horsepower. But if you're talkin' about gas mileage, I wouldn't think ol' Jesus' car would be a smart choice."

After another week or so of hard driving, though, and with the tank still full, Tomlinson began to fret. Maybe his fuel gauge was broken. So he took the car down to Island Amoco.

The gauge checked out just fine.

Amazing.

He drove to Fort Myers Beach, LaBelle, and Estero. He drove to St. Petersburg, Venus, and then to Burnt Store Marina to hang out at the docks and drink at the bar.

The gas needle still pointed to full.

Which was impossible. The Volkswagen was running without burning any gasoline. No logical human being would have accepted that possibility. But Tomlinson, though capable of logical thought, does not embrace a logical view of the world. His beat-up old Volkswagen, he decided, had somehow been vested with spiritual qualities and unworldly abilities.

One night, stoned and very drunk on El Dorado rum, he wobbled up to my house, pounded on my door, and told me, "Doc. I finally figured it out. She's got a soul in her. My car. I think maybe she's an old lover of mine from a previous life. It's a feeling I've got. Like, it just *came* to me, man. That this old lover is now inhabiting my Volkswagen, come back to help me seek enlightenment . . . or maybe screw with me and spy on me, too. Sabotage new relationships, break down on the open road just when I'm horniest—who knows. I've had good women and bad, so it's a crap shoot when it comes to dealing with the new incarnations of old sweeties.

"But my car, she's definitely got a soul. Which is why I'm calling her Stella. That's as good a name as any. I thought about Zeetar, which is one of the hottest monkey-love planets in the galaxy. But how can I explain something like that to spiritual civilians? The point is, my Volkswagen Thing has become a thinking, feeling, sentient being. It's the *only* possible explanation for why she refuses to vex me by burning Mother Earth's fossil fuel."

I'd replied, "The only explanation, huh?"

When I shared with the guides an edited version of what he'd told me, they decided to change tactics. They continued their late-night assaults on Tomlinson's Volkswagen. Now, though, instead of putting gas into the tank, they siphoned gas *out*.

If he drove to Jensen's Marina on nearby Captiva, he had to stop and get fuel. If he drove a quarter-mile to Timber's to hang out with Matt Asen, he had to fill up the tank. He'd been working on wood sculpture in Fort Meyers with Terrence Flannery, a brilliant artist. Every time he turned the key, the gas needle pointed to empty, so he had to go straight to the Hess station on Tarpon Bay Road.

Which shut him up. Ended his windy lecturing on the gas-guzzling cars we drove and the outboard engines we used.

But the guides couldn't trust themselves to be together around him. They'd crack up when Tomlinson came near. They'd cough into their hands, struggle not to squirt beer out their noses, and hurry away.

So it had been a while since I'd heard his anti-SUV monologue. And maybe he was right about me being irritable. Because when he started to belabor the conspiratorial link between the SUV makers of Detroit, the world industrial complex, and Texas oil barons—"The reason's obvious. There're bigger profits in cars that guzzle gas!"—I interrupted, saying, "Why don't you tell Pilar about your Volkswagen? About the amazing mileage it's been getting. There's a pretty good example of what you're talking about."

Tomlinson's jaw got tight. "Uh-uh, don't even mention that back-stabbing, four-cylinder slut to me. Besides, our exit's coming up soon. With all this traffic, I better keep my eyes open."

THE Cacique Restaurant is on West Flagler near Northwest Miami Court, across from the Claude Pepper Federal Building and the old court-house, a Cuban lunch spot in the heart of a city that has been redefined by expatriated Cubans.

We were more than an hour early, so we put the car in a parking barn and walked to Southwest Second Avenue where Pilar said the Masagua consul general kept a suite of offices. She'd been there a number of times in past years.

Good thing we checked. I don't know how many countries maintain consulates in Miami. Many dozens from around the world, no doubt, in-cluding most of the Caribbean and Latin countries.

The Ingraham Building is one of many Miami diplomatic strongholds. The downstairs directory said that the Bahamas, Bolivia, Jamaica, and Uruguay all had offices there. But not Masagua. Not any longer. The Masaguan consulate, a security guard told us, had recently been moved to downtown Coral Gables, next to the Guatemalan consulate on Sevilla Street.

Coral Gables might be twenty minutes away, it might be fifty, depend-ing on traffic.

Heading back to the Cacique Restaurant, among high-rise canyons dot-ted with storefront delis, Italian perfumeries, and Levi's, camera, and passport photo shops, Pilar correctly interpreted my silence.

"You have every right to be furious. It was an easy mistake to make, but

I should have checked. I should have confirmed the address. It would have been simple enough to do."

I said, "In these kinds of situations, it's almost always the simple mistakes that cause the biggest screw-ups. You can't afford to let that kind of thing happen. Never again.

"So let's say we didn't have time to check out the Ingraham Building first. We talk to whoever's fronting for the kidnappers, and he tells us to deliver the money within half an hour. Tells us to drop it at some park or fountain, name a place. He's eyeballed us. He knows we're clean. Securitywise, that wouldn't be a bad move on his part. We produce the money or Lake's dead.

"So we agree, of course—only to find out, ten minutes later, your consulate is in a different city. There's no way to contact the kidnappers, no way to tell them we've made a mistake. We don't have time to pick up the money. We're screwed. Disaster."

Subdued, Tomlinson said, "You're being a little tough on her, man."

Pilar was wearing a navy blue skirt, a starched white blouse, and a white bra beneath. She tugged nervously at the collar of her blouse and told him, "No. He's not. He's exactly right. It was an inexcusable mistake."

To me, she said, "It won't happen again, Marion."

THE guy they sent to meet us was a freak. A muscle freak, and a tattoo freak.

He had a head the size and color of a bleached basketball, skull shaved clean and trapezoid muscles that angled toward his ears so sharply that he was pyramid-shaped.

Plus, there were the tattoos. Tattoos covered his skull, his face and forehead, his arms. He looked like a steroid giant whose skin had been elaborately air-brushed in Easter-egg hues, reds, greens, blues.

We were sitting in the Cacique Restaurant—tile floors, white ceiling fans, bathroom sign in green neon, waitresses in burgundy vests—when the giant strolled in. The place did a busy lunch business, tables full, dishes clattering, but the man was sufficiently sizeable and colorful to cause a momentary lull as people turned to stare.

He wore drawstring sweatpants tied tight around a narrow waist, and a black Everlast muscle T-shirt. His arms looked like overstuffed hams, triceps and latissimus muscles abrading as his arms swung, which gave his walk a restricted, mechanical rhythm.

He had something in his hand—a photo, I soon realized. He stopped in the doorway near the register, looked at the photo, then surveyed the crowded restaurant.

He fixed his dark eyes on Pilar, looked at the photo a second time, then came our way, a big grin on his face.

"Check this out," Tomlinson said. "He's got to be close to six-and-a-half feet tall and three hundred pounds. Why would they send someone so easy to remember? That's weird."

I was thinking the same thing.

But Tattoo was our contact. He came to our table, took the lone empty chair, and swung it around backward so that he could sit cowboy style.

His accent was proud hick, pure palmetto Florida country boy—a surprising redneck linkage in what appeared to be the politically motivated kidnapping of a Central American boy.

Tattoo whistled as if in pain, and said, "Now, look at this fine-lookin' Latin beauty. You're just as pretty as your picture says you'd be." The man checked the photo once more before shoving it into his pocket. "The name I was told you go by is Pilar Foo-went-tays. That the way you say it?"

The lady nodded. "*Fuentes*. You're close enough."

"Well, it sure is a pleasure to make the acquaintance, and I hope you're enjoyin' that fine-smelling food."

Without looking at Tomlinson, the man reached across the table, took a chunk of his fried yellowtail snapper, and stuffed it into his mouth.

"Humm. Not too bad for wetback cookin'. Not too bad at all."

Now he reached, took a piece of bread from my plate, dipped it in a bowl of black beans, saying, "Trouble is, I can't enjoy eating, 'cause my day's already been partway spoiled. Know why? Because I was told you

was gonna be alone, Miz Pilar. Told you *had* to be alone or I wasn't supposed to say boo to you. But now I show up, and here you are with this
hippie who probably ain't washed his hair in a year. And Mr. Coke-glasses
who looks like he sells encyclopedias for a living. So what am I supposed
to tell the people paying me to help y'all close this deal?"

I said, "We're not cops, that's what you tell them. No association with
any law enforcement agencies. We're the lady's friends. She sent an e-
mail, they've been informed. We're just along to make sure that she stays
safe. Which, if your people had any brains at all, they'd appreciate—considering what the deal is. Tell your people that."

Tattoo's brown eyes went round in what seemed to be mock inno-
cence. "Whoa there, hoss. I don't give a tinker's damn if you're a cop or
not. I don't know what kinda deal you people got goin' and I don't care to
know. That's *your* business. What I'm bein' paid to do is just make introductions, do some middle-man work. The Mediator, that's what certain
people call me."

He said it with a smile, *Mediator,* like it deserved a capital *M*.

"A place like South Florida, an ol' boy like me stays busy by playin' Mediator for anybody who comes along. I keep it real simple, no bullshit,
everything step by step. There ain't nothin' in the world illegal about doin'
what *I* do."

He had one of those jowly, globular faces that are quick to show fat as
they age. He leaned his face close to mine now as he added, "So I don't
care if you're a cop. If you're carryin' a gun, or you're wired. But maybe
the people payin' me do. So you wait right here like a good boy while I
go check."

His chair shrieked on the tile as he stood. "Maybe I'll be back. Maybe
I won't."

HE WAS at the restaurant door a few minutes later, pumping his finger at us, telling us to follow him.

I paid the check and we stepped out into the incandescence of a Miami afternoon, heat radiating from sidewalks and asphalt like volcanic vents, a heat so intense that it exerted an acidic, prickling pressure on exposed skin and through the soles of shoes.

In Florida during the hottest months, I don't dress to stay cool. It's impossible. I dress to dry quickly. So I wore featherweight cargo slacks, a short-sleeved shirt of soft Egyptian cotton, tie-on canvas boating shoes, and a blue ball cap with the marina logo embroidered thereon: a tarpon.

Within minutes, my shirt was wet.

Same with Tattoo. His shirt was soaked, sticking to his back as we followed him along Flagler past the courthouse built of gray, fossilized coral.

The back of his bald head, I noted, was tattooed with a jade-blue butterfly, a bright wing opening toward each ear, its lower abdomen expanding into what appeared to be a spiraling Confederate flag that disappeared within his wet shirt.

We followed him across the street to a Starbucks, where we took seats at an outdoor table, the green umbrella baking hot above us.

He said, "I talked to my guys, and they're playin' it careful. So careful I'm almost tempted to ask for a hint what it is you dudes got yourselves into. You don't got the look of snort or herb about ya"—he barely glanced at Tomlinson—"except for the old acid freak here. Which leaves a couple other interesting possibilities. But, like I said, this ol' boy just does his job. I don't *want* to know. So now my orders are, I got to make sure you ain't the law, and that you ain't carryin' nothin' fancy on you."

I said, "O.K. But aren't you worried someone maybe might get suspicious, call the cops, if you pat us down right here?"

I was rewarded with a theatrical grin. "You got a kinda smart-ass mouth on you for a booky-looking squirt. I'm surprised you ain't scarred up more. Instead of pattin' you down, I could grab you by your ankles, turn you upside down, and bang your head on the street just to see what falls out. But that wouldn't be professional. So I got a better way."

Pilar said, "Just tell us what they want us to do. We'll do it."

Tattoo said, "That's a better attitude," then looked from me to Tomlinson. "Either one of you boys carrying a passport?"

We shook our heads. "There wasn't any reason to bring one."

I was surprised when he said, "Good. Saves having to dump them in your car."

Then to Pilar, he said, "What about you?"

"Yes, of course. I'm not a U.S. citizen, so I need to keep mine with me. But we can lock it in the car, if you like."

Tattoo was standing. "Nope, this is workin' out just fine. You folks follow me. We're gonna let our own U.S. government do my security work. And I'll tell you boys right now: If you're carryin' some kinda pop gun and you're a cop, it'll be right there for me to see. If you're carryin' and *not* a cop, you'll be going to jail.

"After that, when I'm sure everything's nice 'n' clean, I'll contact my people again. They'll tell me what they want us to do next."

IF Tattoo had come up with the idea himself, I was impressed. It was an ingenious way of making certain that strangers were neither wired for surveillance nor carrying weapons.

He led us across the street to the Claude Pepper Federal Building, a massive tombstone-colored high-rise, no ground-floor windows, metal barricades at key areas vulnerable to car bombs. Which made no sense until I saw the security cameras, and then signs warning of dire consequences if you were carrying weapons or cameras . . . and then, inside, we came upon a small platoon of armed guards where a line of people waited patiently to get to the lobby and the bank of elevators beyond.

They were waiting because they had to go through a series of security checkpoints that were fully manned and as high-tech as any high-security prison.

Tattoo said, "This here's the main Dade County federal building. Which means security's tighter than a coconut's ass because of all the terrorist crap. Upstairs, you got about every kinda government office there is. So today, Miz Pilar is gonna tell the nice cops she's goin' to Immigration to see about a visa. You boys are goin' to see about an emergency passport.

I'm checking on getting my merchant seaman's ticket. Which'll get us all to the elevators and upstairs, plus frisked with three different types of metal detectors, and at least once by hand.

"We take the elevators up. Then we go to the toilets, wait for a couple minutes, decide we changed our minds. After that, we leave separately."

I said, "Pretty smart."

He seemed pleased by the compliment. "My brain ain't the biggest, but it do got some torque to it."

"You make a habit of coming here?"

He got my meaning instantly. "There ain't no shortage of government buildings in Florida. But what you're really sayin' is, you think because of the way I look, it's a ball-buster in my line of work. That what you're sayin'?"

I said mildly, "Something like that."

"That's just where you're wrong, pal. I'm the perfect choice, 'cause a blind man three days dead could pick me out of a police lineup. So I *got* to walk the straight-and-narrow. That means clients can trust me. If they're breakin' laws, that's their problem, not mine. I *can't,* and they know it. They know I can't screw 'em either. I'm that easy to find."

I said, "Yeah? So what's to keep a tough prosecutor from hauling you in and making you talk about your clients?"

"If I never meet my clients and do everything by phone, there's nothin' to talk about, now, is there, smart-ass? Plus, do I look like the kinda shit-heel who'd squeal?"

As I started to answer, he held up a cucumber-sized finger. "Nope. I don't care to hear no more questions from you, Mister Booky-Boy. You a little too nosy for your own good."

As we got near the security gate, he spoke again in a whisper, "Final warning, dudes—if you're wired or carrying a weapon, they're gonna cuff you and take you to jail. This is your last chance to spook out."

I wasn't carrying a weapon. I'd *brought* a weapon, but it wasn't on me. It was back in the rental car: my 9 mm Sig Sauer, an old and familiar handgun that I usually keep well oiled and locked away in my fish shack. Now, though, it was in a belly pack stowed beneath the front seat.

I'm not a gun fancier; care nothing for shooting. I hadn't told Tomlinson or Pilar about bringing the Sig, but this was one of those rare circumstances when carrying a gun seemed a reasonable thing to do. In fact, it seemed idiotic to meet kidnappers without it.

I told Tattoo, "I've got nothing on me you need to worry about. I don't suppose you'd just take my word for that. Save us all some time."

Tattoo said, "There you go again. Acting like I'm dumb."

EIGHT

OUTSIDE the federal building, after being cleared by security, Tattoo left us for ten minutes. When he came back, he said, "My people say you're supposed to go pick up the package. They want me with you. So that's the way we'll work it. Any complaints?"

Pilar asked, "Did they tell you what we're picking up?"

"Nope. Don't you go tellin' me nothin' 'bout it neither, pretty lady."

We got the Ford Taurus from the parking garage. Tattoo took the passenger seat. The car creaked beneath his weight, listing noticeably to starboard. Without asking, he changed the radio station to Willie Nelson, and then Tim McGraw, Cat Country Radio, 107 FM, radiating out from across central Florida.

I took Eighth Street through Little Havana—coffee shop bodegas, men smoking cigars over dominoes in Maximo Gomez Park—then turned south on LeJeune into Coral Gables.

The Masaguan and Guatemalan consulates were in adjoining buildings, both identified by ornate wall tiles, and next to Mitch Kaplan's Books & Books. Before going inside with Pilar, I gave Tomlinson a warning look— *Keep your mouth closed around this guy.*

I sat leafing through a magazine in the waiting room once an aide, after greeting Pilar warmly, touched the keypad lock, opened a door, and guided her down a long hallway.

Twenty minutes later, she came out carrying a gray photographer's equipment case that looked to be made of some kind of miracle resin, element-proof, but light.

"Is it all there?" I asked as we walked out onto the street.

Pilar told me, "It's in fifties and hundreds. Can you believe a half-million dollars takes up so little space?"

Several steps later, sounding emotional, she added, "There was a note inside. Kahlil, my jeweler friend, he said he couldn't get what he thought my stones were worth, so he added a little more than nineteen thousand dollars of his own money. How many people do you know who would do something so sweet and decent?"

"I'm paying half," I reminded her.

She said it again: "That's not necessary."

The same tone.

TATTOO was getting his instructions from calls that he made from pay phones even though he had a Nokia cell phone clipped to his belt.

The cell phone rang often, playing some kind of show tune. Calliope music maybe, the sort I associate with merry-go-rounds—an odd choice for him. He answered occasionally, always after checking the caller I.D., but none of the calls seemed related to our business.

Once, driving on the East-West Expressway, I listened to him say, "Baby doll, you don't talk nice to me, you ain't gonna get no more a my good sugar. And I sure as hell ain't gonna buy you no more play toys."

Another time, I heard, "There's a reason you need to visit your new lover boy. It's 'cause where I live looks like the Florida you dreamed about before the first time you come down and saw what mosta this ol' whore really looks like."

That told me something. I made a mental note.

Three times we stopped at pay phones. Twice at 7-Elevens, once at a Walgreen's. He'd drop in coins, say a few words, listen, then let the car settle beneath his weight before giving directions.

They had us drive across Biscayne Bay via MacArthur Causeway to

A1A, Collins Avenue, onto South Beach, where Tattoo craned his neck at the girls in thong bikinis at Lummus Park.

He said, "Looky, looky, looky at all the nookie, nookie, nookie," as I drove north in the slow traffic, bumper to bumper, patio restaurant tables full despite the heat, everyone outside to gawk and be seen in the postcard setting, 1950s hotels, pink flamingo Deco, palms, blue ocean, skaters, bikers, and joggers on sidewalks, oiled, silicon breasts on parade along with Porsches, Ferraris, Hummers.

Tattoo knew the area. He barked a steady flow of directions, but never all at once. Never offered a destination, or an explanation.

Once, when I asked, "I assume we're going to meet someone," he replied, "Don't you go assumin' nothin', buster. I'm just doin' what they're tellin' me to do. You're gonna do the same."

At the Howard Johnson's north of Collins Park, he had me pull over and made another call. When he got back into the car, he checked his Rolex Submariner and said, "What you gonna do now is drive us back across the bay again. This time on the Tuttle Causeway, then we gonna take our time and drive north a piece."

That's when I realized what they were doing. And *why*.

I looked in the rearview mirror and caught Tomlinson's eyes. They were bloodshot, watery blue—he'd gone to the Rum Bar late the night before, he'd told me, and gotten very drunk.

In his expression, though, I could see that he now understood as well.

The kidnappers were making us drive back and forth across Biscayne Bay for a purpose. There could only be one reason. Someone was almost certainly in a boat below, watching as we crossed. They were watching to see if cops in unmarked squad cars were keeping track of our movements, setting up a bust. Or to see if they were trailing us from above in a chopper.

Bridges are great isolators, perfect surveillance choke points. In city traffic, it can take three or four cars and a trained team to effectively tail someone. So they'd come up with an ingenious way to check us out, to see if we were double-crossing them.

It told me the people we were dealing with were professionals. I found that at once heartening and daunting. It meant they'd probably be businesslike in their dealings concerning Lake—something that didn't mesh with the burn welt on my son's arm. It also meant they probably wouldn't hesitate to kill the boy if we somehow screwed up on our end.

As we crossed the Julia Tuttle Causeway, I saw several boats moving along the Intracoastal Waterway. I tried to take a fast mental snapshot, doing my best to remember individual boats.

One was a small white tri-hull outboard. It was idling in the distance, beam to the bridge, with what may have been block lettering on the side.

I associate such lettering with rental boats.

There looked to be one, possibly two people aboard, scrunched down behind the windshield.

I didn't want to be obvious about staring. Plus, from that distance, and from a moving car, it was impossible to decipher details.

Twenty minutes later, though, crossing Biscayne Bay yet a third time via the North Bay Bridge, I saw the same boat, positioned to the north but not moving, at least one person hiding behind the windshield. I knew it was the one.

Which was O.K. Whoever was aboard the boat would watch us. They would convince themselves that we were being straight, we hadn't tipped off law enforcement. After that, we'd be able to cut some kind of deal.

Or so I thought.

AT Armando's Service Station on North Shore, Tattoo made yet another telephone call. This time, though, he came back shaking his head, his expression stormy. "Deal's off. My clients say y'all have really fucked this'n up. They say tell you the project's screwed. You ain't gonna be hearin' from them or seein' me ever again."

He gave us a little two-finger salute. "So fare-thee-well, and fuck you very much. I'll catch a ride." Then he turned to walk away.

Behind me, Pilar gave a muffled scream and threw the car door open. She went running after him, calling, "You can't do this! *Why?* We've done exactly what they told us to do."

I was out of the car, too, and then Tomlinson was out. He got his arms around Pilar, who was sobbing, holding her back or supporting her, cars slowing on the busy highway, curious—*See the tattooed giant and the crying woman.*

Which is probably the only reason Tattoo came back to us, making a calming motion with his hands. He didn't want a scene. Didn't want cops arriving, demanding an explanation.

Now Pilar was pleading with him. "I'll do anything they want. *Anything.* Whatever we did wrong, we'll make it right. Just *tell* us."

Tattoo looked from me to Pilar, then back to me, his brow furrowed, his piggish little eyes doing some calculating. Finally, he said, "She really *don't* know why the deal's gone south, does she?"

I said, "No. None of us knows. We have no idea what you're talking about."

He maintained eye contact, telling me he'd know if I was bullshitting, watched my reaction before he said, "You got somebody following you, pal. We was being followed from the time we crossed over onto South Beach. Maybe from the time we left Miami . . . or coulda been Coral Gables. Somebody driving a black Chevy, tinted windows. Every time we crossed a bridge, they crossed right behind us. Five or six cars behind. Sticking right on our tail."

Pilar turned to scream at me, "Marion Ford, if you've gone behind my back and told someone, I'll never forgive you—"

Still holding her, Tomlinson made her stop, saying, "Whoa, my dear, whoa. My man wouldn't do that. It has to be someone else."

To Tattoo, I said, "Call your clients. If we're being followed, we don't know who it is. Tell them we're cooperating. We'll do whatever they want."

The giant was still staring at me, considering. Finally, he nodded. "I got no reason to believe you . . . but I guess I *do.* Besides, the longer you stay in business, the longer I stay in business. I'll call my clients, see what kinda mood they're in."

We waited in the air-conditioned chill of the rental Ford. In the back seat, Tomlinson continued to hold Pilar and reassure her, stroking her hair, speaking softly, "It's cool, it's cool. Your son's all right. I can feel it. I *know* these things. Ask Doc."

She seemed on the brink of emotional collapse.

It was a miserable five minutes that seemed much, much longer.

Finally, Tattoo returned across the parking lot in his swaggering, weight-lifter's gait, his expression showing nothing. When I started to open the door, he shook his head and held up both palms—*Stay in the car.*

Not a good sign.

But when I lowered the front passenger window so he could lean in, he surprised me by saying, "You got yourselves a second chance."

Behind me, I heard Pilar whisper in Spanish, *"Oh, thank you, dear mother of God."*

Tattoo added, "But, Miz Pretty Lady, your two doofus pals here need to understand somethin'. This is also your *last* chance. My clients say you ain't gonna get another one. Don't matter whose fault it is. They say this is it.

"I'm supposed to tell you they'll be in touch in the next day or two. We'll set up another meeting. If someone's still tailing you next time, that's all she wrote."

Her tone wretched, Pilar said, "But we don't *know* who's following us. How are we supposed to stop them?"

Tattoo said, "That's your problem, not ours. But you better figure it out. My advice though?" He looked at Tomlinson, then at me, and gave a little snort of derision. "Your two pals, Mr. Booky and Freaky Creepy here, they ain't the best choices when it comes to a tighty-tight like this."

BEFORE Tattoo told us he'd find his own way home and banged twice on the car's roof, cutting us loose, I told him to tell his clients that Pilar was going to have to dump the satellite phone they'd given her. If a lone car had managed to tail us for more than an hour through all that Miami traffic, the probability was that I'd been right. Some kind of GPS tracking device was involved—probably installed in the phone.

He said he'd tell 'em. But that didn't mean it was O.K.

I drove us west away from the ocean, then south on I-95, keeping my eyes on the rearview mirror, watching for the black Chevy. As I drove, the three of us discussed the maybes. Who might be following us.

Pilar, still shaken, her voice trembling, said there were two possibilities: one or both of the federal investigators she'd spoken to in Masagua. It could be them, or it could be they'd leaked information to people who'd decided to come hunting for what sounded like an easy score.

"Marion's already mentioned the other possibility, too," she said. "It could be people associated with the kidnappers but who're out for themselves. They know I picked up the money at the consulate, and they're trying to take it before I make the exchange."

Tomlinson had one more alternative: "It could be that the kidnappers are lying. Telling us we're being followed just to soften us up, make us more eager to cooperate. If it's one kidnapper, singular, not kidnappers, he was down there in the boat all alone, watching us.

"So, could be he was buying time because he's doing everything by himself. First, he makes sure we're not being followed, then later, he arranges a drop spot for the cash. But he *tells* us we're being followed because he wants to keep us on the defensive. Scared and eager. He wants us to think he's gonna kill Lake, that he can walk away from the deal, no problem."

In my mind, I could see the video, the man in the mask doing everything himself, but telling us over and over that he wasn't acting alone.

I hoped Tomlinson was right.

But what if he wasn't?

Certain inferences could be made if a rogue group in a black Chevy was tracking the satellite phone that Pilar was carrying. Tomlinson was thinking the same thing, because he asked Pilar, "Does your ex-husband know about you and Doc? That he's the father of your son?"

"Yes."

Her flat tone said how uncomfortable she was with the subject.

"Does he know Doc by name, I mean? Where he lives?"

I said, "He knows who I am. Finding out where I live wouldn't take much effort. So, if these people are insiders, we're not going to lose them by just dumping the satellite phone. That's where you're heading with this. They'll find us on Sanibel. Pick up our trail there."

I was still thinking about who might be following us. Who it could be, or where they may have heard about Pilar and the cash. There was yet a third possibility that no one had mentioned. Pilar was mad at me anyway, so I decided to go ahead and risk offending her.

"There's at least one other person who knows. The question is, how much does he know?"

Sounding puzzled, Pilar said, "Aside from the people we've mentioned, there's no one else. Who?"

"Your friend Kahlil. He just sold nearly a half-million dollars' worth of emeralds for you. Did you tell him the reason they had to be sold?"

"Of course. He deserved an explanation."

"Then he's someone else to consider. Maybe he's a talker. Maybe he told a friend. Or a dozen friends."

Oh yeah, she was offended.

"Kahlil is one of the most decent and generous men I know. A moral man. We are . . . Kahlil and I are close. Please don't suggest that he has something to do with this."

Turning to look out the window, she added, "Not coming from you."

NINE

I WAS varying my speed, still watching our rear. There were plenty of Chevrolets, some black Chevys, but none that seemed to be tailing us. If they had an electronic fix on us, though, I knew there was no need for them to maintain visual contact. All they had to do was stay close.

I wondered how they were going to work it. How they planned on separating a briefcase full of cash from Pilar.

I tried to project back: They could've come in from Central America legally by commercial jet. But entering illegally—easy to do by boat, less so by plane, but still doable—would be preferred. It left no tracks to cover later.

Assuming they arrived within the last forty-eight hours, that didn't give them a lot of time to organize, so they'd be winging a lot of it, playing it by ear. They'd come expecting to deal with a lone woman. But now she'd shown up traveling with two, maybe three men.

Maybe they knew Tattoo was a hired middle man, maybe they didn't. That depended on if they had connections with the kidnappers—and they almost *had* to be associated in some way . . . or at least with someone who was leaking good data. Unless I was wrong about the satellite phone, they were well enough informed to secure a GPS receiver that was locked on the right frequency.

But if they *weren't* connected with the kidnappers, or if their source of information had changed, it would then appear to them that the woman had a carload of friends—one of them a formidable giant.

That would make them step back and reconsider.

The question was, would they apply light cover until they got a shot at the woman when she was alone? Or would they try to take us down the first chance they got?

I decided they wouldn't hesitate. For one thing, it seemed likely they'd staked out the Masaguan consul general's office, waiting for us. The Masaguan feds and kidnappers both knew we had to go there to get the money, so it was the logical place to pick up our trail. They saw us exit with the briefcase. They knew we had the money with us in the car. So why give us time to hide it, or lock it away, or deposit it?

They wouldn't, I decided. Not if they saw an opening.

To Pilar, I said, "Where's the satellite phone?"

"In my purse."

"I want you to take it out and leave it on the seat."

"Leave it? I'm not going anywhere."

I'd been watching the green Interstate signs and knew that the East-West Expressway was ahead. I was improvising as I went, following my instincts, heading west toward the wilder, more familiar Everglades.

I said, "Yes, you *are* leaving. I'm going to try and put some distance between us and whoever's back there. Then I'm going to find an exit that looks good, and we'll make a fuel stop. Maybe we'll get a look at the car tailing us. Maybe we won't. Either way, we'll make a show of it, all of us out of the car."

Tomlinson said, "I love the way your brain works, man. Now, all of a sudden, you *want* them to catch us. I don't *understand* it. But I dig the whole opposites thing."

"I want them to see for themselves that we're an easier target than they think. That Tattoo Man isn't with us. I'll be looking for a gas station near a hotel, because the moment the Chevy's out of sight, you two are checking in, getting a room.

"I'm going to leave you in Miami and drive back to Sanibel alone. You can take a cab or a limo if you want. Or I can come back and get you tomorrow. Your decision. And Tomlinson? I'm going to borrow your cell phone."

Pilar said, "I don't think separating is smart. If you confront them, what are you going to do?"

I told her honestly, "I don't know. Whatever it takes to make them stop following us, I guess. I'll have to make it up as I go along."

"Stop following us?"

"That's right. You heard the big man. I have to find a way to stop them. If the kidnappers see someone tailing us again, they'll make the wrong assumption. They'll kill Lake."

"By stop them, you mean . . . well, I know exactly what you mean."

I found her tone and her manner infuriating. Did she have a better plan?

Trying to reassure her, or maybe to get her off the subject, Tomlinson interrupted, saying, "We've got to trust Doc on this one. Let's just let the big horse run, O.K.? He's good at this sort of thing."

Pilar's tone remained severe as she said, "That's true. Now that I've found out, why do I keep forgetting?"

I TOOK the ramp onto 836 west across the Miami River, past Miami International, jumbo jets ascending and descending at mild angles over the highway, flaps flared. I dodged in and out of traffic, accelerating aggressively when I could—which was seldom because it was now a little before four P.M., approaching the rush hour.

Because traffic was heavy, I pushed west, driving hard. I didn't want to risk taking an off ramp, searching for a hotel only to get stuck in some kind of rush-hour jam.

On the outskirts of Miami, though, traffic lightened. I took the Palmetto Expressway ramp and then continued to exit when I saw a billboard advertising a Radisson half a mile away. Only a block or so from the hotel was a Circle K.

It would do.

I swung alongside the gas pumps, and all three of us got out. Tomlinson went inside and returned with bottles of water and Snickers bars. Then we loitered for what seemed a long time before the car finally appeared: a new full-sized Chevrolet with windows too heavily tinted to be a rental.

Thus I knew the people pursuing us also had local friends, local knowledge.

I got the feeling that we surprised them. The car came racing down NW Seventh Street, but braked hard when, apparently, the driver saw us. Then the car accelerated onward. The impression was that they feared they'd lost us, were speeding to catch up, and then were startled when they overran us.

The car had a Florida plate, but it was at the wrong angle, and the car was traveling too fast for me to read.

I looked at Pilar then at Tomlinson before I said, "Get moving. Enjoy the hotel. Lock your doors. If someone knocks, don't answer, no matter what."

As an aside to Tomlinson, I added, "One more thing, old buddy. Don't try to enjoy your little minivacation too much. She'd slap your nose off."

I wondered if that was true or not.

Handing me his cell phone, he sounded frazzled—but also oddly uneasy—when he replied, "I know, man. I'm hopeless. I don't trust myself, either. Mr. Zamboni and the Hat Trick Twins, they won't touch my Zen students. But the bastards are shameless when it comes to all other women. Those three don't listen to *me* anymore."

I told him, "Just a friendly warning," as I got in the car. Then I sat for a moment and watched Tomlinson and Pilar speed-walk toward the covered entrance of the hotel.

Pilar, in her starched white blouse and blue skirt, could have been a coed at some parochial university, sophisticated in her uniform, late for class. Visually and from strong past memory, I noted that she walked with a feline elegance, hips, hair, and breasts moving in countersync cadence, rotating, bouncing, springing.

There were three men standing outside the Radisson's glass doors, luggage at their feet. They'd been talking, but stopped when they noticed her. The men remained silent as she neared, eyes locked on her, seeming to retreat into themselves the closer she got, back-stepping involuntarily from the doorway as if she pushed an energy field ahead of her, or because she merited a deference that common women did not.

I'd seen men behave that way before around her.

I'd reacted that way myself.

Perhaps she still affected me that way. I wondered.

Something else I noted: Pilar carried the photographer's case.

ONLY two roads cross the Everglades, connecting Florida's Gulf Coast with the Atlantic. We'd come to Miami via Alligator Alley, the newest, fastest, and northernmost highway. Now I was returning homeward on the narrow, more southern Tamiami Trail, a less traveled two-lane road that augers through ninety miles of sawgrass and cypress swamp.

The highways travel similar topography, but they are unlike in most other ways. Alligator Alley is a modern freeway, buffered by public land on both sides. There are no homes, no businesses, and only one service station along the way. The Trail, in comparison, is old-time Florida. It is a remote and isolated country road that is interrupted by an occasional cluster of Indian chikee huts, or a lone trailer set back in, or a bait stand. The Alley is six lanes. The Trail is seldom more than two. The Alley is faster, busier. The Trail is slower, shadier, more remote.

I drove westward on the Trail, past tacky Deco roadside attractions at Coppertown and Frog City, eyes shifting from the highway to the road behind. I had to stay far enough ahead of the Chevy to keep them from seeing that I was now alone, but I didn't want to get so far ahead that I gave the impression of flight. Didn't want to tip them that I was aware I was being pursued.

So I drove at a consistent ten miles an hour over the speed limit. Fast enough to keep some distance between us, but not fast enough to attract the attention of the highway patrol.

Getting stopped by the cops now would be disastrous. I pictured myself on the highway shoulder, a squad car parked behind, lights flashing as the black Chevy slowed just enough to confirm that I was alone. I imagined the Chevy driving for another quarter-mile or so before making a U-turn, then heading back to the Radisson exit—the logical starting place to resume their search for Pilar. I pictured the Chevy passing again as an officer handed me a ticket.

Yes, disastrous . . .

Or . . . would it be?

As I sped along, passing slower cars and pickups with bass boats in tow, camper trucks and the occasional semi, I mulled over the possibilities and the potential.

What *were* the options if law enforcement came between me and the Chevy . . . ?

I considered different scenarios, weighing risks.

Beyond the levee at Chekika's Hammock, the road straightened through a dome of cypress trees, water and lily pads on both sides. I slowed for another Indian village. There were thatched huts around a gravel parking lot and a sign that read JAMES TIGER'S FAMOUS REPTILE SHOW AND AIRBOAT RIDES.

James is a friend of mine—and there he was, using a wrench on an airboat engine, the sleeves of his rainbow-colored Seminole shirt rolled high, his old black cowboy hat battling the sun.

I was tempted to stop. If a man lives a long and lucky life, he may meet a handful of people he can trust under any circumstance, in any situation, life or death. James Tiger is one of those rare men.

Still slowing, looking at James, my mind flashed on a different plan, and on how I could work it. I could slide into the parking lot, stuff the satellite phone in one pocket, the Sig Sauer pistol in another, and tell James that the bad guys were after me. Tell him I needed to borrow an airboat, or ask to hitch a ride on his boat to some remote island a couple of miles out in the swamp.

He'd do it. No questions.

Then I'd wait for my pursuers to find me. It might take a while. A couple of hours. Maybe a couple of days. But they'd track me. For half-a-million dollars, they'd figure a way.

I'd be waiting out there with the Sig Sauer, and I'd take them. Put the bodies in a gator hole, never to be found.

It could work . . . if I was willing to do something so extreme.

Which I *was*. If I had to. I've taken similar action before in my life. Hated doing it; loathed myself at the time and for a long while afterward. Despised myself because I was capable of such action, and also because it scared me to the core.

Something inside me is capable of that?

When those memories come slipping back, they produce a sickening and sweaty unpleasantness—which is why I make every effort to live in the present, not the past.

But I've now come to terms with who I am, and what I am. Occasionally for better, often for worse, I have come to terms with that truth.

I sometimes wonder if focusing on marine biology as a life's work isn't a way of justifying, or at least validating, a specific and unsentimental view of existence. From biology's elemental view, human beings, like all species, are not only guided by the tenets of natural selection, we are mandated. In such a world, eliminating enemies, or behavioral anomalies, isn't a decision to be made. It is a necessary process.

I've participated in that process. I can do it again if required. Of that there is no doubt.

Something else, though, was necessary to make my airboat escape work. I also had to be willing to involve my friend James Tiger in what amounted to cold-blooded murder.

That was something I would *not* do.

I touched my foot to the accelerator and sped on.

ONCE, on a long and open stretch of highway, I got a glimpse of the Chevy way, way back there, still on my tail. I wondered if they'd decided to try and catch me.

To find out, I reduced my speed from 75 to 65. The dark car closed briefly, then dropped back.

No. I guessed they'd decided there was still too much traffic. Too many passing witnesses. They were content to stay close. Were probably waiting, hoping there'd be a reason for me to stop in this rural region.

I'd been thinking about doing exactly that, my brain scanning furiously, continuing to inspect variations of what might be a plausible plan, defining, rejecting, then refining.

I could hear Tattoo saying, *If my people catch them tailing you again, the deal's off.* Could hear him saying, *It's your problem, not ours.*

I had to come up with a way not just to shake them, but to lose them. I didn't have to get rid of them permanently, but I did have to make them disappear for a sizeable block of time—several days, and probably longer.

Finally, I settled upon something that might work. I thought about it some more, then finally committed myself to putting the plan into action.

Decision made, I began anticipating details, which presented me with a whole other stack of problems. Not the least of which was, I didn't know how many people were in the car.

So I chose a figure. I chose five because that was the worst-case scenario. It gave me something to work with.

Another troubling possibility was, assuming they *had* entered the country illegally, they could've smuggled in some heavy firepower with them. The prospect of facing a carload of men carrying automatic weapons made my stomach roll.

No matter how many there were, though, and whatever they were packing, I needed to get it right the first time. I needed to pick the ideal place, make a good guess at the timing, and then keep the timing tight.

Ahead, road signs now warned, was an abrupt right curve in what is otherwise a straight road—Forty Mile Bend.

Forty Mile Bend is part of Everglades mythos. It is said that back in the early 1900s, when construction crews were using floating dredges to build the Tamiami Trail across the great sawgrass river, one team started from Miami, to the east. Another started building from below Naples, in the west. The plan called for the two construction crews to meet in the swamp's middle—but the engineering was way off and they missed by many, many miles. Thus a great bend was required to join the two sections of road.

Traveling from east to west, where Forty Mile Bend angles northward, Dade County, which is home to Miami, becomes Collier County, which is home to Naples. Just as Miami and Naples are polar opposites in style and population, so are the two counties. The same is true of the infrastructures that keeps them operating.

Dade County sheriff's deputies, I knew, tend to be metropolitan, even international in demographic. A fair percentage of Collier County deputies, however, are still multigenerational Floridians, proud of their heritage.

Both departments have good reputations, are staffed by competent professionals, according to what I've read and heard. *Most* law enforcement agencies are competent. They must be, because they receive daily, critical public scrutiny of an intensity that few professions would tolerate or could weather.

But between the two agencies, and for my purposes, I favored the cops from Collier County. We had more in common. Our antecedents were similar. I had a better shot at predicting how they thought, how they would react under certain circumstances.

So I took the big curve at Forty Mile Bend, tires squealing, and drove fast across the Collier County line. I kept the accelerator down until, in what seemed to be a horizon of sawgrass and swamp, I came to an old abandoned two-story house built of clapboard, its white paint peeling. The house sat back on a gravel parking lot on the south side of the road, windows boarded.

Because as a teen I'd spent a few years living near the area with my crazed old uncle, Tucker Gatrell, I knew that the place was called Monroe Station. I knew it was built originally to house highway construction crews, then troopers who patrolled the Tamiami Trail, and that finally it was purchased by a family named Lord who operated it for years as a barbecue restaurant.

I'd eaten there many times.

I also knew about the single-lane gravel road just beyond the old house. Known by locals as the Loop Road, it cut deep, southward, into the 'Glades, then circled out twenty-seven miles later.

There were a lot of dead-end trails that exited from the Loop; plenty of remote land eddies that were weighted in silence and shadow.

I was headed for the Loop Road. I knew just the spot where I hoped to stand face to face, alone with the men who were after me. If that place still existed . . . and *if* I could find it.

After checking my watch and noting the time, I slowed and turned left down the road. It was 6:05 P.M.—plenty of daylight before sunset.

Then I picked up Tomlinson's cell phone. I began to dial . . .

MY Uncle Tuck had lived at the edge of the Everglades, on a dilapidated ranch, mostly mangrove and palmetto. He spent his final years bragging to anyone who'd listen that he was among the last of old Florida's cow-boys—cow hunters as they were known—and about the many famous ac-tors and politicians he'd introduced to Florida during his years as a fishing and hunting guide.

It's true that he built a reputation as a guide. He became better known, though, as a smuggler, a shyster, and a transparent con man. Yet Tucker, for reasons I've never unraveled, still sustained the devoted friendship of several good, decent, and remarkably gifted men.

So he must have had some redeeming qualities. Maybe the day will come when I'll discover what those qualities were. *Maybe.* So far, I've never felt the need to try and find out.

One of Tucker's closest friends lived miles deep in the 'Glades, on the road I was now driving. He was a bluegrass fiddler and composer by the name of Ervin T. Rouse. Ervin wrote one brilliant, enduring American classic before retreating to this place to drink whiskey and swap tales with the likes of Tuck and similar 'Glades dwellers. The song was "The Orange Blossom Special."

As a teen, I'd come with Tuck many times to visit; had never heard anyone before or since play a fiddle like that great old man. So I knew the road, and I knew the area well, though it had been years since I'd been here.

As I drove, I felt a curious mix of tension and déjà vu, bouncing along, both hands on the wheel of the Ford, fighting the potholes, unable to see much behind me because of the dust cloud blooming in my wake. The sensation was that of having lived two distinct and separate lives; lives that were now intersecting on this bad road, in this isolated space. That I had returned dragging trouble behind me seemed an additional irony. That there was the potential for violence added to the irony.

I remembered Ervin's shack—for that's what it was, a shack, a plywood and tin shack. I remembered that it was on a sharp curve near a long-abandoned hunting outpost called Pinecrest. I wanted to find it because I needed a section of road that could be easily described to a stranger over the phone, and just as easily found.

If my memory was accurate, the curve was sufficiently distinctive to serve. Not that I expected the shack still to be standing. Didn't need to be. Ervin was long dead, and it was now illegal for people to live in this section of the 'Glades. But I felt confident I'd recognize the curve once I got to it.

Or would I . . . ?

I came to a bend that seemed about right, but I wasn't sure. Opposite it, on my left, was a canal shaded by tall cypress trees. On its mud-slick banks, turtles and small alligators lay in sunlight or shade, regulating body temperature beneath a glittering mobile of dragonflies.

I stopped the car and stepped out.

Visitors don't think of wilderness when they think of Florida, but this was wild country, deep swamp. Insects created an oscillating synthesizer backdrop to chattering, whistling birds and a hammering frog percussion. When I slammed the car door, I also slammed the frogs silent. The silence created a momentary void in the water-weighted air.

I jogged toward an open patch of scrub that once might have been a clearing, and began to kick through rotting wood, limbs, trash. In the weeds, I found chunks of tin. Nearby, I found a wooden sign that read:

GATOR HOOK LODGE
NO GUNS OR KNIVES ALLOWED

It was the sign that had hung on the old bar and restaurant that flourished for years near here. It'd burned, I'd heard.

Then I began to find ruined pieces of album covers, country music titles, and photographs grown over by weeds. The photos were of country music stars.

The walls of Ervin's shack had been papered with the things.

This was his old home site, no doubt.

I was hurrying, but I still took the time to lean and retrieve a fragment of photo that showed a grinning, toothless Ervin T. Rouse posing with a country music icon. Even I recognized Johnny Cash.

The photo had been violated by rain, insects, sun, time. That this once treasured memento had been reduced to roadside litter catalyzed in me a startling sense of transience. Since my early years living near this place, I'd traveled to regions few have been. I'd seen and experienced things few could imagine. Seeing the photo keyed a surprising and reassuring fatalism: If I screwed up, if my life ended here while trying to save my son, that wasn't a bad way to go.

It was the kind of emotional reaction I seldom experience.

Ervin was that kind of man. He was a good one. A real character.

I almost slid the bit of photo into my pocket, but stopped when I realized I couldn't risk the chance of it being found on me and later connected with this location. Instead, I turned and sailed the paper into the canal where he'd once loved to fish. A sort of private farewell.

Jogging back to the rental car, I still felt a powerful tension, but my anxiety over whether the strategy would work or not was gone.

Home field advantage.

If nothing else, I had that . . .

From beneath the front seat, I retrieved my handgun, the 9 mm Sig Sauer. A Sig Sauer is weighted steel-dense, blue-black, and has a look of industrial efficiency that implies precise engineering, exact tolerances. I shucked a round into the chamber as I walked toward the right side of the road. At the sharpest bowing of the curve, I looked both ways before firing three rounds harmlessly into the canal.

Fwhap . . . Fwhap . . . Fwhap

The shots echoed in the tree canopy, then were absorbed by lichen, water, ascending birds.

The handgun ejected the empty brass casings automatically near the shoulder of the road. I noted where the brass fell, and was pleased that the casings were readily visible.

I hurried back to the car. As I turned the ignition key, I checked my watch: 6:28 P.M.

There couldn't be much time left before other vehicles began to arrive.

I put the car into gear, resisting the temptation to floor the accelerator, because I didn't want to leave obvious tire tracks. Then I drove down a straight-away, around a second curve, and toward what I remembered to be the location of a logging trail. At least, I hoped I remembered.

I did. There it was: a rutted, narrow lane overgrown with brush, but still getting some use, still maintained by someone, because the Ford banged down twenty yards or so of trail without difficulty. I drove in far enough to be hidden from the road, but not so far I couldn't back out in a hurry if needed.

Then I shoved Pilar's satellite phone into the crack of the front seat and looked at my watch once again: 6:33.

Under pressure, the brain begins to second-guess itself. It asks questions designed to contrive easy excuses for quitting, for giving up, or running away.

Do I really have time? Is it worth the risk?

Now, though, the questions were meaningless. I was committed. There was no going back.

Head down, arms up to protect my face from brush and branches, I ran as fast as I could to the gravel road. I looked both ways—no cars or engine noise coming from either direction—then sprinted another thirty yards toward what had been Ervin's shack. Standing near the right side of the road, I fired off three more rounds from the SIG 9 mm. Again, I left the brass casings where they fell, clearly visible near the ditch.

After that, I had a hell of a tough decision to make. The safest thing for me to do—and I *preferred* the safest course—was to hide my old handgun away for later retrieval, then stand and wait by the rental car until the black Chevy arrived.

It wouldn't be long now.

The worst my pursuers might do would be slap me around some. Maybe a kick or punch or two. But they wouldn't kill me. They couldn't risk it. Not right away. I knew where Pilar and the money were. No matter how ruthless, they'd make a determined effort to squeeze the information out of me before taking harsher action.

So that's what I wanted to do. Stand and wait. Let them make the first big move, and thus give them the chance to make the first big mistake.

But my brain was still feeling pressured, and so it continued to second-guess. I kept asking myself: *What if they're not armed? What happens if they're not carrying weapons that fire 9 mm ammunition?*

If they didn't have at least one weapon that matched the caliber of my handgun, I was screwed. I was screwed because the people following me had to be at least temporarily linked with the shell casings I'd left lying in the road.

A more reasonable voice reassured: *Of course they're armed. They're here to take your money.*

Something else: *9 mm ammunition has become the world standard. The percentages are on your side.*

And yet . . . and yet, I knew that if I guessed wrong, the entire scheme was doomed. Far worse, I would be putting Pilar, Tomlinson, and my own son in mortal danger. So there was no choice. I had to err on the side of caution.

Erring on the side of caution meant I had to take a big personal risk.

So I checked to make certain the hammer on my SIG-Sauer was down, then popped the magazine. As I did, I trotted along the road, away from the curve where Ervin Rouse's shack had been.

That morning, I'd loaded thirteen copper-blunt Hydra-Shok cartridges, 147-grain, into the magazine. The cartridges, specially designed as man-stoppers, were distinctive in appearance, short and stocky, with stemmed hollow points.

I'm not a gun aficionado. I don't collect firearms, don't frequent gun shows. I don't even enjoy shooting. To me, this handgun, these special loads, were *tools,* nothing more.

I'd fired six shots, so I knew how many rounds remained. But I'm also a freak for checking and rechecking my data. Doing the mental arithmetic wasn't good enough. I wanted to visually confirm that I now had six rounds in the magazine, plus one in the chamber.

Yes, the count was right.

Less than fifty yards beyond the logging road where I'd hidden the Ford, I found a place wide enough for a car to turn around. I pictured the black Chevy slowing at the wooded entrance where my car was hidden; imagined the men inside confirming the location of the rental on their GPS tracker, then squabbling about what to do, how to handle it.

Most likely, they would drive past, pull off the road, then walk back. They'd take their time. Be stealthy. Send just one or two guys to check things out. Or, depending on how they reacted, they might do an immediate U-turn. Come charging back.

Either way, this was the first section of road that was wide enough to turn.

It was here, I decided, that I would ambush them.

On one side of the road, cypress knees protruded from black water. Lily pads floated in shadows beneath arching limbs. Opposite the canal was a dense thicket of Brazilian pepper trees.

I climbed in among the trees, eyes searching the ground for fire ant mounds—ferocious, swarming insects. You don't want to stumble into those when you're trying to hide quietly.

I balanced the pistol in my hand, checked my watch once more.

6:51 P.M.

I was ready.

Pilar had described the man who abducted our son as a monster. A sociopath from a prison for the criminally insane who burned people, and who, I suspected, had used a portable torch to burn Lake's arm.

What brand of sadist could do such a thing to a child?

Standing quietly in the bushes, I thought again of my son. Felt the terror he must have felt the night he was abducted, and wondered about him now, in this instant. Was he still frightened? Was he even alive?

Masked Man, Praxcedes Lourdes, represented the kidnappers, in my mind. The people in the Chevy were more like jackals.

I couldn't deal with the monster until I'd found a way to pen the jackals.

I took Tomlinson's cell phone from my pocket. I dialed 911 for the second time, still thinking of my son.

TEN

SITTING in the Toyota, with the brat bound and gagged in the trunk, Prax told the driver that, as a teenager, he and his parents had been cruising the coast of Nicaragua when the boat they were on hit a reef and sank.

Only he had made it to shore.

Then Prax told him about the night the soldiers came to the village of his adopted Moskito Indian family and set their hut on fire.

His story had changed several times over the years, along with the lies he used to keep the story believable.

As Prax Lourdes talked, though, the truth came into his own mind's eye: the sailboat he'd set ablaze, and the shrieks of his biological parents as he paddled away in a dinghy. Then, two years later, the windstorm *woosh* of his adopted Moskito father, clothes on fire, a human torch chasing him, catching him, as the man screamed, "You witch, you evil witch! You're going to burn *with* us."

To hear that arrogant man crackle was worth the pain that came later.

To set a human being on fire: what an incredible kick; what a sensation of *power*. To trigger an absolute and frantic loss of control in another man was to dominate him completely. A woman, the same thing, only somehow the feeling was more physical . . . sustained . . . *sweeter.*

Fire did that. No method was as instantaneous, more intimate. In the first microseconds, fire stripped away all the crap, all the superiority games and social fakery. Flames unveiled the pathetic little monkey that lived at the core inside all people.

Even thinking about it, hearing his adopted father's cries, Prax would feel again the flooding abdominal tension, and he could remember the very instant when he realized that awesome feeling could be duplicated.

His adopted father caught him, but Prax awoke. He survived.

His adopted father didn't.

Aware he might go to prison, Lourdes spent his waking moments perfecting the details of his alibi. In the burn unit of Managua's peasant hospital, *Hospital Escuela,* speaking through bandages, he told student doctors a detailed story about soldiers attacking in the night.

Unconvinced, they sent a volunteer psychologist to interview him. She was a blond woman who tried to hide her breasts beneath baggy scrubs and vests. She reminded him of his biological mother, whom he'd despised.

Lourdes was so heavily drugged, and in such pain, that he had to concentrate with all his will to lie convincingly. That was nothing new—he was used to dealing with pain. He'd endured excruciating headaches for as long as he could remember. So he managed to keep his answers consistent when she asked her questions in different ways, trying to trick him.

Did he enjoy setting fires? Did he prefer to play alone? Had he ever wet his bed? Had he ever successfully masturbated to completion? Did he feel sorrow that his adopted mother, father, and three sisters had all died in the blaze? Had he ever intentionally burned himself, and taken pleasure from it?

One question, he just played dumb. X rays, the woman said, showed that he'd had a serious head injury years before as a child. Why had he lied to them when they'd ask if he'd had any head injuries?

He said he didn't remember anything about it. Which was close to the truth.

One morning, the nurse brought a tall black woman. The black woman said to him in French, then in English, and, finally, in Spanish, "Why don't you tell us your real name, my love? About your real parents.

From your accent, and when you talk in your sleep, we know that you seem to be French, but that you know a lot of American English, too. Why won't you talk to me?"

Actually, he and his family were French Canadian, though they barned in Florida when not sailing. As with many carnival and circus people, there was a small town in Florida, populated almost entirely by show people, that was their winter home.

The town was on the Gulf Coast, across the bay from Tampa. His family had a mobile home in a trailer park on a little river there, where he learned about boats and water. It was a weird little place, with midgets and clowns, elephants, chimps, and carney freaks for neighbors.

That's why it spooked Prax to learn he'd been talking in his sleep.

Carnival society was a closed society. Had its own vocabulary, and dialect. After ten years working carnivals all across Canada, working his family's sideshow acts, and the center joints and cook shacks, Prax knew that if a savvy person heard him speak English, they'd know right away who he was, the kind of work he'd done.

Not that carnies didn't cover for one another. It was part of the deal. You never gave straight information to cops or strangers, and you didn't give up a fellow carney, no matter what. That didn't mean all or even some carnies were crooked. It's just the way it was among people who were always among strangers, no matter where they were.

That was no guarantee the Mounties or the cops couldn't nail him, though. So Lourdes kept his mouth shut. At night, he slept with a tongue depressor between his teeth.

THE only time he came close to speaking openly was after the black woman had left and the nurse said to him, "I don't understand why you won't tell us. You shouldn't be living in Nicaragua with Indians. We should send you home to be with your people."

Prax replied, "I've spent nearly two years as a Suma. I like way the Suma deal with problems, their assholes, the ways of Yapti Tasba."

It was true. He liked the freedom of the culture. Men were expected to spend long periods of time away from the village, wandering or lobster diving, while women stayed home and worked.

That kind of freedom, always moving, it had a carney feel.

He wasn't surprised when the psychologist answered, "But your village doesn't want you back. We've contacted them. We think they're afraid of you. Why would they be afraid of a boy?"

Prax ignored her, replying, "Then I'll find another village. I'm staying. This is home."

Nicaragua was cool. The place had potential. He was smart enough to realize that. Even though he was only fifteen, Prax was shrewd from years of living on the road, conning money out of local marks.

Better preparation, though, was a lifetime of being *different*. A lifetime of having to give the appearance of being normal every waking minute because if he didn't, he'd be busted, and that would be the end.

Prax knew he was different, had known it since earliest memory. Knew because of the withering headaches that came shooting up his spine a couple hours after sunset almost every night. Knew it because of the rage the pain created in him—a redness that flooded in behind his eyes with a pressure so great that he thought he'd burst.

Sometimes he did.

The first time was when he experimented with a cat that strayed onto the carnival grounds. Then he tried more cats, then dogs. Much later, he doused a sideshow chimp with kerosene.

His parents knew that he was different, too. But different was commonplace in their far-out world. His mother was a *real* freak, which she'd used in various sideshow bits. She had the size and strength of a linebacker, and Prax had inherited both. His father was a runt who, aside from sailing skills, was an idiot.

His parents never associated his strange behavior with his head injury.

Lourdes hated them.

It was mutual.

So Nicaragua was a good bet. The fact that the government's military had secretly adopted a policy of racial genocide against his Moskito Indian tribe, Prax saw as a plus.

Like some sideshow fortune-teller, he'd nailed it.

War, he discovered, excused any outrage. By doing what he was driven to do, enjoying that rush, he became a hero. Then, lured to Masagua by money and more action, Prax Lourdes became *Incendiario.*

He'd done what his sideshow parents had never managed to do. He'd become a headliner.

WHEN Lourdes was done talking, he had checked his watch and said to Reynaldo, "Get out of the car."

Still uneasy, the driver said, "I don't mind waiting. I can stay here."

Lourdes said, "Get out of the car. *Now.* The plane with the early edition of the *Miami Herald*'s just landed. Plus, there's someone I want you to meet."

Reynaldo followed the big man past trash barrels and the smoldering garbage dump to a metal building that had no windows. The chain on the door was already unlocked, and Prax opened it.

The driver was surprised by what was inside.

The building consisted of a main room that was equipped with things he'd seen once before in a surgical operating room in Managua. There was a steel table, gas canisters, a large overhead light, and surgical instruments on a stainless-steel table. On the walls were photos and diagrams of human faces. Several of the diagrams were more like engineer's drawings.

The equipment seemed very old, though. Reynaldo knew nothing about medicine. But even to him, it looked old.

Another surprise was that there was a man waiting for them. A very thin Mexican man with palsied hands and a head tremor. He was wearing a suit coat over a white shirt, and he looked even older than the surgical equipment.

Reynaldo expected to be introduced. Instead, Lourdes said to the man, without any explanation, "I don't think his skin's worth a shit. Too much time outdoors. What do you think?"

Whose skin? Such an odd thing to say.

The Mexican was sitting, sweating, his entire body shaking—a drug addict, Reynaldo realized.

The man peered at Reynaldo intensely for a moment before sagging back, seemingly disappointed. "Why do you even waste my time? I can't work with material like that."

He added very quickly, "Did you bring my stuff?"

Lourdes said, "Yeah, but later," as he stepped to the table and dropped a cotton swab that had a swash of red on it, and a vial that contained what looked to be a tiny amount of black liquid. "Stick this under the microscope and get me a blood type on this as quick as you can."

Before the Mexican could speak, Lourdes added, "No, you old quack, it doesn't belong to this asshole. He's just my driver. It's someone else, so cross your fingers it's O-positive. You keep telling me eight out of ten people should match, so why have we had such shitty luck the last few tries?"

Reynaldo realized that the blood must belong to the boy, and the Mexican must be a doctor of some sort. Because now the man stood and, showing some authority for once, motioned for Lourdes to take off the mask.

Lourdes' back was to Reynaldo, but the driver still felt a neural chill as the big man stripped the mask off and rubbed at the patches of curly blond hair on the back of his head with his scarred, banana-sized fingers. He did it all with the same exaggerated mannerisms that nagged at the driver's memory and reminded him of something he'd seen as a child.

At a long ago circus?

Yes, that was it. The way the man moved, used his voice and hands, the fast, big gestures, it was the way clowns had behaved beneath that huge tent.

The clowns, Reynaldo remembered, had terrified him then, too.

The driver wanted to open the door and run, but he felt frozen as he watched the doctor reach expertly to touch places on Lourdes' face, his eyes focused, lips pursed. It was an expression he'd seen before on the faces of doctors when they were examining a patient.

"The nose is looking better. The eyelids are coming along. But the nose is definitely looking somewhat better. Discoloration doesn't always mean dead tissue, and a little infection is always to be expected when you have to work under these conditions."

His tone showing only contempt, Lourdes replied, "Especially when the quack's a heroin junkie. Which is why I'm going off and finding my-self an expert, you pathetic little weasel."

The doctor had apparently heard the abuse before, because he only replied, "Yes, the nose seems better. Some color is coming into it. It may take yet. But this man—" He indicated Reynaldo. "He'd be of no use to us even if the decay had continued."

Reynaldo remained frozen as Prax Lourdes then turned, showing him his full face—a big smile there—and used an elegant sweep of the arm, as if to introduce himself.

With the other hand, he tapped at something that sounded metallic in his pocket.

"Hear what the man said? The quack's got no use for you. That's kinda rude, don't you think, Reynaldo? So why don't we leave the asshole here, walk out by the trash dump, just the two of us. We can have ourselves a quick smoke?"

ELEVEN

SEVERAL minutes after I dialed 911 for the second time, I heard a car approaching from the distance. I hoped it was the Chevy driving into my trap. As the car neared, I could hear its shocks hammering, the vehicle going way too fast on the bad road.

It's the way law enforcement people sometimes drive on an emergency call.

Not good. It was way too early for the cops to show up. For me to pull this off, timing was key.

I stood tense, weapon in hand, panting, taking shallow gulps of air, hoping to hell it was the Chevy and not a sheriff's deputy. Hoping that I'd soon hear the car slow as it neared the logging trail . . . expecting it to decelerate because the Chevy's GPS tracker told them the rental Ford was hidden there. Then I expected the car to speed onward in my direction, searching for a place to turn around.

I'd get my first look at the jackal types who were after my son's ransom money, because there was only one place to turn around. It was this wide place in the road immediately in front of me. They wouldn't suspect a thing until I stepped out, weapon raised.

I willed the car to keep coming my way.

It didn't.

I heard the car slow as it closed on what I guessed to be the logging road. Then, after a short and sudden silence, I heard a single, muted *clunk*, followed by more silence, then . . . nothing.

For a minute or more, I sat stupidly in my little hiding place. The silence should have told me more than any amount of shouting or slamming of doors.

Then I knew: It wasn't a sheriff's squad car. It was the Chevy, all right. But the men inside hadn't behaved as anticipated. When they'd realized they were near the hidden Ford, they'd stopped. Decided to sneak in without a sound, but for the *clunk* of a single, closing car door latch.

When I comprehended, I lurched out of the pepper thicket, running but staying low, digging hard for traction in the sand and gravel . . . hoping I could still find a way to take them from behind. Take them by surprise, before they saw or heard me coming.

I shadowed the tree line as I neared the bend, then slowed to a walk before I peeked to have a look.

There it was, the black car. They'd parked the Chevrolet across the logging trail's entrance, blocking what they presumed was our escape route. They'd pulled the car into the brush in a hurry. The driver's door and a back door were open.

So, counting the two open doors, plus the muffled *clunk* of a door closing, there were at least three people . . . though none visible.

Still near the tree line, ready to dive for cover, I approached the car from its blind rear quarter, gun at eye level, combat position, both arms extended. When close enough, I swung to bring the muzzle onto the area of the car's back seat. Did it from an angle that would allow me to fire into the front compartment.

Nothing. No one inside

I relaxed momentarily, feeling a rivulet of sweat gain speed as it traced my spine.

Velcroed to the car's dashboard and plugged into the cigarette lighter was the GPS tracker, its color screen the size of a Palm Pilot. The screen remained illuminated, still communicating with satellites overhead, even though the engine was off.

On the screen was a detailed map that showed the Loop Road where it bellied away from Monroe Station. Near Ervin Rouse's curve were two blinking cursors nearly touching.

One cursor was a black X. I realized that it represented the rental Ford. The other cursor, a blinking white arrow, was the Chevy.

I'd been right, at least, about the tracking system.

I took a step closer to the Chevy, disgusted with myself. If only they'd stopped where I'd expected. All I needed was a quick look from the bushes. If they had weapons that fired 9 mm rounds, no problem. If they didn't, that was O.K., too. I could've surprised them, taken their crew down clean. Once they were disarmed, I could have arranged any kind of incriminating scenario I wanted.

Who were the local deputies going to believe? Central American nationals who were probably in the country illegally? Or me, a local and a respected marine biologist?

Not now, though . . . now I had to improvise. I had to get lucky fast.

I looked into the empty car once more. Saw a Spanish edition of the *Miami Herald* scattered on the floor of the back seat. I leaned into the sour odor of cigars to look: Monday edition.

I saw McDonald's wrappers and crumpled cans of a Colombian beer, Aguila, smashed cigarette butts in the ashtray, an open box of Remington 12-gauge shells—I didn't like that.

There was a wrinkled automotive magazine, a small Igloo cooler, clothing on a hanger, a road atlas, and other indications that several men planned to live out of this vehicle for a while. On the floor in front of the passenger seat, I also saw a pair of leather gloves.

That caught my attention.

Gloves.

That's when it came to me. I knew how I could make the plan work. *Maybe* . . . as long as I was willing to surrender to them unarmed. Make myself an easy target for the 12-gauge shotgun I knew they were carrying. A shotgun at the very least.

Put myself at risk for my son?

No indecision there. No thought required.

Pure, that was the feeling. I'd never experienced an emotion like it in my life. I felt no fear, no hesitation, not even a sense of duty or obligation. I felt resolve. It was something to be done.

Fatherhood. I was learning about it late, but at least I was learning.

For an instant, Dewey's face flashed in my mind—a baffling lapse in concentration, it seemed . . . until I understood the association.

I brought the test strips thinking we could have a private ceremony. Find out if I am or not . . .

It reminded me of something: There was reason for risk. I also had reason to be smart, stay alive.

A full-time father . . . what would that be like?

Yeah, I had reason.

I peered over the roof of the car to make certain the men weren't on their way back. Then I tilted my head, listening for other fast cars approaching.

Were there?

Maybe . . . could be there was a car rumbling toward us from the distance.

There was still time, though. Not a lot, I hoped. But some.

I reached, put on the gloves, and used them to smear fingerprints that covered my old semiautomatic pistol.

How long had I owned the thing?

I had to think about that.

Years.

The Sig Sauer had been with me through some tough times. In several distant and dangerous countries.

It had been with me in Masagua during the Revolution, I remembered. I'd used it at least twice in the months before I met Pilar. In fact, I'd looked down the barrel of it at a pompous, self-serving, and diabolical little man named Don Blas Diego.

There was additional irony in that.

Now I'd have to part with it.

I reminded myself that I don't care about firearms. I don't care about *things.* I also reminded myself that I'm not the superstitious type. I told myself that Marion Ford doesn't cling to objects, and he certainly doesn't believe that guns can be good-luck talismans.

I once believed that I was incapable of lying to myself. It's a delusion I no longer maintain.

THERE weren't five of them. There were three. Three Latin-looking men, two squat and broad, one tall and angular, their backs to me as they approached the Ford.

As they neared the car, I tailed them.

They thought we might still be in the car. They were moving along the logging trail, hunched down in the classic way that hunters do. The man to the left carried a short-barreled, semiautomatic shotgun. It was the 12-gauge I'd expected after seeing the box of ammunition.

The taller man—white guayabera shirt worn outside expensive-looking sailcloth slacks—led from the middle, and appeared to be unarmed. Wasn't showing anything obvious, anyway. He had dense black hair, professionally styled. The clothing, the hair, the way he carried himself all suggested money. Privilege.

Like the guy with the shotgun, the third man had the look of hired muscle. He carried what, from a distance, looked to be an automatic pistol—a submachine gun.

The main difference between a submachine gun and an automatic rifle is that a sub gun fires pistol ammunition. These days, the most common caliber is 9 mm.

I'd been right when I guessed they'd be carrying something similar. So why hadn't I followed my instincts?

Good men I once trained with had an axiom that offered advice to anyone charged with making a battle plan: Keep it simple, stupid.

KISS is a handy acronym.

I hadn't trusted my own instincts, which is stupid. Worse, I hadn't kept my trap sufficiently simple.

Now, though, I felt like things were back on track . . . if I could keep from getting shot.

I was behind the men, walking the center of the trail, making no effort to hide or move quietly. The last thing I wanted was to startle them. When humans are startled, various muscles in our bodies contract involuntarily. The trigger finger is among them.

So, when I was within thirty yards or so and they still hadn't noticed me, I called out, "Hey, guys? Hello. *Hello?*"

All three whirled to face me, shotgun and Uzi at shoulder level—I recognized the sub gun now—both men leaning toward me ready to shoot while their taller companion surprised me by using his momentum to throw himself into the bushes, out of sight. He apparently assumed I had a weapon and was diving for cover.

It seemed a cowardly reaction. Let the others stand in the open while he hid.

Still, I was looking down two gun barrels. I had both hands high, calling to them, "Don't shoot, guys! *E-e-e-asy. Easy*, for Christ's sake! I don't have a gun, a knife . . . I don't have *anything*."

I kept the tone timid, talking like I was a typical suburban citizen, harmless, friendly, but nervous facing men with weapons. Which I *was*. I'm often told I look like a professor at some small Midwestern college. I was trying very hard to match my tone to that nonthreatening image now.

Because they kept their weapons trained on me, I continued babbling, "Seriously, I don't know what you guys are doing . . . not that I *care* what you're doing. It's none of my business. Or—hey—maybe I'm *trespassing*. If I am, I didn't see any signs or anything. *Honest*. I was just out for a little hike. Fellas, could you *please* not point those guns at me?"

Very slowly they lowered their weapons, looking at me full-faced now over the barrels. Both men could have been sculpted out of the same stocky Latino tree. The stunted oak variety. They were a foot shorter than I. Their faces, shoulders, and thighs were proportionally wide, tannin-dark, so they had the collective structural grace of twin butcher's blocks.

Each had a mustache, too. Could have been fraternal twins. But their clothes set them apart. One wore a white straw Panama hat and a silken shirt that had a metallic sheen in strobing neon pinks and blues. The other preferred black. A guayabera shirt, black slacks, and shiny white shoes.

They might have been dressed for a night of salsa dancing—or running a string of prostitutes. Stylish in a gaudy ethnic way that is sexually emblematic. Striking colors compete for sexual attention.

I watched White Panama exchange looks with White Shoes, both of them now swinging weapons between the rental car and me. For all they knew, Tattoo and Tomlinson were hiding inside the car, part of a trap. They also shifted glances toward the bushes where their companion was keeping his head low. But he was also moving, I noted, maybe trying to get a look at me from cover.

The impression: Two bodyguards were seeking guidance from their boss man. A boss who either lacked courage or had good reason to fear an attack.

White Panama motioned with the Uzi and said to me in broken English, "Put your hands on your hair. Make it so your back turn to see my face in this way."

I heard *"see mi fees theeze way,"* as he gave me a rotating demonstration with his index finger.

I folded my hands atop my head and turned my back to them as White Shoes asked in slightly better English, "Are your friends still in the car today? Where is *Generalissimo* Balserio's wife, Pilar? What have you done with the wife?"

Pilar and Balserio's marriage had been annulled years ago. That he still referred to her as Balserio's wife told me something. Suggested they were allied with the General, and probably the original plan to kidnap Lake. In the video, Masked Man had also referred to Pilar as Balserio's wife.

I replied, "I'm alone. I don't know anything about a wife. *Whose* wife?"

"Don't lie to us, mister. You lie, I shoot you here. Let the crocodiles eat your heart. Are your people in the car? Tell us something for my second question!"

"There's no one in the car. I'll show you myself. You can follow me and I'll prove it."

"Then where is the giant man? The giant with the painted tattoos on his body? If he's hiding in the trees, we shoot you first if he comes out."

I wasn't surprised they were nervous about Tattoo. But why didn't they know he was a hired go-between? That suggested they *weren't* involved with the kidnappers. Which meant they weren't allied with Balserio.

Now nothing made sense.

Before I could answer, though, a third voice commanded me in articulate English, "Shut up. Quiet! I want to get a better look at him. You. *Yankee.* Do what I say: Turn toward us a half-turn—keep your hands where they are. Don't look at me! Turn *now.*"

Tall Man was giving orders from his hiding place.

I turned until I heard, "That's far enough. Stop there."

Then, after a studied pause, I listened to him whisper in guttural Spanish, "It *is* you, you Yankee filth . . . you *sewage,*" before saying to me in a louder voice, "Turn your back to us again. Now!"

I thought to myself, *Uh-oh, big trouble.*

TROUBLE, no doubt about it. Serious trouble . . .

For one thing, he hadn't bothered to speak to me in English. He knew enough to realize it wasn't necessary. Something else: His voice touched a long-ago memory. It took a moment for my brain to match the voice with a name. When I recognized who it was, I didn't want to believe it. But there was no doubt.

I thought, *What the hell is* he *doing here?*

Tall Man and I had met only twice, but I'd heard his voice many times. During the Revolution in Masagua, I'd heard him give impassioned speeches over jungle radios, and from the balcony of the presidential palace. I'd listened to his voice enough to know there was no mistake.

Now I heard the voice say, "Keep your weapons pointed at this lying son-of-a-bitch. If he moves, if he raises a hand, shoot his kneecaps off. But make goddamn certain you don't hit *me,* you fools."

There was a rustling from behind, then the sound of a big man walking toward me through the brush.

I wanted to throw myself to the ground, tumble, and come up running. Take my chances with the shotgun and the Uzi rather than stand there and let him put a knife or bullet in me from behind. He was certainly capable of murdering me like that. In fact, shooting someone in the back was exactly the man's style.

So I gambled. I kept my hands on my head, but turned toward the three men, a confident smile on my face, and said as if surprised, "My God. Is it really you? General *Jorge Balserio*? Why didn't you *say* so. We haven't talked since the Revolution. You look *great.*"

Like we were old long-lost friends.

The expressions of momentary confusion on the faces of the bodyguards were encouraging. But they weren't bewildered enough for me to attempt to run. And Balserio was still striding hard toward me, his eyes glassy, fists clenched.

"Dr. Marion Ford, you . . . you shit pile. I swore I'd find you one day—now I have. You cheating, sneaking whore of a man. You *screwed my wife.* You *touched* my woman. Now you're going to pay!"

I was looking at the bodyguards, trying to read them, hoping I could risk dropping my hands to defend myself. But then Balserio squelched that possibility, repeating, "Idiots! I tell you again: Move closer with your guns so you won't hit me. If this pig touches me, shoot his feet, his knees, but don't kill him yet. That's an *order.*"

He was banking out around me to give his bodyguards a cleaner angle of fire. I turned at the same pace, continuing to face him. The guards were moving toward me, too. White Shoes, I noted, had pulled a little semi-automatic handgun from somewhere, choosing to use it rather than risk hitting his boss with shotgun pellets.

Balserio's face was flushed a monoxide purple, his expression demented. He was digging in the pocket of his slacks. I watched him pull out a bone-handled knife. He snapped the blade open, still striding toward me, eyes still blazing. Jesus, now he was *grinning*, a coyote sort of leer on his aristocratic face.

During the Revolution, Balserio had been the subject of whispered rumors. His temper tantrums were legendary. The bloody atrocities supposedly sparked by them were infamous. Twice, there'd been formal inquiries from investigators with the International Human Rights Commission.

In Central America, giving people nicknames is a cultural pastime. One of his was the Crazy Machete.

I'd had an affair with Balserio's wife. Now here he was, coming at me, waving a knife in his left fist. All those years of hating me seemed to be shunted into that stainless-steel blade, and it glittered like a laser. I couldn't take my eyes off it.

I went from feeling shock to a strange, energized numbness. It was as if electricity had immobilized my nervous system. No weapon scares me more than a sharp steel blade. Fight someone who's armed with a knife, and even if you manage to win, you're almost sure to come away with ruined hands, holes in your skin, damaged tendons.

Years ago, they taught us the techniques, how to survive that kind of attack by using rubber knives and a multitude of scenarios. Made us train for hours. I'd never been in a position desperate enough to need the training, thank God, but I'd seen men who'd actually fought and survived knife fights.

The memory sickened me.

But now I either had to run and risk being shot—or wait meekly while this crazy man started hacking away.

I'd called 911 twice. *Where were the cops?*

Desperate to buy time, I said in Spanish so his bodyguards would understand, "General—stop right where you are or you're not going to get the half-million dollars. I don't have it here. But I'll take you to it. Put that knife away, I'll cooperate. You and your two men, you can have it all—"

But the Crazy Machete had snapped.

"Screw your money! Do you think we came to find Pilar because of money? I *have* all the money I need, you worm!"

They weren't after the money? Then why follow Pilar?

Survival, though. That's all I could think about. If I survived, maybe I'd get the chance to find out.

He was nearly within arm's reach now. I was backing away, hands still on my head, eyes focused on the knife that he was now passing between his left hand and his right.

Was that supposed to confuse me? The knife always ended up in his left hand. When he made a move, I knew it would be with his left.

And he soon would.

Balserio was working himself into it—he *was* going to kill me, that was clear. He was ranting as he began to circle. Ranting that I'd been naked with his wife, that I'd humiliated him. Ranting that I was finally going to get what I deserved. There was only *one* punishment that fit my crime.

"It's something we do to pigs," he said. "You're a pig, and now I'll make you a sow."

Castration.

Jesus . . .

Was he serious?

Oh yeah—I could see it behind his eyes: something freaky in there fired by hatred. And ready to do it *right now* as he extended the knife blade slowly toward my chest, getting ready to charge me—I could see that, too; could read it in his muscle tension, face, and forearms.

I had to do something. The bodyguards had their guns aimed. I knew I'd *rather* be shot than stand there and let him stab me, but . . .

Make a decision, Ford . . .

I risked backing away faster as Balserio continued his purge, taunting me, "I'll do the same thing to that bastard son of yours, too, when I get the chance. He's next. On the day he was born, I should have had him drowned like the mongrel he is—"

That did it. Suddenly, I was moving, no longer in doubt.

I stopped backpedaling and dropped my hands. Surprised, Balserio froze for just an instant. In that instant, I lunged toward him, shooting in low on one knee, trusting instinct and muscle memory . . . just letting it happen . . . and I caught his left wrist clean with my right hand as he tried to drive the blade into my face.

I was already snapping his wrist and palm skyward as I stood, locking my fingers on his left elbow, which added lift and leverage. I could have broken his arm without much effort, which made it easy to spin Balserio so that his body shielded mine from the guards.

"*Shoot him!*"

The bodyguards were shouting for him to duck, to get down, and I expected to hear gunfire. Instead, all I heard was Balserio's whistling scream of pain as I brought his left arm up behind him, then grabbed a handful of his hair for additional torque.

"He's *hurting* me. Fire!"

I'd hoped he'd managed to hold on to the knife. I had a vague notion that if I took the knife from him, then held the blade to their boss man's throat, maybe I could bully the bodyguards into dropping their weapons.

But nope. No knife. He'd lost it when I popped his wrist askew.

Even so, I still had their general . . .

As the two guards moved cautiously toward me, their weapons raised, I shifted my grip from the man's hair and arm to a modified choke hold, so that my forearms cradled Balserio's head.

As the General wrestled with me, again commanding, "Shoot him! You idiots, kill him!" I said to the guards in a much calmer voice to make certain they listened: "Come one step closer, I'll break his neck. I know *how* to do it, believe me."

I could have done it, too. But for what?

It was a bluff, and it didn't work.

The bodyguards had finally maneuvered themselves so that there was one on each side of me. Now Panama Hat touched the barrel of his Uzi submachine gun near my temple, and said in Spanish, "Yeah, dude, that's cool, go right ahead. You break his neck, I shoot your head off. Then you and the General can go to hell together and finish your fight. People down in that place are probably already selling tickets, man, making bets."

Panama Hat was far more subtle and articulate in Spanish.

I had no choice. I released Balserio, pushing him roughly away. He turned immediately and charged. He kicked at me once, hard—I blocked it with my hands and hip—and then he began to slap wildly at my face with his open hands.

"You think I'm done with you? I'm *not* done with you."

As he slapped at me and kicked, I covered my head with my arms, ducking and weaving until his men pulled him away.

But when Balserio then dropped to his hands and knees, searching furiously to recover his knife, it occurred to me: *Maybe I shouldn't have bluffed.*

He seemed determined to use the damn thing.

TWELVE

PANAMA Hat was Elmase. White Shoes was Hugo. The men could communicate without speaking. Eye movement, a shift of the shoulders, a re-angling of the jaw. That's all it took.

They had some history, judging from their easy familiarity. Way more going between each other than with the General. Were probably partners in some intricate way. Maybe family.

Balserio was a mental case, and they seemed to recognize it. Or maybe he was just acting crazy, playing out years of despising me, but taking it beyond the edge.

This was the General who'd imported a sociopath into his own country for political gain. A serial killer who set people on *fire*. Did they know?

Maybe. I noticed that they distanced themselves from Balserio in subtle ways. One was by demonstrating exaggerated patience.

The General was still on his knees, crawling in the tall scrub where the knife had vanished. There were plant colonies I recognized as giant leather ferns—ancient sporangia coated—and alligator lilies with stalks toothed sharp enough to cut skin.

Balserio had cut himself a couple of times, cursing, then sucking blood off his fingers.

"You don't have knives? One of you has to have a knife!"

"No, General. We have guns. Why would we need anything else when we have good guns? We can shoot off his *cojones,* if you wish."

From the tone, the flat subservience mixed with sarcasm, I got the impression they wouldn't have admitted carrying knives if they had them.

Balserio was practically frothing. "I'm paying fools like you? Then grab that pig's arms while I find *my* knife. Tie him to a tree and strip his pants. I'm going to cut his balls off. I swore I'd make him a sow if I ever got the chance. I'll do it now. *Then* we'll find Pilar."

Elmase and Hugo looked at me, expressions mild but now interested, a bedrock contempt held in ready. To be terrified was to be debased. Maybe contempt shielded them from the humiliation of other men they'd seen begging. How would I react?

Hugo said, "Then I guess we'll need some rope. Do we have rope in the car?"

Elmase said slowly, "No, but there's tape. We could tape his arms and legs to a tree. Tape could work . . . if you're sure you want to do this thing."

Neither sounded enthusiastic. More silent communication was taking place. Their focus on me, though, remained intense. How would this man react when threatened with the ultimate male humiliation?

I was furious. Too enraged to be frightened. Furious that Balserio would not only threaten me, but also threaten to maim my son. He intended to *do* it. Really wanted to cut me. Tomlinson has written a few things that've stuck with me. One is, *To make a fool of a tyrant, refuse to submit.*

It had a brand of kiss-my-ass wisdom that now flooded through me.

So my reaction was aggressive, and it wasn't an act.

The bodyguards had put some space between us. White Shoes—Hugo—had slipped the pistol back into his pocket and was relying on the shotgun again.

When he said, "Yes, then I guess you should get the tape. I'll hold the big man while you do his hands first, then his—" I silenced him, snapping, "*Enough.* Stop right there. Not another word."

Both paused, looking at me, expectant.

I pointed my index finger first at Hugo, then Elmase, before I continued, "Don't waste your time with the tape. What you need to do is, go ahead and shoot me. I mean it. Do it *right now.* Because I'm not going to let you lay a finger on me. No one's tying me to a tree. And that lunatic's sure as hell not getting near me again with a knife. So go ahead and shoot."

I jabbed my finger at Hugo for emphasis. "I'll tell you one thing, though. You'd better aim high and shoot straight. And you'd better hope my hands don't live any longer than my brain. If they do, *you're* gonna die with me."

Hugo sobered for a moment, his contempt fading as he translated the meaning of that. He and Elmase exchanged facial expressions, then a shrug.

The exchange seemed to go: *Is he acting?*

No . . . he's for real.

Then: *Yeah, man. I'd die before letting any man take a knife to my private parts, too.*

Hugo looked at me with his wide face and began to chuckle. Then Elmase began to laugh, too.

"If your hands don't die before your brain," Hugo said. "Man, that's a good one. Like in this old movie I saw. This hand go running around on its fingers, choking dudes. Scary. And the way you said it. That was kinda scary, too. Like you could make it *happen.*"

We'd locked eyes, my eyes telling his: *Yeah, I can make it happen.* Still furious, I believed it.

I didn't look away until Hugo had turned to Elmase, who was saying, "Yeah, but the Yankee is so *right.* Take the bullet, man. Before I even let some dude put his hands on my balls, I'd take the bullet. Shit, I'd grab the gun and do it *myself.*"

Behind us, Balserio was on his knees still searching for the knife, frustrated now, and yelling, "Didn't you hear me? I told you to take him and tie him to a tree. That's an *order.*"

Hugo made a waving motion with his hand, not dismissing the man but evading. "That's what we're *doing,* General. But first . . . I think, we need to check out this dude's car. Who knows? Maybe your wife's hiding in there. Or that giant dude with the tattoos—if he's around, he's so big, we'd have to shoot him ten, twelve times to bring him down. Like those rhinos you see on TV. Be cool, General. Be cool. We know our jobs."

Spanish profanity can only seldom be translated literally into English. Try, and it sounds silly. That's because it relies on so many simple, inoffensive words that, when used with subtle or sinister emphasis, become offensive. The words *cork, rope, papaya,* and *bug,* for example, can also be graphically profane.

Balserio knew all the words and subtleties, and he pelted me with them as Hugo and Elmase steered me at gunpoint toward the rental Ford. He used the foulest, sickest phrases. Translated, though, he was telling me that I was a billy goat who slept with young billy goats on rusty mattress springs in my mother's house.

Something perverse in me found that funny—or maybe I was just crashing emotionally after being threatened and assaulted—and as my anger dissipated, I began to laugh. Really laugh.

I was a *cabrón?* A billy goat? The man who might soon be president of Masagua was calling me animal names.

Hilarious.

Hugo and Elmase seemed surprised, then puzzled. I might not be tied to a tree, awaiting the Crazy Machete, but they still had me captive at gunpoint.

But then Elmase stopped walking, head tilted because he heard what I'd already heard: the raceway sound of cars revving too fast around a curve.

"What's that noise, man?"

"Shit! Cars coming, hide your gun!"

Then we could see them, white cars heading our way, seeming to flatten themselves at speed over the gravel road: county sheriff's vehicles, green on white, no sirens or lights, which is procedure when a person calling 911 says he thinks he'll be killed if the bad guys hear help coming.

To Hugo and Elmase, I now said, "You'd better throw your weapons down. Quick."

When they didn't react immediately, I added, "When the police jump out, see you two guys dressed like pimps, holding automatic weapons—down here in the Everglades? They *might* think you're dangerous."

Convinced, they swung their guns into the bushes as I added, "But you're going to jail anyway. I know you helped me out with that crazy asshole, but it's still gotta be jail."

Elmase seemed not to hear that, replying, "Pimps? Dressed like *pimps*? That's not a very nice thing to say. These clothes got style, man."

Standing there in his white Panama hat and metallic shirt, neon pink and blue, offended. About to be arrested, but his expression still telling me: *You hurt my feelings, man.*

DIAL 911 and tell them you're a respectable Sanibel Island resident crossing the Everglades in a car being pursued at high speed by strangers who are shooting guns, and the dispatcher will send out the cavalry.

The cavalry had assembled: sheriff's deputies, state troopers, and plain-clothes detectives in unmarked cars, all vehicles jumbled in a line, the Loop Road blocked shut, emergency lights strobing high in the shadowed domes of cypress trees on this late South Florida afternoon.

Sunset was at a little after eight P.M. Probably less than an hour away. No way for me to know for certain, because I was handcuffed. Couldn't see my watch.

Back on Sanibel and Captiva, the ceremonial cocktail crowds would al-ready be gathering at South Seas Plantation, the Mucky Duck, Casa Ybel, among others, and at our little Dinkin's Bay Marina. Same would be true up and down the Gulf Coast of Florida, Key West to Pensacola Bay.

It would soon be social hour in the dawdling May heat. The pearly time when friends meet with cold drinks in small, local places to watch the sun orbit into the Gulf and spark its universal blaze.

I wanted to get back to Dinkin's Bay for sunset. Wanted to share some stories and laughs with Mack, Jeth, JoAnn, Rhonda, all the fishing guides, the live-aboards, and the rest of the marina community. That's exactly what I needed to neutralize the image of Balserio coming at me, knife in hand, with that leering grin on his face.

It had been too close. Too ugly.

I wanted faces of friends to replace his in my memory, before the image seared itself.

But there wasn't much chance I'd make it back in time.

Despite the handcuffs, and out of habit, I tried to check my watch anyway. I flinched to move my arms from behind me and sneak a glance. Impossible. Not sitting alone in the back seat of a Collier County Sheriff's deputy's vehicle.

I'd been placed there by a uniformed deputy with the briefest of explanations—"Relax. We'll get back to you."—and so had been waiting and watching a small army of law enforcement people move in busy silence outside my air-conditioned space.

I was thirsty. I also had to pee.

They'd treated Hugo, Elmase, Balserio, and me all the same.

When the first three squad cars came skidding toward us, the officers bailed with weapons drawn and pointed, screaming, *"Get down! Show us your hands ! Get down! Get down!"*

So much for my theory that I'd be singled out as an innocent local and given special treatment.

We were approached cautiously, asked the whereabouts of weaponry, then handcuffed, frisked, I.D.s taken, then separated.

Because firearms were involved, they explained, and because there was a report of shots fired, everyone had to be constrained until officers figured out who was who and what had happened.

It took a while.

Finally, a woman in a starched deputy's uniform opened the door and asked, "You're the gentleman who called nine-one-one?"

Then she asked, "Do you mind answering a few questions?"

Sitting in the back of the squad car, I repeated my story separately to two different uniformed deputies. They were both articulate, professional.

After the first interview, I was told I had to remain in the back seat, but the handcuffs were removed, my driver's license was returned, and I was allowed to take a whiz.

As I returned to the car, I noted that Elmase, Hugo, and the sadistic General were in separate vehicles, all getting lots of close attention from people both in uniform and out. They were still handcuffed, too, judging from their posture.

I was pleased.

After telling my story a second time, I was asked politely if I wouldn't mind sticking around long enough to tell it again to a couple of officers from the Major Crimes Division who'd soon arrive.

It sounded like a request, though it wasn't. I pretended to be magnanimous and cooperative.

In my account, I doctored the truth in several places. I didn't mention that Tomlinson and Pilar had been with me, nor that my son had been kidnapped. I told them that while I was being pursued, someone had shot at my car on two different occasions from the Chevy.

Because I knew it was possible that Balserio had used a fake passport to enter the country, and because I didn't want to risk being linked to press accounts about a Masaguan *politico* being arrested, I didn't volunteer his last name.

"It was the tall guy," I said. "The one who fired the shots is the same one who came at me with the knife. I could see him in the rearview mirror, shooting. I'll swear to it."

The knife idiocy was enough to put him in jail, but I had to include the shooting incidents. I'd already told the dispatcher it was happening when I dialed 911.

Aware that it's the rare citizen who ever hears a weapon fired with lethal intent, I stammered and rambled to seem sufficiently upset, but managed to tell the officer precisely where Balserio had popped off the rounds: the curve where Ervin Rouse's house had once stood—easy to describe—and then again on the straight-away.

I knew they'd go looking, and I knew they'd find the spent brass casings. Three rounds at each place, near the ditch, on the passenger's side of the road.

I also knew they'd search the Chevy and find the weapon that had fired those rounds: my Sig Sauer. I'd slid it beneath the car's passenger seat.

FNALLY, at ten till eight—when I would have much preferred to be roaming the marina docks of Dinkin's Bay, cold beer in hand—two plainclothes detectives from the department's Major Crimes Division tapped on the window, then opened the door and introduced themselves.

I followed them to their unmarked car and sat in the back.

They'd been assigned the case, they told me. What they didn't say was that all the other cops I'd spoken to that day no longer mattered. These were the people I had to convince.

There was a woman with a name that sounded like *Gartone*. She was early thirties, maybe Cuban American, with shoulder-length black hair and a stylish pantsuit. It had a tailored look, expensive. Same with the makeup and jewelry. Tasteful. She could have been on her way to a country club function.

I got the clear impression that her clothing had been selected as carefully as the weapon she carried in a shoulder holster beneath her jacket. Dressing the way she did, she automatically had a psychological advantage over anyone she dealt with. The lowlifes would confide in her, eager for the approval of someone they considered a superior. The upper-class types would connect as equals and cooperate just as eagerly, hoping for unspoken perks from a peer.

As she slid into the seat beside me, I thought to myself, *Watch your step with this one.*

The other detective was an old guy. Retirement age. Or maybe he was one of those senior citizen volunteers you sometimes see riding with cops.

I was undecided until she introduced him as Detective Merlin T. Starkey.

He could have been in his late sixties or seventies. Moved slow and creaky, like he'd taken some hard shots in his day. Silver hair, balding. Dressed like a cattle rancher, with Red Wing boots, pearl button shirt, green suspenders, string bowtie, and a Stetson hat. The hat looked like it had spent some real time on real trails.

"Starkey" is a common name everywhere, but especially in South Florida. Early settlers named Starkey were a tough, fertile, and hearty folk.

"Call me Merlin, son," he said in a slow nasal accent that was pure mangrove and sawgrass. He sat in the front seat, without a notebook.

Merlin, I decided, would not be sympathetic to foreigners riding around the Everglades with illegal weapons, assaulting solid citizens such as myself.

But it was Detective Gartone's case. Starkey was just along for company. That seemed obvious.

She asked all the questions, taping the interview on a digital recorder the size of a cigarette lighter. For more than half an hour, we sat in the back of the car, sharing that small space, talking. That's the way she made it seem: as if we were having a conversation. She had that easy kind of manner.

I felt as if we were building rapport. She seemed to believe me. Seemed to be empathetic. I had to keep reminding myself that she was also one very smart cop, and it could be an act.

When she asked me to describe again, step by step, how I'd disarmed Balserio, she gave me a concerned shake of the head, muttered, "You're very lucky," then asked permission to use a digital camera to photograph the scratches on my face and hands.

A question that she lingered on was the identity of the man who'd fired the shots from the car. I'd told the uniformed deputies that I was willing to swear that it was Balserio. But a little alarm went off in my head, keyed by the way she asked—a subtle change in her tone that seemed to coach me—and I modified my answer.

I said I thought it was the man I knew as Jorge.

"You *think* it was him," she said.

"I was scared. Everything happened so fast, it was kind of blurry. But I'm pretty sure."

"You're willing to swear shots were fired, but not who the shooter was."

"I guess that's the most honest way to put it."

For some reason, that seemed to raise my stock. Brought her fully on my side.

In the front seat, Merlin T. Starkey stirred and cleared his throat, as if he'd been dozing.

Now I noticed something new in Detective Gartone's manner when she said, "You also allege that, during the knife attack, the assailant accused you of having an affair with his wife. Were there grounds for the accusation?"

What I noticed was, she added an extra curtain of professional reserve, as if to further insulate herself from the subject. To me, though, it suggested that she found the topic uncomfortable, which, in turn, suggested a sexual awareness. In that instant, I became conscious of her as a woman—her legs, the intensity of her reserve, eyes boring in, the shape of her. I wondered if, in the same abbreviated space of time, she'd become conscious of me as a man.

She was not the sort to permit even a subtle sign, despite the fact that she wore no wedding ring. Too professional. And I had more than enough going on in my life now, struggling not to lose Dewey. Still . . . when you meet the rare independent ones, the strong professionals with uncompromised standards, you note their existence and file the details away. On lonely nights, it's a good thing to go through those files and remember that good women are out there.

She rephrased the question. "I'm trying to establish a motive here, Dr. Ford. You say that the man accused you of having an affair with his wife."

I said, "That's correct. The taller of the three, Jorge."

"Yet, you say you don't know Jorge's last name."

"I know *her* last name. I'm not certain they share that name, and I see no reason to risk revealing the identity of an innocent third party."

I could see that the detective approved of that.

"Then you *were* having an affair with your alleged attacker's wife."

Her eyes continue to bore in as I replied, "The marriage was annulled long ago. It's my understanding that, in the Catholic religion, an annulment doesn't end a marriage. It decrees that the marriage never existed. They were never husband and wife, so there's really no way to respond to your question."

She said, "For the first time, I think you're being evasive."

"The lunatic who tried to cut me up with the knife, what did he tell you?"

Gartone started to reply, caught herself, then closed the notebook in which she'd been jotting shorthand. She held the recorder to her lips, saying, "This concludes the interview with Dr. Marion Ford on the date as stated," and turned to face me. "All three men deny they attacked you. Not with a knife, not with a gun. They say you made up the entire story."

"Really."

"Does that surprise you?"

Trying to sound fretful and a little naïve, I said, "No-o-o-o. I guess not. I suppose that's what criminals do, huh? Lie about breaking the law. But you had to find their guns in the bushes. That should tell you something. People aren't allowed to carry around guns like that, are they?"

"We found a fully automatic assault pistol and a shotgun lying in the bushes in the Everglades. Even if they acknowledged ownership—which they didn't—it's not a big deal. Tobacco Firearms might get around to it in a month or so.

"The man you call Jorge had no identification, no passport, and refused to give us his name. The other two, all they had were Nicaraguan driver's licenses."

She shrugged. "Even if all three are in the country illegally, that's no longer a big deal, either. Our borders are so wide open, the Department of Immigration doesn't want to hear a peep from us unless we catch a busload." Sounding stern, she added, "I'm trying to tell you something here, Dr. Ford."

"You're telling me that I shouldn't be evasive. That you're trying to help."

"We don't want men with knives who try to . . . mutilate people running around loose. Let's put it that way."

I said, "So, I guess it's my word against theirs . . . unless . . . well, you find some evidence that supports my story. When they shot at my car—can't you tell if a gun's been fired? It'd be missing bullets, right?"

Detective Gartone's laughter was like mid-low notes on a piano. "You really *are* an academic. Yes, we can tell if a weapon's been fired. That's why you and I are having what amounts to a private conversation."

Talking now as if the old detective in the front seat wasn't there.

Then, opening the car door, unfolding long legs as she exited, she added, "The two places on the road you say they fired at you? We found shell casings that match a weapon that was hidden in their vehicle. Backs up your story."

I said, "Shell casings? You're *kidding*. Jeez, I was beginning to worry you'd think I was hallucinating or something. It was a hell of a scary experience."

"If it's any consolation, I don't think many men would have handled themselves as well as you. For an amateur, I mean."

Maybe the detective lady *was* giving me a little signal. And maybe, under other circumstances, I would have given her a signal in return.

Gartone wasn't pretty in any conventional way, but her face had an interesting complexity in this late, sunset light. It was a face that became more appealing when her mask of formality vanished into a smile.

She smiled now for just a moment before telling me that we were nearly done. She had to put me under oath, I had to sign some papers. After that, I was free to drive the Ford back to Sanibel, where, she suggested, I put iodine on my scratches, then get some sleep. I could rest easy, she said, because my assailants wouldn't be released from jail until I was notified.

Handing me her card, dark eyes showing no emotion, she said, "In fact, I'll call you personally. It's my job."

THIRTEEN

I THOUGHT that concluded my dealings for the day with the Collier County Sheriff's Department until, from inside the car, Detective Merlin Starkey spoke for the first time since the introductions.

"Miz Tamara? You mind if I walk Dr. Ford back to his vehicle?"

Tamara. An interesting first name to go with the face.

"If he's the Ford boy I'm rememberin'," he said, "the one lived in Mango for a spell, it's possible I knowed his uncle pretty good. Maybe some of his other people. Is it O.K.?"

I thought, *Not another one of Tucker Gatrell's old redneck pals . . .*

But it was worth it because I was rewarded with a second sampling of the woman's piano laughter. "Oh, Merlin, I thought you'd fallen asleep. Of course you can go with Dr. Ford. I've got paperwork to finish. But come straight back to the car, O.K.? You know how I worry about you. In a place like this, I'd almost bet there're snakes."

Talking like a granddaughter would talk to her lovable, bumbling old grandfather.

"Could be snakes, ma'am," the old man said. He was using a silver-headed walking stick to leverage himself out of the squad car, putting on his Stetson. Looking at me then with dark, piercing eyes that did not mesh with his soft drawl, he added, "Yes, ma'am, this here's real *snaky*-lookin' country."

The old coot had just insulted me. Was it intentional? It seemed too obvious not to be. But Merlin T. Starkey had no reason to offend. Or did he?

I found out soon enough.

I walked with him slowly along the gravel road toward the logging trail. He nodded to the few deputies who remained, calling them by their first names, or touching the brim of his Stetson if the officer was a woman, saying, "Howdy-do, miz."

Otherwise, he remained silent. Didn't respond when I remarked upon the lady detective's professionalism. Continued to walk, using the cane, staring straight ahead. It was as if he couldn't hear. Seemed to ignore me, doing it intentionally as with the insult. But he was quick to answer when I suggested, "Merlin, I can make it the rest of the way on my own. When I'm not in such a hurry, maybe we can get together and you can tell me about the old days."

"You ain't goin' any durn place till we have us a private talk, boy," he snapped. "And never mind what I said back there. My name ain't Merlin to you. It's Detective Starkey. Or *sir*. In my line a work, if I wasn't protectivelike, I'd be on a first-name basis with every crook, hustler, and con man scum between Marathon and Cedar Key. So you allow me my propers. Hear?"

Oh yeah. He'd taken a dislike to me for some reason.

I replied patiently, "O.-K. Whatever you say. But I'm tired. I want to get home to a shower and a few beers. You can understand that." Said it respectfully, too, thinking, *What's going on here?*

Starkey shot back with a nasty chuckle, "Oh, I'll make 'er quick, sonny boy. Nearly fifty years carryin' a badge in the 'Glades, and I was never known to ramble when it come to settin' a lying fraud straight."

He was baiting me, maybe. Even so, I stopped for a moment, irritated, watching him as he continued to limp along, using the walking stick as a third leg. We were several meters into the logging road. The shadow of cypress trees had changed the dominate odor from gravel and dust to moss, and dropped the temperature ten degrees.

"Hold on a second there, Mister . . . Detective, *sir*. I don't know what I did to make you mad. But if you've got a problem, why didn't you get it on the table while we were in the car? Instead, you tell me you were a friend of my uncle to lure me out here—"

The old man whirled to face me with surprising agility. He had a round, Santa-like face, which somehow seemed to make his expression even more fierce. "I never said I was a friend to Tucker Gatrell. I said I *knowed* him, and I did. I think your uncle was a lying, conniving, dope-smuggling son-of-a-buck. I'd use stronger language, only I never seen a need to lower my-self to that kinda garbage-mouth talk.

"Oh, I *knowed* Tucker. If it warn't for what that swindler did to me, I'da been sheriff of this county long back, and I'd be retired already. Probably be shooting quail with the governor and a couple senators right now. Instead, I'll never make it past captain. Your uncle double-crossed me. He ruined my life."

I was so taken aback by his words and his fury that it was a long, be-fuddled moment before I responded. "You're giving me a hard time now because you're still . . . pissed off at something my uncle did years ago?" After another moment, I added, "You're *serious.*"

"Serious as a snake bite." The old detective pointed his walking stick at me, and jabbed it, saying, "But I think you're a bad'un for your own sake. You got a full dose of Gatrell snakiness in you, boy. You're a little too cute and tricky for your own good. Well, sonny, you ain't got *me* fooled. So you want to talk, jes' the two of us? Or you want me to talk public?"

I wasn't sure what he meant, but I didn't like the sound of it.

I looked behind me: Tamara Gartone was sitting in her car, hunched over a clipboard, waiting. Balserio, the two Nicaraguans, were gone, presumably on their way to be arraigned and then to jail. The last two squad cars were pulling out.

I looked at my watch. The sky was grape and molten brass through the lace of limbs, but I had to squint to read the numerals here in the swamp gloom: 8:42 P.M.

With luck, I'd be back at Dinkin's Bay Marina around eleven. Maybe in time to have a beer with Tomlinson before . . .

But no. Tomlinson, I remembered, was at the Miami Radisson with Pilar. Pilar was maybe getting a break from all the terrible stress. Probably having a few glasses of wine, spending quality time with her new best friend, my randy Zen Buddhist pal who was always eager to offer solace and comfort to distraught ladies—me, the hypocrite, thinking hypocritical thoughts.

I made Merlin Starkey walk with me deeper into the logging trail before I said to him, "Go ahead and talk. But no more comparisons with Gatrell, O.K.? I'm not a fan. I never was."

He snorted. That nasty chuckle again. "I know about that, too, sonny boy. I know why you hated the man."

"Oh?"

"Um-huh. It's 'cause of what you think he done to your parents. They was killed in a boat fire back when you was a kid. I knowed 'em both. Not well, but I'd met 'em. Good folk. You always faulted Gatrell for the fire. You decided he'd installed one a his idiot inventions as a fuel valve. A bad valve coulda caused that boat fire."

Suddenly I was straining to listen to his every word. "You're right. How do you know that?"

"'Cause," Starkey said, "I was one a the deputies who investigated the deaths. Gatrell'd already ruined my career by that time, and I was itchin' for ways to hang the slippery dog. Involuntary manslaughter at the least. I wanted to get him.

"I studied that fire from every angle. Found out you was doin' the same—just a young kid at the time, but smart. I'll give you that. You and me even met once. I come to your uncle's place to look at what was left of the boat. You'd been piecing her back together. Remember?"

I stared at the old man; studied his blotched, penetrating old eyes. It jogged a vague recollection of a young, athletic-looking man, military haircut, business suit and briefcase, who seemed to know in advance that my uncle was away. I'd gotten the impression he wouldn't have visited otherwise. But it hadn't been that many decades ago, and Merlin Starkey looked ancient.

As if reading my thoughts, he said, "Time don't scar a man nearly as bad as his failures. I failed to get my revenge on Gatrell. I wanted to prove he was to blame for your folks dying. Instead, I proved to myself he warn't."

After a pause, he added, "A *different* person was to blame for that fire, that's what I figured out. So you've been wrong all along. I was so disappointed, I lost interest and let 'er drop. I warn't in charge of the case anyway. No one asked *my* opinion."

Unaware that I'd even moved, I'd walked so that I was now standing face to face with the old man. He was leaning against the silver trunk of a cypress tree, and had his stick braced beneath one hip like a sort of unipod stool.

"Who was it? The person who killed my parents. Was it . . . accidental?"

Starkey smiled, his head bobbing. "Whoo-wheee! I just saw somethin' behind your eyes there, sonny boy, that I don't like. I seen it before. Men on death row up to Raiford, they got the same little thing that flashes back there. Not all of 'em. Just the good'uns, the real pros. Kind of a glow, like water over ice." He hooted again. "Whoo-whee!"

I said softly, nearly whispering, "Knock it off. I asked you a simple question."

Starkey held up an index finger, correcting me. "My propers. Show proper respect when you're addressin' me." He'd plucked a tin of Copenhagen snuff out of his shirt pocket, and thumped it between his fingers, waiting.

The old asshole was enjoying the leverage he now had on me.

I said impatiently, "O.K., *Detective* Starkey. Tell me what you found out. Who was it? I'd . . . appreciate your help."

"Maybe I'll tell you. But first, you stand there and listen to a few things just so you know you ain't so smart—*Doctor* Ford. Tamara Gartone? I reckon she's just about the finest young woman ever to come to our department. She got the brains, she got the heart to do anything she wants. If I had me a daughter, I couldn't want her to be no finer person than Miz Tamara."

Confused—why was he now on this tangent?—I said, "I agree. Ten minutes ago, when I was telling you how impressed I was, you wouldn't answer me. What's your point?"

"You lied to the woman, that's my point, sonny boy. That story about shots bein' fired at you from the Chevy. Pure cow manure. They never fired a round. But she believes you, and she's sent men to jail 'cause of it. You're settin' her up to make her look like a fool. I don't know what you're into, but if it's bigger'n it seems, it could come back and hurt her. Ruin her career. Just like your uncle did to me."

The old man was still looking at me, but seemed uninterested in my response. He knew the truth. Because he knew, there was nothing to learn from my reaction. But *how* did he know?

I said carefully, "If that's supposed to make sense, you lost me. Even if it did, I wouldn't intentionally put her in jeopardy. I just met her, but I like her."

"But that's *exactly* what you're doin', boy. Which is why you're gonna go bang on her car window right now and tell the lady what really happened. Don't mention that I give you a boot in the pants. I don't *want* credit. People in the department now, they think I'm half-senile, which is just the way I like it. So you set her straight like it was your own idea.

"After that, then maybe we'll get together and I'll tell you what I learnt about that boat fire. After all these years, you'll finally know."

He had the snuff tamped down between cheek and gum now. He cleaned his fingers on his pants and spit, waiting.

There had been a time, long, long ago, when I was obsessed with discovering the exact cause of the fire and resulting explosion that killed my mother and father. Now, I seldom thought of those two.

I thought of them now.

To celebrate their twelfth anniversary, my parents took a cruise into the Ten Thousand Islands along Florida's Gulf Coast. The last time I saw them, I was standing on the dock of the Rod & Gun Club, Everglades City. My father was big-shouldered on the fly bridge, and my mother was facing me, waving goodbye.

I hadn't tried to recall that parting in years. Now a forgotten scene came back to me. I remembered how pretty my mother looked in the light of a morning river. Her face, her beauty—the clarity of those few seconds— was so vivid that I could smell the water, could hear her voice. Then my father turned toward me. He grinned and flashed a hand signal that he said only the two of us knew.

The memory was so detailed, the emotion so powerful, that I was startled. A weird feeling.

The vessel they were aboard had an inboard gas engine. If someone tampers with or damages an inboard's fuel system, gas fumes collect easily in the bilge. An arcing spark then becomes a detonator.

I spent more than a year after what was dismissed as a boating accident reassembling bits and pieces of that boat like a puzzle, fixated on determining the exact cause of the fire. *Who* was responsible?

I have been relentless about assembling meticulous data, observing and recording precise detail, ever since. That stuck with me, too.

THE old man said again, "Sonny boy, Miz Tamara's in the car all alone. Tell her the truth, and I'll tell you the truth. The person responsible is no one you ever suspected, I promise you that."

The rage to learn who or what had killed my parents was still in me, I realized. Surprising—I'm not a sentimental person. Yet, I wanted to know. The desire swept through me in the same way fear or fury sweeps through the nerve tendrils. I felt like grabbing the old man and shaking the information out of him. I also gave serious consideration to giving him what he wanted.

But I couldn't. I'd promised Pilar that I wouldn't involve law enforcement, just as she had promised Lake's abductors. More compelling, I couldn't put the safety of my own son at risk just to satisfy the obsession—or maybe put right the wounds—of the boy, and the son, I had once been.

Balserio had to stay in jail.

I was shaking my head—a private reply to Merlin Starkey—as I said, "You seem so sure. Would you mind explaining why you don't believe me?"

"That's 'cause I *am* sure. You want to play it tricky? Then I'll spell it out for you." He grinned again—he'd wanted me to ask. "You swore to our deputies the tall one was the shooter. The one you called Jorge. Say you saw him clear in your rearview mirror."

I said, "That's right. But when Detective Gartone asked me, I changed my—"

"I know how you changed it," he interrupted. "I know why, too. Let me finish!

"When I searched the Chevy, it was before we met, but the deputies told me your story. You swore the tall one fired from the passenger window. Which sounded O.K. until I noticed that both front seats was slid way forward. Our people didn't move them, so I asked the suspects. They all said the same. The two Nicaraguans are short, but Jorge's six-four, six-five. He always rode in the *back* with them two up front, seats way forward."

I shrugged. "I was scared, confused. I made a mistake. So Jorge must have fired from the back seat. If it *was* him."

Starkey was still enjoying it. "That's not the only mistake you made. All the spent brass we found landed on the right shoulder of the road. That worked in real good with your story about him firing from the passenger window. It still works in pretty good with him firing from the back seat, right side. But I noticed something different about Jorge. Know what that was?"

I gave it a moment, thinking, then swallowed hard—*uh-oh*—because I was remembering how Balserio handled the knife, passing it back and forth from hand to hand.

"What I noticed," Starkey said, leaning toward me, his voice rising in a sort of victorious intensity, "is the man you say fired at you woulda never done it the way you said. There ain't no way in Hades. That's because the man's *left-handed*. Ain't no way a left-handed man is gonna fire from the right window of an empty back seat.

"Just to be sure, I had the deputy undo the tall man's cuffs. I made him take the little test where you sight a target through your fingers with both eyes wide open—" The old detective formed a circle with thumb and index finger, holding it away from his face, to demonstrate. "Close your left eye, and if the target stays in the circle, your right eye's strongest. Jorge's not only left-handed, but he's got a dominant left eye. No lefty with a dominant left eye shoots right-handed. *Ever*. So I knowed you was lyin' even before we met.

"You staged the whole dang business, Ford. You fired them rounds.

That spooky old SIG-Sauer with no serial numbers we found in the Chevy was planted by you. For some reason, you want them boys jailed real bad."

I was thinking to myself, *Tucker Gatrell outsmarted this guy?* as he continued, "I told Miz Tamara all that before we got you in the car. But something clicked between you two. Man and woman stuff. I seen it happen to some of the best. They get a gut feelin' about who they can trust, and their brain stops. I knowed it when she started askin' questions in a way so you knew how to answer. Poor girl didn't even know she was doin' it. So I'm gonna give you one last chance to do the honorable thing. The right thing."

I shook my head slowly again—*No*—saying, "I'm not involved in anything that's going to hurt her or her career, I promise you."

He snorted, spit as he banged his stick on the ground hard, like a gavel. "That ain't gonna cut it. So here's the deal: If she takes any grief because of your lies, I'm gonna come down on you like a marble ceiling. I still never got my revenge on your uncle. Not *yet*, anyway. Maybe I'll get 'er through you."

I looked at my watch—8:57 P.M.—then looked at the black cypress canopy above, a pearling sky beyond, thinking, *All I want to do is get home. Back to my fish and boats and books—and find my boy.*

Even so, I still had to ask the question. Had to ask because I needed to know how much hatred I was dealing with. How far was this old man willing to take it? In getting him to talk, I also hoped maybe he'd soften a little and give me a few hints about who was responsible for the boat fire.

Even though I was exhausted, I tried my best to sound empathetic when I asked Merlin T. Starkey about Tucker Gatrell, and how, exactly, that old con man had managed to ruin his career.

And he told me.

FOURTEEN

AS I pulled onto the Tamiami Trail, headed west toward Sanibel, I got the number from information and had the girl at the Miami Radisson's front desk ring Tomlinson's room.

No answer.

The first time, I left a message for him saying, "I've got a classic Tucker Gatrell story that you're not going to believe. Actually, you will believe it. It's so typical. Plus there's interesting news about the black car."

I think I sounded upbeat. Not a hint of suspicion in my voice.

How Tucker had ruined the career of Merlin T. Starkey—I told myself that was the reason I tried Tomlinson's room again ten minutes later, then redialed a third time a few minutes after that. Told myself I was eager to share the wild tale, and also confirm that Pilar and Tomlinson were safe. That seemed reasonable. Hadn't I told them not to leave the room?

True, Balserio, Hugo, and Elmase had probably already been booked into Collier County jail. But my friend and my former lover weren't aware of that. They should have been inside the Radisson with the bolts latched.

I checked my watch: 9:30 P.M.

So where were they?

Or . . . maybe they *were* in the room, but ignoring the phone. Inside all alone, but having too much fun to answer.

Yeah, that was certainly possible . . .

I plucked up the cell phone, hit redial again, and told the irritable desk clerk, "This is kind of important. Would you mind trying that room one more time?"

Nothing.

My primary concern was that they were in some kind of trouble. Someone had gotten to them. But I was also aware of an undercurrent of adolescent-grade suspicion.

My behavior, I lied to myself, had nothing to do with Tomlinson and how he behaved with women. I also told myself it wasn't because of the secret, sexual Pilar that tumbled out under a lot of stress, and after a couple of glasses of wine.

I simply wanted to let them know that it was safe for them to unlock the door and leave Miami. That maybe they should get on the phone and grab the first fast cab back to Sanibel.

I'm not the suspicious type. Too mature, too rational to be jealous, so that's not why I kept calling.

That's what I told myself.

I also wasn't already regretting exchanging my Sig Sauer for Balserio's freedom, nor did some secret part of me consider that gun a mighty good-luck talisman.

Right.

In the next few minutes, I received two calls. But it wasn't the missing couple. First time, it was one of Tomlinson's Zen students, who told me in a rush that she felt the mantra he'd assigned her just wasn't working because, she now realized, it was similar to the name of an old boyfriend.

"Please tell the respected Daishi it's becoming a real downer, picturing that asshole's face every time I work on my *sutra.*"

I said I'd pass the information along if and when I ever spoke to the great Daishi again.

The second caller didn't pause even when I tried to interrupt.

"Hey, man, how're you doin'? Nothing urgent but my outboard's about bone dry. Hear what I'm tellin' ya? We need it at the Marco Island store. I hear a buck fifty a gallon sounds right. So I'll take two bags. *Gallons,* I mean. Only if it's high test, though; got a big race tonight. Catch you at the shack. Same place—and tell your delivery boy not to be late this time."

As I said "Huh?" he hung up.

AT ten till ten, I slowed for the orange blinker and gas station fluorescence that is the turnoff to Everglades City at the intersection of Route 29. Down that rural two-lane was the Rod & Gun Club, the classic old fishing lodge where I'd waved a last goodbye to my parents.

Suddenly, I wasn't thinking about Tomlinson and Pilar anymore.

To the southwest, beyond mangroves, the lights of the village reflected off clouds. Once again, the image of the departing boat, my father, my mother, her eyes and smiling face, appeared. My father's secret hand signal. Once again, the freshness of detail startled me.

Had that scene ever come into my mind before?

No.

I was certain it hadn't. Not as an adult, anyway. Yet, how could I have forgotten a moment like that?

It seemed impossible, but I had. Until today.

It was a psychological anomaly that I'd never experienced.

I have little patience for nostalgia; seldom linger in the past. I've lived an independent, self-reliant life in which family hasn't played a role. After so many years on my own, my recall of those long-dead people had faded more completely than the photo I'd found of Ervin Rouse.

Yet on this day, they'd reappeared, alive in memory.

I found that puzzling and remarkable. It also seemed somehow important.

Why?

I couldn't fathom. What I'd learned about Tucker Gatrell wasn't a factor. No, it was more personal than that.

I considered making the turn to Everglades City, traveling the four or five miles to the Barron River to stand beneath the old moon-globe streetlights. To stand on the dock once again, where I'd said goodbye a final time. That reconnection might suggest an answer.

I decided against it. It was a little too touchy-feely for comfort. To me, self-exploration has always seemed an excuse for self-absorption. I'm too interested in the world outside to waste time on dramatic introspection.

I kept driving.

Still, the question lingered: Why had I experienced such a vivid recollection—especially after what I'd been through earlier? The leering face of a crazy man, threatening castration with a knife, is not easily displaced.

But it *had* been displaced. It had been replaced by the forgotten memory of my final few moments with my parents.

I thought about it as I drove.

I was in a wild section of Everglades called the Fakahatchee Strand. Traffic was sparse. I had windows down, peepers and bullfrogs rioting as I burrowed through their darkness at speed. The moon, nearly full, had been up long enough to saturate the flora with incandescent current. The sawgrass was luminous, a plateau of blue. Isolated tree canopies glowed cellularly—a kind of lunar synthesis.

I continued to wrestle with the question: *Why?* What had caused that buried moment to reveal itself?

I tried to cut through all the emotional, sentimental BS, seeking a rational explanation. I've read that internal, emotional anomalies are often catalyzed by external change. My life had changed dramatically in the last few days.

Key elements came to mind, then key words: son . . . parents . . . heredity . . . genetics . . . *blood.*

Yes, that seemed a sensible linkage.

It had only been in the last year or so that Lake had accepted me as his father, and I'd come to accept and value him as my son. The man and pretty woman who'd returned in memory with such startling clarity were my son's *grandparents.*

I'd never thought of my parents in that context before. In fact, I no longer even thought of myself as having parents, nor of being someone's son.

Family? I think of the cheerful live-aboards and fishing guides of Dinkin's Bay Marina as my extended family. But to be a member of an actual family, a blood kinship? With the exception of my cousin and friend, Ransom Gatrell—Tucker's daughter—having relatives, being part of a family, was something I'd never coveted.

Maybe shock caused by Lake's dilemma had sparked the forgotten memory. If so, it had also sparked the realization that I *was* the member of a family.

What was left of one, anyway.

I'd lost my parents years ago. Now I was confronting the possibility of losing their only grandson. As a biologist, the enormity of such a loss hit me for the first time. Two generations, two bridges in a family hereditary chain, wiped out.

As a father, the possibility of losing yet another generational member hit me much harder. Lake was my son. He was a great kid who loved science and baseball, and he was a hell of a lot more than just some genetic bridge.

I don't use a lot of profanity, but I used a couple of rough words now, banged my hand on the steering wheel, and yelled into the night, "Where are you? *Where are you?*"

I've never thought of myself as an orphan. Nor will I—too much self-pity in that word. But after a lifetime spent living alone, I had the frailest suspicion of an understanding that it meant something very different to *exist alone* in the world.

I now faced that possibility.

I had to stay smart and hope for the right breaks. We had to make contact with the kidnappers at the first opportunity.

I had to find my son.

THE satellite phone was beside me on the seat. With Balserio and his men put away, I felt there was a window of time in which it would be safe to carry the thing. In a couple of days, maybe three, I'd destroy it. Hadn't the lady detective told me I'd be notified before they were released from jail?

Yeah.

So the phone remained a tenuous link.

I glanced at the thing now, willing it to ring.

It didn't, of course.

Why hadn't they called? Maybe they'd given Pilar the phone only so they could use it to track her. It seemed plausible, but I was desperate enough to hang on to it anyway. They *might* call.

Tomlinson and Pilar came to mind. I checked the dashboard clock—
10:04—as I picked up the cell phone. Maybe they'd returned to the hotel
room. Or . . . maybe something really had happened to them.

I squinted to touch Redial, then stopped myself as my mind transferred
data. There'd been another recent, surprising change in my life. There
was yet another person who might become a part of that linkage that
joined Lake and me.

Those key words again: heredity . . . genetics . . . *blood*.

This much I knew: The well-being of the woman who'd slipped into my
mind was a hell of a lot more important than an ex-lover.

Quickly, I dialed Dewey Nye's home number. She's the early-to-bed
type during the week, so I expected to catch her reading before turning off
the light.

I didn't. She not only didn't answer, her message machine didn't intercept. Odd.

So I tried her cell phone. I decided I must have dialed wrong, because
a recorded message told me, *"The number you have reached is no longer in
service."*

I felt a little chill when, after dialing carefully, I got the same message.

Dewey had kept the same cell phone number for years. A dummy
number she called it. The last four digits were all sevens. Lucky sevens,
she called it that, too. She wouldn't have canceled her service.

I dialed once again just to be sure, and got the recording.

She *had* canceled it.

Or did wireless phones, when broken, respond in that way?

I didn't know.

I'd been driving the speed limit. I'd been considering turning back to
Miami. Instead, I pushed the car up to eighty.

Now I had to find Dewey, too.

I REACHED the four-way stop at Tarpon Bay Road, Sanibel Island,
at eleven-thirty. But instead of turning right onto the narrow road that
leads to Dinkin's Bay Marina, I continued on toward Captiva.

I crossed Blind Pass Bridge, noticing that the bar at 'Tween Waters was still open, and the Green Flash, too. At Twin Palms Marina, it looked like the Jensen brothers were having a midweek cookout and party. There were colored lights and a bonfire that glazed boats, docks, people, coconut palms with oscillating gold.

I knew that if I stopped at any one of those places, I'd find friends and a drink, and sympathy, too.

Normally, the idea would have been appealing. Not now. During times of personal calamity, even the most familiar of safe harbors can seem as foreign as a far planet. Emotional chaos has its own trajectory. Until the energy of that path dissipates, and we arc back into the customary orbit of our normal lives, nothing feels or appears quite as it should be.

Until I found Dewey—knew that she was safe and that we were on good terms again—my life, and these familiar islands, would not be the same.

Off Mango Court, I turned down the sand drive to her home. I felt even more pressured than on my last visit, but I drove slowly, watching for local pets, driving along the high ficus hedges, headlights glaring off security signs, and then I swung into her drive hoping once again to see the Lexus parked beneath the carport.

Once again, it wasn't.

There was activity at the house, though. The front door was open, lights on. A Dodge Ram pickup was parked out front, some kind of white compact, too, plus a smaller red pickup—all the vehicles seemed familiar—and there were people inside the house, moving across the lighted windows.

My first impression was that Dewey was having a little party of her own, and maybe her car was gone because she had had to run to the store to fetch more ice or mixer.

But then I recognized the bumper stickers on the Dodge. Knew it was Jeth Nichols, one of our marina fishing guides, and so I instantly knew the owners of the other cars, too.

This was no party, and the Lexus wasn't gone because Dewey was on a quick trip to the store.

I got out of the rental Ford in a rush and jogged toward the house, thinking, *Don't let them be here because she's sick, or hurt, or because someone broke in . . .*

Those weren't the reasons.

As I got to the porch, I surprised Jeth, who was backing out the door carrying one end of Dewey's king-sized mattress. Lugging the other end was Javier Castillo, a fishing guide from Two Parrot Bight Marina, and one of Jeth's best friends.

When I saw the mattress, I knew. I knew why they were here. I also understood why Dewey's phones weren't working. This close to midnight, men load beds into pickups for only one reason. Not only that, but the back of the truck was nearly full of my girl's furniture.

But I asked anyway.

"*Jeth.* What are you guys doing here so late? Where's Dewey?"

Jeth looks like an all-state linebacker who never stopped taking good care of himself, a great-looking guy with the truest of hearts. His mild stutter is an endearing quirk, although it is seldom heard these days—unless he's upset or nervous.

The man was nervous now.

"Goddang, dah-dah-dah-Doc! You 'bout scared me to death sneakin' up-p-p-p like that." He'd dropped the mattress and was holding a big hand to his chest. I got the feeling, though, I hadn't scared him that badly. He was trying to buy a little time; needed space to figure out what to say to me.

I said, "Javier—where is she? What's going on here?"

Javier is a lean black man, average height, thin lips but a broad African nose and short black hair. He floated over from Cuba years ago in an inner tube, worked sixteen-hour days to get a foothold. He now has a gorgeous family, the community's respect, and an equal amount of pride. But when I spoke to him, trying to hold his eyes, he just shook his head and looked away.

"Jeth, damn it, *answer* me. Where's Dewey? I'm not going to ask you a third time. Is she all right?"

I realized that my tone was threatening. Dominant and demanding—it was that, too. I instantly regretted the way I'd spoken to him.

So did Jeth. His voice sounded as pained as the expression on his face as he replied, "Oh, Dewey's fine, she's just fine, don't you worry about that. We're takin' some of her personal stuff to a storage place off-island 'cause . . . well, 'cause that's what she *asked* one of us to do. But I don't want to be the one ta have ta tah-tah-tell you about it, man. Dang it, Doc, why'd you have to show up here now?"

Jeth and I are close friends. Old friends. I didn't know the details of why he and Javier were helping Dewey move, but I resented that the two of us had been put in this situation. Friends should not be drawn into the middle of romantic troubles. Because of this, it would be a while before Jeth and I felt comfortable around each other again.

From inside, I heard a woman's voice call to them, "You guys quit gabbing, and get that mattress loaded. It's already late, and we're not even close to being done. Get going!"

It was a familiar voice, with a Midwestern civility built into her inflections, and so her bossiness seemed intentionally exaggerated, as if she were joking.

She wasn't.

As I made room for them to pass, Jeth said, "I'm sorry, Doc. I truly am."

I said, "No, no, I'm the one who should apologize. I shouldn't've come on so hard."

"Oh hell." His tone said, *Forget it.* But there was also a little chill there. I'd offended him. "We'll grab us some beers." Now Jeth was stepping up into the back of his truck, making it look easy. "Maybe tomorrow night if you got some time."

I knew it'd be a lot longer than that, but said, "Sure. Tomorrow should be good."

As they drove away, Javier smiled and called to me in Spanish, "In Cuba, we had a saying: If it wasn't for a woman's love, a man could go his entire life without hearing of his faults or being punished for them."

I smiled and nodded. My friendship with Javier, at least, was unaffected.

He'd reminded me of an even more cynical Latin maxim: The real magic of love is that, for a short period of time, it blinds two people to the pain it will surely cause.

FIFTEEN

SEEING Dewey's mattress bouncing away in the back of a pickup not only hurt, but it created in me a kind of emotional numbness. Her bed was such an intimate symbol of the time we'd spent alone in her house. That she had made the decision to move so impulsively—irrationally, it seemed to me—was a measure of the pain I'd inflicted.

I went to the open door and, stupidly, knocked before entering. I expected to see Janet Mueller, and there she was, dressed for sweat and hard labor in baggy shorts and a man's shirt, sleeves rolled up.

She stood in the center of a room full of boxes, and garbage bags, and stacks of Dewey's clothes still on hangers. Her mousy hair was piled under a ball cap, a couple of curls touched with gray hanging out. She's always been on the chubby side. In the last six months or so, though, she'd lost too much weight, and her face was gaunt. It'd aged her.

I said, "I can't believe she's done this. All in less than twenty-four hours?"

Janet finished taping a box closed and pushed it aside. "You've always said you like strong women. Dewey was never the indecisive type. I guess there has to be a downside to a man dating his equal."

"I need to talk to her, Jan. For just a few minutes. It's important. Where is she?"

She started to reply, but then stopped, studying my face. Janet's a close friend, too. In ways, closer than Jeth. She knows me well, and so probably accurately diagnosed my coloring, or my expression.

"Are you O.K., Doc? You don't look good. Have a seat, take some deep breaths, and I'll get you something to drink. I haven't cleaned out the fridge yet."

"Janet, please. Tell me how to contact her."

"No. I can't do that. Please don't ask me again. Dewey's gone. She'll be in touch—she said to tell you that. She also said to tell you not to try and find her."

I put my hands on her shoulders. "She's gone *where?*"

"Gone, that's all. She's moved to another place. That's all I'm going to say. So no more pressure. O.K.?"

She turned from beneath my hands and went to the kitchen. I heard the refrigerator open, then the carbonated signature of bottles being opened. After a moment, she poked her head out and said, "That doesn't mean I'm not your buddy anymore. I know it's a heck of a shock, so let's go talk. Just you and me, out there in the Florida room. But no more prying. You've got to promise."

I followed her through the kitchen, out the sliding doors toward the lighted pool. It was a rectangular plunge pool floored with black tile, so the water appeared iceberg blue. The pool lights projected shimmering lines onto the area's high-screened paneling, illuminating the deck, showing potted plants, barbecue grill, weight machine, wet bar. On the other side of the screen were silhouetted trees, and stars.

I accepted the beer. She went back to the kitchen, returned with chunks of cheddar, chorizo sausage, a bottle of hot sauce, and crackers. She took a seat beside me in a deck chair while I tried not to look at the water, because I could see Dewey floating naked after a tough workout, or late at night, just the two of us, after making love.

I said, "We were together here just last night. I talked to her. She didn't mention doing anything this drastic."

Janet sipped, swallowed, chewed, nodded. "I know."

"She told you?"

"Not the details. Just that something happened between you two. That it was serious. And that she needed to get off the islands for a while to think clearly. I can understand that. Sanibel and Captiva are like luxury liners with palms and a beach. Leave your cabin, and you can't help but run into the same old fun-loving crew. There are times, though, when you need a little distance."

I said, "If I write her a letter, can you see that she gets it?"

"Yes. I can do that."

"I really screwed up, Jan. No one's ever called me talkative, so why is it my mouth that always gets me in trouble with the women I care about? I think she may be gone for good."

Janet stirred beside me, and I felt her hand pat my arm then come to rest atop my hand. "Do you know why women like quiet men? Because it's easier for us to believe they're really listening. Relationships are a pain in the ass, Dr. Ford."

I said, "Yes, they are, Dr. Mueller," laughing softly with her, and realizing that she'd already helped dissipate some of the emotional trauma, which is exactly what she was trying to do.

"After the last time I got dumped, I swore I'd never get any closer to a permanent relationship, or marriage, than going to a sex store and telling the sales clerk 'I do' when she asked if I wanted to buy a vibrator."

I was laughing harder as she added, "But nothing shocks me anymore when it comes to relationships. *Nothing.*"

She gave it so much emphasis, I knew she was referencing something recent and personal. Which meant she had things in her own love life she wanted to talk about, too.

AS MUCH as anyone I know, Janet reminds me why I like women as people. She is also my secret reminder that, for women who are not born with great looks, or who are past a certain age, the world is an unfair place.

Men can compensate for their genetic bad luck by being successful in business or politics. The same is not true for women. Inequity becomes a fact of life. Some of the very best of them end up settling for guys who are not their intellectual or emotional equals, and lead lives that never offer them much challenge or reward. These are the private ones, the undiscovered treasures whose gifts are forever concealed by an oversized body, or a facial conformation that's a few centimeters off the current Hollywood ideal.

As we sat and talked, and had another beer, I thought about this good person and all that she'd endured. Maybe she hoped that's what I'd do. It certainly reduced my feeling of being overwhelmed.

Most people stop maturing long before they stop aging, but not this lady. Whatever her own rocky life had demanded, she'd evolved and grown in whatever way it took to compensate. I admired that. Same with everyone at Dinkin's Bay.

Janet had arrived at the marina a few years back with lots of emotional baggage, after losing her husband in a car wreck, then their unborn child to a miscarriage. Many people move to Florida hoping to save themselves or to reinvent themselves. Janet's one of the few resilient enough to have succeeded at both.

While she healed, she worked regularly in my lab and lived aboard her little blue houseboat. After a split-up with Jeth, her on-again-off-again love, she'd moved her vessel to Twin Palms, but continued to work for me and remained a part of the Dinkin's Bay community.

Janet was always the quiet girl with glasses, the sisterly type who was there when you needed her, but was never glib or showy. She was the one with the frazzled hair and heavy hips, but a cute face; the one who liked to laugh and socialize. If you were a man, you wanted to protect her, just as women, on first meeting, knew immediately they could trust Janet and confide in her.

She was nice, but lacked confidence. She could be outgoing, but never assertive.

That changed.

Not so long ago, Janet, along with friends, had been set adrift in the open sea after a boating accident, only to be picked up by the worst sort of people.

Once again, she'd endured. Then she'd prevailed.

I remembered what Merlin Starkey had said about his life being scarred by his failures. Janet has too much character and courage to allow herself to use such a transparent excuse.

The woman who sat next to me now was a very different Janet Mueller from the soft-spoken lady who'd come shy-eyed into the marina years back. There was no shortage of self-confidence, she had no problem being assertive—but my friend had also lost something during the process.

There's always a price.

AS I finished my second beer and the last of the food, she said, "If you don't feel better, at least you look better. You were so pale, I thought you were going to pass out on me."

I said, "Years from now, when I'm older and even more decrepit and you're nursing me through my dotage, maybe I'll tell you the whole story about my day. Finding out about Dewey wasn't the worst of it, but it's close."

"I'm tempted to ask."

"Like I said, down the road, when you're feeding me with a spoon."

"Another one of Doc's secrets," she said, musing. "The marina folks wonder about you sometimes, you know. You disappear for a week or a month at a time, then come back and never say a word. Like last November, you show up with your hand bandaged and your tan almost gone. They whisper behind your back."

When I didn't reply, she stood—my signal to leave. "It's going on one o'clock in the morning, sweetie. The guys'll be back soon. They're gonna make another trip, then call it a night."

I wasn't ready to leave yet, though. There was one last thing I wanted to do.

I dropped my bottle in the recycle bin, said, "Gotta use the head first," then walked down the hall, past the guest bath and bedroom, to Dewey's master suite. I turned on the bathroom light and locked the door behind me.

The wastebasket hadn't yet been emptied. It's what I'd hoped. I flushed the toilet to cover the noise, then knelt and pawed through the bathroom detritus. I didn't expect to find what I was searching for, so I was enormously pleased when I did: A small blue box that read CLEARBLUE HOME PREGNANCY TEST.

I touched index finger to glasses, adjusting them, before I looked inside.

Empty.

The printing on the box said that it had contained two test strips. Where were they?

I knelt over the trash again and sifted more carefully. I found a plastic wrapper that had held one of the strips, but nothing else.

What did that tell me? I stood, thinking about it.

Dewey had used the kit. Once, at least. Maybe twice. That meant that she knew. She knew if she was pregnant or not.

Would she have decided to leave Captiva if she was *not* pregnant?

Possibly. The woman had a temper, and she also had as much willpower and pride as anyone I've ever met. So what could I infer additionally, if anything?

Not much, I decided. Positive or negative, she could have done the test twice just to be certain.

From the front of the house, I heard Janet call, "Doc? Hey in there. What'd you do, fall in?"

I shoved the box deep into the trash, then flushed again.

JANET stood on the front stoop outside, lights off, looking at the sky. A commercial airliner, was transecting airspace between Pine Island and Sanibel, on the standard landing pattern into Regional Southwest Airport. With its landing lights fired, the plane looked like a bright planet descending

I stopped beside her and said, "What's Dewey going to do with the house? Am I allowed to ask that? She's leaving it empty, I hope. She *is* coming back."

Still looking at the plane, Janet replied softly, "Jeth and I are moving in. For a while, anyway. A few months. Just to see how it goes."

I said, *"What?"*

The rollercoaster affair between Janet and the good-looking fishing guide had ended forever, we all thought, when Jeth had fallen in love with Janet's younger sister, Claudia. Claudia was a funnier, rowdier edition of Janet. She was athletic, more of a guy's girl, and a better match, it seemed. But that hadn't made it any easier for Jeth when he tried to break the news to Janet. He stuttered so badly that Claudia had to take over.

I said, "How long have you two been back together? Usually, I at least hear rumors."

"A couple of months. We kept it quiet. We knew how damn foolish we'd both look if it didn't work out. There was something the big goof had to find out for himself about Claudia. All our lives, whatever big sister had, little sister wanted. But once she got it, Claudia got tired of it real quick. Jeth caught her in the bedroom with not one, but two other guys. Tourist guys down from Boston. That's something else he didn't know about Claudia. She's always been on the kinky side."

Now it made sense, the way Janet said that nothing surprised her about relationships.

Because I was her friend, I had to say it. "So Jeth came back to you on the rebound. How's your pride dealing with that?"

"Pride? I really don't give two hoots about pride anymore. What's the worst that can happen? I get hurt?" She made a fluttering sound with her lips: *As if I haven't been hurt before!* "Doc, after all the crap I've been through, here's about the only thing I've learned for sure: It's one hell of a short and lonely life. If I can make it a little happier, and a little less lonely, by forgiving someone I care about, then I'm going to risk it."

I put my arm over her shoulder, the two of us standing, looking into the late sky and at the airliner. "Do me a favor. Pass that little gem along to Dewey, would you? I could use some forgiveness." After a moment, I added, "What time did her flight leave this morning?"

Janet started to answer, "She didn't leave this morning because—" but caught herself and stopped. Using two fingers to lift my arm away as if it were soiled laundry, she then turned and said, "Don't do that to me, pal. I've worked with you, I know how that little calculator you call a brain functions. If I give you the flight time, you'll figure out all the possible destinations, then start narrowing it down from there. Don't you dare get tricky with me. So show a little respect. Or maybe we're not as close friends as I thought."

The last was added with a real edge—a verbal slap that told me how serious she was.

I said, "You're right. I'm sorry. That will never happen again." I held out my hand. "Forgiven?"

The woman shook her head at me severely, smiled, ignoring my hand, and gave me a quick hug—"Of course I forgive you. Because I love you."—then paused, listening. "Hey—do you hear something ringing? Kind of a weird warble?"

I listened and heard it, too. Muted, rhythmic. It seemed to be coming from the rental car.

Then I realized: *The satellite phone was ringing.*

I sprinted toward the Ford.

SIXTEEN

BY NOON Thursday, Prax Lourdes and Laken Fuentes were on a DC 10 cargo plane to Pinar del Rio, western Cuba, just them, the pilot, plus several tons of Masaguan rice in burlap sacks. By ten P.M., they were boarding a beat-up old fertilizer freighter that was registered in Monrovia, Liberia, a ship named *Repatriate*.

For the last six or seven years, when the cops or the Nicaraguan military were really on his ass, Lourdes hopped a freighter. Didn't matter where it went. Pay cash, no questions. Nothing touched the privacy of a ship that was transporting fertilizers.

He preferred the tramp freighter *Repatriate*. The ship's captain was a 250-pound Bahamian white woman named Micki who would do anything for money. *Anything.* She'd been born in Detroit, grown up in the slums of Nassau, chain-smoked Pall Malls, drank cane liquor, despised women even more than she did children, and probably hated men, too.

Men, at least, though, she could tolerate.

Not that she gave much of a shit about any human being on earth.

Once, in Bluefields, Nicaragua, she'd asked Prax, "Is it true? Do you really do what they say you do? I'd fuckin' like to see it. Elsewise, I'm thinkin' you're jus' one more freak fulla shit. With my own eyes, I'd like to see it happen."

That was a first.

Prax had said to her, "You got anyone in mind?"

Micki told him, "Not really. But how about our Greek cook? He ain't worth a shit, and he's got so much grease pourin' out of him, you won't even need no fire starter."

Captain Micki was close to right. The woman *enjoyed* it, watching the drunken Greek sprint toward the dock, ablaze. He was a *burner.*

Not at all like his driver, Reynaldo. The man had been a disappointment. Too stoic, some of those mountain Indios. Reynaldo, he'd run a couple steps, then just sort of balled up and smoldered.

His heroin junkie plastic surgeon, Fernando Delgado, hadn't gone up much better. He was too strung out to run. Just slapped at himself and screamed, as if he might have been imagining it.

That took the fun out of it.

Killing the doctor had been a snap decision. It happened that way sometimes. It was after getting the good news about the kid's blood type, and while looking in the mirror, seeing what a mess the quack had made of his face. That's when he felt the sudden headache begin to move up his spine, and then the rage came flooding in behind his eyes like a scarlet starburst.

So he'd done the doctor, too.

Talk about burning bridges.

AFTER the way the fat sea captain, Micki, had set up the Greek, Lourdes almost always used the *Repatriate.* Used it exclusively for trips to Florida. He went there whenever the feds in Central America got too close.

Micki was a psycho bitch, but she was also a hell of a captain. She had the routine down. She could get him off the boat and back aboard without the local cops ever having a clue. Micki, he could trust.

One thing Prax had learned working carnivals was that people who didn't bother to pretend that they had morals or ethics were the only people who could ever be trusted. You always knew where they stood, and what they were after.

That was Micki. Cash, that's all she cared about. Prax could do any damn thing he wanted aboard her vessel as long as he didn't get in her way or piss her off.

Another reason the *Repatriate* was his vessel of choice was because there were seldom more than a handful of seamen aboard. The ship always carried a skeleton crew because everyone on the docks despised Micki. Seamen desperate enough to stick it out were exactly like her: They'd do anything for cash.

That made doing business aboard *Repatriate* easy.

All he had to have was money.

Prax had some cash now. He'd stolen Balserio's $75,000—he *loved* that; only, the shit-heel had short-counted him. Plus, he had another $25,000 or so he'd copped during the last year traveling around the Masaguan countryside doing his thing.

So he'd flown out of Central America with close to $100K. But the cargo pilot had taken a chunk of that. Then Micki had taken a much bigger chunk.

At the freighter docks in Mariel Harbor, Cuba, she'd called him up to her cabin—the place was too filthy for pigs—and said, "I got all three of those things you said you ordered. Plus the instruments. But they'uz double what you said they'd cost. Even the Russian stuff, and it was used. It all cost more."

Prax had expected this.

When he asked, she told him what the price was. The numbers had about doubled. He'd expected that, too, and had privately figured it into his expenses. Which was a relief.

Micki reminded him that the cost of the ship, her, and the crew, plus doing all the bullshit he wanted, was a hundred percent markup of the stuff for the infirmary, plus the usual nut, but times two. Cash.

A lot of cash.

She said, "You got that fucking kid locked in one of the cabins. I swear to Christ, if he starts to cry, or whine, or ask for shit, I'll throw the little motherfucker's ass overboard without slowing a knot. And I'm still gonna charge you the fuckin' nut for his passage."

Micki. You had to love her. She was one of the few people in the world whom Prax actually enjoyed hanging around with. The woman could make him laugh!

Still standing in her stinking cabin, he had listened to her return to the subject of the equipment they'd loaded aboard in Mariel, saying, "Jesus Christ, when you said you wanted a surgical microscope, I pictured something that would fit on a desk. We had to use the fucking ship's derrick to get the thing aboard. Crew about busted its ass getting the damn thing into the infirmary."

Prax had said, suddenly very serious, "You found the microscope I wrote to you about in the e-mail? It's a Carl Zeiss, the floor model. Weighs about three hundred pounds. They had a couple in Havana, 'cause I checked on the internet. It's important you got the right model. Same with the surgical instruments. Doctors—the great ones—they're very damn fussy about what they use in their work."

Micki had just lit a cigarette. Now she intentionally blew smoke in his face. Prax wasn't wearing one of his masks. Aboard *Repatriate*, it wasn't necessary—another reason he liked the ship.

He leaned into the smoke, tried to suck it in and blow it back at her— which made her smile. The two of them got along pretty good.

She said, "If that face of yours didn't look like a map of the world, man, you might have a shot at ol' Micki—but don't ever be givin' me orders aboard my own ship again."

Prax had replied, "If you lost a hundred pounds and took a bath, I might *take* a shot. I'm not giving orders. I'm just telling you it's important I get the right stuff. I know what I want."

Actually, he knew what surgical equipment that Dr. Valerie Santos used. She'd told him in her e-mails.

THE *Repatriate* left Cuban waters before midnight on Thursday, May 1, crossed the Florida Straits into the Gulf of Mexico, and twenty-three hours later, was being piloted by U.S. authorities into the shipping channels of Tampa Bay.

By three A.M., Saturday morning, the ship was moored at a wing of isolated phosphate loading docks on a river near a highway bridge, and Micki was finishing the last of the paperwork so the two Port Authority inspectors could go on their merry way.

They knew Micki, they knew the ship, and their inspection had been no more thorough than others.

When they left the *Repatriate,* the U.S. authorities stationed a single male security guard at the bottom of the gangplank, on the starboard side of the vessel, so the crew could not disembark.

There was no security of any kind, not a soul watching the port—or river side—of the ship. And, at this hour, there was almost no car traffic on the usually busy highway bridge.

Micki was smart. That's the way she always timed it.

By four-thirty A.M., Prax was ashore in his own double-wide trailer, and the boy was safely locked away in another.

The kid hadn't been any trouble at all. In fact, the little brat actually seemed to get into the adventure of it, climbing down the rope ladder, sneaking around in boats at night.

Ashore, in the weird little trailer park where Prax had grown up, the kid had even stopped outside in the moonlight, taken a good look around and started identifying early morning bird calls and shit, insect noises and frogs, too. Like he was a damn little scientist or something.

Oddball kid. A nerd who didn't look like a nerd. Not with that gorgeous face of his.

NOW HOME, the first thing Prax did was take a satellite phone from his bag and put it in its charger base. He would be needing the phone soon because he'd be needing a lot more cash very soon. Micki had told him she'd be back in a week, maybe less, and he'd better damn well be ready with the money, or she'd leave his ass.

The number of the phone he'd left for Pilar Fuentes was taped to the back of the charger, and he also had the number written down in a couple of other places.

Next, he poured himself a tumbler of Scotch over ice, lighted a big

Cohiba—an El Presidente—and sat at his laptop computer. He had the fast DSL system here in the States—it wasn't like using those shitty, slow phone lines back in Masagua—and he was instantly on the internet, checking and sending e-mails.

Yes! There was one from Dr. Valerie Santos.

The famous Dr. Valerie was so attentive. Was very free with information to a correspondent who claimed to be a poor young South American burn victim.

PRAX had first written to the "Contact Dr. Valerie" link on the surgical group's web page nearly six months ago. It was a con that he'd thought might work, but he'd had no idea how far he'd be able to take it.

He'd written,

> Forgive the bad English of mine, but my name is Mary Perez, and I am a 19-year-old female film student at the University of Nicaragua. I read about your brilliant work in People magazine, Edition Español. I find your work fascinating because my face was badly burned as a child when soldiers attacked our village during the Revolution . . .

After giving details about that, using stuff he knew—like the burn center in Managua—he'd continued:

> As a film student, I'm working on a script, and you're one of the few in the world who can help me. In my script, your character (yes, you are in my film!) must perform a complete facial transplant, but under Third World or even jungle conditions. There's been a plane crash. The donor is still alive, his face is perfect, but he has no hope. The patient's face has been burned beyond recognition. I want to make this film as accurate as possible because, as a burn victim, I want the world to know . . .

The first couple of replies came from the woman's assistant, Prax could tell by the wording. But then he uploaded and sent a photo that he'd found on the internet of some teenage Latina crispy critter whose face had been scorched by napalm.

That did it. Prax started getting personal attention from "Dr. Valerie," as she signed her e-mails. Sometimes, she wrote to him daily.

The e-mail he opened now began,

My Dear Mary,

I have very bad news for you, and it's important that you take action immediately. I have done some checking and have found out that your physician, Dr. Fernando Delgado, is not qualified to do your surgery, or to give you advice about the screenplay you are writing. The Mexican Medical Board revoked his license several years ago because of his terrible mortality record as a plastic surgeon . . .

Prax deleted the letter, thinking, *No shit.*

Two days later, responding to a note he'd written earlier, Dr. Santos replied:

Dear Mary,

I don't doubt that you are who you say you are, but I simply cannot share personal information with patients (yes, I consider you my patient now, dear) such as where I live, or about my husband and family. I will tell you, however, that I live close enough to Tampa General Hospital that I jog to and from work every day. I keep dress-up clothes and heels in the physicians' locker room just in case!

Lourdes found that useful.

Then, the next evening, when he was pissed off at Pilar Fuentes and her new asshole pals, and whoever the hell it was following them in the black Chevy, he received a very valuable e-mail from the nice doctor lady:

Another example that you must leave Fernando Delgado's care immediately is that he has given you bad information about medication that is out of date by a decade!

> *Yes, transplant patients take medications each day to prevent organ re-jection that are called "immunosuppressants." They help suppress the im-mune system to prevent or reverse rejection. But not the drugs you were told. All wrong, young lady!*
>
> *Today, cyclosporine is one of the most commonly used antirejection drugs, and it's usually combined with prednisone. Cyclosporine is a very potent immunosuppressant. Most of our transplant patients prefer the cap-sule, but the odor, however, leaves something to be desired!*
>
> *There are also some new, recently approved immunosuppressants that I prefer and use exclusively on my patients . . .*

A list of medicines followed. All sophisticated stuff that was new to him. *Shit!*

How in the hell was he going to put his hands on all those drugs?

Lourdes had brought the boy into the trailer with him. He'd done that the last couple of nights, which he didn't mind so much. It gave him somebody to talk to; take his mind off it when the headaches and the fa-cial pain came.

The last few years, the facial pain had been as bad or worse than the pounding inside his head. When the headaches came shooting up his spine, the first jolt now seemed to bathe his face in acid. Fucking miser-able. So talking took his mind off it.

Otherwise, all the kid did was read. About the only time he opened his mouth was to ask for more books, or to do research on the internet—which Prax allowed, as long as he was right there to keep an eye on the little brat.

The kid was reading now, sitting at a chair in the corner. Some book about bugs or snakes or some damn thing.

Prax watched him for a second before he said, "Have you ever heard of drugs called cyclosporine or prednisone? I've never heard of the fuckin' stuff."

The kid looked up from his book and thought about it for a moment before he said, "Cyclosporine, no, but prednisone, yeah. I remember reading about it because the body produces its own form of prednisone, a chemical called cortisol."

"Really?"

"Um-huh. I've been reading a lot about medicine lately, because . . . well, a friend of mine has some emotional problems. There are so many new drugs coming out that can help—almost always from the United States— it's kind of interesting. The chemistry of it, I mean. I think I'm going to be a doctor."

Prax said, "No shit? A fuckin' doctor."

"Yeah, no shit."

The kid was like that. A smart-ass, but *smart*.

Maybe the brat would have some ideas on how to get his hands on those brand-new drugs. . . .

SEVENTEEN

EVEN though I seemed to be moving in slow motion, the satellite phone was still ringing when I got the car door open.

The phone was made by Motorola, cased in black plastic, the size and shape of a standard cell phone, but it had an oversized antenna and a flat face with no keypad. There was an On-Off button, a menu key, and a couple of other buttons. Stupidly, I hadn't bothered to familiarize myself with the thing.

It rang once more, green face plate flashing, as I held it beneath the car's dome light, trying to figure out how to answer.

Damn it, how's this work?

Finally, I pressed the largest button and slammed the phone to my ear. "Hello. Hello?"

There was silence on the other end. Silence . . . but it was an inhabited silence. Someone was listening.

After a few seconds, I realized that the silence may have been catalyzed by surprise—because the caller was expecting Pilar to answer. Quickly I said in Spanish, "My name's Ford. I'm the boy's father. *Laken's* father. I'm all alone, no police. The mother's . . . indisposed right now."

More silence.

"Hello! Talk to me. Let me talk to my son."

Then I heard *click*.

I kept talking until I was certain they'd disconnected. Then I hit the Off key.

Shit.

I was aware that Janet was watching me from the house. Because I didn't want to have to explain, I waved goodbye, got in the car, and drove slowly back toward the beach, the satellite phone in my lap.

Call back, give me another chance. Ring, damn you, ring.

The phone still wasn't taking my telepathic commands.

It was nearly one A.M., but I was so hyped-up, I knew there was no chance of sleep. Besides, there were still a few proactive steps to take, I decided.

The reasonable thing to do now, and what we *should* do, was check Pilar's e-mail to see if the kidnappers had supplemented their call with another written message. Trouble was, Pilar—and her password—were in Miami.

I was justified in asking her for it. No question about that. She and Tomlinson had to be in the room by this late hour, so I grabbed the cell phone, dialed the Radisson.

No answer.

I was furious.

I redialed the hotel immediately and asked the clerk, "Are you sure they haven't checked out?"

He used a practiced, polite and frosty tone that showed disdain, but from a safe distance. "Oh yes, sir, I'm positive, sir."

"Then make sure they get my message the instant they get in."

"Yes sir!"

As I drove, I rehearsed some of the bitter, cutting things I would say to my old pal and to the mother of the boy who, for all we knew, was fighting for his life at this very instant. I indulged in that ugly rehearsal for several miles before I recognized the kind of emotional spiral I was in. Negative cycling is as irrational as Pollyanna optimism.

I stopped and made myself review. Tomlinson is a flake and a womanizer, but he is also brilliant, decent, and one of the kindest people I know. Pilar and I had issues, but I had no reason to doubt her devotion as a parent.

Quite the opposite. Neither of them would put their own pleasure ahead of our son's well-being. If they weren't in their hotel room, or weren't answering the phone, there was almost certain to be a good reason.

Now . . . what the hell that reason was, I couldn't imagine. But I decided that I should, at the very least, give them a chance to explain before I passed judgment.

So back off, Ford. Settle down.

I was hyped, all right. Juiced on a day of adrenal overload. It was O.K. to stay aggressive, but I also needed to stay constructive.

I took it easy through the curves south of 'Tween Waters, then slowed to a crawl at Blind Pass Bridge.

To my right, the moon was enormous over the Gulf of Mexico. It was a gaseous sphere, meteor scars showing, sitting on a rim of atmosphere that buffered Captiva Island from the emptiness of outer space. Beyond the bridge, white surf rolled out of a far horizon that touched Yucatan and the jungles of Central America.

I stared, eyes soft-focused, thinking that only water separated me from a shore where someone held my son prisoner. Islands may be isolated by water, but they also seem more intimately linked to a wider world because of the uninterrupted plane. Lake seemed close. Just over there. Just beyond the moon.

I'm coming. I'll find you.

I touched my foot to the accelerator.

As I drove, I concentrated on how to take the next necessary step: check Pilar's e-mail. Lake's well-being was too important to let it wait until morning. The kidnappers might want us in Miami the next afternoon, and we wouldn't know about it until too late. But how could I get the woman's password at one A.M. without talking to her?

I knew a way. Maybe.

I had a friend I could call. A man by the name of Bernie Yeager. He could help—if he was home, and if he was agreeable. An elite and distinguished member of the U.S. electronic warfare and intelligence community, Bernie didn't qualify as law enforcement. Not by my definition, anyway.

Under my agreement with Pilar, contacting Bernie was permissible.

On the way back to Dinkin's Bay, there was someone else I decided to telephone: my cousin, Ransom Gatrell.

Under any other circumstances, I wouldn't have bothered her so late. But Ransom's a night owl—she's always up at odd hours—plus, my sensitivity to the power of blood linkage had been heightened.

Her second cousin, Lake, had been kidnapped. Aside from my son, she is my only living relative, and so I dialed her number.

Ransom was born and raised on Cat Island, one of the remote cays in the Bahamas. She works on Sanibel now, lives just across the bay from me, but her Bahamian accent remains just as strong as her Cat Island attitude.

When I told her what had happened, I heard her say with great emotion, *"Aw, me brudder, I knowed I wuz piddlin' 'bout diz hour far a reezin, mon. I comin' to yer hose jus' as fas' daht li'l boot kin kirry me sweeet broon awss. 'N I breengin' a jar o 'soop, mon. Daht ain' no beeg dill."*

What she'd told me was, she was going to get in her boat and meet me at my house, and that she was bringing along a jar of soup that she'd made.

I was smiling mildly when I punched off, but then I stopped smiling.

The satellite phone was warbling again.

THIS TIME, when I answered, there was a voice that I recognized on the other end. It was Masked Man, the voice from the video. It was Praxcedes Lourdes, my son's abductor. It was the one Pilar called "monster," the man who burned men.

In Spanish, Lourdes said, "We don't want to kill this beautiful brat of yours, but our people in Florida tell us you're not cooperating. Why aren't you cooperating?"

I started to say, "We are cooperating. The car following us today wasn't police. They were—"

But Lourdes interrupted, screaming, "Shut up! You're giving me a fucking migraine!" followed by a string of ranting profanities spoken in such a tone of agony that it sounded as if he really might have been in pain.

I thought to myself, *The man's insane.*

After a short, gathering pause, when he'd regained some control, he continued, "Cooperating? What are you, some kind of moron? The woman's supposed to answer our e-mails immediately. We sent one three hours ago and still haven't heard back. The bitch is supposed to be *alone.*"

I said, "I'm the boy's father. I'm Laken's father. We've got the money. All we want is the boy—"

"Shut your fuckin' mouth and listen!" His voice had that anguished quality again. "We want more than cash, now. We're fighting a war. We need medical supplies. Some of the new breakthrough drugs not easy to get. One that's experimental—for our wounded. The brat tells me you're some kind of big-shot scientist. He says you know all about medicine, and can do just about any fucking thing. So that's your new job, finding the drugs and delivering them with the money."

Lourdes had been told I was a scientist? It was the first indication that Lake might still be alive. I wanted more than just an indicator, though. I wanted to find a way to apply at least some light leverage; was hesitant to risk it, but knew I had to try.

Medical supplies. Something about the way he said it suggested that he had a personal interest. They seemed important to him. Maybe that's why Lake had told him "scientist." He'd hedged intentionally. Made me sound more important than I was—a finesse on Lake's part that gave me a fine surge of optimism. My son was working the guy instinctively, helping to set him up for me. Why Lourdes believed I had connections in the medical field didn't matter. As long as he thought I could be useful, it gave me a tiny opening.

I began, "I'm not a physician. I've got access to medicines; prescription stuff. Experimental drugs, though, could take some time. You need to understand that. You don't just go to the store and place an order."

"You have until Sunday. No later."

"I have to know what you need, and the quantities. First, though, let me talk to the boy. That's not negotiable. I'm giving your people drugs and cash? Let me hear his voice. After that, I'll do what you say—but I want daily e-mails so we know you're keeping him alive."

"*You* want? Why the fuck should we care what *you* want? Maybe we'll just kill him now, big shot."

I had to force the words out of my mouth: "Because then you wouldn't have any leverage. Personally—well, the kid and I aren't that close. He's costing me a lot of money. Now you want drugs, experimental medicine, which, frankly, I can't get legally. Even trying to *get* experimental drugs could put my career in jeopardy. I want to be sure I'm getting something in return."

I had heard his coughing, bully's laughter on the video. I heard it again now. "Hooh, a tough guy, huh! O.K. . . . O.K. Go ahead and talk to your brat, tough guy. But I want those fucking drugs!"

A few moments later, I heard my son say, "Doc? *Dad?*" and then add in a rush, "Doc, you need to do what he says. His friends will hurt Mother. They have someone watching her all the time. Please do what he says."

Lake sounded hoarse, frail. I found it heartbreaking that he was more concerned for Pilar than for himself. Because I knew I had only seconds to talk to him, and because I suspected Lourdes or someone else was listening in, I replied, "I'll follow their orders, you do the same. They're going to let you send me e-mails. Don't be tricky. Write about the usual stuff: baseball, birds, plants. Just so I know it's you. Things just the two of us know about. *Science.* Understand?"

On one level, I meant exactly what I said. On a more subtle, second level, I was trying to tell him there might be a way for us to pass information secretly.

Science is its own language. We'd written that back and forth often enough.

Did he understand?

He didn't seem to. Didn't even seem to hear me, because after a beat or two of silence, he replied, "Mother needs to be protected—"

He didn't finish. Lourdes' loud voice cut him off, saying, "Happy, asshole? Check your e-mail tonight. You better get what I want."

There was a click, and they were gone.

MY COUSIN, Ransom, was already in the galley of my little house, heating a pot of soup on the propane stove when I walked in.

"Brother, my brother," she said, holding her arms out to me, "I be worried about you so much."

I hugged her tight, lifting her so that her toes pointed to the wooden floor, letting her know how much I appreciated her boating over to keep me company.

"He's alive!" I told her, delighted, and then explained why I was certain.

"We got to find my nephew," she said when I'd finished. Her tone was solemn. "What those fools down there in the jungle don't be suspectin' is, you got yourself a sister who knows the words. Who's got the *power*. I can throw a spell on them Latino trash that'll ruin 'em from here. Fact, that's jes what I'm gonna do, my brother. Throw me a spell on them bad boys."

I smiled, stood away, then kissed her on the forehead. "Thanks, sis. You do that."

As Tucker Gatrell's daughter, Ransom's not my real sister, of course. But because she has introduced herself that way ever since arriving on Sanibel—"How you doin', mon, I'm Doc's sistah!"—many have come to accept it as fact, and so I no longer correct them, or her.

If people believe that I am the brother of a lanky, buxom, coconut-brown woman who casts spells, wears voodoo beads braided into her hair, and who makes blood offerings at midnight, that's O.K. with me. It's flattering. Flattering because I've come to care for Ransom like she really is my sister. She is smart and perceptive, with a bawdy sense of comedy. She's also as tough as they come, and a raging independent.

"I know you don't believe in my power, man. But it's real. You tell me about the men who took our boy, I'll make it happen."

When the woman talks, it's more like she's singing, so I heard: *Ah-no-ya doan ba-leeve en me-paawh-er, mon!*

I kissed her a second time, then told her, "You make your magic, and I'll make mine. Yeah, the bastards will regret it before we're done."

I took my address book from the little teak secretary next to the reading chair, found the number I needed. As I dialed, I watched Ransom moving gracefully around the kitchen. She was wearing pink satiny shorts and a black tank top that showed her breast implants, of which she is so proud.

Tucker Gatrell had been a tropical bum and a Caribbean junkie. It was illustrative of Tucker's life that Ransom, one of the few good things produced by his wanderings, had been accidental. She'd grown up poor, fatherless, and carried her poverty into adulthood, along with a severe weight problem.

Sometimes good things come out of tragedy, and for Ransom, it was her decision to fight back against what seemed inevitable. She decided to change; to prepare her body and outlook for what she calls her "Womanly Life." The implants, she says, were symbolic.

As I dialed, she looked at me severely and said, "Man, who you callin' this late at night?"

I told her it wasn't nearly so late in Scottsdale, Arizona, where a certain friend lived. I did not mention that I'd dialed a Virginia area code to reach my friend's Arizona desert adobe, nor that the friend was intelligence wizard Bernie Yeager.

She swung her head away, irked at my secrecy, and the Obeah beads braided into her hair added a clattering rebuke. She also wore strings of beads around her neck, I noticed: strands of red and white beads, as well as strands of white and yellow.

Ransom is a believer and a practitioner.

Obeah is a complex religious stew of voodoo, Catholicism, and old African lore. It uses complicated symbols referencing many gods. The red and white beads she wore honored the god of destiny.

I'd often seen men wear them in Cuba and the Bahamas.

But only women wore white and yellow beads. They celebrated Ochun, the goddess of rivers and love and female sensuality. I found that combination—river, love, sensuality—charming, and I never looked at Ransom without thinking of that word.

Ochun.

I looked at her now as the phone began to ring. Watched her turn to me and pantomime eating with a spoon: Did I want my soup now?

I shook my head quickly and touched finger to lips because Bernie Yeager had just answered.

IN ANY phone conversation with Bernie, you have to first go through the ceremonies of security, and then through the social pleasantries.

I had to wait for him to return my call from his office—could picture him in a space crowded with computers, satellite dishes, electronic maps—then we chatted for a time while he recorded then matched my voiceprint to confirm I was who I said I was.

"Marion," he said apologetically, "in a world so crazy as this? Even with an old friend like you, Bernie doesn't take chances."

I would have been shocked if he had.

Bernie is a legend among the world's elite intelligence community—the few members familiar with the man's work, anyway. It was Bernie who'd consistently intercepted radio and internet communications between the Taliban in Afghanistan and terrorist cells during the Iraqi war. It was Bernie who'd invaded and compromised computer communications between Managua and Havana during the Sandinista wars in Nicaragua.

A year or so ago, I read that he was given a lifetime achievement award by an esoteric organization called the Association of Old Crows. The AOC has thousands of members, all engaged in the science and practice of electronic warfare information operations. Because his accomplishments could not be listed, Bernie's introduction was short, but the ovation was long.

Years ago, I did the man a favor. He's repaid me many times over. Yet now, after inquiring about my health, and then about a couple of mutual friends, Bernie said to me, "When you call such an old man as me, and at an hour such as this, I know it's serious. I know it's because you need something special. With you, Marion, the answer is yes. It is always yes. If it's an arm you need, a leg you need—God forbid. The answer is still yes."

I said, "I wouldn't ask if it wasn't important," and then told him what I wanted.

When I'd finished, Bernie allowed a space of silence to communicate to me that he was taken aback, before he deadpanned, "A password. A simple password. You are asking me, Bernie Yeager, for a lady's password. The kind that gets her into a civilian internet server so she can trade stock tips and recipes and gossip with old sorority pals. Marion"—he scolded me—"that's like asking a concert pianist for 'Chopsticks.'"

I said, "It may be more than that. But there's not a lot else I can tell you."

"It's something you can't tell me? Your friend who has every level of government security clearance outside maybe a certain Oval Office in a certain building that I'll let you guess the color of, thanks very much. It's personal, that's what you're saying."

"That's right. It's personal."

"Marion . . ." He seemed to be choosing his words carefully. "Marion, I shouldn't even ask someone like you such an offensive question. But in such a business—" He shrugged his shoulders with vocal inflection. "Offending people is part of the job. I want you to tell me that you don't want this lady's password because you think she's cheating. Because you think she's writing love letters to another man.

"All around the world," he said, "people are trying to steal the passwords of their unfaithful lovers. So sad. This may sound strange coming from someone who does what I do, but I still believe that a man and woman's privacy is sacred."

I said softly, "If I told you, departmental statutes would require that you pass the information along to other offices. It has to do with my family, Bernie. If I don't get the password soon, someone might die."

He said slowly, "But the only family you have is the son down in . . . Masagua . . . oh my God, Marion!" He said the last horrified and heartbroken. "Oh, my dear friend! *Jiffa*, that's what I am. Such a *putz*. I make jokes while you're dying inside. Of course you can't give me the details. But what you can do, right this instant, is go get on your antique computer and send me the e-mail addresses you want hacked. Everything you have. Do it now.

"So I stay up past midnight. I turn into a pumpkin, what's the worst that can happen?" He'd shrugged his shoulders again with a sharp upswing in pitch. "Such terrible things go on in this crazy world of ours. I'll call you the moment I have anything."

EIGHTEEN

WHEN the phone rang forty-five minutes later, I came rushing out of the lab to answer. Got to it on the third ring, picked it up, and said, "What'd you find, Bernie? Did you get the information?"

After what turned out to be momentary surprise, a woman's voice replied, "This isn't Bernie, but I do have some news. Dr. Ford? You *are* Marion Ford."

I realized I was speaking to Detective Tamara Gartone. After I'd identified myself, she apologized for calling so late, but said she was required by law to contact the victim.

I said, "Huh?"

"You," she said. "You, the victim. Normally, someone at the county jail would have made the notification. But I told you I'd call personally, so I am."

What was she talking about? I was still flustered by my blunder answering the phone.

"The man who assaulted you is going to be released from jail within the next few hours," she said. "Don Jorge Balserio. That's what we're required to let you know. Personally, Dr. Ford, I think it's a hell of a mistake, and I can't believe we're doing it. Turns out, though, we've got no choice. Balserio—it's *General* Balserio—holds a diplomatic passport. Nicaragua."

Finally, I'd caught on. "You're letting Balserio out of jail tonight?"

"Later on this morning. I know, it feels like the same day. I'm not certain of the exact time he'll be released. It's because of his diplomatic status. Are you aware of what that means?"

I told her I was. Diplomatic immunity has allowed rapists, thieves, and DUI killers to leave U.S. soil and live happily ever after without trial or punishment. It's well documented that a serial rapist, the son of a Ghanaian attaché to the United Nations, waved and laughed at police from his Newark departure gate, while his last victim lay near death in a Yorkville hospital. Because of an archaic treaty, neither our county, state, nor even the federal government can detain or prosecute a foreign official who holds a diplomatic passport.

She seemed impressed that I was so well informed. "It's been that way since the Vienna Convention of 1961," she said. "Because we're so close to Miami, we deal with it occasionally. Just like this guy Balserio, they're always pompous jerks, and they never cooperate, because they know they're going to walk no matter what."

"What about the other two? The ones with the Nicaraguan driver's licenses."

"No, they don't have diplomatic status. But the charges against them aren't nearly as serious. They'll be out soon anyway. General Balserio, though. I make him as the bad one."

Her agency had followed procedure. They'd contacted the U.S. Department of State, which had contacted the Nicaraguan embassy, formally requesting that Balserio's immunity be waived. The request had been denied, so the man would soon be free.

I could hear the beep-beep of my telephone's call-waiting alert as she added, "On the bright side, he has to leave the country. They're flying him out, probably this afternoon. So he shouldn't give you any more trouble."

I thought: *Unless he decides to return illegally.*

She paused, listening. "Are you getting another call?"

I said, "Yeah, and I'm afraid I'm going to have to take it. Can we talk another time?"

The lady sounded professional, even chilly when she said, "You're a busy man, Dr. Ford. Such unusual business hours. Give Bernie my best."

IT wasn't Bernie.

I touched the flash button, answered with a more restrained, "Hello?" and heard the voice of Merlin T. Starkey say, "Ford? Tell me you don't know why I'm callin'."

I said, "Detective Gartone just hung up. I know how disappointed you must be. So why don't you have a glass of warm milk and crawl back into bed?"

The old man didn't sound the least bit sleepy for 2:20 in the morning. "Not before I'm finished tellin' you what I got to say. The guy you framed so he'd get jailed? Turns out he's some big, important foreign diplomat. Someone like him, he ain't gonna let it slide. You really hung Miz Tamara out there on a limb all by her lonesome, didn't you, sonny boy?"

Ransom was sitting in the reading chair, the marina's black cat, Crunch & Des, curled in her lap. With a mortar and pestle she'd been grinding bits of blue rock, powder, leaves, occasionally pausing to add a few drops of turpentine. But she now stopped. She seemed to know that someone hostile was on the other end of the line. Her intuition was good that way.

Ransom was watching me closely as I said, "He's not going to blame her, so stop worrying. And she's not going to hear any more about what happened on the Loop Road."

"That's what you keep sayin.' But here's what I want you to know. I think something real dirty's goin' on between you and them foreigners. And it ain't done yet. So what I'm thinkin' is, someone needs to keep a real tight eye on you, Ford. I still got a few connections in Tallahassee. I can get Florida Department of Law Enforcement to assign me temporary duty. They'll let me roam all over the state with my nose on your butt. In fact, I think I will do that. You and those Latinos, I got the feeling something real bad's gonna happen soon."

I said quickly, "Starkey, don't do that. Believe me, you don't understand the situation."

My sudden eagerness pleased him—he was back in control. "See there,

I *knew* I was right. I'm gonna call my friends tomorrow and get me assigned TDY."

One nasty old bastard.

Because I could tell he was ready to hang up, and because I was too pissed off to think it out, I said in a rush, "Hey, Merlin? That story you told me about how Tucker Gatrell ruined your career. I thought it was funny as hell."

The man who never used foul language said, "Fuck you, sonny boy," and slammed the phone in my ear.

I was in the midst of explaining to Ransom how and why the old man had infuriated me, when the phone rang again.

She returned to mixing her powders, saying, "I'll put that ol' fool on my juju list, too," as I picked up the phone and said carefully, "Hello . . . ?"

BERNIE had Pilar's password, said it was no problem. Passwords, actually. She had two internet accounts. Her personal account was through Hotmail.com, which was free and the most commonly used server in Central America. Her other account was used mostly for business and more formal correspondence. It was through the Masaguan government and a thing called ISTMO Communication Group.

"It's an internet presence provider," he explained, adding that it offered hosting services and domain registration, with headquarters in Panama, and offices in Costa Rica, El Salvador, Guatemala, and Miami.

Bernie told me the big international accounts were the easiest for someone like him to hack. "At AOL, Yahoo, Hotmail, even stuff that's deleted—passwords, name it—is stored on the archived internet service provider's hard drive. That's in case the FBI or someone like me wants to come looking."

This early in the morning, I wasn't certain I wanted to hear all the details, but did my best to sound interested. Like most great artists, the man took joy in the intricacies of his craft.

"I downloaded all her files and sent them to you as an attachment. I don't know if you're worried about being caught spending time online by the real subscriber or not. They gonna send the internet police up from

Central America to slap you on the wrist? I know, I know—so why should we care?"

The note Pilar had received telling us to meet the tattooed giant in Miami was from *xyxq37@nicarado.org*. Bernie referred to that person as "X." Retrieving X's password wasn't so easy, he said.

"Nicarado's the server used by libraries and schools in Nicaragua and Masagua," he said. "All the accounts are free, and there's an unlimited number of accounts a person can set up. If this person's smart, doesn't want to be tracked, doesn't want his e-mails hacked, he can just keep changing names and accounts, traveling all over Central America. Sure, I can get you passwords. But that's not going to help if the account address keeps changing."

I said, "You couldn't get his password?"

Bernie sounded hurt. "He asks me such a question. A man I've known so many years, he asks a question like that. Yes, Marion, I *do* have X's password. Yes, it took me all of twenty minutes, but I got it. It's a strange one, too. It doesn't sound Spanish, but you speak the language so well, you maybe know it. The password is *Bozark*."

I said, "Bozark? No . . . not Spanish. *Maybe* Tlaxclen Maya, but nothing I know in Spanish. It sounds American. Regional."

Which made sense. Lourdes spoke with an American accent, plus a hint of something else.

Bernie said, "I did a web search on it. Ran it backward, rearranged the letters. Bozark's a common family name. Nothing else came up. Same thing I found in X's files. Nothing. Which is what I was telling you. The password may be worthless because X left nothing to read. Nothing that I can access without physically going to the main computer, anyway. There's a history of one transmission to her address, and that's it. So I think we're dealing with someone who knows the system, who keeps changing accounts to hide his tracks."

I asked, "Bernie, is there any way you can narrow down *where* in Central America the e-mails are originating?"

What I'd been considering was grabbing a plane to Masagua and hunting for Prax Lourdes while Pilar and Tomlinson took care of the ransom demands here in Florida. I liked the thought of that; moving in on him while he thought I was still back in the States, hustling drugs for some wounded revolutionary.

In a singsong voice, Bernie answered, "Maybe yes, maybe no, maybe. Which I was just about to tell you if you'd show a little patience. Every e-mail has a routing code. How it reads depends on the server, but internationally, it's a mess. It's not like zip codes or telephone routing numbers. It varies with the place and the server. Take . . . well, for instance, if you send me something over the internet, I can tell it's from Florida in the United States. But Nicarado, it's a mess with a capital M."

Even so, he explained, there was still enough routing information for him to have a pretty good idea, geographically, where it came from. I listened closely as he added, "But I noticed something very fishy in the coding," he said. "A little time delay indicator almost no one in the world would have caught but me—excuse me for bragging, but true. The person who sent this e-mail? I'd bet he or she was in the country of Masagua. Almost definitely on a public computer. A library; a school. But the person who *wrote* the e-mail, the place where the e-mail originated, I'd say he's probably *not* in Masagua. Maybe not even in Central America."

I said, *"What?"*

"I think he sent the e-mail to a confederate in Masagua who then forwarded it on under the Nicarado address. Maybe the confederate copied it, maybe retyped it. I can't say; I'm going simply on an anomaly in the routing code."

So much for the idea of flying to Masagua and beginning my search. That would come soon enough, though. I was counting on it.

I said, "X writes the e-mail, and sends it from someplace unknown to a library or school in Masagua. X's partner then forwards it to the States under a Nicarado address."

"Exactly."

I checked my watch as I thanked Bernie for his help. I was eager to get into Pilar's e-mail and see if Lourdes had sent her anything more.

There was nothing surprising about Pilar's password. It was *Ixku-ixku*—another Mayan word that she was fond of, the name of an ancient goddess.

THE guilt of a voyeur has an uneasiness attached; a slimy feel . . .

That was the sensation, scanning Pilar's e-mail.

Pilar had something going with her jeweler friend Kahlil in Masagua. There were nearly a dozen unread e-mails from him in her in-box. Some of the subject headings were "Missing my love," "My heart is with you," "Long for your touch."

Or maybe Kahlil just had it bad for Pilar. I hadn't checked her Mail Sent file. Maybe her replies weren't as sappy.

Not that I opened and read the man's letters. Nor would I. I agree with Bernie: A person's privacy is sacred. And I didn't like that voyeur feeling.

There were two e-mails, though, that I opened immediately. Like the earlier e-mail Pilar had received from the kidnappers, the subject heading was blank, and both notes came from addresses that seemed to be a random series of letters and numbers. Both also came from the server Nicarado.org.

The first was dated the previous day, Wednesday, at 11:10 P.M. At that exact moment, I'd been on my way back from the Everglades after dealing with Balserio. The second e-mail had just now arrived; was delivered electronically only a few minutes before I sat down at the desk in my lab and signed on with Pilar's password.

I was tempted to open the new e-mail first. Instead, I forced myself to read them in the order they arrived:

Rich bitch. Florida called us and said you were being followed, which is so fucking stupid of you. Trick us again, the brat dies. No more warnings. Tomorrow night, drive to St. Petersburg. Be in the downtown area no later than 10 at night. Have the satellite phone, someone will let you know. If you threw it away, you're the losers because you didn't get our permission. The money better be packed in a hard photographer's case exactly like you were told. Make sure of that. No more fuck-ups. Answer this message immediately so we know you have it.

I kept the e-mail as new and saved it to my filing cabinet, wondering about the photographer's carrying case. Why was that so important? When Lourdes mentioned it on the video, I'd considered a couple of vague explanations, but didn't linger long enough to think them through. Maybe the pick-up man would be posing as a photographer. Or . . . a camera case was rugged, durable, which made it ideal if they intended to bury the money until they were sure law enforcement wasn't waiting to nail them. The cases were also shockproof. They could send us down some lonely road and have us throw the case out the window on command.

Tomlinson would be a good one to ferret other possibilities—if he and Pilar ever resurfaced.

I opened the second e-mail.

Maybe because I'd just gotten off the phone with Lourdes, I could hear his voice as I read:

> *Big-shot scientist. The brat says you can do anything; well, let's see. Your industrialist whores up there are paying for the bullets killing our peasants, so I feel good about you stealing the medicine to help keep some of them alive. One of our important people got hit bad and has an operation coming up, but the doctors say they don't have the best medicine, and that's where you come in. We want the following supplies, and you have until Sunday afternoon to get it, and don't even ask for more time because the answer is "Fuck you." When you get it, pack it good in the same kind of case as the money. The hard photography kind that seals tight without having to lock. Don't go to St. Petersburg tonight because we'll do the exchange all at the same time. Answer back fast.*

A list of several drugs then followed. I was familiar with only a couple of the names. Because he demanded relatively small quantities, it seemed to support his story that they were needed for a specific operation.

Lourdes' e-mail ended,

> *You should have seen the look on your brat's face when I told him you said we should go ahead and kill him, Papa didn't want to pay all that money.*

I thought to myself: *Lake had to know it's not true. That I said it only to get leverage.*

I kept the e-mail as new, then forwarded it to my own business address at Sanibel Biological Supply. If I wanted to send him a question about the drug list, I wanted to be able to do it without going into Pilar's account. As I did, I told myself that Lake understood, hoping the boy was secure enough and smart enough to know I had to play it tough from my end. Even so, it made me feel sick inside—and furious, too.

I'd thought about it before, but now I thought about it again: Praxcedes Lourdes would one day feel a tap on his shoulder and turn to find me standing there, the two of us off all alone.

Imagining the moment displaced the anger, made it fade.

I BEGAN to write a note confirming that I'd received his e-mail, but then stopped. Lourdes wanted a fast response, but it didn't have to be *that* fast. Why not take a little extra time and maybe think of a way to make my reply work for me? Use it to my advantage if I could.

I knew nothing about several of the medicines he'd demanded, had no idea if I could get them—but Lourdes didn't know that. I decided to do some cursory research. If I sounded authoritative, if I convinced him I knew what I was talking about, maybe it'd give Masked Man a little extra incentive to keep me happy.

There were several common antibacterials on the list. I didn't bother with them. I went to work looking up the medicines that were less common. One was cyclosporine. He wanted five hundred 100 mg capsules, plus 50 mg of cyclosporine for intravenous infusion, packaged in 5 ml sterile ampules.

Another was prednisone. He wanted five hundred 20 mg capsules. He also wanted drugs named ATGAM and Thymoglobulin, and something called OKT3, all in intravenous infusion bags or ampules, plus the needles and tubes required as delivery systems.

Maybe one or all three of these were the experimental medicines he'd talked about.

My impression of Lourdes was that he was vicious and shrewd but poorly educated. This was an extremely sophisticated and detailed list of supplies, and he'd put it together very quickly. Who was he fronting for? Or who was supplying him with data?

Using internet search engines, I began to research the drugs one by one. I started with what might be the experimental types first.

In a medical journal, I read an article about OKT3:

> The antibody OKT3 blocks the functions of human cells that re-ject foreign bodies. We explored its effectiveness in treating the rejection of renal allografts. Of 123 patients suffering acute re-jection of cadaveric renal transplants, those treated with OKT3 daily for a mean of 14 days, 73 percent experienced marked re-coveries.

Cadaveric renal transplants? Lourdes wanted the drugs for someone who needed a kidney transplant?

Well . . . not necessarily.

I ran the names of the others. Except for the more common drugs on the list, the rest were antirejection or immunosuppressant drugs. They were medicines administered to patients either during or after receiving a trans-planted heart, limb, liver, or lung, a skin graft, or any other procedure where a foreign organ is introduced.

Someone was getting a transplant. Soon, apparently. He needed the most powerful immunosuppressants available.

Ruined organs and lost limbs are not uncommon among battlefield casualties.

But something about the scenario bothered me. I've spent much of my life dealing with the military, and military people. For Lourdes to tell me, an American civilian, that one of their top military people had been wounded and was about to undergo a serious operation seemed to be a terrible breach of security. What kind of army was Balserio run-ning?

If the story was true, not a very good one, I decided.

AT ten minutes until three in the morning, I wrote a note to Lourdes confirming I'd read his demands. I wrote it in English to see how he'd react. If I could get him to reply in what I suspected was his native language, I'd learn a lot more about him:

> *Reception confirmed. Please consult your doctors again before I waste my time getting all this stuff. Our people here usually recommend ATGAM and Thymoglobulin over OKT3, particularly for acute rejection episodes. Side effects are similar to OKT3, but are usually less severe. Do your doctors know what they're doing? None of it's going to be easy to find, so make sure it's what they want.*
>
> *I'm not doing anything until we start getting e-mails from the boy. His letters need to include a reference to something current so we know they weren't written in advance. They also need to be personal enough so we know only he could have written them. This is nonnegotiable, and we expect his first e-mail later today.*

I read the thing over more than a half a dozen times, wondering if it was too tough. Decided it needed to be tough.

Finally, I inserted the sentence *"Natural history is a familiar topic"* just before the sentence that began, *"This is nonnegotiable . . ."* I hoped Lake would see it; that it would give him the hint he needed.

If he could get outside, or see outside, there were ways for him to tell me where he was geographically. Narrow it down, at least.

I sent the e-mail unsigned.

I GOT UP, stretched, walked through the breezeway that separates the lab from my house, and peeked through the screen door: Ransom and the black cat were curled up in the chair, dozing. She'd transferred the concoction she'd been creating into a clear glass beaker. It was my smallest Pyrex boiling flask from the lab. A boiling flask has a bulbous bottom and a tubular neck. Filled with the turquoise potion, it was as exotic-looking as a genie's lamp. The flask sat atop my old transoceanic short-wave radio—a bizarre combination. Looked like it really could perform voodoo magic.

I wondered how she was going to use the stuff. Did her victims have to come in contact with the goo?

I should have been exhausted, but still felt wakeful, so decided to make a more careful search of Pilar's e-mail. I didn't know how many times Lourdes or his accomplices had communicated with her via the internet—I hadn't asked—so there might be more to learn. I returned to the lab, cleaned my glasses, sat at the computer, and began to scan.

Pilar is a methodical woman. She's also extremely private. I was not surprised to discover that she saved many—maybe all—of the e-mails she'd written (for her records, of course), but preserved few of the e-mails she'd received. Nearly everything in her Old Mail file had been deleted. With the exception of several messages from Lake—his *Chamaeleo* address jumped out at me—and a dozen or so others, the file was empty. None had a Nicarado.org address, so I went into her Mail Sent file and concentrated on studying the subject headings and addresses there.

Her replies to the kidnappers might well tell me the content of their messages to her.

On Thursday, May 1, the day she discovered Lake missing, she'd written to a lot of people. Same was true of Friday, May 2. The numbers suggested a kind of emotional frenzy. Understandable.

Judging from the recipient addresses, many of the letters had to do with inquiring about travel, contacting the Masaguan counsul general's office, and also arranging for people to look after her private affairs while she was away.

Several were to *Kahlil39*. Her correspondence with him was busy. Not as sappy from her end, but still something serious going on. Subject headings were: "One heart," "Dear Man." On the day that Lake disappeared, it was "Desperate!"

I was tempted to actually read one of her earlier letters to him, but that ugly voyeur-guilt stopped my hand on the mouse. I wondered how Kahlil would feel if he knew she'd vanished with one of America's horniest, most sexually active Zen Buddhist monks.

Pilar had even saved the note she'd sent to an ex-lover she now reviled—me. I saw my Sanibel Biological Supply e-mail address; saw the subject heading—"Personal/important"—and opened it so that I could re-read:

> Greetings to you. I'm arriving in Miami on Monday, and would very much like to speak to you in person about an important matter. May I visit you Tuesday afternoon on Sanibel? Please give my warm regards to Tomlinson . . .

It had seemed chilly when I read it then. It seemed chillier now.

Several of the recipients had Nicarado.org addresses. That got me excited, but my excitement was wasted. I opened each to find that Pilar was usually replying to a teacher or a librarian who had a public account.

Now I *was* tired. Her stack of sent mail was so lengthy that I decided I'd done enough, and I'd had enough. I'd been awake for slightly more than twenty-one hours—twenty-one very active hours—and so I moved the mouse for a final quick scan of subject headings before signing off . . . and then I stopped, confused . . . then baffled.

On the afternoon that Pilar discovered Lake missing, she had written an e-mail to *Tinman@Fight4Right.org.* The first two words of the subject heading were the same as on her note to me, "Personal/important." But added to that were three incongruous words: "About our son."

About our son?

Whose son? Lake, *our* son, was her only child.

Confused, I looked at the top of the page. Maybe I was dopey from exhaustion. I checked to make certain I was still in her Mail Sent file.

Yes, I was.

I checked to see if she was forwarding a letter from someone else.

No.

Had she actually written the e-mail and sent it?

Yes, hers was the source address. The subject heading was Pilar's: "Personal/important about our son."

One of the first symptoms of shock can be a roaring sound in the inner ear.

Nearly deafened, I clicked on the subject line. Then I opened the e-mail to read what was inside.

NINETEEN

I T   W A S written in English, and the beginning of the letter was very similar to the note that Pilar had written to me:

My Dear Tinman,

Greetings to you. I'm arriving in Florida on Monday. If we can work out the logistics, I would very much like to speak to you in person about an urgent matter, even though I realize it may be awkward . . .

Its contents then changed dramatically:

I've written you several times over the last year, yet you've never replied. I beg you to please answer me now.

A terrible thing has happened, and you should be informed. My son, Laken, has been abducted and is being held for ransom. I am terrified and don't know what to do. Can't we please talk? More than ever, I now need to ask you those questions.

We were once friends, and I still think of you fondly. I know that neither of us has wanted to acknowledge the possibility that you are Laken's father. I have always wondered. There's something you don't know. Slightly more than a year ago, I received information about MF that made me hope that it's true you are his father. Now, I really do have reason to believe you are the one.

This is the sixth time I've written you in the last few months, and you have not replied. Please answer me now when I am so desperate for your help. Years ago, when I gave you the chance, you chose to disappear from our lives. Don't disappear now.

P

I whispered two words. Two soft profanities. Then I stood slowly and walked on shaky legs to the lab station. I removed my glasses and ducked my head beneath the gooseneck faucet, and let the cold water run. I turned, buried my face in a towel, rubbing hard, drying hair and face, feeling a bizarre sense of unreality, seeing swirls and starbursts of color behind my eyes.

I said another whispered profanity—a rhetorical question—then returned to the computer and read portions of the letter again.

Tinman . . . We were once friends, and I still think of you fondly. I know that neither of us has wanted to acknowledge the possibility that you are Laken's father. I have always wondered.

Who in the hell was Tinman? And why hadn't this woman—a person whose ethics I'd admired for years—had the decency to tell me that such a thing was a possibility?

I didn't feel betrayed. There has to be a covenant before there can be a betrayal. Pilar and I had none. What I felt was a terrible sense of potential loss. I was already fighting to save my son. Now these new, outrageous circumstances were threatening to take him in a way that was beyond any hope of change or my control.

There's something you don't know. Slightly more than a year ago, I received information about MF that made me hope that it's true. Now, I really do have reason to believe you are the one.

Slightly more than a year ago, someone had shown her files concerning my work in Central America. She'd learned the truth about Marion Ford—

or believed she had. That had changed everything, as far as she was concerned.

In my mind, I replayed the first minutes that we'd been alone together; could hear Pilar saying, "Do you know what concerns me the most since I found out? That Laken calls you 'father.' If he believes your blood runs in his veins, will he try to emulate you? Already, he's becoming more and more like you. At night, I go to sleep worrying about it. Will that part of you be in him? That gene, that kind of . . . of evil? Is there a killer inside of my child, waiting?"

Her odd wording now made sense.

I could also hear her say, "You're not the good man I fell in love with. You couldn't be. How could you have done those things?"

Did she really believe this guy could be Lake's father? Or was it simply because she now preferred to believe that it was true?

I knew I'd want to read the letter later, study the nuances, so I saved the e-mail to my computer's personal files. I then moved the cursor so that I could read the second e-mail she'd written *Tinman*. It was sent on Sunday, the night before she left for Miami.

It was as shocking as the first:

> *My dear Campañero, I write a final time begging you to answer. Do you remember the good days when we called each other by that name? It honors peasants, not politics. I ask you to reflect on those days, and so agree to help. I know you must still have loyal connections in Central America. We all admired your heart and brain so much. I ask you to call on those connections now and ask them to look for a monster named Praxcedes Lourdes, the one who abducted my son, and to pass the information on to me.*
>
> *I wonder if you are getting my letters? Or maybe you don't respond because you still feel guilt because you encouraged MF's friendship with the hope of gathering information about his country's illegal activities. In this way, we are the same, my dear Tinman. I also felt much guilt. Unlike you, though, I no longer feel any remorse. One day, when we are together and alone, I will tell you why. Perhaps, then, you will finally answer me. What happened that night? I remember laughing and laughing, and being very*

dizzy. I think you know the truth. Are you Laken's father? His face reminds me of yours.

P

I'D recently taken delivery of the finest microscope I've ever owned. It's a Leica Selectra Trinocular, with extraordinary resolution, variable zoom, and a vertical photo tube. I turned away from the computer and seemed to float across the room, where I reached out to the microscope as if it were a lifebuoy.

I removed the scope's cover and found a glass slide on which I'd already mounted a cross section from a piece of loggerhead sponge. I'd found the sponge while collecting on the flats a few days earlier. I fixed the slide on the scope's stage plate, touched the light toggle, and removed my glasses. Then I leaned toward the viewing head's eyepieces, eager to escape into that bright world of exacting focus.

I had to have a break. My brain was so fogged by what I'd just read, I felt dizzy, even nauseous. It couldn't be true, but it *was* true. Pilar had become friendly with me, and then ingratiated herself, in order to gather information about my covert work. So she *had* known. Or, as she'd told me, at least suspected—but not the extent of the things I'd been ordered to do during the revolution that was going on in her country.

Tinman had done the same thing—whoever the hell Tinman was. He, supposedly, was also a friend. At least, that's the way her letter read.

I'd gone over the sentences only a couple of times, but they'd already been seared into my memory:

I also felt much guilt. In this way, we are the same, my dear Tinman. Unlike you, though, I no longer feel any remorse.

Yeah, there was no room for doubt.

But which of my male friends? I'd had several good ones during my time there. At least, I'd thought of them as good friends.

Are you Laken's father? His face reminds me of yours.

That certainly narrowed it down.

If Lake and Tinman actually did resemble one another, then Tinman also had to be distinctly non-Latin-looking. In his photos and in person, Lake could pass for a Midwestern farmboy.

The possibilities made me feel wobbly. I needed an emotional retreat. The microscope awaited. I touched my eyes to the twin eyepieces and was instantly transported. I took one . . . two . . . and then a third full breath.

Magnified by the fine optics, the protein fibers of the sponge's osculum—its excurrent water opening—seemed large enough so that a model city could be erected within its perfect convexity. There were vast corridors and safe hideaways that, to me, were alluring. I longed to climb inside.

I touched the glass plate, and the view changed. There was a curling flagellum, a hairlike paddle that pulls in water . . . and the crosshatched symmetry of the animal's silicate skeleton. The skeleton was an intricate pattern of fluted ramps on a curving honeycombed infrastructure. I increased magnification until the sponge fibers became an extraordinarily modernistic sculpture. A single filament might have been a stairway designed by Dalí.

I was looking into a world that was no less chemically complex and biologically diverse than my own. Sponges consist of cooperating communities of different cells. We have counted as many as sixteen thousand animals, and many species, living in the canal systems of a single sponge.

Complex, yes. But not nearly so complicated.

My mind cycled away from this articulate microuniverse, back into the murkier world that was my own. I stood suddenly, and lowered my glasses.

I'd scanned my memory synapses over and over, and the results were always the same. During that general time period prior to Lake's birth, there were only two men whom I considered friends, who'd also known Pilar in Masagua, and who were unmistakably Anglo-Saxon.

One was my old partner, Thackery, the crazed Australian surfer and SAS operative. I remembered that he had a Ph.D. in oceanography, was a passionate environmentalist. Part of his cover was that he'd infiltrated an ultra-left-wing environmental group that was helping to fund the guerrilla fighters. Or supposedly infiltrated them. Could Thackery actually have been working for the enemy? Could he, in fact, have been a double agent, fighting for the other side?

I hadn't seen the man in years. Wondered how I could track him down. And if he was Tinman, I would have to find him . . . or at least make certain that people in the American intelligence community knew about him. Even though several years had passed, it was still a serious security breach, and it would have to be dealt with.

Yet, the truth was, I hoped that Tinman *was* Thackery.

There was only one other possibility. That was Tomlinson.

AT a little after four in the morning, I opened the screen door and stepped into my little house to see Ransom curled in the chair, still holding Crunch & Des. But instead of sleeping, her eyes were open wide, staring at me. She looked alarmed.

She yawned, stretched, still staring, and said, "My brother. I just had me a witchin' dream, and you was in it. Now I open my eyes, and here you are in front of me lookin' so pale, like you just seen a ghost."

I told her, "In a way, I just did."

I've spent a lifetime maintaining my own counsel, and keeping secrets. Even if I believed in the value of psychoanalysis, emotional purging— name a popular term—I swore an oath to a covenant long ago that bars me from any such therapy. So, after living such a long and solitary internal existence, I discovered something new in Ransom. She's become a friend and confidante who, because she actually does treat me with the unconditional love of a sister, has earned my unconditional trust.

So I told her. Told her about Pilar's e-mails, and that I might not be Lake's father. Without getting into my clandestine activities—information I can never divulge—I told her all that I could about Thackery, and then added, "The only other possibility is Tomlinson."

I'd felt sick. But the expression of outrage on her face rallied me. "You *serious.* That ol' hippie-stork needs someone to tie his cock in a knot. Or throw a potion on him that makes his Willie Johnson limp as boiled yarn. Maybe tha's just exactly what I'll do. Came close to doin' it back the time we dated those few times and I found out he was already diddlin' other womens."

I nearly smiled.

I said, "The thing is, the timing with Tomlinson and Pilar doesn't work out quite right. He was in Masagua with me before Lake was born, but it was only five or six months before he was born."

Sounding cynical, Ransom asked, "Were you there when that baby born?"

"No."

"Know anybody who was?"

"I didn't even know she was pregnant."

"Uh-huh. Sometimes a woman lie about when a baby come out when she not sure who the daddy be. Who the one that told *you* about the child?"

I had to think back. The answer surprised me. "It was . . . *Tomlinson?* . . . Yeah, it was. He brought me a newspaper that had a photo of Pilar and Lake. It was taken not too long after she gave birth. He had blond hair back then, so I just naturally assumed . . ."

Ransom was nodding, still saying, "Uh-huh, uh-huh . . ." Then she asked, "When did the woman tell you that you was the daddy?"

I had to think about that, too. "Because of where they lived, Masagua, I couldn't go back to that country for a long time. There were . . . *reasons*. On my end, not hers. So I guess it would have been in phone conversations. I remember waiting for her to mention it; figuring that she would. And she finally did. When Lake was maybe three or so, she said something like, 'He's at an age where he's asking about his father. So we need to have a talk.' She put it like that. She said she thought I'd be a good father when the time came for us to be together."

Ransom said, "Uh-huh, uh-huh," in the same knowing tone. "Why you think the timing's so far off with that ugly Stork Man, Tomlinson?"

I said, "It might not be. There's a chance Pilar met Tomlinson before she met me."

To explain, I had to tell her things about the man that I'd never shared with anyone.

AS FAR as I know, even Tomlinson isn't aware how far our relationship goes back.

There's a good reason for that. But because of things that I'm obligated to keep confidential, I couldn't lay it all out for Ransom. I had to blur the edges. I tried to say little but imply a lot.

Ransom has a first-rate intellect and great intuition. She seemed to understand that I was constrained by something, and she reacted to those limitations with only the occasional, careful question.

Stroking the black cat's ears, she listened intently as I told her that not so long ago, in this same room, nearly in tears, Tomlinson had confessed to me that, many years before, he'd participated in a crime that had killed a friend of mine.

I told Ransom, "I already knew. I pretended like I didn't. But I'd found out long ago that Tomlinson was involved. Even before I came back to Sanibel and started leasing this place."

I could see that she wanted to ask, *How?* Instead, she just nodded.

Tomlinson, I told her, had been a member of a political extremist group responsible for sending a bomb to a San Diego naval installation. The bomb had killed three people and injured another.

One of the sailors killed was a naval Special Warfare officer. The officer had been a good friend. He'd had a wife and a child. I took it personally.

I couldn't tell Ransom that I was a member of an organization that also took the murders very personally. A secret organization so small and select that we took orders from three or fewer people at the very top of the political ladder, and conducted operations that were never officially documented or acknowledged. Not that we knew where our orders originated.

I found that out much later.

Our group had exceptional resources, and few legal or political boundaries.

Tomlinson hadn't sent the bomb. He hadn't participated in the making of it, nor had he been aware of the plan. But he hadn't tried to stop them or have them stopped, either. He'd been a member of the group. As far as we were concerned, there was blood on his hands.

We didn't know it at the time, but he felt the same. It was more guilty blood for the heir to a fortune soaked in the blood of others.

It was then he began to study Buddhism, and that he secretly created a scholarship fund for the children of the murdered sailor.

It was also then that Tomlinson fell apart. He went insane. He was institutionalized by his family for many months, and given shock treatments, and kept heavily drugged.

I told Ransom, "Being locked away like that saved his life. But not in the way you might think. It saved him because it got him off the street. The group responsible for the bombing had thirteen members. Within two years after the explosion, six of the thirteen had been either killed in freak accidents or badly injured. Two others—*poof*—vanished. No trace ever found."

The woman understood my meaning. I could read it in her expression—a look of growing, uneasy dismay—as she said, "Like this here cat when it be after a bird. Someone was huntin' them folks down and murderin' them."

I corrected her. "I don't think you can call it murder. Not if it's sanctioned."

Now her expression had saddened, seemed to say, *Oh Lord, I don't want to believe you said that.*

IT SEEMED wiser to continue talking than to risk a pause that might invite her questions. So I said, "When I came back to Sanibel and found out this stilt house could be leased, I had no idea that Tomlinson sometimes used Dinkin's Bay as an anchorage. Quite a coincidence, huh? I didn't think so at the time.

"When he showed up and I realized who he was, I was suspicious as hell. I figured he had to be suspicious of me, too, though he never showed it. In fact, he came on like the same sweet, brilliant flake he seems to be today. Like maybe the shock therapy had changed his wiring or something. That's what I thought could've happened.

"But I was still on my guard. The group that sent the bomb wasn't the only radical organization Tomlinson had been involved with. I . . . *knew* about him . . . for reasons I might tell you down the road. So I thought maybe someone had sent him after me. Or maybe some government agency had leveraged him and was using him against me."

Ransom asked carefully, "There's a reason some government might do that to you, my brother?"

I barely nodded twice—*Yes*—before I continued, "I got my chance to test Tomlinson's motives when a pal of mine got into some trouble and I had to go back to Central America. I invited him along. You get a man in the jungle, all the little tricks and gimmicks fall apart after a few days. Once I got him in the jungle, I knew I'd find out the truth."

I made a grunting sound of derision. "At least I thought I would. So maybe there were some clues I could've picked up on. He knew a lot about the people, the customs. Maybe more than he should've. Another was that he talked about the Maya like a university scholar. So it could be that one of the organizations he belonged to was a thing called Fight-4-Right, and he'd been in Masagua before. Fight-4-Right is an underground radical group that raises money for violent political causes, and works closely with the village populations of Third World countries."

Ransom said, "The Stork Man, our Tomlinson, he be workin' for some group that preach violence? My brother, he be like the least violent human soul I ever met. The only weapon he ever use is that big dick a his, and that a happy-makin' thing. You know that."

I said, "It was a different time. People, politics, philosophies, and Tomlinson got caught up in the dynamics of his generation. Me?"—I shrugged—"I've never cared about politics. Never will, and I've never felt a part of any generation. So I never understood the behaviors."

I'd been pacing as I talked. I stopped now, looked at my watch, and said, "So, see why I had to give you the background? It wouldn't've made sense without it. The point is, Tomlinson may have met Pilar before I met her, or around the same time—only I wasn't aware of it. Because of their past political associations, there may be reasons for both of them to still keep secrets from me. At least, think they should."

I began pacing again as I added bitterly, "Which means maybe neither of them were the friends I thought they were."

Ransom said, "That ugly Stork Man, he may be a crazy ganja-smokin' fool, brother, but he always your friend. You know that, too. I think that always safe to say. He almost like your brother." Her tone of gentle rebuke said I was wrong to doubt him so quickly.

Still angry, I replied, "I'm not accusing him. I'm just saying it's possible, that's all. If he and Pilar were here, I'd be tempted to stick my nose in their faces and ask just what the hell the truth is. But I wouldn't. I can't. There're too many—"

I caught myself. I'd almost said that there were too many security issues involved to confront them. I couldn't. I couldn't even hint that I'd uncovered the information until I was absolutely certain of the identity of Tinman.

So I finished lamely, but still bitter, "I can't ask them because they're holed up in some hotel room in Miami. They won't even answer my calls."

Shaking her head for some reason, Ransom was suddenly up, getting something from the galley—a piece of paper. "That where you're wrong. I meant to tell you. I come inside the house before you got here, and found this note on the door. It from the Stork Man."

TOMLINSON'S penmanship reminds me of the eloquent ink craft that I associate with previous centuries—beautifully formed and slanted loops and swirls. *Spencerian script,* he calls it, and credits his writing hand to a former life in which, he says, he worked as a shipping clerk, eighteenth-century London, on the Thames River.

The note read:

Doctor, my Doctor,

We took a shuttle back to the island about an hour after you dropped us at the hotel. Pilar started worrying we might get an important e-mail, and said we should check it. Guess you must have stopped somewhere or got hung up. Bring some beers and come on out to No Mas if it's not after 11, man. My corporeal ass is dragging, so will hopefully be drunk, stoned, or asleep very soon. Abrazos, mi hermano!

As I looked up from the note, Ransom asked, "I already read it. What's that last part mean?"

I said, "It's an affectionate way of saying goodbye. Spanish. 'I give you a hug, my brother.'"

Ransom told me, "Jes' like I said, your brother. What kinda person gonna say that and not be your friend? And you talking about them like they was shacked up together in some hotel."

"I don't feel real apologetic right now. Maybe it has to do with finding out I'm maybe not the real father of my son."

Ransom began, "Let me ask you somethin', Marion Ford"—using her serious voice, the one she employs when making a point or assuming a platform of wisdom—"did you feel like the boy's father before you read them letters? Course you did. Then tell me, how can a few words change a man's feelin's for his child? Where's it say you got to have the same blood to be a father? Hell, man, I ain't your *real* sister. But, 'cause of the feelings I got, I am your real *sister*. See what I'm sayin'?"

I was tempted to share the irony with her. It was only in recent hours that I'd had my first insights into the power of blood kinship—the first to which I had ever attached any emotion, anyway—and now those feelings were already being challenged.

I shook my head wearily, made a flapping motion with my hands, and began to undress. "You're right. He's my son. No matter who the real father is, he's still my son."

"Yeah, that a healthy way to think of it. Now, get them clothes off. You so bone weary, you get you some sleep now. I stay and rub your back maybe. Say—why you not wearing the gris-gris bag I give you? That good luck, man!"

I had my shirt off, so she could see that I wasn't wearing the little leather sack of herbs and who-knows-what-else around my neck. I never did.

I let my fishing shorts drop to the floor, stepped out of them, turned, and walked to the west window, then stopped, looking out, as she said,

"Something else you need to make you feel better, I can get some goofer dust. Put a little on you, then pray over it every day for nine days. I got some nice lotion, too—turpentine and rose petals mostly—that make the heart pains go 'way."

I said, "Do you have any magic dust that'll make Dewey come back? Or at least call."

I'd told her about that, too.

"Oh yeah, man. The bring-me-lover-home spell, that an easy one. When the moon full? We do it then, and that girl, Dewey, she soon back in your arms."

I was standing in my underwear, looking out over the mangroves, the marina lights off to my right, a wedge of moon showing over the trees. The moon would soon be setting over the Gulf; setting almost exactly at the same time the sun was rising over the bay. Decided that, as long as I was up, I might as well stay up to see it.

I told my sister, "I'm too tired to sleep. I think I'll jog down Tarpon Bay Road to the beach, do a short run and swim."

I could picture myself swimming toward the moon on a lane of silver light, the island widening behind me. What a temptation, to just keep swimming toward the moon.

I wondered if Dewey was awake, thinking about me, thinking about us.

Yeah, the mood I was in, that would be better than trying to sleep.

TWENTY

I SAW Tomlinson briefly late that afternoon at the marina. He'd puttered ashore in his little dinghy so he could drive to Bailey's General Store and buy supplies. The encounter was as uncomfortable as it was unexpected.

Unexpected because he makes shopping runs less frequently these days. Too much risk of being recognized. He has a garden variety of phobias, and the newest is the fear of being mobbed by foreign-speaking strangers.

It's happened because of his growing cult status as a Zen teacher. His adoring groupies come to the marina to seek him out, and the attention makes him edgy. Until Mack, who owns and manages the marina, put a stop to it, they'd hang around the docks, hoping for a glimpse of their beloved prophet.

That's the way they think of him, too. It has to do with a religious treatise that he wrote years ago when he was still a university student, *One Fathom Above Sea Level*. A fathom is six feet, so the title refers to the universe as viewed through one man's eyes—Tomlinson's.

The paper was published in Germany, enjoyed a brief European vogue, and then vanished. But a while back, it was rediscovered. It was translated into Japanese, then Chinese, and began to circulate around the world on the internet. The internet's great triumph is that it is successfully joining us as one race, even while inviting dependencies that amplify our vulnerability, and that may well destroy us as a modern society.

Anyway, Tomlinson has his faults, but ego isn't among them. Except for an understandable wariness, he's been unchanged by all the attention. The problem is, he says, he can't *remember* writing *One Fathom,* nor what inspired it.

It used to trouble him: not remembering what he'd written, or what had moved him to that level of virtuosity. As he explains it, heavy drink and drugs were involved, so the brain cells that did the actual creating are long since dead.

It bothered him so much, in fact, that around Christmas, he disappeared for a couple of months on what he later described to me as his personal quest to rediscover the source of that lost inspiration. When I asked for details, he demurred, though I noticed that he stopped speaking of *One Fathom* as if it had been written by an unknown person.

And he was forced to change his lifestyle because of the unwelcome fame. Tomlinson has always kept his sun-battered Morgan sailboat moored only a few hundred yards offshore from the docks, and just across the channel from my stilt house. Now, though, he's moved it near the middle of the bay to discourage his followers from attempting to swim out to meet him. It's a considerably longer distance, and one of the reasons he makes fewer trips to the marina.

Which is why I was surprised to run into him that afternoon. I'd seen him ride by earlier that day—probably to pick up his cell phone, which I'd left for him behind the counter in the marina office. With the phone, I'd also left a note that listed the medical supplies we needed, and a brief explanation. I couldn't help adding a postscript reminding him that he had hipster doctor buddies who were happy to sell him sevoflurane gas and laughing gas to sniff for recreational use, so maybe they'd come through with a couple of drugs that were actually intended for medical purposes.

The sevoflurane gas he used was the worst. Smelled exactly like anchovies to me. But Tomlinson loved the stuff, and would walk around giggling for hours, stinking of marijuana and fish.

I'd told him where to find his cell phone in a brief exchange on the VHF radio. Other than that, I saw no need for us to talk.

We had no pressing business.

Pilar had called me from her hotel room early that morning just as I returned from swimming, and I'd already told her about my e-mail exchange with Prax Lourdes. I'd described the bizarre call on the satellite phone. Told her a lie—that he'd demanded my e-mail address, and that he'd written me directly. Explained it all without mentioning that I'd broken into her internet account, her personal e-mails, and that I'd already read Lourdes' earlier demand that we drive to St. Petersburg.

I'd let her find that letter for herself, then act surprised when she told me.

Behaving as if I were surprised—after all the experience I'd gotten in the last few hours, that'd be no problem.

I'D slept off and on during the day, Ransom keeping me company. She works at Tarpon Bay Marina, managing the little store there, and also at the Sanibel Rum Bar & Grille. She said things had been so slow, taking a day off was no big deal.

That indicated to me the degree of her concern.

It was showing. The turmoil, all the stress, were getting to me, or she wouldn't have taken a day away from work.

I found myself worrying about Dewey—Where was she? Why hadn't I heard from her? And Lake—Would they let him write me? And when?

I thought about Tinman. Who the hell was he?

I knew a man who might be able to tell me. . . .

I have a satellite phone of my own. Seldom need it; keep it packed away because I can use it to contact only one man: a guy named Hal Harrington.

Hal's with the U.S. State Department. He's also a member of a covert operations team that is known, to a very few, as the Negotiating and System Analysis Group—the Negotiators, for short.

Because the success of the team requires that members blend easily into most societies worldwide, each man was provided with a legitimate and mobile profession when he joined. Harrington became a computer software wizard.

Another of the group's members became a marine biologist.

The trouble with becoming a Negotiator was that, once you were in, there was no getting out. You could never be free again.

Whenever I talked with Hal, he reminded me of that.

"Quid pro quo," he would say, granting most technical favors I asked, but always giving me an assignment in return.

I hadn't talked with him in a while.

I decided not to talk to him now. But I did send him an e-mail, asking for information on Thackery. Did the crazed surfer ever go by the alias "Tinman"?

I knew that, ultimately, it would mean another assignment from Hal.

AFTER THAT, I paced; checked my AOL account over and over for e-mails. I paced; glared at the phone, willing it to ring, hoping that I would hear Dewey's voice on the other end.

I telephoned Janet Mueller twice, pressing her to contact the woman, each time stressing how important it was that I speak with her. When I picked up the phone a third time, I stopped and had to vow to myself I wouldn't pester Janet again.

There was something else I was obsessing about, too: Tomlinson.

Except for his quick trip into the marina, he'd spent the day out there all alone aboard *No Mas*. From the windows of my lab, I could see the vessel's old white hull at anchor, pointing like a slow weather vane against the tide. With all that was going on in my life, I had to ask myself, under normal circumstances, wouldn't I have sought out his opinions and advice? Wouldn't I have hopped in my skiff and gone a-calling? Or invited him in for an early beer?

The answer was an unqualified yes. He would have been the first person I would have turned to for help. Ransom was correct. The man had come to seem like a brother to me.

That had changed, though. For now, anyway. Maybe for all time.

WHICH is probably why, that afternoon when I nearly collided with Tomlinson as I exited the Red Pelican Gift Shop, I tried way too hard to mask my uneasiness—which, of course, just made my uneasiness more obvious.

The most startling thing, though, was that Tomlinson's manner was just as stilted.

"Whoops, sorry . . . *oh*. Hello, Tomlinson."

"Doc? Hey, great to see you, *compadre*. Just really . . . great."

"In for supplies?"

"Oh yeah, man. Beans and beer."

"Food and beer, well . . . you need those."

"Absolutely. Food, yeah . . . even for me, eating is, like . . . mandatory."

"Yeah, sure. Food. Um. Did you . . . did you get the note I left about the medical supplies?"

"Oh yeah. My doctor buddies are already working on the list."

"Good. Good. Well . . . nice seeing you."

"Right back at you, amigo!"

Walking away from him, I could feel sweat beading on my back, and I knew that my face had to be flushed. I was already dreading our next meeting, when from behind me I heard him call after me, "Doc. Hey, Doc? Hold it just a sec, would you?"

I turned to look. I was standing in the parking lot. He'd stopped just outside the marina office, next to the doorway that led up the steps to Jeth's upstairs apartment. He was conservatively dressed for him: shirtless, khaki British walking shorts belted with a rope, and a knitted Rastafarian cap, red, black, and green, holding his hair in a bun.

I said, "Something wrong?"

I couldn't remember ever seeing him looking so melancholy. "Yeah, Doc. Your aura, man. It's impossible for me not to notice. You don't even have to tell me, and I already know."

"Know what?"

"I know something's happened."

I said, "I don't understand what you're talking about."

"What I'm talking about is you. That something very heavy has gone down. It's like—*ouch*—iceberg country. A solid cold wall has dropped. That's the vibe I'm getting. Emotional cataclysm; bridges burning." He seemed to be thinking it through as he spoke, feeling the words. "An event has taken place that has changed the entire social interactive structure. You've . . . discovered *something*. A real mind-bender. Is any of this making sense?"

My tone flat, I said, "No. But that's not unusual when I listen to you."

"Are you sure? Then why is it I get the feeling you're pissed off at me?"

I said, "I don't know. Is there some reason I *should* be pissed off?"

He still wore that poignant expression, but there was now also a spark of awareness. "O.K. I'm beginning to tune in. Like clouds moving away from the void."

"I'm glad one of us understands, because I don't." I turned to leave.

"In that case, I'll walk along with you, if you don't mind. Maybe we can hash it out."

I didn't want him to walk with me, but couldn't think of a quick excuse that made sense. I looked from one to another of the marina's main roofed structures. There are four: the combination office and take-out restaurant, the Red Pelican Gift Shop, Mack's house, which is beyond the docks at the edge of the mangroves, and the storage barn and repair shop behind it.

I was on my way to the storage barn because Mack, for mysterious reasons, had invited me and some of the guides to a private meeting there. So I used that. I said, "I'm in kind of a rush. Mack wants to see me about something—it's important; I'm not sure what. And I'm late."

I've known Tomlinson so long that I can read his mannerisms nearly as well as he can read mine. The gentle smile on his face told me, *I know you're lying, but it's O.K.,* even as he spoke, saying, "It won't take long, and I'll walk fast. Promise."

I began to walk again and he joined in step. "I heard about Dewey splitting. Man, I am so sorry. As you know, good women can't dump me fast enough once they catch on to how truly weird my act is. So that kind of emotional pain is something I've got a handle on. Like, if you need an ear to listen?"

I said, "What I need is to find out where she went. She's so damn stubborn. I need to discuss something with her. There's a very important *reason* that we need to talk. But she won't. So, if you know where she is, I'd appreciate your telling me."

He was shaking his head. "I told everybody I don't want to know. That's 'cause if you asked, I knew I'd tell you, man. It's the lady's gig; Dewey's secret. Not mine to share. But Doc—" He seemed to put additional meaning in his emphasis. "There's nothing in the world you couldn't ask me. Not if I knew the answer. Or do for you. The same deal, man. *Anything.*"

I stopped walking. Stood there looking into his blue and ancient mariner's eyes. "It makes me nervous when friends put little messages between the lines. It's like they're trying to make me guess. Or find out what I know. If you want to tell me something, just come right out and tell me."

He thought about that for a moment, considering, before he said, "You're in a hurry. You've got that meeting with Mack. So maybe tonight, we can have a few beers, sit out and feed the mosquitoes. Yeah, Doc"— this was added reflectively—"I think we've got a few things we need to discuss. Maybe clear the air a little, huh?"

Not wanting to sound too unsociable—he was already guarded—I told him, that reminded me: I had a Tucker Gatrell story for him that he was going to love.

THE junk and marine litter that has accumulated around the storage barn and repair shop is screened from the parking lot by a wooden fence that runs back and along the mangrove swamp that encircles the marina and Dinkin's Bay.

The marina's fishing guides—Jeth, Felix, Neville, Alex Payne, Dave— were already there when I arrived, sitting on packing crates or leaning against savaged outboards, all looking at Mack, who'd been speaking. Mack was wearing green Bermuda shorts, a yellow tank top, and a massive straw hat, and was smoking a cigar that was just long enough to extend beyond the brim.

When I appeared, Mack paused long enough to relight the cigar and say, "See? I invited Doc. That proves I'm not crazy."

I wondered what that meant.

Mack is Graeme MacKinley, a New Zealander who sailed to the States years ago and took a flier on a marina. He is stocky, plain-spoken, and a superlative businessman who's tight with a dime but big-hearted when it comes to philanthropy, and with the quirky cast of characters who live and work at his marina. Like many foreign nationals who've done well in the States, he's both ardently patriotic and also a raging libertarian who despises government regulations and interference. When it comes to marina business, he rarely asks opinions or takes polls.

Unaware of the meeting's purpose or what he meant, I replied, "Sorry to disagree, Mack, but I've come to the conclusion that almost everyone at this marina is a tad crazy—including me," which got a small laugh and, to my own surprise, seemed to lighten my mood a little.

Mack said, "Oh, you got a point there, mate!" and then added to no one in particular, "Fill 'im in, gents. Tell the doctor what we're doing here."

Big Felix Blane took charge. "You wanna talk crazy, well, Mack's come up with one of the craziest ideas of all time. You know the Sanibel police boat? That shitty little tri-hull they keep moored next to the *Island Belle*? They almost never use the thing, and the engine's about shot."

I said, "Sure, I know the boat," picturing a stained hull with an older Evinrude outboard. I'd heard the department had gotten it in some kind of sting a few years back.

Captain Felix said, "The boat just sits there, they don't keep the bottom clean, but it could be an O.K. little skiff if they cared a little more about it. Which they don't seem to. So maybe that's why the police department hasn't paid their wet-slippage rent in a couple months."

"Seven months," Mack corrected sharply. "For seven months, their bean-counters have been stringing me along. They don't return my calls, they ignore my letters. I'm sick of being treated like a fool."

"That's what this is about," Captain Dave said. "The Sanibel Police Department hasn't paid their rent, and Mack's on the warpath. Now he wants us to do something that's just plain nuts."

"Seeking justice isn't nuts," Mack said priggishly. "Do you remember what country you're in? Or a thing called the Constitution? I've called them, I've sent notices. I've gone down to City Hall in person; wasted hours trying to collect that goddamn debt. They made *me* fill out forms because *they* haven't paid their bills.

"How long would I be walking around free on the streets if the tables were turned? If I owed the city money? If I told them to go piss up a rope when they came to collect?" Mack had been gesturing with his cigar, but now jammed it back in the corner of his mouth. "It's the principle of the thing, damn it! When the government starts ignoring the basic rules of commerce, we're all taking it up the bum. The department owes me money. They refuse to pay, so I've had it. I've given them every chance."

I could see that Mack had been worked up about it for a while.

I asked, "So what are you going to do?"

Jeth Nichols had avoided eye contact after our minor confrontation the night before, but that was now forgotten as he said to me with emotion, "He wants us to *steal* the Sanibel Police Department's boat. *All* of us. We could get in a lot of trouble for doin' something like that, couldn't we, dah-dah-Doc?"

Sounding as if he really were a little crazed, Mack said, "I want you to *sink* the son-of-a-bitch, not just steal her. Punch her full of holes, tow her out, and make a reef. We'll catch enough grouper and snapper off that piece of junk to pay their tab twenty times over. Just what the bastards deserve, too." He said the last as if he could feel the satisfaction it would bring him, already anticipating how he was going to feel.

Captain Felix said to me, "He says we all have to help sink the boat, 'cause that way no one will talk. Every single one of us has to have a hand in it. We've already pulled her onto the canoe trail, out of sight, so the live-aboards won't know."

"If we don't all hang together, we'll all surely hang separately," Mack said, paraphrasing the famous Benjamin Franklin quote.

Jeth appeared stricken. "Jesus Christ, they can still hang you for stealing shit from a police depa-pah-partment?"

Mack calmed him with a look and a gesture before adding, "I've al-

ready locked the marina gate, so there's no chance of any outsiders coming around. What I suggest you gents do is take axes, crowbars—" He
pointed to the repair shop. "We've got all the tools right here. Knock
plenty of holes in the hull. Take out all the flotation and fuel, then plug
the holes with something temporary."

Puffing on the cigar, he looked at me. "Rags, maybe? Old life jackets?
Whatta you think, Doc?"

Sounding calm, but a little helpless, too, Captain Felix said, "He wants
us to do it tonight before the moon gets up too bright. Tell him he's crazy,
Doc. Steal the freaking police department's boat? Jesus, what are we
going to say if we get caught?"

Mack, all the guides, everyone was looking at me. Under any other circumstances, in any other mood, I would probably have used some gradual,
delicate line of reasoning so that Mack would finally decide for himself
that it wasn't a good idea. But it wasn't a normal circumstance, and I was
in anything but a normal frame of mind.

I looked at my watch—I could spare a little time before checking e-mails
and meeting Tomlinson. Plus, I was aware, on some subtle level of con-
sciousness, that this was a good thing for me to be doing; a healthy diversion,
interacting with the marina family. Earlier, as I'd driven past the party the
Jensen brothers were hosting, I'd thought about how emotional trauma
distorts our normal orbit. But now the strong, not-so-normal gravitational
power of Dinkin's Bay was pulling me back into line again.

To Mack, I said, "What I don't understand is, we get along fine with the
police. They're a good bunch, from the top right on down. It doesn't have
anything to do with—"

"It's not the uniforms," he interrupted. "It's the bloody bean-counters.
The suits. It's not the cops themselves."

"How many months are they late?"

"Eight, if you count May. And I think I will."

I said, "You've tried all the formal steps to try and get them to pay?"

Nodding, Mack replied, "They enjoy making me jump through their
bloody little hoops. They could pay. The bean-counters know they *should*
pay. But I can't sue 'em, and the bastards know that, too. So when they

come lookin' for their boat, I'm gonna say I don't know what happened to it, and I don't care. That boat stopped being my responsibility when they stopped payin'."

I looked from Jeth to Felix to Dave. I felt more like myself than I'd felt in days, yet what I said to them was way out of character: "Guys, I can't believe I'm saying this, and I know you never expected it. But Mack's right. Let's go sink that son-of-a-bitch."

A FEW minutes before moonrise, I ran my 21-foot Maverick flats skiff past Woodring Point, the big 225-horsepower Merc blasting a platinum rooster tail toward the stars as I ran throttle-heavy toward the pocket of lights that marked the marina. I left the channel at Green Point, just before the old fish house ruins, touching the jack plate toggle to raise the engine, then increased trim and steered straight toward my lab, running fifty miles an hour across the flat in two feet of water, sometimes less, sometimes more.

As I expected, Tomlinson was in the house waiting on me. His dinghy was tied up next to my 24-foot trawl boat, the old cedar plank netter I bought in Chokoloskee and use for dragging up specimens. The moon was already so bright that I could read the words SANIBEL BIOLOGICAL SUPPLY painted on the stern.

As I tied my skiff, he called from inside, "I was about to give up on you. Or come looking. Since we met, I can't remember you ever being late before."

I called back, "I'll be right up. Help yourself to a beer."

"I've already helped myself to three. I'm doing the fifteen-minute dosage tonight. But thanks anyway."

He meant a beer every fifteen minutes.

I ignored the urge to hose and flush my skiff, and the guilt that went with ignoring maintenance, and went upstairs, taking the wooden steps two at a time. Tomlinson was in the galley, kneeling at the little refrigerator when I came in. He looked at me for a moment, then looked again, his expression a mix of surprise and uneasiness . . . but then the uneasiness changed to unexpected relief.

"Holy shitskee, what happened to you?"

I looked at my arms, looked at my legs, and saw that I was streaked with gray marl, bits of turtle grass, and that my shorts and shirt were a mess of mud and shell. There was some blood involved, too.

Stripping off my shirt, I said, "Have you ever tried to sink a boat? Intentionally, I mean. I had no idea, but it's damn near impossible. You know that cheap tri-hull runabout the cops use sometimes? It's like a damn floating vampire. It just won't die."

Tomlinson grinned—oh yeah, he was very relieved that I'd provided some amusing way to neutralize the discomfort between us. The fact was, I was glad, too. But I also wondered if, after this meeting, there would ever be an easy moment between us again.

After he'd assured me that Pilar hadn't heard anything new from the kidnappers or from Lake, Tomlinson asked, "You were intentionally trying to sink the police department's boat? *Why?*"

I explained the reason, and then how we'd gone about trying to sink the thing, as I changed into dry clothes—I'd shower later, after checking my e-mails. Just because they hadn't contacted Pilar didn't mean that I hadn't been sent a note.

We'd knocked holes in the runabout's hull, I told him. We'd removed all the foam flotation—or so we thought. We plugged the holes with old life jackets and rags, then connected all the plugs with a complex network of fishing line so that we could remove all the plugs with a single yank.

I said, "We towed it out into about ten feet of water near the mouth of the bay—you know the spot. When we pulled the plugs, the damn boat filled halfway up and wouldn't sink any farther."

We'd spent the next forty minutes hacking, chopping, and then finally, with all of us in the water, physically trying to stomp and pull the hull under.

"The guides are still out there. When I left, the tri-hull was sitting with its bow out of the water, just high enough so you could still see the Sanibel Police Department reflector stencil from, oh, say, no less than a quarter-mile away. I thought Jeth was going to start bawling, he was so upset. But then he got caught under the boat's stern somehow and nearly drowned, and that seemed to calm him right down."

I was tucking in my shirt, hurrying toward the computer in my lab as I added, "The last I heard, they were sending a skiff back to the marina to load up that old stove that's piled with the storage junk. How they're going to fit a stove on a fishing skiff, I don't know. But the plan is to shove the stove off onto the deck of the police boat, and the weight of the stove is supposed to take it under. You know, finally kill the bastard. A stove through the heart."

Tomlinson and I were both laughing as I sat at the computer and began the process of signing on to AOL. But then I stopped laughing and turned to look at him, suddenly serious. "You know something, Tomlinson? Even with all the crap that's going on in my life, I realized something tonight. Just hanging out with the guides, doing something as idiotic as trying to sink a stolen boat, it reminded me. We've got great lives here. Dinkin's Bay's a great little place. A bunch of fun people who don't take life too seriously, but with enough fabric and character to give a damn. To know that other people's lives matter. Plus, they really seem to care about us."

He was nodding, listening carefully but not making eye contact as I continued.

"For a couple of tropical drifters like you and me, it's probably the closest we'll ever come to having a home. I'd hate to see anything screw that up because of old . . . old *stuff.* Things that happened in the past. Events, or old promises. Alliances that maybe seemed the right thing to do at the time. Bullshit like that is absolute poison, and it always comes out sooner or later if you try and keep it hidden."

Now he was looking at me, his eyes wise and old as he tugged nervously at a strand of frazzled, sun-bleached hair, still nodding, and I could see that he understood.

He said softly, "I was right this afternoon; right about you changing. So there's something I wish I'd've told you a long time ago. Back when I figured out I could trust you. Back when I realized that you and I—about the two most unlikely nerds in the world—were going to be friends. I'm damn sorry about that, Marion."

I said, "From one nerd to another, we all make mistakes. I've got scars from dealing with my scars." I studied his face evenly for a moment before adding, "But that doesn't mean everything can be forgiven. Some mistakes, there's no statute of limitations."

I waited through his long, thoughtful silence, then watched him stand a little straighter before he said, "I know that. I realize the risk. Even so, there's something I need to tell you—"

Listening, I turned, glanced at the computer screen . . . and then did a quick double-take before interrupting, "*Whoa*. Hold it right there," stopping Tomlinson in midsentence.

I was holding up a warning index finger, my eyes fixed on the screen again as I added, "If you've waited this long, it can wait a little longer. There's an e-mail here from Lake. I've got an e-mail from my son."

TWENTY
ONE

THERE was an old, blind, black carney who lived in the trailer park, and who owned a utility van that had once been a phone truck. He'd bought it so neighbors could drive him places when he needed to go. Lourdes used the van to get around Tampa, and the old carney stayed with the boy when he was away.

On Sunday afternoon, Prax had driven through Tampa, then across the bridge onto exclusive Davis Island, where Tampa General Hospital was located. It was a huge complex, eight stories or so high, a pink-looking color, with helicopter pads and a multistory parking garage. The hospital was right there by the water, and within easy jogging distance of lots of older, classy-looking million-dollar homes.

He'd spent some time driving the streets, getting to know the area in daylight so he'd be comfortable there at night, looking at the mansions set back on shady lawns, all the rich assholes probably out playing golf or tennis or some other bullshit game.

On Monday, he'd come to the same area, but in the 22-foot Boston Whaler Outrage he'd bought for cash and kept at a marina on the Alafia River, which was just down the road from his trailer. Nice boat with twin 150-HP Yamahas, and the bastard could fly.

He'd cruised back and forth by the hospital, then cruised the canals looking at the mansions again, wondering which one was owned by his e-mail pal, Dr. Valerie. He kept his face covered with a bandana—not unusual for fishermen with skin cancers in Florida

That was the afternoon he was pretty sure he spotted her. Her e-mails hadn't given him any information about where she lived or her personal life, but she'd mentioned a couple times that she was close enough to the hospital to jog to and from work. So Prax had idled around the car bridges pretending to fish when, a little after sunset, there she was: a fit-looking, middle-age woman in fancy turquoise and black running tights, wearing a pink visor. She came jogging out from what seemed to be the back of the hospital, across the parking lot, then took a left toward the island's cozy little business district.

She looked smaller than he had imagined her to be. In fact, Dr. Valerie looked tiny. It was weird how fame always seemed to make people look smaller in real life.

Prax had gotten the boat up on plane, trying to follow along in the general direction. The last he saw her, she'd turned down what he found out was Magnolia Street, which led to a handful of the island's largest homes, all right there on the waterfront.

He was pleased. That narrowed things down.

HE SPENT Wednesday in a rental boat, charging around Miami Beach. Now, on Thursday afternoon, he drove the van once again, but this time straight to the hospital and parked in the parking garage, third level. He had his face expertly wrapped with gauze bandages, one of his hands, too, and he was wearing a green hospital gown over his shorts and T-shirt, as if he were a patient.

Screw it, if someone stopped him, asked him any questions, he'd just say he was a burn victim who wanted to take his own private tour of Tampa General's famous burn center.

What's the worst they could do?

He entered the hospital's East Pavilion wing, walking through the bricked patio—people were eating at the outdoor tables there, blackbirds whistling above them in a tree. It seemed more like a modern shopping center—Christ, there was even a McDonald's, along with other kinds of shops and crap.

Inside, he found a directory on the wall, then took the elevator to the sixth floor. He stepped out into a wide, well-lighted hallway to see a black sign with white lettering that read: WELCOME TO TAMPA GENERAL REGIONAL BURN CENTER.

Visiting hours were listed below, followed by: BURN ICU VISITORS MUST CALL BEFORE ENTERING.

Prax decided to try and get into the ICU area anyway, just to see how far he could take it.

He did, too—but only long enough to take a quick look. He saw the nurses' station—counter and walls done in blue pastels—with staff sitting and standing, talking or hurrying past, everyone wearing surgical scrubs and sometimes plastic, elastic hair coverings. Behind the counter, above a computer monitor, was a glass case filled with personal photographs: sons and daughters and grandbabies.

It gave the place a personal touch that made Lourdes oddly uneasy.

Beside and behind the nurses' station, in a separate but open room, was one of the things he'd come hoping to find. It was an entire wall of medicines and medical supplies, everything stored in tall metal lockers, on shelves faced with glass so that you could see what was inside.

Prax realized that he didn't have a chance in hell of getting into the room unnoticed and stealing the drugs he wanted. Even if he pulled the fire alarm and caused a panic, there were too many security people roaming around.

A disappointment.

Something that didn't disappoint, though, was the surgical schedule he found on a clipboard that was hanging on a wall. This was down the hall, near a far less busy Nurses' Station C3.

He read: *Thursday: Dr. Santos, 2000 hrs, Operating Room II.*

He scanned down to read also: *Thursday: Dr. Santos, 1400 hrs, Operating Room II.*

So maybe the famous lady was in the hospital right now, working her magic?

He followed the signs until he was outside the double doors of Operating Room II, looking at signs that warned he could not pass through the electronic doors without being scrubbed.

Coming through those doors, from inside the room, he could hear music playing. Loud music. Some kind of opera-sounding stuff, which always sounded like make-believe tragedy to him and which he hated. But maybe someone famous and sophisticated like Dr. Valerie would like opera.

So maybe she was in there. Judging from the schedule, it looked like she'd be in the same operating room that night, too, working late. Would probably have to jog home alone in the dark.

He wondered if she'd take a break, go home between surgeries, or just stick around the hospital.

Prax returned to his van, drove to the little business district, and waited. At 4:15 P.M., Dr. Valerie jogged by; waved to people eating at outdoor tables, a big smile on her pretty face. Seemed to know everyone.

Yeah, she was tiny. A little miniature woman who photographed like a full-sized fashion model.

He gave it a couple of minutes, then followed her down Magnolia Street to a pale yellow three-story mansion, with columns and fountains and a black wrought-iron fence. He watched her stop, still jogging in place, and punch in some kind of code before opening the gate. It took a while.

Hillsborough Bay was right across the quiet street, with a cement seawall to knock down waves if it was blowing.

Micki, the pushy freighter captain bitch, had called him earlier that day and told him she and her boat would be back in Tampa Bay tomorrow, Friday, and would probably return to Nicaragua very early Saturday morning, or during the day on Sunday.

"But stay on your toes," she'd added. "If they get us loaded and on the transit schedule, we could be casting off earlier. And for me to get your weirdo special cargo aboard's gonna take us a little time. So have everything all set."

They'd already discussed it. The fat captain knew what he was planning to bring—not who, but what—and how to make it work.

She would have two empty 50-gallon drums waiting.

But the jump ahead in schedule had made him feel tense, rushed.

Not now.

Prax could picture his Boston Whaler tied to the seawall in the darkness next to the doctor's house, and the miniature surgeon having to stop to punch in a code at the gate.

He thought, *Perfect.*

LATER that afternoon, Lourdes rushed back to the trailer park, where he put duct tape, a big pillow case, and a rope into the back of the van. He also loaded a fresh gas canister into a mini-blowtorch. He'd bought the thing at Sears. It wasn't much bigger than his hand.

There was something else that he hid in the glove box: a small bottle of ether, wrapped in a hand towel.

After that, he brought the kid inside the trailer with him again. The skin of his cheeks was already on fire, and he could feel the first shock wave of pressure that preceded his headaches.

If Dr. Valerie had the operating room scheduled for eight P.M., there was no telling how late she'd get out. Even so, he wasn't going to risk screwing this up. He wanted to be right there in the boat waiting outside her house, no matter how early or late she was.

Even so, he still had time for a couple of drinks and to lie down on the couch. The combination sometimes made the pain disappear faster.

As he walked toward the living room, the kid said to him, "Let me get on the computer, there's something I've been thinking about. Something I want to show you. I found it yesterday, but you didn't give me time to follow up."

Prax screamed at him, "Fuck off! It's getting so you're starting to give the fucking orders around here, which is bullshit!"

But then Prax remembered that he *had* to let the kid on the internet. He'd told the kid's stubborn asshole father that he'd get a personal e-mail from the boy. So, a short time later he watched Laken sign online.

He felt like slapping the boy out of his seat. The smug little prick always seemed to get his way.

After a few minutes squinting at the monitor and typing fast, the kid stood and said, "Have a look at this."

His head pounding, his skin screaming, Prax sat and read:

Trigeminal neuralgia, often associated with burn scarring, is among the most terrible of chronic pain conditions. The trigeminal nerve is the fifth cranial nerve, and has three branches that are designated as 5-1, 5-2, and 5-3. This nerve supplies sensation to the face.

Neurogenic pain is awful, of a burning quality, and incapacitating. It is also sometimes associated with cluster headaches. Medications may lessen attacks, but seldom work.

The article then went into specific detail.

When Prax had read it through twice, he leaned back and said, "Shit, I think that's *exactly* what I got. I had a doctor in Masagua, a plastic fucking surgeon he called himself, and he couldna figured it out in a hundred years. The stupid damn quack!"

The man tended to get louder and more animated as his pain increased. Now he slapped at the screen. "But what fucking good does it do me to know? It says right here medications don't work. As if I haven't tried every fucking pill on earth! Why'd you even bother me with this bullshit?"

The more furious he became, the calmer the boy always seemed to get. He was very calm now as he said, "That's where you might be wrong. There's a whole new class of drugs, they haven't been out long. They were developed as anticonvulsion medications, but doctors are finding all kinds of ancillary benefits. They're finding out that the medicine changes the chemistry of the brain in some way—it's hard to explain—but these new meds can stop chronic pain. Back pain, pain from scars, that sort of thing."

Christ, now the smug little son-of-a-bitch was talking down to him, like he was stupid.

"I've got a fuckin' brain, asswipe! If you can understand how a pill works, I sure as shit can understand how it works. For all I know, you're making this bullshit up."

The red color had flooded in behind Lourdes' eyes, and he was thinking: *If the little prick talks back to me one more time, I'll drag him down to the river and set his shirt on fire.*

Still very calm, the kid said, "I'm not making it up. This new drug is also helping people who have severe emotional problems—chemical imbalances in the brain. I have a friend who has some problems like that. I'm trying to get her to try them. I think you ought to give it a try, too."

With the kid looking over his shoulder, Prax found information on the internet about the new class of drugs. He spent half an hour reading.

Son-of-a-bitch if the brat wasn't right!

After that, Prax let the kid write the e-mail to his father. But he read it carefully several times to make certain the smug little bastard didn't sneak in any clues about where they were.

When he was convinced that he hadn't, Prax sat at the desk and sent the kid's e-mail to Nicaragua so it could be forwarded.

TWENTY
TWO
_____

THE sender's address was the familiar random mix of letters and numbers at Nicarado.org. But on the subject line, I read "Message from *Chamaeleo.*"

I opened the e-mail, and with Tomlinson leaning eagerly over my shoulder, we read a note written by my son in English:

Hi Doc,

They're letting me write and not giving me much time, but at least it's allowed to be personal. I bet you and Mr. Tomlinson are getting ready for baseball season, huh? I sure like that Wilson catcher's mitt. Why do you think the White Sox ever traded Moe Berg to the Indians?

I've been eating O.K., and been allowed to continue some of my science studies. I think I heard an alligator last night, a series of grunts, and I've definitely seen reddish egrets feeding on the mature tadpole. I also found a gray parakeet nest nearby, even though they prefer coconut palms. But, like lots of places in the mountains of Central America, there don't seem to be any coconut palms. The moon was so bright before sunrise this morning, I could see birds roosting.

Oh, there's another medicine you need to get. It's Neurontin, capsules in the highest dosage. It's important. That's all for now. Today's front-page *headline in the Latin American edition of the* Miami Herald *was about the Chinese increasing their control on the Panama Canal.*

> *Caio, Pescado,*
> *Lake*

Excited, I jumped up and turned away from the computer to see that Tomlinson was beaming, as excited as I was. I grabbed him by the shoulders and shook him as I said, *"Unbelievable.* Do you realize the importance of the things he's saying? Jesus, what a boy!"

Tomlinson was talking at the same time, jumping up and down as if I were bouncing him. "Moe Berg, man! That's the farthest kind of far-out. *I* told him about the dude, man. And now he's *using* it. The kid's a blessed genius."

I said, "On the satellite phone and in my e-mail, I dropped a couple of hints, and he picked right up on what I was asking him to do. He's smuggling information to us. He's trying to tell us where he is through the biological references. That's the only interpretation I can . . . ."

I had begun to sit back at the computer to reread the letter, but then I paused, thinking about it, suddenly worried. "Hey, I just thought of something. What are the chances, do you think, that Lourdes—anybody associated with him—would know who Moe Berg is? That they'd figure it out? Lake would be in even more danger than he is now."

Tomlinson created a circle with thumb and forefinger. "Zero. Hardly anyone in the States even knows who the man was. Central America, it's got to be zilch."

Moe Berg isn't well known, I couldn't argue that. He'd never been a great baseball player, was remembered by only a few—but he was one of the baseball greats of the twentieth century.

Intellectually, Berg had been massively gifted. Athletically, he had not. About Berg, sportswriters of the time said that the oddball catcher could speak seven languages, but couldn't hit in any of them, which was an exaggeration, but close. He'd played more than a dozen years in the major leagues, mostly as a benchwarmer and bullpen specialist, yet somehow he'd managed to be chosen for the 1934 All-Star team, and he'd toured Japan with Babe Ruth, Lou Gehrig, and all the other greats.

It wasn't until decades later that the truth had come out. The .243 lifetime hitter hadn't made the All-Star team because of his skills on the field. He'd made it for the same reason he'd been sent to pre–World War II Germany, and then into Latin America on "goodwill" baseball missions. The catcher was a spy for the OSS.

In Tokyo, when he hadn't been in the bullpen, he'd been out roaming the city, speaking Japanese like a native and using a movie camera to take film of Tokyo Harbor, munitions factories, and the city skyline that would later be invaluable to American bomber pilots.

In Nazi Germany, he'd become "friendly" with nuclear physicists who were also baseball fans.

Berg never married. He died in 1977. His last words, to a hospital nurse, were, "How'd the Mets do today?"

I had to agree with Tomlinson. Berg's name was the perfect signal flag. My son was telling me that his e-mail included imbedded information.

Now it was up to us to decipher it.

TOMLINSON and I both reread the letter several times, the two of us exchanging knowing glances—Lake had given us a hell of a lot of data in just a few sentences—but we kept quiet at first, letting our brains process it.

Finally, Tomlinson said, "What might be helpful is for you to print out a couple of copies of the letter, one for each of us. Make one for Pilar, too. That way, we can read it over a little bit of geography, not tied to one place the whole time. The way my noggin works, the thought process latches onto a kind of rhythm. It seeks its own little beat. So I'm better off loosey-goosey."

As I printed the e-mail, Tomlinson went to the galley. He'd been shirtless, but he returned wearing one of my white lab coats, his bony chest showing.

It was nearly eleven P.M., and the May night was finally cooling.

He was also carrying two cold bottles of beer, each wrapped in a brown paper napkin. As he handed one to me, I said, "When I found this e-mail, it interrupted something you were about to tell me. If you want, go ahead and get it off your chest. Clear the decks so we can concentrate."

He chugged a third of his beer, then wiped his mouth with the back of his hand. "Ummm . . . I'd sorta like to wait, if it's O.K. with you. From a couple of things the boy wrote, I've already got some theories working. My neurons are firing, man. I'd hate to switch turbines now."

"Is that true, or are you just saying that because you've got a case of the jitters?"

He smiled, gave me a what-the-hell shrug, and said, "Little of both. You mind?"

I'd already thought it over, considered the options before I brought it up. It was possible that whatever Tomlinson had to tell me might be so injurious that I wouldn't want him involved with the search for Lake. Could be the end of a friendship. I hoped that wasn't the case—it was unlikely—but there was still that potential.

For now, though, I didn't want to risk losing the use of that big brain of his, so I said, "Yeah, let's get to work on the e-mail now. We can talk later."

Relief. I could see it in him, and he relaxed a little as I continued, "You've read the thing at least as many times as I have. What do you think Lake's telling us?"

"A bunch, man. I think he's told us approximately where they are, geographically. If I don't miss my guess, I think he's told us close to everything we need to narrow it down." He finished his beer with another gulp, placed it on the epoxy counter of my lab station, and began to pace, occasionally glancing at the letter. "First off, though, Doc, I've got to make sure of a few things. You have knowledge and expertise in areas I don't, so I'd like you to tell me a couple of things just to make sure we're working from the same premise. How do you rate the boy's English?"

"Better than most kids here in the States. He's had to study it, really work at getting it right."

"That's what I was hoping you'd say. From his e-mails to me, I've got the same opinion. O.K. . . . so I read this thing assuming that, while there might be a typo or two, Lake wrote exactly what he meant to write. He's probably been thinking about what to say ever since you planted your subliminal message—science is a *language*. And he's being careful. He can't risk giving them a hint he's being cute. He's probably scared shitless. I know I'd be."

Tomlinson was washing his hands together, his concentration intense, getting into it. "Even so, he pulled it off. What I think is, all four animals he mentions, they have a specific double meaning. A place where coconut palms don't grow? That tells us something. Bright moonlight early in the morning! He's got a clear view to the west, which tells us even more."

Then Tomlinson added with the kind of enthusiasm that makes him so endearing, "What I'm willing to bet is, we'll know where your boy is within the next half an hour or so. You're the biologist, and your Spanish is a lot better than mine, so I need to ask you a few more questions, or we can check out a few search engines on the internet for answers. But keep your chin up, amigo. Remember, this is only his first e-mail. If Lake writes us again tomorrow, he'll nail it down."

I was already worrying that, in trying to give us more detailed information, my son would take additional risks, get found out, and be made to suffer for it.

TOMLINSON asked all the right questions. Most I'd already posed to myself.

In reply to his questions, I told him that there was no exact translation for "alligator" in Spanish. Told him that *caimán* was the Spanish word that came closest. *Cocodrilo* was next. And yes, I added, a person who spoke primarily Spanish, when writing in English, might incorrectly translate *caimán* as "alligator," even though they were two very different species of reptiles.

I also told him that, in my opinion, no one would have noticed anything suspicious about the use of "alligator," including Lourdes, who I was certain spoke English.

After listening carefully to my answers, my old friend's eyes were glittering when he then said, "I didn't know about the difference between *caimáns* and alligators until years ago, when the two of us were down in Masagua. I mentioned something about one or the other, and you told me there were no alligators in Central America or South America. That was a shocker. I figured there were gators all over the tropical world. Do you think Lake knows that?"

I said, "I'm sure of it. We exchanged e-mails that had to do with salt-water crocs. About how passive the American croc is compared to the ones in Australia and Africa. He knows about gators, too."

In Tomlinson's expression, I could see it: He *knew*. Understood the significance of that one word.

"So the alligator's a good biological locator. What's the farthest south it ranges? Mexico, maybe?"

I said, "It's an excellent locator. There are many dozens of species of crocodilians worldwide. But there are only two species of alligator. There's a species in China, and then there's our species, the American alligator. You find them in all the Gulf Coast states, Texas, Mississippi, Louisiana, and a few others. But I doubt if they get into Mexico. That far south, I think it would be an anomaly."

Tomlinson said, "So the question we need to answer is, did Lake use the word 'alligator' accurately and with intent?"

I replied softly, "I already know the answer to that. I think he used it correctly. I think he knew exactly what he was doing. There are a couple things in his e-mail that've convinced me. Listen—" I held up the paper and read directly from the letter. "*'I heard an alligator last night, a series of grunts.'* That's important because crocodiles don't bellow or bark. They're quiet animals. So are *caimáns*. Only male gators make the loud grunting sound that you and I've both heard. They make that display during mating season. This is May, Tomlinson. It's mating season."

I continued, "There's something else that suggests to me that Lake wanted us to be sure we understood he meant alligator, nothing else. The way he signed the thing. *Ciao, Pescado.* Literally, it means 'Goodbye, fish.' But it's also slang. Chilean slang. It means 'See you later, alligator.' It's adolescent enough, it wouldn't draw a second look from Lourdes. But very subtly, he's stressing the point. Wherever it is they're hiding, I think Lake actually heard an alligator. He wrote about it because it suited our purpose perfectly."

Tomlinson said carefully, "Then you're saying they've split. They are . . . they're *not* in Central America anymore. The mountains, when he mentions the region, that's a red herring to please Lourdes, make him think he's leading us off the trail instead of to them. Or maybe Lourdes made him stick it in."

I rubbed my forehead, thinking hard, going through the data methodically. "I think he's telling us that he and Lourdes have crossed over the border into the United States."

Whispering, as if he felt a little chill, his eyes slowly widening, Tomlinson said, "Oh my God . . . reddish egrets, and a place where coconut palms don't grow. And the moonlight being so bright just before dawn. I know where they are, man, where they have to be. *Approximately,* I'm saying—"

Tomlinson has a knack for making brilliant, intuitive leaps in what would otherwise be a process of logical thought. Because I didn't want to hear his conclusion now, though, I cut him off, offering a more obvious conclusion: "Yeah, they're on water. Lake's on or near water, with no mountains to the west."

Trying to make him go slower, I added, "I know, I know, we're probably thinking the same thing. But we need to do more research. I want our proofs to point to a conclusion, not the other way around. It's a hell of a mistake to come up with a theory before you're sure of the data. I don't know the exact habits of the reddish egret, and I'm not even sure what a gray parakeet is. Where they're even found. There's a lot more we need to know before we risk bending facts to fit our conclusion."

"There are feral parrots and parakeets all over Florida," Tomlinson said. "I'd bet anything they're here, Lake and the Masked Man. I'll bet Lourdes is running a one-man show, and they're in Florida."

I had a Google search page on the screen. I typed in *reddish egret northernmost range* as I said, "It's a possibility. Let's see what we come up with," before I turned to him and added, "Would you mind checking the library, bring my *Peterson's Field Guide to Eastern Birds,* and the one on reptiles? And the Audubon guides, too. I think there's one entirely about Florida."

Tomlinson's smirk said I was hopelessly backward, but he approved.

When it comes to research, I still prefer books.

TWENTY
THREE

STEP by step, we eliminated all of the Gulf Coast states except for one, because only one met all the requirements detailed in Lake's e-mail: He was being kept on or near a body of freshwater, on a plateau of land or coastline that had an unimpeded view westward. The area had a population of alligators, gray parakeets, reddish egrets, but no coconut palms—which, to me, certainly implied that he was also near saltwater, and on a landmass where coconut palms grew somewhere.

Tomlinson was right. *Florida.*

That established, we tried to hammer down a more exact area in the state. It wasn't easy—but not impossible, either.

Many states have zones of varied flora and fauna—differences often linked to elevation—but few have lines of demarcation as abrupt as those of Florida, a delicate peninsula that is supersensitized to frost, salt, sea wind.

An example: Draw a line across the state. Draw it, roughly, from the northern tip of Key Largo on Florida's east coast to the state's southwestern horn, Cape Sable. The region south of that line includes the tip of the peninsula and all of the Florida Keys. This is the only true tropic zone in the United States. Tropical trees, shrubs, flowers, many mammals, mollusks, crustaceans, corals, insects, and birds otherwise found only in the West Indies, and deep in the Caribbean, flourish here.

Another example of Florida's abrupt demarcations of floral diversity:

Draw a second line from Cape Canaveral on the Atlantic Coast to an area south of Sarasota on the Gulf. It will not be a straight line. Because of the Gulf Stream, the line will move inland from Canaveral several dozen miles, then south to Lake Okeechobee and, finally, across the state to approximately fifteen miles or so south of Sarasota. All land and water below that line is considered a subtropical zone. As in the Florida Keys, many tropical plants, animals, birds, and insects thrive here, including key limes, papaya, mangoes, gumbo limbos—and the coconut palm, which is not considered an indigenous plant, but is emblematic of the tropics.

Twenty miles south of Sarasota, coconut palms grow beautifully—tall with slender dinosaur necks, heavy fronds feathering down, almost always leaning toward the strongest intersectings of sun and water. A few miles north of Sarasota, however, coconut palms seldom survive for long, if they grow at all.

Tampa seems to be the final transitional. The weather there is superb, but you don't find mature coconut palms in Tampa.

The reddish egret is equally emblematic of the American tropics. It is an uncommon, medium-sized wading bird that looks a lot like its relative, the little blue heron. It's easy to identify on the flats, however, because of its bizarre feeding techniques. Most herons stand motionless, like snipers, or stalk their prey with exaggerated slow giraffe-steps.

Not the reddish egret. It runs and lurches with wings held high, like some drunken kung fu expert, jabbing at fish and shrimp with its stiletto beak.

I wondered if that's how Lake had identified the bird he saw. *If* he saw a reddish. Could be he just invented the sighting. Saw it in a book and realized that it was a far more exacting locator than the American alligator.

From the little I'd seen and heard, Prax Lourdes didn't strike me as the Audubon Society type. He'd be oblivious of wildlife around him. Lake could probably make up any wildlife sighting and get away with it.

Tomlinson seemed pleased for both of us that the internet was not nearly as informative as my excellent little library. I felt a sharp adrenal charge when I opened my *Peterson's Field Guide* to the range map for the reddish egret, illustration 91, and saw that the bird lived and bred almost exclusively along the southwest coast of Florida.

Once again, Tampa was the final transitional. With rare, rare exceptions, the reddish egret did not venture north of there.

The gray parakeet reference was not as instructive. It is more commonly known as the monk parakeet because of its hood of green feathers. The hood is sharply contrasted by the bird's gray face and golden breast. The rest of the bird, whether male or female, is chartreuse green except for its orange beak and a fringe of blue feathers on tail and wings. Monk parakeets are known for their complicated, chambered nests.

I've seen them all over the state—particularly around baseball diamonds—flying in chattering flocks, wobbly in flight as if the ancestral memory of pet stores and cages has made them unsteady.

Like the coconut palm, the monk parakeet's not a native, but unlike the tree, the hearty animal ranges all over the country.

We wondered if Lake had avoided calling the bird by its more common name because Lourdes, at least occasionally, wore monk's robes.

The reference in the e-mail that neither of us could decipher was the line that read, *"I've definitely seen reddish egrets feeding on the mature tadpole."*

A mature tadpole is a frog. Lourdes may not have known that, but my son certainly did. In Florida, we have pig frogs, leopard frogs, barking dog frogs, bullfrogs—all kinds of frogs. And larger wading birds, which are fierce predators, sometimes feed on them, just as they feed on snakes and lizards. Why hadn't Lake just come right out and used the word "frog"? Why was it to be avoided?

Tomlinson and I discussed the odd wording—*feeding on the mature tadpole,* singular—and decided it was, most probably, an accidental error in syntax.

If there was additional meaning, we could not grasp it.

"That's O.K. We're closing in on them," Tomlinson said. "The map's getting smaller and smaller."

He meant that literally. Because I've traveled so much, I have a good collection of maps. We had a map of Gulf Coast states open on my stainless-steel dissecting table. Each time we eliminated an area, we would fold it out of sight. The map was now the size of a thick paper towel, and showed only the Gulf Coast section of Florida between Cedar Key and Englewood.

Now I watched Tomlinson bracket Tampa Bay with thumb and fore-finger. He touched Tarpon Springs to the north, Anna Maria Island to the south. "They're somewhere between here," he said. "Maybe on some is-land. Just because Lake didn't see coconut palms doesn't mean there might not be a few around, so let's hedge a little to the south. But more likely they're in the Tampa–St. Petersburg area. That e-mail message that Lourdes canceled, the one that told us to drive to St. Pete? That's sugges-tive. That tells me Lake and the Masked Man are hiding out somewhere close to there."

I agreed. "When he had us driving around Miami with that tattooed giant, he kept an eye on us from a boat. Do you think it's reasonable to as-sume, if he is holed up in the Tampa area, that he has access to a boat? Be-cause if you think he does, I'm going to load my skiff and run up there in the morning. I can poke around and maybe get a lucky break or two while you and Pilar stay in touch on this end." I glanced at my watch: 11:20 P.M. "Hell, I'm tempted to go tonight."

Tomlinson said, "Even if he doesn't have a boat, we know they're near the water. So, yeah, your fast stinkpot might be just what the doctor or-dered. But wait till morning, man. We've got too much other stuff to do. Or you know what might make more sense? You trailer your boat, and I sail *No Mas* up the coast. That way, we have a water base, water transport, and ground transport."

It was a perfectly reasonable proposal, so I couldn't refuse, but I found it oddly disappointing. There's something freeing about stocking a boat with food, drink, and ice, then heading out over unencumbered water. After all the stress I'd been under, it's what my instincts told me to do.

Which was why it was difficult not to grab the keys to my skiff, just get in the boat, and go. I kept pacing to the lab's north window and staring out into the moon-bright bay. My son was almost certainly out there. Not so far away in this night. Beyond a few islands, removed by a few bays.

So, to keep my mind occupied, I used Tomlinson to talk a couple of subjects through. A few things were troubling me. They just didn't add up. Like Lourdes' motives for coming to the United States. It'd been on my mind since I first began to suspect that Lourdes was in Florida, so it was my turn to pose some question to Tomlinson.

I said, "Why would he take the risk? And *how?* You saw the photos of what his face looked like. Even if he managed to smuggle Lake into the country on a private plane or boat, how could a man with those kinds of injuries travel around unnoticed, unquestioned, with a kidnapped boy?"

Tomlinson said, "I've been thinking about that ever since Pilar first showed us the photos of Lourdes. Since Tuesday when you said you couldn't understand how a man with a face like his could blend in with the general population and avoid the Nicaraguan cops. Doc, what I keep coming back to is, you're *right.* I suppose that, in fact, it's possible that he could do it. But, in reality, it's a statistical improbability. There's a fine difference between the two, which I'm sure you realize. What's the Arthur Conan Doyle line that you like? Eliminate the impossible, and whatever remains—however improbable—is your answer."

I was nodding, tracking the logic, because I'd been thinking the same thing. "In the video, he put off a weird, theatrical vibe. He could be dressed up in some kind of costume, something that covers his face. Or he could bandage his face as if his burn scars were still fresh."

Tomlinson said slowly, "Yeah . . . I suppose. And, yeah, you're right about the theatrical business . . ."

I was listening to a fast boat outside heading in our direction, slowing on its approach, as I added, "Aside from that, I agree with you: It's highly improbable that a man wearing a mask, or with a face that's been scarred, can travel around incognito. So a reasonable hypothesis is that either his face has been changed in some way, or . . . or the man we are dealing with is not Praxcedes Lourdes. We haven't thought about that. What if it's *not* the same person?"

Both of us were now listening to the approaching boat when my telephone began to ring—I'd just signed off from the internet, making the phone line available for the first time in more than an hour.

I walked across the lab to answer the phone as Tomlinson walked to the window to see who was coming up in the boat.

It was Dewey calling.

I **LISTENED** to my estranged lover say, "Jesus Christ, you talk on the phone for hours. Like some old woman jabbering to Thelma about her damn gall bladder operation or something. Or some old fart rambling on with some dugout buddy about his last woody, it was so many years ago he can barely remember, and how he shoulda blown it a kiss goodbye because that would have been the last action he ever got. The older you get, the more pathetic you are, Ford. I think dumping you may've been the smartest decision I've ever made in my life."

I was grinning, but I felt a welling of emotion, too, that made my voice tight. "You're as sweet-natured as ever, Dew. It's so good to hear your voice. Where the hell are you? We need to talk. I . . . I miss you a lot."

"We *are* talking, numb-nuts. We'd have been talking an hour ago if you'd shake the moths out of that billfold of yours and pay for a designated computer line. I *know* you, you hate talking on the phone." Her voice softened—tough jock act over—and she nearly broke into tears as she added, "So I know the real reason the line was busy. You were tunneled into that computer of yours, doing some kind of research, into your Thoreau act, oblivious to the current century and everything else. And I . . . I miss you, too, Doc."

Judging from the poor reception, she was calling long distance from someplace with antiquated service, or she was on a cell phone. The way her words faded in and out, I got the mental image of telephone wires strung across desolate countryside, swaying in the night wind.

So maybe Europe, returned to visit her old lover, Walda. Or the wilds of New York. Or someplace in the Midwest where she'd once said her family had roots. Or maybe, just maybe, calling from a cell phone aboard a boat only a few marinas away. Impossible to tell.

When Tomlinson realized it was Dewey, he'd given me a double thumbs-up and left me alone in the lab. Even so, I walked to the wall of aquaria so that my voice would be muted by the sound of bubbling aerators before I said, "Where are you? I'll fly to where you are, or I'll meet you halfway. Or I can—"

I stopped in midsentence. Realized that I couldn't go anywhere to meet her. I was heading to Tampa in the morning.

She interrupted as if reading my mind, "The thing you need to concentrate on is finding your son. I know that this must be a terrible time for you. He comes first. There's nothing more important. So maybe the timing's exactly right for this, you and me taking some time apart. Is there any news?"

I gave her a condensed version of the progress we'd made in narrowing down the search for Lake, ending, "The truth is, the timing couldn't be worse. I need you here. I miss you, I miss our friendship. I realize how much now. I also realize that the things you overheard me saying to Pilar the other night—they were absolute bullshit. It was ridiculous. It was fantasy. I didn't mean any of it."

"Doc, I don't want to go back over that. It hurts too much. But what I've got to wonder is, would you be apologizing to me now if the lady had said yes to you instead of no. It hurts like hell coming in second in the Marion-Ford-picks-a-lifetime-love contest."

I said, "Give me a chance to prove you wrong. Come home, I'll show you." And because I could think of no delicate way into the subject, I added, "We have lots of important things to discuss. Like the pregnancy test. What were the results? I think I have a right to know."

It was the wrong thing to say.

"*Right?* Don't talk to me about rights, pal. Not after the hell I've been through in the last two days. Besides, I told you I wasn't going to take the test, so what makes you so sure I did?"

My stumbling silence seemed to infuriate her even more. "Stop assuming things about me, Ford, O.K.? Because that really pisses me off! I'll call you again when I feel like it. That's *my* right."

The phone went dead.

Shit.

I don't have caller I.D., but I knew that our local service had a feature that makes it possible to dial Star 57 and retrieve the number of the previous caller. I pressed the three digits, got a recording that said I would be charged for the service, then listened to an automated voice tell me that the caller's number had been blocked.

Shit!

I walked out of the lab and let the screen door slam behind me. Tomlinson was on the lower deck, standing in moonlight near the big wooden fish tank with Jeth Nichols and Captain Alex. The outdoor porch light was on, so he could apparently see my expression, because when I stopped on the deck above them, he said, "Are you O.K.? You don't look so good, my amigo. Why don't I trot inside right quick and grab you a beer?"

I said, "I'm fine," snapping at him without intending to. Then to Jeth, I said, "Are you guys still having problems with that runabout?"

Captain Alex said, "If you and Tomlinson have the time, we need help real bad. We got the stove loaded on Jeth's old Suncoast, *Jacks or Better,* but the stove was too much weight, and now his old boat's out there taking on water, she's about to go under. The only thing keeping her on the surface is, we've got her rafted to the police boat, and you couldn't sink that son-of-a-bitch with dynamite."

Jeth put in miserably, "Come the morning, the cops is gonna find my bah-bah-boat tied to theirs. I just know it, I just know it. Find their boat all chopped full of holes, my fingerprints all over the place, and some of my blood, too. I'm gonna get arrested again, and they still hang people for doing this kind of idiotic shit. And it's all Mack's fault!"

Sounding serious, but loving it, Tomlinson said to me, "I don't see how we can refuse. Not if there's a chance Jeth may be executed."

Before I changed back into my wet clothes, I told Tomlinson, "We're not done with our talk yet."

He told me, "I know."

TWENTY
FOUR

THE next morning, Friday, I walked through my lab, going over the things-to-do list I was leaving for Janet Mueller, who'd be watching the place for me, and checked my big fish tank a final time.

Then, carrying my canvas duffel and a briefcase containing a half-million dollars in cash, I walked the creaky boardwalk through the mangroves to where my blue Chevy pickup sat, Maverick flats boat already racked on its galvanized trailer astern . . . and I stopped, frozen.

Leaning against my boat were the twin Nicaraguan hoods, Elmase and Hugo, the two stocky butcher-block thugs, beards heavier around their mustaches, still dressed in the same gaudy clothes.

The black Chevy was parked next to my pickup, the GPS locator right there on the dash, color screen aglow. Pilar's satellite phone, I remembered, was locked inside my pickup, along with Tomlinson's borrowed laptop.

So why was I surprised?

Judging from the beards and the wrinkled clothes, it looked like the Nicaraguans hadn't been out of the Collier County jail for long. I hadn't checked my phone messages, and so, presumably, had missed Tamara Gartone's notification call.

Maybe Merlin Starkey's call, too—if he hadn't already fulfilled his threat and been reassigned to temporary duty by the Florida Department of Law

Enforcement. In which case, he might already be in line behind these two, following me around.

Grinning at me, showing a golden tooth, wearing his black guayabera and shiny white shoes, Hugo said in Spanish, "Well, well, well, we been waiting for you. Waiting for the big gringo with glasses. Señor 'If your hands don't die before your brain'—I still think that such a funny thing to say, dude."

Elmase was not smiling. Maybe that fresh black eye and swollen lip had something to do with his foul humor. He stood there with thick fists on thick hips, looking grim, his white straw Panama hat pulled low, his neon pink shirt torn in places. "Yeah, man, but callin' us pimps, man, that not such a funny thing. Why you go and say something so mean like that? A pimp, man, he hangs out with whores, man. Hugo and me, we don't got to pay the women we hang with. Hardly never."

I would have chuckled if I hadn't been so edgy. If these guys charged me both at once, I didn't have much of a chance. They'd take the money, no problem.

I said, "You know what, Elmase? You're right. That was a damn thoughtless thing for me to say. So please accept my apologies." I touched my gray shorts, my blue chambray work shirt. "As if I know anything about clothes."

Elmase looked at Hugo out of his swollen eye, placated, his expression saying, *At least he admits it. He don't know nothing about style.*

As I stood there, I was trying to decide my best out if they came at me. I was gauging the distance to the boardwalk, estimating my chances of making it down the walkway and jumping into deep water before one of them caught me. If I got one or both of them into the water, the odds were instantly changed. The advantage was mine.

They'd come to finish the job for Balserio—why else would they be there?

So I was surprised, and momentarily relieved, to hear Hugo say, "The reason we come to find you is, we got a message for you from the General. Hey—*relax*, dude. It ain't nothing bad. It's our one last job for that crazy fool."

I didn't relax, but I swung my duffel into the back of the pickup, pretending as if I had. "Oh really? What's the message?"

Elmase said to Hugo, "We supposed to give it to the woman, man. The General's wife. Not just this dude." Then to me, he said, "Where is Pilar Fuentes, man? We give you both the message, we're outta here, I promise. All I want to do, man, is get back to Miami and change clothes. Like, we're in a *hurry*."

Pilar was aboard *No Mas* with Tomlinson, but I said, "I have no idea where she is. I wouldn't tell you, anyway. You know that. So just give the message to me. I'll pass it along."

The two of them had a short visual exchange before Hugo shrugged. "You're O.K., dude. We kinda like you. And Balserio, hey, he's a crazy fuck. So here it is. The crazy dude who kidnapped your son, he's double-crossed the General. The Man-Burner—that's what we call him in Nicaragua—he was supposed to kidnap the kid, but then make it easy for the General to rescue the kid back. Make the General look like a big hero. You know? Help make him be more popular and win the Revolution.

"Instead," Hugo said, "the Man-Burner stole eighty grand or so of the General's money and took off with the kid. He's somewhere in Florida, we think. He had fake passports, all the papers. We found the pilot who flew them to Havana. He says he thinks they maybe hopped a freighter. Which the General says is probably what happened, because Lourdes— that's the crazy dude's real name—Lourdes got a thing about traveling on ships. The guy can just up and vanish sometimes—" Hugo snapped his fingers for emphasis. "The General's people think maybe it's because he sometimes works the maritime ships. Or at least travels that way because, with a face like his, he don't want to be seen."

"Have you ever seen his face? Or a photo?"

"Nobody sees the dude's face and lives," Elmase replied softly. "They say he's the devil. They say if you see his face, you gonna burn in hell, man."

I said to him, "I'll let you know about that," before asking Hugo, "Do you have any idea where they might be in Florida? Or where they would have come in?"

Hugo said, "That's why we were following *you*, man. We thought you'd lead us to him. Trouble was, the General lost his cool when he figured out who you are. But he's back under control; still wants to help.

'Cause if Lourdes kills the boy, Balserio'll never see the inside of the presidential palace again. People down there are gonna hate him, man, and he knows it."

I said, "Balserio's not planning on coming back to Florida, is he? I sure as hell don't want to see him if he does. His kind of help, we don't need."

Hugo said, "No, he's not allowed to come back. But if he gets information, he wants to be able to get it to you. He wants to *help* you, man. Or if you find out where Lourdes is, the General says he'll pay Elmase and me to . . ." The stocky man shrugged and smiled. "He'll pay us to take care of the problem. Make sure the Man-Burner never burns nobody again."

I had taken two business cards from my billfold and was adding the phone number of my hotel on each. As I did, I said, "Does this mean you're going to stop tailing me?"

"You got that right," Hugo said. "Last thing we want, dude, is to end up in jail again. First night we was in the cage, a coupla big brothers said something about Elmase's pink shirt. He's touchy about that, you know. We ended up fightin' four or five guys, just the two of us."

Taking my card, looking at it, Elmase said, "They just like you, man. They don't got no taste when it comes to dressing very cool."

AT A little after eleven A.M., I pulled my old blue pickup truck into the circular drive of the Renaissance Vinoy Resort Hotel, downtown St. Pete. It was a blustery, salt-heavy morning, and I stepped out into a southwest wind that smelled of ocean squalls and waterspouts.

Gray days are unusual for St. Pete. The city still claims to hold the world record for most consecutive sunny days: 764. In fact, for many years, the St. Petersburg *Times,* a great newspaper, was given away for free if the day started out cloudy.

The *Times* business office, on this day, would have made no profit on paper sales.

Looking at the Vinoy, though, with its Moorish gables and stucco columns, a four-story palace painted beach pink, trimmed in green, with its four hundred rooms quartered on lush grounds of gardens and pools, the day radiated a vivid tropical ambiance.

Florida still has a stock of classic hotels that have carried the atmosphere of previous eras into this new century. The Vinoy is one. It and resorts of similar distinction were designed for the peers of Roosevelt, Vanderbilt, Gable, Kennedy, Capone, and Dillinger, and the elegance of that era has been preserved. Places like the Vinoy seem to have absorbed enough sunshine and Caribbean heat over the years so that even on cloudy days, the land and water around them seem brightened via conduction. The Vinoy-era hotels are preserves of the tropics on their own private tropical preserve.

I've spent enough of my life hunkered down in jungle camps and Third World flophouses so that, when I have occasion to stay in a hotel, I splurge on good ones. I'd chosen the hotel for that reason, plus a couple of others. It has its own little marina, with instant access to Tampa Bay. I could keep my Maverick flats boat there in a wet slip. Could walk out the hotel's ornate tile and marble lobby, across Fifth Street to the floating docks, step aboard, and be gone in a minute.

Another reason was that Tomlinson and Pilar were sailing up from Dinkin's Bay, planned on arriving sometime early the next morning, and the marina basin had electric, water, and all the other modern umbilicals that most un-Tomlinson-like yachtsmen require.

It was Pilar's decision to travel with Tomlinson. I was neither surprised nor upset.

The main reason I'd chosen the hotel, though, was that I'm a fan of downtown St. Pete, and nearby downtown Tampa, and their outlying barrier islands. The area is among Florida's great, unheralded metropolitan treasures, and the two cities have much in common. I appreciate their eclectic architecture: bootlegger 1930s meets the twenty-first century; Little Havana meets Manhattan; Southern Californian beach Deco joins Steubenville-by-the-Sea.

I like the copper and earth-tone colors of space-age skyscrapers standing girder-to-dormer with churches built of stone and handmade brick. I like the funky backwater canals with rusting shrimp boats that lead to elegant waterfront neighborhoods, plus all the great restaurants, cigar factories, museums, galleries, beaches, and bars.

Tampa and St. Pete have all those things. And St. Pete's downtown baseball park, Al Lang Field, is one of the great ball yards of the world. I used to love playing there at night, under the lights, so close to Tampa Bay that the smell of chalk and rosin and Bermuda grass would sometimes mix with the smell of a prevailing Gulf Stream breeze and warm, ballooning gusts of air that drifted northward out of Cuba.

So I'd chosen the Vinoy.

I'd already launched my skiff at the city boat ramp, idled to the marina, then jogged back for my truck—the logistics of trailering a boat always requires similar pain-in-the-butt maneuverings.

So now I handed my keys to the valet. Listened to him say about my old Chevy pickup, "I bet you're into fixing up antique cars. Is that right, sir?" before I went to the front desk, checked in, and got a receipt for the briefcase that I had them put in the hotel safe.

I had a second, bigger briefcase, as well. On the drive to St. Pete, I'd stopped at a photography supply and bought a shockproof case big enough to hold the medicine, as I'd been directed.

I checked that at the front desk and got a receipt for it, as well.

I then proceeded to order something that I thought I'd never order in my life: a cellular telephone.

I told the concierge to get me a rental phone and to set up a temporary account. Because I didn't know where I was going to be using it, or under what conditions, I told him I wanted all the little cellular phone options I wouldn't have considered in my normal life: micro headphone set for hands-free use, caller I.D., and call waiting.

I told the concierge he didn't have to explain it all to me, I'd figure it out as I went.

The reason I wanted the phone was simple: I wanted a way for Dewey to get in touch with me. I didn't want to miss an opportunity to talk with her, and this was the only way.

When I was finished signing the papers, I carried my single canvas backpack, satellite phone therein, along with Tomlinson's borrowed lap-top, to my water-view Room 578.

I am a methodical person with orderly habits. When I settle into a hotel, the ceremony seldom varies. If I'm in an equatorial region, I turn the air on high, open all the windows, hang my shaving kit so it's ready when I need it, put beer atop the air conditioner if it's appropriately con-figured, then change into shorts and go for a swim.

Now, though, I immediately checked my e-mail, then Pilar's.

Nothing new.

Next, I walked to the balcony, slid the door open, and stepped out to see the view from my fifth-floor room.

I could look over the tops of palms and see the St. Pete skyline: high-rises and stadium lights, and the Jell-O-lucent swimming pool below. And there was the bay, a waterscape nine miles wide, Tampa's skyscrapers and storage tanks on the other side, barges and tugs and ocean liners moving out there on the Intracoastal Waterway, working their way to and from Florida's busiest west coast commercial port.

Slightly to the south, the horizon dropped to a rim of blue-green: man-groves and pines mostly, only a few radio towers and smoke stacks show-ing above.

To celebrate a recent birthday, I'd swum across Tampa Bay; started a few miles north of where I now stood, then finished four miles, and a little less than two hours later, wading ashore at a park above the Howard Frankland Bridge. Even though I'd done the swim on a ragged, windy day, the bay and surrounding city had seemed a safe and cheerful harbor; an extension of my Sanibel homeplace. Now, though, the area seemed shadowed with grim and dangerous potential.

Standing on the Vinoy's balcony, searching the horizon, taking it all in, I thought of Lourdes, and of my smart, smart son who was being held captive.

They were out there.

The exercise had perverse appeal: If I moved my head back and forth, I knew that at some unrealized intersection, my eyes made contact.

Where?

WHEN you've spent a lifetime running around in small boats in the worst kinds of conditions, at night, in fog, and in squalls, you come to understand early on the importance of learning your area of operation and, as best as you can, memorizing key range markers and landmarks *before* you get on the water.

So I changed into jogging shorts and took swim goggles plus my brand-new nautical chart of Tampa Bay down to the hotel pool. Swam a few hundred yards to relax, then sat with a huge glass of ice water with lime, and studied the minute details of the chart as if their importance could mean the difference between life and death.

Fact of the matter was, they might.

Uncharacteristically, though, I had trouble concentrating. It was difficult because early that morning Tomlinson and I had gone for a long walk down the beach toward Sanibel's lighthouse point. Walked slowly, side by side, past occasional stoop-shouldered shell hunters and joggers, and past shore birds that skittered like pockets of ground fog, moving rhythmically in and out with the wash and fall of waves.

During that walk, he'd finally confessed to me what he should have confessed long ago. He also told me some things that he could not have shared in a more timely fashion. There was a reason for the lapse. I believed his excuse, and what he told me.

Some of the details of my talk with Tomlinson kept banging around in my skull, interrupting the mechanics of the memorization process as I tried to imprint details from the chart onto my brain.

Finally, I said to hell with it. When things aren't going well in the classroom, it sometimes helps to get out into the field. So I went back up to the fifth floor, where I changed into fishing shorts, tank top, and boating Tevas.

As I was getting ready, my cell phone arrived, battery already charged. I checked out the little headphone set. It seemed comfortable enough. I could drop the phone in my pocket and chatter away.

I called my lab immediately, hoping to get Janet Mueller, but I got my recorder instead. Using the remote function on my home answering machine, I changed the out-going message so that anyone who called would hear my voice recite my new cellular number. I did it for Dewey, no one else.

Maybe Tomlinson's right. Maybe it's inevitable that we will all end up slaves to the microchip.

Next, I tried to call Harris Lilly, an old friend of mine who is in naval intelligence. Tried him first at his home, and then on his cell phone.

I got lucky. He just happened to be deployed on some kind of duty for U.S. Central Command—he didn't say what, of course—and was working just across the bay from me at MacDill Air Force Base. MacDill is a massive military preserve that takes up much of Tampa's southern peninsular tip, and it is from there that the United States military ran the wars in Afghanistan and Iraq.

I said to Harris, "I'm in town for a few days, so how'd you like to go boating?"

As if I'd just invited him on a Sunday picnic, he replied, "Ah, a *boat* ride. As if I don't spend enough time on the water. And what a pleasant day for it. Gray and windy, and it's almost certainly going to rain. Sounds *lovely*."

"A perfect afternoon," I said, playing along. "Maybe I'll pack a lunch. There's a lot I need to see. Just you and me banging around Tampa Bay."

Suddenly serious, he said, "Screw lunch. Neither one of us is the recreational type, so you wouldn't be asking if you didn't have something interesting going on. I'm assuming there's a damn good reason you want me to go."

"Exactly right, Commander. It's called local knowledge. You've got it. I need it. I trailered my skiff up. Do you have some time this afternoon?"

"I can manage. If it's that important."

"It's that important. So do you want me to pick you up at MacDill? I think I can find my way to the docks at the southeast inlet. I *ought* to be able to."

Laughing, Harris Lilly said, "Yeah, blindfolded, I think you could find those docks. But these days, our security teams get very nervous about civilian vessels approaching the base. They're prone to blow little boats out of the water with great big guns. Even someone like you. So why don't you pick me up somewhere around Ballast Point, just up from the base? At the Tampa Yacht Club or the fishing pier. I'll give you the tour from there."

I said, "How about the Yacht Club. In an hour?"

Harris said, "An hour, yeah. That'll give me time to change out of my Superman suit into civvies. Which will allow me to pound down several of the excellent beers you'll be bringing in deepest gratitude for my help."

TWENTY
FIVE

HARRIS Lilly is in his early forties, half Anglo, half Vietnamese, but entirely American. He looks more like someone well groomed and well satisfied in one of the solid professions—a physician, a judge—rather than the shit-hot reserve naval intelligence officer that he is. He's lean, with soccer-player legs, and gives the impression of boyishness, childlike enthusiasm, even naïveté—until you get a good look at his eyes.

Look into Harris's eyes and you will see that his enthusiasm is real, his energy level is unbelievable, but that the boy in him disappeared long, long ago.

Reserve officer does not mean that he is a "weekend warrior." It means he does special assignments. He will sometimes drop off the radar screen, out of sight for weeks, sometimes months, at a time.

In his words, when he's not "playing Navy," he is employed as a pilot for the Tampa Port Authority. When most people hear the word "pilot," they think of airplanes. Around ports, though, the word "pilot" describes a highly trained, state and federally licensed maritime captain who boards and takes command of all incoming and outgoing freighters, tankers, and cruise ships, and makes sure they make safe passage through the tricky, narrow local channels.

Tampa pilots have been operating out of Egmont Key since the early

1800s, yet few people even know their profession exists. What they also don't know is that, like all pilots worldwide, these pros play an essential role in maintaining the safety and security of the region.

For instance: Tampa is the largest fertilizer port in the world, so ships often bring in highly volatile anhydrous ammonia and sulphur. Tampa is also the import destination for all jet fuel, gasoline, and diesel used from Orlando south to Naples and north to Crystal River. Many millions of metric tons of petroleum products cross Tampa Bay annually.

Put a foreign skipper who is unfamiliar with the waters at the helm of an ammonia tanker or a jet fuel tanker in a raging squall, in a narrow channel, and suddenly, two hundred thousand unsuspecting people in downtown Tampa are at great risk.

To be a Maritime Harbor pilot, you must be a consummate professional, so I'd lucked out by getting my pal Harris to tour me around the bay.

Few men had more detailed knowledge of the area and local waters.

I BOWED up to Tampa's classy yacht club at a little after one P.M., and Harris stepped aboard while I was already backing away. Because it made sense, I slid over into the starboard swivel seat and let him take the wheel.

In my own skiff, it is not something I often do.

I've got a 225-Mercury mounted on the transom, but it's quiet enough that he didn't have to raise his voice much to say to me, "Are we looking for people or places?"

I told him, "In a way, both. If you don't mind, I'd sort of like to get an overview first. A general look around. I want to get to know the area a whole lot better than I know it now."

He nodded. "In that case, I'll start by showing you how Tampa works; how the port works. For a general overview, the first thing we'll do is make the loop through the city. The scenic route." He looked at the silver Submariner on his left wrist. "It's still around lunch time, so all the beautiful women execs and secretaries will be out strolling the streets. After that, I suppose you have something more specific in mind?"

I shrugged, turned, and opened the live well, in which I'd stored block ice and drinks. I opened a bottle of Steinlager for him, took a bottle of water for myself, and said, "Let's do the loop. After that, yeah, we'll talk specifics."

It is a pleasure to ride with a good small-boat handler. Riding with a poor boat handler is like taking a physical beating. Harris is one of the rare good ones. We had a southwest wind gusting between fifteen and eighteen, but he got the boat trimmed just right, tabs and engine angled precisely, bow down and hull listing ever so slightly to starboard, and we cut our way smoothly toward the skyline of downtown Tampa.

As we neared Davis Islands, he began a steady commentary, pointing out landmarks with a tactical brevity that bore no resemblance to anything typically offered by a sightseeing guide.

"See that point straight ahead, all the masts sticking up in front of that row of beautiful houses? That's the Davis Islands Yacht Club. They take it seriously, just like the Tampa folks. Real sailors, not phonies. Just beyond is the seaplane basin . . . and the municipal airport. If you ever get in a real tight situation and need a fast egress—the civilian variety, I'm talking about—I'd make the right phone calls, then make a beeline for this area. Chopper, seaplane, a fast car. If someone's on your tail, it'd be tough for them to be certain how you spooked out."

That's the way it went. Him talking, me listening, making mental notes. Much, much better than hanging around the pool at the Vinoy trying to memorize the chart.

Off to our right was Hookers Point. There were ocean-going freighters, barges, and tugs moored alongside avenues of commercial dockage, cranes and semis working. On shore were acres of storage tanks, some for liquids, some built as elevators for fertilizer. Many of the containers were painted with seascape murals: dolphins, breaching whales, sharks. Others were industrial gray or green.

Looking as the shoreline swept past, I listened to Harris say, "Tampa is part of a long peninsula that hangs down into Tampa Bay. The Port of Tampa is made up mostly of a second, smaller peninsula to the east, closer to the mainland. Kind of like a miniature Tampa hanging down"— he had a chart out now, folded into a square, showing me—"so it's an ideal

location. The port's a couple thousand acres, so it's isolated from downtown and all the residential stuff, but it still has almost instant access to the
city and the Interstates."

He told me about some of the freighters he'd transited in and out recently as a pilot, and the many cruise ships, adding, "The big cruise lines
love the city. They're investing more and more—Holland America and
Carnival—because here's what a lot of people don't realize: Tampa's closer
to the Panama Canal than Miami. It's faster access to Havana, too. When
Cuba opens up? Our cruise business is going to boom off the scale."

He ran us up Sedon Channel, the pretty houses of Davis Islands off to
our left, and directly into the skyscraper-heart of the city: Convention
Center, high-rise hotels with marinas and patio bars, WFLA television station, cars streaming over bridges with plasmic rhythm, condo-sized cruise
ships moored off to our right, canyons of steel and glass towering over us
now in a narrowing waterway that seemed built for gondolas.

Harris was right about the women. Lots of beautiful executive types in
business dresses and stockings.

He continued to name key landmarks. Tall buildings, mostly, that
could be seen from far offshore.

At one point, he indicated an eight-story, salmon-colored complex next
to the Davis Islands Bridge, and said, "That's Tampa General Hospital.
Did you hear about what happened there last night?"

A woman surgeon, he said, had been abducted as she'd walked from
the hospital to her home on the south tip of Davis Islands.

"Her name's Valerie Santos," he said. "I've seen her on some of the
local talk shows. This drop-dead gorgeous plastic surgeon who works in
the burn unit, and some asshole snatches her."

Harris told me that a while back, he and another pilot happened to be
first on the scene at a local marina fire that had injured a friend of theirs.
The hospital staff, he said, had done a hell of a job saving the guy.

Harris added, "I visited him a couple of times in the unit—half-hoping
I'd get to see the beautiful doctor lady in person. Never did. But there
were some good-looking nurses that made up for it. Shit, now some
freak's got her."

Harris mentioning Tampa General—particularly the burn unit—reminded me of another freak, Prax Lourdes, which, in turn, reminded me of the esoteric list of drugs he'd demanded.

Thanks to a good and dear thoracic surgeon friend of mine, I'd stopped on my way out of Fort Myers and picked up the boxes of cyclosporine and prednisone that he'd assembled, plus Neurontin capsules in the highest dosage.

The Neurontin was not so easy for him to get. "It's an antiepilepsy medication," he said. "We don't use it in my field."

Giving away prescription drugs to someone who's not a patient wasn't something he did lightly, and I took it as a testament to his confidence in me that he'd made an exception.

When he asked why I needed the meds, I'd told him the truth as I'd been told it: The medicines were for casualties of the war in Masagua and were desperately needed. The request for antiepilepsy med, though, I didn't understand.

Tomlinson had worked his sources, too. He'd already gotten the immunosuppressant drugs Thymoglobulin and OKT3, all in intravenous infusion forms, and given them to me for safe-keeping.

When I'd told him I was impressed he'd secured them so quickly, he said, "With the medical people I know, all the business I've done with them? No worries, man. Don't be vexed at me, *compadre,* but my doctor pals also threw in a cylinder of nitrous oxide gas. When I get to St. Pete, you should give it a try. *Really,* Doc. To me, sevoflurane gas is kinda like eating an anchovy pizza, but without the calories. But nitrous, man, is just good, clean fun. Take a couple whiffs, drink a beer. Then just sit back and watch the world get goofy. Next thing you know, you're crawling around in the bilge, laughing your ass off."

More seriously, he added, "After what I told you this morning, maybe it'll help us be friends again."

STILL in my skiff, we headed away from the city, out toward the shipping channels of Tampa Bay. Without mentioning the e-mail from Lake,

I'd told Harris that I was looking for an area of land and water in which I might find a specific combination of wildlife.

I'd written the list on a sheet of hotel stationery and handed it to him: reddish egret; monk parrot; monk parrot nest; mature bull gator; a place where toads or frogs might lay eggs.

He read it, squinted, then read it again. The sidelong look he gave me would have been hilarious if the situation wasn't so serious.

"Please don't tell me we're out here because you're on a freaking snipe hunt or something, Doc. What the hell is this all about?"

I said, "It's no game. There's not much else I can say. I'm looking for someone. Finding this person is as important as anything I've ever done in my life. I wouldn't tell you that much if I didn't trust you. But I can't ask for your help or anyone else's beyond a certain point, and I can't involve law enforcement." I let that sink in before adding, "I suspect that you've been in the same situation."

He thought for a moment before nodding. "Yeah. So let me look at the list again—" He did. Studied it for a moment, shielding the paper from the wind before saying, "O.K. But what you need to remember is, I'm not the biologist. So you're going to have to help me out. An alligator? Sure, I can take you to a couple places where we might see a gator or two. But those birds—a red egret? I don't think I've ever seen one. How the hell would I know?"

So I tried to describe the sort of area it might be: a place where brackish water meets freshwater. A place where mangrove fringe transitions into buttonwood, then changes to live oak or piney woods upland. There also had to be a creek or river that connected to a bay.

I told him, "It's not on the sheet I gave you, but there's also a reference to tadpoles in the data I have. I didn't write it down because I don't understand it. A place where an egret was seen feeding on a mature tadpole, that was the context. But it doesn't seem to make much sense because all frogs and all toads lay eggs that develop into tadpoles, and you can find frogs and toads all over Florida. Plus, when tadpoles mature, they're no longer tadpoles. So the reference seems to be from out of left field."

Harris didn't want to let it go so quickly, though. He asked, "What's the difference? I always wondered that. Between a frog and a toad, I mean."

I said, "A frog spends most of its mature life in water, a toad doesn't. A frog's skin is slimy, a toad's skin is dry. A frog's designed to jump, most toads hop or walk. Little things like that. A toad has poison glands behind its eyes, frogs don't. But they all hatch out as tadpoles."

He said, "So a mature tadpole could be a toad *or* a frog?"

"Uh-huh. That's the source of some of the confusion. Which is why I think it's best we concentrate on the elements we do understand."

But he continued to ponder the subject a little longer before he asked, "The way you got this list. Was it oral, or written, or some other way?"

I reminded myself I was being questioned by a top naval intelligence officer as I said, "It was in an e-mail."

"The person who sent it, could they give information freely? Or were they trying to stick information between the lines?"

"Surreptitiously. It was a dangerous situation with no room for error."

"Was the other data good? Accurate, articulate?"

"It was better than good. It was great, really brilliantly done."

Harris said, "So what you're telling me is—I'm talking from my own experience here, in these kinds of situations—all the other words in this list have meaning but one. So, to me, it's a little flag waving. And what I'm wondering is, maybe the person who sent the e-mail tried to jam a little extra meaning into what he was telling you. He or she couldn't use the exact word they wanted—it would be too obvious—so they shoot for a double meaning."

The man had something on his mind; a specific angle. What?

I said, "Well . . . the person I'm discussing was trying to communicate a location. I'm sure of that. And, yes, it's true that every reference but one seemed to have an intended meaning. So the problem is probably on my end, I agree. Is there something I'm missing here, old pal?"

He ignored the question, still deep in thought. "Doc, what's the *exact* line from the e-mail? Are you allowed to tell me?"

We were in the middle of Hillsborough Bay now, riding south in growing swells, beneath a scudding gray sky, my skiff seeming to shrink as the bay widened around us. I thought about it for a moment, trying to recall the sentence exactly, before I said, "The person wrote to me that he saw a reddish egret feeding on a mature tadpole. No, wait"—I paused to correct myself—"the wording was odd. The person wrote that the bird was feeding on *the* mature tadpole."

"On the mature tadpole."

"That's correct."

"Any other odd errors like that in the letter?"

"Nope. That was the only one."

My savvy intelligence officer friend smiled, seemingly pleased with himself. "O.K., then maybe the wording's not so odd after all. So try this: Replace the word 'tadpole' with the word 'toad.' And if that doesn't make any sense, try 'frog.'" He nodded suddenly, his smile broader. "Yeah. See, that one really works. Better yet, try replacing the word with 'bullfrog.'"

I said, "Why? What the hell are you talking about?"

Harris had the chart atop the console. Without looking at it, he tapped his index finger on a section of mainland around the little town of Gibsonton. "You're looking for a place where saltwater meets fresh. A place that's got creeks and rivers and gators. The red egret? Like I said, I don't have a clue. But there's a little spot here where someone could watch a bird feed on *the* frog. The person who wrote the e-mail couldn't come right out and use the word because it would be too obvious."

He tapped the chart again. "Take a look, Doc. Probably doesn't mean a thing but what the hell, we'll give it a shot. And if it's not this one, there's another one we could try."

I lifted the chart closer to my glasses and saw what he meant. Just south of Gibsonton was a winding blue ribbon of water named Bullfrog Creek.

TWENTY
SIX

THE narrow mouth of Bullfrog Creek was shaded with mangroves, sable palms, Brazilian pepper. Mounted in the water on a piling was a red-and-white sign that read DANGER.

Probably to relieve my own anxiety, I said, "That seems a touch dramatic, doesn't it?"

Harris had my skiff in idle, drifting, looking at the sign, the bay, and the skyline of Tampa behind us.

"Depends," he said. "Not if you do what I do for a living. Almost seems appropriate—especially if you've ever tried to run a freighter down that channel we just crossed."

He'd already told me about the commercial channel north of the creek. It was the waterway into the Alafia River, a narrow, east-west shipping lane that my master pilot pal had described as the "scariest three miles of water in the entire bay." As a pilot, he often had to make the run to get freighters to the phosphate plant located up the river at Gibsonton.

Now Harris nudged the skiff into forward, and we idled into the creek past the DANGER sign, as he said, "What it probably means is, the creek's not marked. There're no channels. Or someone's trying to keep it private. That kinda fits with what most people think about Gibsonton. They're not right. But it's what they think. Do you know anything about the place, Doc?"

I knew about Gibsonton. Knew more than most, anyway, because

Tomlinson had a fondness for it. He'd told me his daughter had been conceived in what may be the quirkiest little town in a state that's known for quirkiness. Conceived there in some 1950s-retro motor court with his renegade Japanese feminist girlfriend who now despised him, and who'd had numerous restraining orders served on him.

Even so, I sat back and listened to Harris tell me about the oddball little town of Gibsonton as we motored up the creek, my skiff's bow transecting then shattering the mirror reflections of overhanging trees that crowded in around us as we wound our way inland.

Since the 1920s, Gibsonton—or Gib'town—has been the favorite winter home of circus, carnival, and sideshow people, both performers and support staff. What attracted them was the weather, the good fishing on the Alafia River, and also a population of locals who didn't seem to have the usual prejudices against carnies or sideshow attractions such as giants, monkey-faced women, human pincushions, dwarfs, and other curiosities. Instead of staring, the locals accepted them for the good and decent people they happened to be.

In time, county officials made Gib'town even more attractive to that small nomadic society by granting the village "show business" zoning, which meant residents could keep Ferris wheels, trapeze gear, or even caged lions on their property. The post office installed a special mailbox for the ever-increasing population of midgets.

The arrival of the Ringling Brothers' circus train each November to unload performers and performing animals, who were winter residents, became a notable event on the Gulf Coast of Florida.

"Several years back," Harris said, "Gibsonton got a lot of bad publicity because of the Lobster Boy murder. Did you hear about that? Lobster Boy had some kind of disease that made his hands and legs look like flippers, and he'd been exhibiting in sideshows since he was seven. His wife said he was a mean drunk, an abuser, and she paid some teenager to shoot him.

"Other than that," he said, "you never hear anything bad about Gib'-town. They're good people. They have their own tight little society. I've heard they even have their own kind of language. Different words that outsiders can't understand. So the carney folks, the circus people, they're different. But they're O.K. I've known 'em most of my life. There are a lot of stories about foreign tankers being moored up the river waiting to be loaded with phosphate, and the crews sneaking into town to party with the show people. You know, dwarfs and bearded ladies and things. The Gib'town phosphate docks are so isolated, security has never been real tight—just one cop on the docks so the crew can't go marching down the gangplank."

I asked him, "How's security now?"

"For all of Tampa, if you're an inbound foreign commercial ship, it's tighter than it used to be. If a skipper's smart, and willing to risk it, he can still slip in just about anything he wants. And Gibsonton, it's still the same—a single cop on the dock when a foreign ship's in town."

"How about security for outward-bound foreign vessels?"

I was thinking about how Lourdes might travel if and when he decided to return to Central America. And about where a man with a disfigured face might blend in easily.

"It's a lot easier. You've got to clear customs, but they don't really look for anything *leaving* the country. They never have."

Abruptly, he pointed toward shore. "There you go. There's an example of what this town's about. Welcome to Gib'town."

We'd rounded a bend, and the mangrove fringe opened to reveal a small trailer park on the south bank and a camper-trailer park on the north. The park to the south looked like it dated back to the days of black-and-white television. There were rows of old mobile homes, bread-loaf shapes with peeling aluminum, some with TV antennas sticking up, the wire corroded by years of heat and *I Love Lucy* reruns.

Along the border of the trailer park were wobbly finger docks and a few inexpensive boats, aluminum mostly.

Lourdes had used a rental boat in Miami. What looked to be a 20-footer or so.

There was nothing like that moored here. But there was a cement ramp. Instead of someone offloading a boat, though, a shirtless man with the biggest handlebar mustache I've ever seen was hosing down a young Indian elephant, allowing it to wade in the shallows of the river.

Ashore, parked along the narrow streets of the mobile-home park, I could also see a cage built on a flatbed trailer, its wooden façade painted neon orange and green, with a banner advertising the spectacular Parnell Monkey Act. Nearby, there was another canvas banner draped from a tree, as if recently painted, that read:

SEE TO BELIEVE!
RAGTIME KURT AND KATHLEEN STOCKER
THE AMAZING AERIALISTS
FIRE BREATHER ROBBIE ROEPSTORFF
KONG, THE WORLD'S STRONGEST TATTOOED GIANT.

A tattooed giant?

That got my attention.

Turning, I watched a snowy egret, standing one-legged on a low limb, stab its yellow beak into the water and skewer a wiggling, silver minnow.

Except for its white feathers, the bird looked very much like its relative, the reddish egret.

Overhead, I heard a wild screeching, squabbling, and I lifted my eyes to see a flock of parrotlike birds seem to tumble past, then crash, bounce, and cling to the high boughs of a pine, still squawking.

They were bright green birds with dark heads—monk parakeets.

I leaned, scooped a handful of water and tasted it: fresh, tannin-sweet.

Gator country.

I had been in this situation many times in my life—closing in on some unsuspecting target of choice—but I had never felt so charged with purpose, or so focused.

My son was here. He was somewhere nearby. I was convinced of it. Could feel that it was so with an atavistic certainty that held no currency or rationale in the frontal lobe of my brain.

When I looked from mobile home to mobile home, window to window, my vision now had a searchlight intensity, and my eyes moved with the same tunneling focus.

In one of the trailers, I noticed curtains move . . .

In a patch of front lawn of another, a woman in a baggy dress and wearing a huge straw hat seemed to watch us peripherally as she swept her sidewalk . . .

In the distance, silhouetted in the shade of trees, a large man stood facing us, his face unseen . . .

Near him was a modern circus wagon with a huge marquee painted in red and blue that proclaimed THE WORLD OF WONDERS awaited inside, including the Half Girl, Half-Snake; the Bear with Three Eyes; and Dezi, the Talking Wonder Dog.

I stared at the marquee, thinking about it as Harris said, "Don't let these old trailers fool you. The carnies don't live here, most of them. They make a lot of money in the business. They've got a lot nicer places on up."

He was right about that. We crossed under the U.S. 41 bridge, fast traffic passing overhead, Bullfrog Marina alongside, and motored another mile up the creek and into a pretty lagoon. There were palms and oaks, Spanish moss hanging like fog in the shadows, expensive houses set back, a couple of gators drifting, eyes periscoping above the mirror skein of water.

It was a beautiful area. Backcountry Florida idyllic.

Seeing a place so pretty caused me to recall something that a tattooed giant had recently said into the phone while he was directing us around Miami. He was saying to some woman that the reason she needed to come visit him was because he lived in a part of Florida that still looked the way people dreamed it should.

Here was that little chunk of Florida.

My association between the two was not random or coincidental: There he was, the tattooed Mediator. From the boat, I could see him jogging along the street, beneath shading oaks, unmistakable with his head the size and color of a bleached basketball, skull shaved clean and trapezoid muscles that pyramided to his ears, his skin dyed in Easter egg hues, reds, greens, blues.

So now he also had a name and a title. He was Kong, the World's Strongest Tattooed Giant.

To Harris Lilly, I said, "Commander, I'm going to ask you to dump me off here, then bug out and take my boat back alone. Do you think the Tampa Yacht Club will let you moor it there for the afternoon? Maybe the night?"

He looked from the jogging giant to me, then back to the giant, concerned. "Are you sure? You know, old buddy, I have just about every kind of security clearance there is. I can tag along, watch your six, and never tell a soul. Promise."

I was pointing toward a section of seawall where I could step off as I gathered my gear back out of the forward locker. "I wish I could. I really do. But I can't."

As I stepped off, I told him, "I'll let you know how it goes."

I GOT the impression that the tattooed giant had seldom been surprised in his life.

He was surprised now. His eyes went wide, and he jumped a little, startled, when I jogged quietly up behind him, tapped him on the shoulder, and said, "Hey, Kong, I think it's time we had a little talk."

He liked the Everlast muscle shirts. This one was blue. He wore a belly pack and red shorts, but they didn't seem as colorful as the fire-bright tattoos that covered his legs: dragons, snakes, and gargoyles.

I jogged alone for a few steps as he stopped, jamming hands on hips, getting himself under control before he said, sounding cheery, "Well, well, well, if it ain't Mr. Booky-Boy. Where's your long-haired hippie pal, Mr. Freaky Creepy?" Then he added, not the least bit cheerfully, "It is very uncool of you to track me down, buster. Very uncool. It ain't gonna help your cause one bit."

As he started to jog away, I reached out and put my right hand on his chest, stopping him.

He wasn't used to that, either. Being touched. Being told what to do. His face reddened as I told him, "You're not going anywhere. Not until we have our talk."

Kong said, "The only place you're goin', Booky-Boy, is the hospital to get ya a new arm if you don't take your paw off me right now. I done told you: I got nothing to say 'cause I don't know nothin'. People hire me for middle-man work."

Before I could reply, he pivoted, swatted my hand away as if it were nothing, then lunged, grabbed me beneath the arms, and lifted me without much effort until I was nose to nose with him.

My options were to go for his eyes . . . or maybe pop his eardrums, then go for his throat . . . or to let it play out and just listen.

I decided to listen.

The guy was *strong*.

Holding me there, nearly a foot off the ground, he told me, "I don't want to know what business it is you got going down. Not listening is how Mr. Kong keeps his pretty ass out of trouble. Like I told you, my brain ain't the biggest, but it do got some torque. So why don't you just run along—and leave *me* alone."

He'd just told me the only way I could involve him. *If* he was telling me the truth. *If* he wasn't part of the deal already.

If he was lying? It wouldn't matter anyway.

Talking fast, I said, "The guy who hired you kidnapped my son. A guy named Praxcedes Lourdes, but he's probably going by something else. I think they're hiding out somewhere here. Somewhere around Gibsonton, and he's going to kill my son if I don't find him."

I continued before he could interrupt, "Maybe you're being straight with me. Maybe you *don't* know who you're working for. But Lourdes knows you. Which means you probably know who he is even if you don't realize it."

Kong shook his head, expression pained, and dropped me to the ground. He seemed to rub at a knot behind his ear, saying, "*Kidnapping?* You're kidding."

"No. It's the truth. That's who you're helping."

"Jesus Christ, I don't get involved in anything heavy like that. The guy hinted around it was some kind of extortion deal. Like maybe he had naked pictures of the pretty lady or something. Or blackmail. Dope deals and bribery. That's mostly what I do. But kidnapping someone's kid? Jesus Christ!"

"He's Pilar's son and mine."

Kong was still shaking his head, a little dazed by what he was hearing. "You just had to tell me, didn't you? Not only that, you just cost me like ten, maybe fifteen grand. 'Cause now I got to walk. Wash my hands of the whole deal, both sides. I can't listen to another word, because if the story gets around, I'm out of the mediator business. Which is not a good thing, asshole. Not good at all because this late in the spring, a guy like me, a guy who works carnivals, I'm not exactly rolling in cash."

I said, "My son's life's on the line. So don't expect any sympathy. I'll pay you, if that's the only problem. I'll pay you what Lourdes was going to pay if you'll help."

Kong made a face, thinking about it, then sighed. "If I was to double-cross a client, cut a private deal, that really would screw me."

I said, "I'll pay you double. If you find a way to help me, I'll pay you cash."

The World's Strongest Tattooed Giant said, "Double, huh?" He looked at his watch, mulling it over. "I guess, we can at least walk up the street and have a drink. We can talk her over. But *kidnapping*. Goddamn!"

KONG said he'd missed lunch and would have preferred to go to the Giant's Camp Restaurant because they had such good collard greens, but a car had smashed through the place recently, and temporarily shut it down.

"The giant," he told me, "was Big Al Tomaini. He was 'bout eight-four, a lot bigger giant than me, and his wife, Jeanie, was less than three feet tall. Nice lady. And great collards."

Kong, I could tell, enjoyed the carney business.

Instead, we walked along U.S. 41 to the Showtown Bar & Grill, with painted clowns on the door, a jukebox on a cement floor inside, and lots of circus posters and murals on the walls. There were a dozen or so people inside, and I stood in Kong's shadow while he said hello to Peti, the fire-eating midget; Chuck, the owner; and some other show people. I listened to them talk about the latest controversy: Land developers wanted the county to revoke Gibsonton's special show-business zoning so they could put in big-ticket subdivisions and not have to worry about rubbing elbows with cotton candy wagons, Ferris wheels, and sideshow exhibits.

"That'll be the end of us show people," one of them said.

I heard another say in reply what sounded like, "Giz-iz-bye ciz-iz-arney tiz-iz-own . . . ," speaking in what seemed to be a kind of pig Latin that I couldn't understand.

Talking their own secret language, maybe, because I was there.

Then Kong ordered a beer from Rocky the bartender, nothing for me, and I followed him to a corner table. First thing, he said, before he'd talk about anything else, he wanted to know how I'd found him.

"Coincidence, "I said. "That's the truth. I saw a banner about Kong the Tattooed Giant, then saw you jogging. But it's no coincidence that I think my son's in the area. I have some pretty good sources."

Kong was nodding. "So what I could do is, contact the guy who's paying me, tell him you're closing in. The boy dies, but I still get paid. What's to stop me?"

I said, "A prison sentence. If you help Lourdes, or anyone who's working with him, you become an accessory. If you aren't already, legally speaking."

Because he knew I was right, Kong said, *"Shit,"* the way guys say it when they're in a corner.

Then he said, "O.K., Booky-Boy, the truth is, I don't know who hired me. It's a voice on the phone. The caller I.D. number's always blocked. But, yeah, it's probably someone who's in on it. In on it—that's carney talk for being part of the carnival business. 'Cause he left my first payment—two grand, cash—in my box at the Showman's Club, our private place just across the river."

"Was the voice familiar?"

"Never heard it before."

"The guy I'm talking about was badly burned as a teen. Maybe terrible scars. Or always wears something to cover his face." Looking at the posters on the wall of the Showtown Bar gave me an idea. "A clown maybe. Always in costume. He might try to pull something like that."

That made Kong smile. "Buster, there are about ten thousand circus people, sideshow exhibitors, and show business folks who spend winters in this little town. We don't make a habit of talking about each other to outsiders. But I *will* tell you this is the best place in the country for a person who looks bad, or scary, or dresses weird to live, because nobody asks him any questions, and he'd never get a second look."

As I said, "Yeah, that's just what I've been thinking," the cell phone inside Kong's belly pack began to ring. The calliope music that seemed so odd in Miami fit here.

He looked at the caller I.D., raised his eyebrows. When Kong answered—"Talk to me"—he listened for a moment before looking across the table, then pointing at the phone.

I watched Kong mouth the words: *It's him.*

TWENTY
SEVEN

I LISTENED to Kong say into the phone, "Uh-huh. I can give them the message. Uh-huh. Uh-huh. You've sent the e-mail, so then I follow up by phone. Hey, hold on a sec. Let me get something so I can write this down."

It felt weird hurrying across the bar to find paper so the tattooed giant could take a message from my son's kidnapper that was intended for me.

A minute later, Kong shut off his phone, cleared it, and said, "The guy's a fucking weirdo, man. That's the only bad thing about being a mediator—some of the scum I've got to deal with. People think carnies are bad? In sideshows, all we do is stick a spotlight on things that you rubes, the townies, dream about doin' in the dark. It's people outside of the gates that're the scary ones."

I said, "The person you just spoke with burns people because he enjoys it. Kills them by setting them on fire. He's a serial killer from Central America."

That got Kong's attention. "You're shitting me. For real?"

I nodded. "And he's got my son."

Kong said, "There was a freak act a while back. Sideshow geek stuff. A guy would shoot fire out of his butt, his tallywhacker, then blow himself up. But this dude really sets people on fire?"

"Yeah. He really does. What's the message you're supposed to give me?"

Kong had written on the back of a lunch menu. He looked at the menu as he said, "The big bridge that crosses over from the mainland to St. Petersburg, the Sunshine Skyway. On the St. Pete end, there's a little place called Maximo Park. Do you know it? He wants you and your pals there by seven-thirty tonight with the money and—this is him talking—'with the money and the other stuff.' That's a little before sunset."

Sunset, I knew, was a few minutes after eight.

Kong spun the menu across the table toward me. "As long as you're fucking up my mediator business, you might as well tell me the rest. How much money, and what's he mean, 'other stuff'?"

I told him about the money and the medicine, adding, "I've got both with me, but Pilar and Tomlinson can't make it. They're under sail, on their way here by boat. I can't let Lourdes know that, of course. But why should he care who makes the delivery?"

Kong said, "That's a good point." Back in his role as mediator again.

"Do you have a way to contact him?"

"Yeah, I call a number that has a Nicaraguan country code. But he's not going to like it. He sounded very hyper. Pissed off; almost like someone sounds when they've got a hell of a headache. Know what I mean?"

Yes, I knew what he meant.

Checking my watch, I said, "He was supposed to give us until Sunday to get the medicine together. Now all of a sudden, he's in a rush. It's twenty till five now. It's a two-and-a-half-hour drive from Sanibel to St. Pete, yet he expects you to get his message to us, then for us to pack and get on the road in time to be at the Skyway by sunset? That's cutting it damn close."

Kong had a huge, dumb-looking face, but he had perceptive amber eyes that didn't miss much. "You think he knows that you're here? That we're together?"

"Maybe. Shoving the deadline up like this, he's acting like something's spooked him. I came up Bullfrog Creek by boat. I have a strong suspicion that Lourdes and my son have been staying somewhere on or near the creek. Are you absolutely certain you don't know where he is? Not even a guess?"

Kong got an ugly look on his face. "I ain't tellin' you again, buster. I don't have a clue. Far as I know, I've never seen him, and don't know where he is."

I said, "Then maybe he got a look at me when I was coming up the creek. Or maybe he's got neighbors helping as lookouts. There are a couple of old trailer parks I came past. How easy would it be for him to get other carnies to help him out?"

Kong said, "If they knew he was a kidnapper? Zero. But if he convinced them he was in the business, and if he gave them some bullshit story—his asshole ex-wife wants his car repossessed—there's a kind of carney code. We don't help outsiders get inside, and we protect our own from the outside."

"Then maybe that's it. Someone saw me, got suspicious. Now he's panicky."

"That doesn't sound good for your son."

"No. Not good." I had my billfold out. From it, I took the plastic key to my room at the Vinoy and slid it to him. "You're working for me now. O.K.?"

The huge man shrugged. "The idea of some kid getting burned alive don't exactly appeal to me. So, yeah, I guess I don't have much choice."

"Good. Then here's what I want you to do. Call Lourdes right now and tell him that you made contact with me. Tell him that we've got everything, and we can deliver it tonight. But it's just me and you making the drop. Also, tell him I want to know how we're doing the exchange. I'm supposed to get something in *return*. I'm supposed to get my son—which you know nothing about, of course. Tell him I want to know how it's going to work."

Kong said, "I can ask him, but I think he'll do it like before. Tell us what to do step by step, over the phone, while we're driving."

I said, "Call and ask anyway. After that, I want you to drive back to my hotel, get the money, pick up the medicine. You're going alone. You're going to pretend like I'm with you, because I'm staying in Gibsonton . . ." I paused, thinking it through. "Hold it, that won't work—"

Boats and cars. The logistics were always difficult. Plus, there was an additional problem.

After another moment, I said, "That won't work because the hotel isn't going to give you anything from the safe, even if I call and tell them it's O.K."

Kong had a bitter sense of humor. "You're kiddin'. They're not gonna hand over a suitcase full a money to a nice-lookin' guy like me?"

I stood, now in a hurry to leave. "Which means that you're going to have to drive me to the Vinoy. Fast. Then drop me at my boat. You take the money and the medicine. You let Lourdes drive you all over town, jump through all his hoops. You're still going to be consulting me—every time you make a move, call me on my cell phone. But don't let him know I'm not with you. You keep him busy. That'll give me a chance to take a close look around those trailer parks."

"But what if the guy really plans on swapping you the kid for the money? He'll have your son with him. Or somewhere staked close by."

I said, "I hope he does. If that's the way it goes, take good care of my boy till I get there. But I don't see it happening that way. Not this early in the game."

Twenty minutes later, as we crossed the Howard Frankland Bridge in Kong's black pickup truck with the silver-tinted windows and monster tires, country music blaring, he said after fifteen minutes of silence, "You gonna go off and trust me with a half-million dollars cash. Just like that?"

I'd been thinking about that, too. "I've got a friend in town named Harris. I might ask him to ride along with you, just for the hell of it. But if he's busy? Well, Kong, I found you once. I can find you again."

AT THE Vinoy, Kong waited outside in his truck while I signed for the two gray photographer's briefcases made of shockproof miracle resin and carried them upstairs to my room. I opened the smaller of the two just to make certain: looked at the neatly packed stacks of U.S. fifties and hundreds, each bound in paper sleeves that read *Banco Nacional de Masagua*.

Early that morning, Pilar had bristled when I'd asked if she'd done even a rough count. Her friend Kahlil, she said, had already counted it, and that was good enough.

With my son's life potentially on the line, it wasn't good enough for me, but I couldn't take the time to count it now. So I snapped the case closed and began to strip off my clothes, while at the same time, I walked to the desk and used Tomlinson's laptop to sign on to the internet.

Wearing only undershorts, I sat at the desk when I saw that I had a new e-mail from an address that was a random series of letters at Nicarado.org.

I opened it to find a note from Lourdes. It had been sent less than an hour earlier.

He'd written in English for the first time:

> Our Florida people want you to be at the north side of the Sunshine Sky-
> way, St. Petersburg, at 7:30. Have everything. A person you will recognize
> will meet you. He'll be in a black pickup truck. You'll get your brat back in
> a week or so. After you deliver another half-million cash. How's it feel to be
> the fuckee for a change! Here's a couple of words from your brat.

After a series of spaces was a very short note from Lake. It read:

> Dear Doc,
>   The Cubs have been hitting like they have an extra eye, so maybe another
> World Series run? So you know this is really me, I was thinking about our
> talk concerning Charles Darwin when he discussed why only certain pri-
> mates can talk and why other mammals can't. Hope to see you very soon,
> Laken

I reread the note several times, trying to control my breathing, trying to stay calm. It wasn't easy.

Lourdes' note, I took mostly at face value. The exception was his threat to continue the extortion for another week. It was possible that he meant it, but my instincts told me it was a red herring. He was planning on moving. Planning to take off. Tonight, probably, after he got the money and the medicine.

My son's note was more subtle, but contained far more interesting information.

If I thought about my trip up the river into Gibsonton, Lake's words and references took on exceptional meaning. There was a key word and a key reference in those few sentences that were too telling to be coincidental.

"Cub" was one of those words. That he referenced mammals that cannot talk was another.

My brilliant son had done it again.

I dug through my overnight bag and pulled on dark blue twill slacks and a black T-shirt. I jammed my old navy blue watch cap into a pocket as I grabbed the money and the medicine, and headed toward the door.

I knew where my son was being held captive.

But then I stopped. I made one more phone call.

THE World's Strongest Tattooed Giant dropped me at the Tampa Yacht and Country Club on Interbay Boulevard, just north of Ballast Point Park, at 6:45 P.M. Harris Lilly was there waiting. He told me where my skiff was moored, then got in the truck with Kong. I watched them drive away toward the rendezvous in St. Petersburg.

From the phone in my hotel room, I'd given my naval intelligence pal the short version of what was going on. By telling him, I'd broken my word to Pilar, but that meant nothing now. Rescuing Lake was all that mattered.

Harris listened in silence, asked a couple of good questions, accepting what I had to say without much emotion or comment. There's a strong sense of brotherhood among the international intelligence community. Nothing he heard seemed to surprise him.

I finished, saying, "When Lourdes was bouncing us around Miami, he did it by boat. It's an easy way to orchestrate things and make sure your target's not being tailed. I think he'll do the same thing tonight. If I don't find my son in Gibsonton, I think I'll find him somewhere on Tampa Bay. I want to be on the water, waiting for him. That's why I need you taking care of things on land."

Harris said he was not only willing to help, he was eager.

"It doesn't sound like I have to do anything illegal," he said. "Just ride around in a vehicle and pretend like I'm you. That can't be too hard. What about the guy I'll be with, though. Do you trust him? Should I be carrying?"

By that, he meant should he carry a concealed firearm.

I told Harris, "I don't really know him. He's a huge guy, a muscle freak. And kind of a redneck jerk. But in a weird way, yeah, I think I do trust him. I think he'll play by the rules."

I told him that I'd carry the gun anyway, though.

So now I watched my naval intelligence buddy ride away with Kong before I walked toward the club's modern marina, past a complex of tennis courts—which reminded me of Dewey. She'd almost certainly played here many times during her years at the tennis academy in nearby Bradenton.

I felt a genuine longing for the girl. I missed hearing her voice. Missed being able to tell her what was going on in my life.

I wished I could now take the little rental cell phone that was in my pocket, dial her number, and say, "I think I finally know where he is."

TWENTY
EIGHT

THE wind had calmed, as if suctioned through a hole in the earth's atmosphere by the westwarding sun. It was orbiting low in the sky astern as I ran my skiff at speed across Hillsborough Bay, the sun's color the smoldering yellow of a tropic moon. Its starburst rays touched the Tampa skyline—a random geometric, like a Wyoming geode—and it set ablaze canyons of tinted glass and steel.

I kept my eyes focused to the southwest: the tall navigational towers that marked the channel into the Alafia River, and the entrance to Gibsonton.

Earlier, during my trip up Bullfrog Creek, I'd paid attention to detail. I remembered what I saw there. I remembered the old trailer park where a woman had watched us while sweeping in her yard. Remembered that a large man had stared at us from the shadows. And I remembered the carnival wagon with the gaudy marquee that advertised a bear with three eyes and a dog named Dezi who could talk.

My son had written that the Cubs were hitting as if they had a third eye.

He'd also invented a discussion that he and I had never had concerning something Darwin didn't write: the inability of certain mammals to talk.

That would include a dog named Dezi.

Lake was being held somewhere within the vicinity of that carnival wagon. Maybe in that very trailer. He couldn't have described it to me more plainly.

Did he know that I'd been nearby? Had he seen me? Or had he somehow read it in Lourdes' behavior?

I wondered.

I checked my watch: 7:15. There was still slightly more than forty-five
minutes until sunset. I didn't want to start searching the trailer park until
after dark. But if Lourdes had a boat somewhere up Bullfrog Creek, I
knew there was a slim chance of getting a glimpse of him exiting the
mouth of the creek, heading for the Sunshine Skyway.

I'd be able to see if he was alone, or if he had my son with him.

I was running at a comfortable 4700 rpm, which is around 50 statute
miles an hour. I trimmed the big 225-Merc slightly and ran it up to 5700
rpm, flying across Hillsborough Bay at close to 60 miles an hour, blasting
a rainbow-colored rooster tail.

At 45 mph in an open boat, the eyeballs begin to flutter. At 55, they
begin to get teary. I turned my head away slightly to spare my vision.
Off to starboard, I could see a decrepit-looking freighter, rust-streaked,
green paint peeling beneath a dusty coat of phosphate. It was riding
low in the water, outward bound. It had just exited the Alafia River
Channel. What Harris called the scariest three miles of commercial water
around.

Two muscle-bound tugs had just released the vessel, from the looks of
things. The tugboats *Colonel* and *Tampa* had their sterns to me, heading
north toward the port as I planed closer to the phosphate ship.

All freighters have descending numbers painted vertically like measur-
ing sticks on the outside of their hulls, a strip located forward, another
amidships, and a third just forward the stern. These 6-inch numerals are
called "draft marks." Water was waking midway along the faded "29" on
this vessel, so I knew it was drawing twenty-nine feet or so of water. I also
noticed a pilot ladder hanging off the side of the ship—a solid-looking
rope ladder with wooden rungs. Every fifth rung was a spreader, which is
an extra-wide rung to prevent the ladder from twisting.

One of Harris's Tampa pilot colleagues was aboard. It was his job to
navigate this ship several miles offshore, and then, without the freighter
stopping, he would skitter down that ladder and onto a local pilot trans-

port boat, which would take him home to Egmont Key, an island five miles to the west of the Sunshine Skyway Bridge.

I crossed behind the freighter close enough to read the big gray letters on its stern:

REPATRIATE

MONROVIA, LIBERIA

An appropriate name, considering that country's history. Maritime companies who own unsafe, outdated commercial vessels usually register them in countries like Liberia, where inspectors are more easily bribed—if there are inspections at all.

I waved at the wheelhouse just in case the American pilot was looking. A fellow pilot of his was doing me a hell of a favor.

I steered sharply east again, quartering the freighter's long, rolling wake. Ahead, in the far distance, was a small sailboat, its sail a gilded ivory in the late sun.

It was about the size of *No Mas*, but I knew that it couldn't be Tomlinson. It was much too early for my purist sailor friend to be arriving in Tampa Bay.

But it brought his image to mind. Brought back the talk we'd had early that morning, the two of us walking the beach toward Sanibel's Lighthouse Point.

It gave me something to think about as I crossed the last three miles of open water to Bullfrog Creek.

OUR talk had been more like a confession. Tomlinson's confession.

He was right. What he had to tell me put our friendship at serious risk. Knowingly, what he told me also put his own freedom, even his life, at risk.

"We should have had this conversation months ago, Doc," he said. "I feel guilty as hell, man, because I've been putting it off. I know it's cowardly, but it's because I'm scared. I know that what I have to say might change everything between us. Forever."

It had to do with the realization that he'd suffered a severe memory loss earlier in his life. Tomlinson told me that no one seemed to take him seriously when he said he couldn't remember writing *One Fathom Above Sea Level,* but it was true.

He said, "Look man, I realize I'm a figure of fun around the marina. That's fine. I dig the role. Hell, I *play* the role. But when I read *One Fathom,* I went into a kind of identity shock. Some of the stuff I'd written all those years ago, it was so powerful. Some of it was so pure. It scared me. How could I possibly have created something so beautiful, yet have absolutely zero memory of doing it?"

Tomlinson added, "I began to wonder, and fret: What other important events in my life had totally disappeared from my memory. And *why*? It had to be more than the drugs, man. Not even I used that many drugs."

As we walked the beach, he told me about it. He was so troubled by the mystery that he began to do research into his own personal history. Finally, as I knew, early the previous winter he disappeared from the islands without telling anyone where he was going, without saying goodbye. He'd was gone for nearly four months, and then returned without explanation.

"I went to try and find out what happened to me," he said. "I went back to my old university. Hung out with some of my old friends. I wanted to pick up the trail because it was during college, during that time of my life, that I lost my own personal trail. I lost my path, and I also lost great big chunks of my memory. It didn't take me long to figure out what'd happened."

On the beach, he had stopped abruptly, lifted his scraggly hair, and pointed to a burn scar on the side of his head. The scar was shaped a little bit like a lightning bolt—ironic because he'd gotten the burn as the result of lightning.

"Electricity did it to me. Wiped parts of my memory bank clean, and it also screwed with my personality. Maybe for the better. Because, from what I discovered, I was a serious candidate for Asshole of the Decade before it happened."

I said, "Before you got struck by lightning? That was only a few years back."

"No. The memory loss, the personality change, were both caused by the electroshock treatments. I've told you about it. The ones I got a year or so after writing *One Fathom*. It was just after the bomb that killed the sailor at the San Diego naval base.

"The guilt, man, seeing those smoking bodies on TV. I went insane. No other way to put it. They gave me shock treatments when my father had me institutionalized. Strapped me down on the table every day for weeks. I think they way overdid it. I was so screwed up, I'd write letters and sign them 'Sincerely as a fucking loon.' And I *meant* it."

He continued, "It took me a while, but I tracked down the physician who'd administered the shock treatments to me. The zapper. The guy went on to become a brilliant psychiatrist, a great healer. I have something I want to show you. To explain what happened to me. He wrote me this letter."

Tomlinson handed me two pages typed on the personal stationery of a California physician. We were standing on a section of dune near the Sanibel Beach Club. This early, people were already up there playing tennis, hanging out by the pool. I adjusted my glasses and read the letter quickly, skipping some of the more detailed portions:

Dear Mr. Tomlinson:

I must have administered electroshock to at least a thousand patients as a resident. I detested doing it. I apologize to you now. I wish I could apologize to them all individually. . . .

The nurses would bring the patient in on a rolling cot, get an I.V. going, and I would put in sodium amytal. I remember that many of the patients had severe halitosis and I had to hover over them, close as a lover, and I felt guilty and obscene. . . .

Then I would place the electrodes on their heads, two shiny steel plates, about 1.5 inches in diameter, fastened tightly above the ears, and add a gel sticky with saline for good contact. . . .

When all was ready, I took a rubber doorstop, usually red, sometimes brown, shaped like a wedge and wrapped with sterile gauze. I placed that thing in their mouth so when they bit down they would not break their teeth. . . .

On the electroconvulsive therapy machine, there were two dials. One was the strength of the current and the other was a timer for the duration of the shock. I set the parameters according to the age, sex, weight, and medical condition of the patient.

I would then give a couple of whiffs of oxygen to the patient, inject Anectine, and watch until the patient stopped breathing. That meant all the muscles were paralyzed.

I would then reach back behind me, hit the contact switch, and watch a small muscular tremor in the patient that indicated electric current passing through his brain.

The usual course of "treatment" was two weeks, every other day. Judging from the severity of your memory loss, however, Mr. Tomlinson, I suspect you are one of the few who received a far more aggressive course. Some doctors insisted on administering ECT twice a day for as long as it took to get the patient to be incontinent. Those people became zombies.

Again, Mr. Tomlinson, I apologize. It was my duty as a resident to carry out the orders of those above me. If I objected, my residency would have been over.

It was the accepted treatment of the day.

I have many stories of things that happened. Some horrid, some funny, always poignant.

I enclose an article from a medical journal concerning memory loss caused by ECT. You may find it enlightening.

I folded the letter, handed it to Tomlinson, saying, "He sounds like a good man. Like he genuinely regrets what he did."

Tomlinson handed me the copy of the magazine article, saying, "Me, too. Regret it, I mean. Except that it changed me from Asshole of the Decade to who I am now, apparently. Wait until you read this."

TWENTY
NINE

I SKIMMED the article on electroconvulsive treatment, skipping much of it due to my own impatience. The interesting parts included:

> During World War I, physicians noticed that mentally ill patients who suffered convulsions during bouts of malaria sometimes seemed cured of their depression or other emotional problems. This led to the use of the drug Metrazol to induce seizures.
>
> In 1938, Ugo Cerletti, an Italian psychiatrist, while observing slaughterhouse pigs being shocked unconscious, came up with the idea of using electroshock to create seizures in his patients.
>
> For the next forty years, many hundreds of thousands of patients of all ages, and around the world, received electroconvulsive therapy (ECT) for all kinds of mental "disorders" from depression, to mania and schizophrenia, to even homosexuality and truancy. . . .

I skipped down a page to read a segment that Tomlinson had high-lighted with a blue marker:

> It has now been documented that memory impairment, and sometimes total memory loss, is the most serious side effect of electroconvulsive therapy, and is the one most frequently trou-bling to patients.

Sometimes the memory loss is temporary, and includes only the days or weeks around the time of the treatment. In other patients, entire blocks of memory have been erased. Some patients have reported near complete amnesia regarding their lives prior to the therapy. Many patients lose specific or general memory for many months, and sometimes of a year or more that preceded receiving ECT.

As one patient said, "More than a year prior to entering the hospital, my wife and I had bought a new house. When I left the hospital, I had absolutely no recollection of that house. Entering every room was a new experience."

I skipped a little further because Tomlinson had highlighted and bracketed the following:

It has also been documented that a substantial number of ECT patients have been able to recover sizeable blocks of lost memory by the careful reconstruction, or registration, of key life experiences and places. . . .

I handed the article back to Tomlinson as he told me, "That's what I decided to do—revisit and re-experience key elements and experiences in my life. I was still trying to remember writing *One Fathom Above Sea Level.* That became my focus."

He told me that the only remaining memory he had about writing his now-famous work was connected to a popular song. It was a song by a classic rock band named America.

He said, "You know their stuff: 'Sister Golden Hair,' 'Ventura Highway,' 'You Can Do Magic.' The band's got two genius writers, so they've had a ton of hits.

"Back when I wrote *One Fathom,* though, the song that haunted me was 'Horse with No Name.' Everyone knows the lyrics. 'I've been through the desert on a horse with no name . . .'"

He sang a portion of it softly, then whistled for a while before explaining, "The line that just rocked me, though, was, 'The ocean is a desert with its life underground, and a perfect disguise above.' Are you familiar with the line, Doc?"

I know very little about rock music. Tend to listen to Latin music, Caribbean basin stuff, and Buffett, of course, and lately have taken an unexpected liking to an extraordinary folk singer and composer, Wendy Webb. But even I knew the song he was discussing, though little else about the band.

He repeated the lyric: "'The ocean is a desert with its life underground, and a perfect disguise above,'" before adding, "For someone like me, a sailor, that line was like a three-pronged probe. It hit me in the marrow, the brain, and the heart. All the far-out implications, all the very heavy vibes and duality it communicated. That song, it just sent me off on a whole new spiritual trip."

Tomlinson combed long, bony fingers through his hair and said, "The line was the seed that started *One Fathom*. That song. 'A Horse with No Name.' That's all I remembered. The rest of my memory from that time period was a blank sheet. So when I disappeared from the marina? I got a piece of pure karmic luck. I called around, found out where the band America was playing. I met their road manager, Erin, and finagled a job as a roadie. So that's where I went when I disappeared. I was working for the band America. Can you believe it? A really cool experience, man."

I watched him smile, enjoying the memory of it for a few seconds before he continued, "They had no idea who I was, why I was there. A great bunch of people. They do more than a hundred gigs a year, all first-class, and it was pure good karma that put me in the right place at the right time. So I helped them set up in L.A., Phoenix, Chicago, little towns in Iowa and Wisconsin. Yeah, and San Diego, too."

San Diego, he said, that's where his memory started coming back to him.

WHAT Tomlinson remembered, and now confessed to me, was that he hadn't just been a member of the radical group that had sent the bomb to the San Diego naval station. He'd been the group's founder. He'd also helped design the bomb. And build it. And send it.

"We got the directions from *The Anarchist Cookbook*," he added. His voice sounded weary. I couldn't remember ever hearing him so sad. "In other words, I am directly responsible for the death of your friend. I guess the electroshock wiped out my recall; every single detail. Or maybe I wanted it wiped out. I've come to the conclusion that, in me, a clear conscience is the first symptom of damaged brain function."

I'd stopped walking. Stood looking out over the Gulf of Mexico: green water, pearl horizon, copper morning sky. I said, "He had a wife and children."

"I know. I've been helping them secretly for years. Financially, I mean."

I knew that was true.

I said, "I gave you documents from another friend of mine that legally exonerates you from any responsibility. I did that for you."

"I know that, too."

"There are no statutes of limitation on murder. If you turn yourself in—or if someone turns you in—you're going to jail for a very long time."

Tomlinson had been looking at me. But now he turned so that we stood side by side, both of us looking out to sea. "I plan to turn myself in and confess. I'm responsible. It's the moral thing to do. Spiritually, it's what I'm *obligated* to do.

"But Doc"—his voice choked slightly—"I don't think I could take it. Jail, I mean. Being penned up. Not being able to get out on the water aboard *No Mas*. What I'd rather have happen—my spiritual *preference*—is I'd rather just . . . *disappear*. Like the other members of my organization did years ago. Back when someone was hunting them down. I'd prefer that. Rather than go to jail, I wish the man assigned to make me disappear would just . . . *do* it. Get it over with and make it happen."

I hated the inference, and the implicit obligation. How could he ask such a thing of me?

I said, *"Stop it."* Then changed the subject immediately by becoming aggressive, wanting him on the defensive, asking, "What else do you remember? What other nasty little secrets were in there hiding? How about this: Were you ever a member of a second radical group? One called Fight-4-Right? And did you spend time working for them in Central America?"

He shook his head. "No. I don't think so. But it's *possible*. I lost about two entire years of my memory. I have no idea what I did during most of that time period. Only part of it's come back."

"Did you ever know an Australian oceanographer named Thackery? He was a big environmentalist and a surfer."

I was thinking about the e-mails I'd found, written by Pilar.

Tomlinson had to think about that. "Maybe I did know someone named Thackery. It . . . it sounds familiar. But I can't be sure. I'm sorry."

"What about Pilar? Did you know her before I met her? Or has she said anything to you, sent you any e-mails, or asked you anything that suggests that you did know each other?"

He grimaced and took a deep breath. "No-o-o-o. I don't think I ever met her before you and I went to Masagua together. If I was ever in Central America before that, I have absolutely no recollection of it. But there is something I need to tell you about that woman. About Pilar. This isn't easy, man. And there's no way to sugar-coat it."

I thought: *Uh-oh, here it comes.*

But it was not what I expected.

I WAS still standing, looking at the water, but I had turned away from Tomlinson slightly. I waited through a long silence before he said, "The thing about you, Doc, is you tend to see the good in everybody. You're analytical, sure. But you focus on what's productive in people, what's positive."

I said, "So? The exact same thing's true of you."

"I know. I know. But the difference is, there's no rational explanation for malice or impiety. Because of that, rational people like you are slow to recognize it. But someone like me, I know intuitively if a person's basically good, or basically bad. You've always thought Pilar was one of the great women in the world. I knew the moment I met her she was just the opposite. She's one of the bad ones. Not evil, just bad."

I was more than taken aback. It was a shocking thing to hear from a man whose judgment I valued, and who rarely said an unkind word about another human being. Tomlinson's demons have made him reluctant to judge.

Yet, he continued, "She's self-obsessed. Huge mood swings. Delusions of grandeur. Think about it, Doc: She associated herself with a Mayan goddess. *Ixku*? Remember her taking that name? Trouble is, when your best friend is in love with a witch, you can't risk the friendship by telling him."

As we resumed walking back to Dinkin's Bay Marina, he continued to tell me things about the woman I thought I knew but, as I would discover, I didn't know at all.

Years ago, he said, in Central America, while I'd lain unconscious, they'd taken a break together, smoked a joint, and she'd tried to seduce him—unsuccessfully.

"I didn't even know you that well back then," he said, "but I had this gut feeling you and I were going to be *hermanos*. It's one of the few times Zamboni and the Hat Trick Twins didn't win that particular sort of face-off. A buddy's girlfriend is a line I've never crossed."

Two nights ago, in Miami, she'd tried to seduce him again—which is why he'd insisted that they return to Sanibel. It's also why he'd stayed aboard his boat most of the day, fretting over whether he should tell me or not.

Tomlinson's a flake, but he's a brilliant flake, with Ph.D.s in philosophy and sociology, and he keeps up on the professional literature. Judging from Pilar's behavior, he said, she was driven by a disorder that he called "acute bipolar mania," which is the severest form of what was once called manic depression.

"They don't love anyone," he said. "They're not capable of the emotion. They only play roles that advance their own delusions."

Pilar? Could it be true?

I questioned him in detail. Most of the questions were clinical. What symptomatic behavior had he observed? Could he name specific things she'd said and done?

Yes—he could. And did.

I have no training—and little interest—in his field. Yet, listening to him, I realized that I'd observed many of the symptoms myself, but hadn't recognized them for what they were.

In hindsight, Pilar's conduct *had* been disturbing at times. I remembered sudden rages quickly masked if strangers appeared. I remembered overhearing her cooing to herself as a baby might talk when she didn't know I was listening. I remembered making a joke of the fact that, after four years, she still didn't know my birthday. I remembered her telling me things that I knew were untrue, and that I thought were her intentional exaggerations.

"That's part of the sickness," Tomlinson said. "They may lie intentionally if it suits their needs, or their delusion can bend the truth any way necessary to advance their own cause. Either way, the lie becomes real to them."

Odd references in Lake's e-mails also now made sense to me. At least twice he'd mentioned that he was worried about his mother, and that he was trying to get her to "talk to someone."

When I'd inquired about what, he hadn't responded.

Ultimately, I was convinced that what Tomlinson was saying about Pilar was valid. It was a startling revelation that left me, for those few minutes at least, emotionally numbed.

He further surprised me by adding, "My personal opinion about you and Pilar has always been that you never really loved her, Doc. You maybe *believed* you loved her, but that's because she was safe. There was no chance you would have to marry her, or that she'd show up one day at the lab with all her luggage asking to move in. She lived in a different country, had her own life. You rarely saw her or spoke with her, so you could use her as a sort of mirror to project your own female ideal."

When I said, "You're describing a guy who's not only selfish and shallow, but emotionally blocked," Tomlinson replied, "Well, pal, for all our good qualities, we both live alone for a reason, don't we?"

Smiling, I told him I'd have to think about that. But, yeah, it was possibly true.

As we neared Tarpon Bay Road and the mangrove lane that leads to my lab and to the marina, he insisted on returning to the subject of the San Diego bombing, to the guilt he felt, and to his moral obligation to turn himself in to authorities.

I reminded him, "You said that you were a different person before you were institutionalized. When pathology is involved, a person's behavior can't be judged as either moral or immoral. Sickness is a form of disability. Like Pilar—you said she wasn't an evil person, just bad. So stop blaming yourself. Leave it in the past where it belongs. My friend Johnny's long dead, and his wife Cheryl's happily remarried. So just leave it be."

Sounding harried, confused, Tomlinson said, "I don't know, Doc. I don't know. Do you really believe that? Do you believe that moral responsibility can be mitigated? I don't think I buy it. Spiritually, man, I don't think I can allow myself to go on as if nothing happened. I took a human life! I think I have an obligation to let the legal system decide how I should be punished."

When I put my arm over his shoulder, pulled him to me roughly, and said in a joking tone, "Let's put it this way: If you try to turn yourself in to law enforcement, I won't kill you, but I may try to slap a little sense into you," my friend Tomlinson's knees buckled for a moment, and he began to sob.

He'd reacted the same way not so long ago, the afternoon I'd given him papers that exonerated him from the crime he now knew that he'd committed.

RUNNING my boat fast across Hillsborough Bay now, Tampa behind me and the St. Pete skyline now off to my right, it was painful to think about Tomlinson. Painful to think that he seemed determined to carry out what he saw as a spiritual obligation to confess to that long-ago murder.

What a loss that would be to the marina. What a loss to everyone who knew the man—particularly to his best friend.

Oddly, though, about Pilar Fuentes, I now felt no sense of loss whatsoever. To have her perplexing behavior explained so rationally had, in the instant of my understanding it, purged me of all emotional sensations attached to her.

The woman I thought I knew did not exist. She was a fiction. Therefore, my history with her was also an illusion, and so no sensation of regret, or joy, or bitterness could be assigned.

It was the weirdest feeling. One moment, the Pilar I thought I'd cared for had existed in memory. The next moment, she'd been vaporized by the truth.

"She loves no one," Tomlinson had said.

It was the saddest of phrases, but also freeing. In that instant, she disappeared from my past. In that way, at least, I could relate to Tomlinson. It was a little like having a block of memory wiped clean.

Dewey was still there with me, though. Thoughts of her remained, along with the deep, deep regret I now felt that I hadn't recognized the truth about Pilar before I spoke the idiotic words that Dewey had overheard.

Off to my left were spoil islands, and the rectangular green mountain of phosphate spoil that marked Gibsonton. I slowed to 40 mph and cut in close to an island furred with pine and a few scraggly cabbage palms, before slowing to idle near a section of white beach that looked like it might have a creek near shore.

I checked my watch: 7:25 P.M. on a Friday, early May.

A little more than a half an hour before sunset.

So should I run up Bullfrog Creek, get closer to the trailer park, and risk meeting Prax Lourdes coming out? Or should I assume he was already sitting somewhere near the Sunshine Skyway, waiting for me to arrive by car?

Meeting him, I decided, might not be such a bad thing.

I pushed the throttle forward, jumping my skiff onto plane, and headed for the creek.

THIRTY

DR. VALERIE Maria Santos remembered very little of what had happened late Thursday night, the night that she'd been abducted. The details failed to imprint on her brain because the perpetrator had nearly killed her accidentally, he was so freakishly strong, plus he knew almost nothing about administering ether as an anesthetic.

Dr. Valerie remembered being in Operating Room II—her favorite—and that she'd told the techs to play opera, loud.

That was standard. Dr. Valerie was well known for scheduling late surgeries—she was a night owl—and also for playing unusual music while she operated.

There was a brilliant thoracic surgeon in southwest Florida who required that AC/DC's heavy metal rock be piped in through the surgical theater's Bose speakers when he cut a chest. (Physicians who succeed in the esoteric fields of surgery are artists, after all, as well as technicians.) But Dr. Valerie's musical selections—Peruvian flute, Cuban jazz, and now opera—were the favorite among the staff.

When Dr. Valerie operated—with her fast and gifted fingers, and with Bocelli's "Our Prayer" echoing in the operating room—it was like attending church but at the same time watching a brilliant composer conduct her own symphony.

With opera as a backdrop, and charged with the sensation of playing accompanists to her solo genius, the nurses and techs, when finished, would sometimes leave the room and head to the lockers or lounge in tears. Dr. Valerie's choice of music seemed an indicator of the famous woman's intellect, as well as the empathy that the doctor invested in each and every patient.

The little woman really could perform magic, seemed to be able to make burned tissue rejoin itself and heal.

Lately, Dr. Valerie's music of choice was exclusively opera. Almost always sung by Andrea Bocelli. But on Thursday night, the night she was abducted, her selection was *Madama Butterfly*—appropriate, considering not only what happened, but her own screwed-up romantic life.

She also remembered that the case was a skin transplant on a five-year-old who'd pulled a pot of boiling water off her mother's stove. Dr. Valerie let her assistants do most of the close-needle work, which was increasingly common—spread the skills. It was a tiny patch of skin, and the little girl was going to be just fine.

Then the woman's memory skipped, and she was downstairs in the female doctors' locker room, standing at her locker, C-217, changing into her running clothes. Because it was a hot night and very late—close to midnight—she just wore shorts, a knit shirt, and a pair of well-worn New Balances.

She'd stopped into the doctors' lounge—the business sections from half a dozen newspapers were spread everywhere; that's all her colleagues seemed to read—and took a couple of bites from an apple, then chugged a bottle of water before heading out the hospital's rear exit, past the little rose garden.

She'd dreaded going home. For years, she'd disliked spending time alone with her husband, Edward. But in the last few weeks, it was worse than ever because, she felt certain, he had finally found out about her two-year affair with a local nurse anesthetist.

Sooner or later, the man would confront her. It was inevitable. And when he did, Dr. Valerie had already decided, she was going to tell him the truth. Which meant divorce, and also meant headlines in the rag newspapers.

Ed had been staying up later than usual, sullen and moping, spoiling for a fight. She felt that Thursday might be the night.

That's all she remembered until she was standing at the electronic gate outside their home. She had a good sweat going, was running in place as she typed in the combination, when from behind her, she heard a man's deep voice say, "Dr. Valerie? Do you have time for a patient?"

She'd turned to see a huge man wearing a hospital gown, his face wrapped in gauze. There was the strong odor of ether on him.

"Do I know you?"

"Kinda. We've written some e-mails back and forth. Say—do you know anything about a skin condition called trig-eee-minal neur-al-gia? That's a fuckin' hard word to say."

She remembered feeling a chill at the inappropriateness of his language; remembered backing away, but the damn gate was still locked.

"Yes," she said, "I know about trigeminal neuralgia. It's terrible. The pain can be even worse than the original burn. But I don't discuss medicine away from my office. I'm sorry."

She'd turned sideways and was trying to punch in the gate combination while still keeping an eye on the big man.

"What about those new anticonvulsion drugs? Someone told me they might work. Might take away some of the pain."

The doctor's steady hands were shaking. She couldn't get the combination right!

"Yes, that's true with the anticonvulsives. We've been getting excellent results. I'm very interested in your case, but I've got to go now. Call me at the office. We'll talk about it."

She heard the man say, "I'll be damned. The fuckin' boy is right again!"

Because she loved children, she asked without even thinking about it, "What boy is that?"

The big man said, "The boy. The kid I wrote you about in the plane crash deal. The kid who's gonna be my donor." Talking as he stepped toward her, he lifted her as if she were no heavier than a pillow, the stink of ether suddenly overwhelming.

There were then a few blurry memories of lying on the bottom of a fast, open boat . . . and then of being sealed tight in darkness; cramped in a space no larger than a coffin . . . or a 50-gallon drum.

Terror.

Dr. Valerie Maria Santos remembered *that.*

IF SHE hadn't been wearing her digital cross-trainer's watch, the one with the heart monitor, the famous plastic surgeon wouldn't have known that it was Friday morning close to noon when she awoke. She was in a steel room that was painted gray. There was the muffled rumble of an engine, and the room was rocking gently.

She was on a ship.

She lay on a cot, her arms and legs bound with duct tape. Fortunately, whoever had abducted her hadn't also gagged her.

There was vomit on the cot, and on the floor of the boat.

The doctor was thirstier than she could ever remember being.

She called out weakly, "Hello? Can someone help me? I need help. Please."

She called out a few more times over the next ten minutes before she heard a clanking at the door, and a hugely fat blond woman stepped into the room. The woman was wearing a baggy T-shirt, sweatstains at the armpits, and smoking a cigarette. Without taking the cigarette from her mouth, the woman shook a warning finger as she said, "You fancy little bitch, if you open your mouth one more time, make the slightest fucking sound or fuss, I'll stick you back in that can and dump your ass overboard! I 'bout busted my ass getting that fancy microscope of yours into sick bay, so I ain't in the mood to take your shit!"

Vicious. The woman meant it.

No one had ever talked to Dr. Valerie like that in her life.

"Please. Just some water. That's all I want. *Please.*"

The big woman made a noise of disgust and came back a few minutes later with a liter bottle of water. The doctor's arms were taped in front of her, so she could hold the bottle. She lifted it to her lips.

Still smoking, the woman watched her drink. The expression on her face was scary.

"Why are you doing this to me? Where are you taking me? I have money. I can pay."

With startling agility, the big woman jumped across the room and slapped the bottle out of the doctor's hands, hissing, "I told you not to make another sound! You say one more word, and I'll lock the two of us in here. I'll do you *myself.* How'd you like that, you fancy little bitch?"

When the woman was gone, door closed behind her, Dr. Valerie buried her face in the pillow and wept.

AT 6:15, Friday evening, the sound of the engine changed from a rumble to a vibrating roar, and the boat began to move. Dr. Valerie had dozed on and off through the day, feeling sick from the ether.

She was still thirsty, but felt stronger now.

With her teeth, she began to alternately chew at the tape on her hands and unwrap the tape that bound her ankles. Within half an hour, she was free.

But the door was locked from the outside. She considered pounding on the door, trying to get someone's attention, but the fat woman so terrified her that she didn't risk it.

There was nothing in the room to read, so the doctor began to pace. She continued to pace, her brain scanning frantically for a solution. Why was this happening? The woman had said something about her microscope being moved into the ship's sick bay. What could that possibly mean?

Over and over again, Dr. Valerie went through her fragmented memories of the night before. Picturing what she could visualize of the man who had abducted her. Trying to recall his every word.

He'd said that he was a patient. Was he?

No. She became certain of that. She remembered her patients. She would have recognized something about him: his voice, his size, the rough language.

He'd also said they'd exchanged e-mails. But that wasn't true either. She had so little free time that, aside from close friends, she seldom wrote to anyone.

There were a couple of exceptions: the Nigerian pre-med student that she was mentoring, and the Central American girl who'd been badly burned and who had the terrible, outlaw doctor as a physician. In fact, she'd written to Mary Perez the previous morning, offering more technical advice for the film script the poor girl was writing for her class at the University of Nicaragua.

Dr. Valerie's name was signed to all of the correspondence they received on the web page, but her staff handled all that.

So, the answer was no. They had not exchanged e-mails. Yet, one of the few things she remembered clearly was that he'd said that he had e-mailed her about a boy. The boy who was his *donor.* Clearly, the boy was real— he'd apparently told the big man about the new anticonvulsion drugs. And the man had said something about a plane crash.

None of it made sense.

Valerie Santos was an articulate, brilliant woman and, like most overachievers, obsessive. She continued to pace, her mind scanning for some explanation, until the ship began to lift and roll too much, and she had to lie down on the cot.

That was around eight-thirty P.M.

At around nine, she stiffened, then leaped to her feet, whispering to herself, "Oh my God . . . oh my God. No! My *surgical* microscope?"

All the little pieces of the puzzle had suddenly drifted into place. Mary Perez's screenplay had to do with a plane crash. The main character was a plastic surgeon who had to do a full facial transplant under Third World conditions. The donor was a boy who was supposedly beyond saving. The recipient was a very large man; a film star, in the girl's script.

Pacing again, the doctor began to chew at her nails, desperate to find another explanation.

Oh God. No . . .

She couldn't.

She hadn't been e-mailing a girl named Mary. She'd been corresponding with her abductor. He was Mary Perez.

The last thing Dr. Valerie had written to him was:

My Dear Mary,

I am so proud of the progress you are making! Yes, as I wrote to you, after a full facial transplant, the recipient will look almost exactly like the donor, with the exception of eyes and teeth.

But there is one serious flaw in the premise for your script that you need to fix. No ethical surgeon would ever allow a living human being to be used as a donor for that procedure. Doesn't matter if they think the boy in your script is sure to die. I certainly wouldn't do it under any circumstances. Never!

No, the boy character must already be dead before the surgery begins. Something else: Under the conditions you are describing, he can have been dead for only an hour or two if his skin is still to be suitable for harvesting . . .

THIRTY
ONE

I TIED my boat to an overhanging limb in a mosquito drainage, jammed the key in my pocket, and stepped off the bow onto the trampoline roots of red mangrove trees. I climbed through mangroves and then highland scrub toward the trailer park, keeping pace with the slowly lengthening shadows of new darkness.

It was close to nine P.M.

Soon, I could see lighted windows through the trees, people moving within: rows of illuminated rectangles embedded in shoebox files of larger aluminum rectangles, human theater going on within those small containers.

Inside one of the trailers, I saw what appeared to be a woman with an Abe Lincoln beard lean to hug a man with a massively fat face: sideshow exhibitors carrying out their lives; public people living privately, intimately in this small, protected world.

The park was its own province of rich smells and unexpected sounds. Pork chops were frying in a pan, spaghetti was simmering in someone's kitchen, there was a trash fire smoldering, and manure from the Indian elephant I'd seen earlier was somewhere nearby.

Once, I stopped when I thought I heard the low, organic rumble of distant thunder. I stood and listened to the strange sound until my memories of Africa finally correctly identified the noise: There was a caged lion not far away, purring and grunting, trying to communicate with wild lions thirteen thousand miles away across the Atlantic.

At least, I hoped the lion was caged.

The trailer park had a one-lane asphalt street that circled through it. The street was lighted by occasional bare bulbs suspended beneath tin-can shades. I avoided the pools of light, and made my way to the circus wagon with its gaudy marquee that proclaimed that THE WORLD OF WON-DERS awaited inside, including the bear with three eyes, and Dezi the Talking Wonder Dog.

Its windows were dimly lit, while the trailers around it seemed inhabited; normal.

Perhaps it was dimly lighted for a reason. I decided to check out the wagon my son had identified.

The street I was on was empty and quiet but for the lion's low rumble and the distant barking of a dog. I gave it a moment, then slid into deeper shadows beside the wagon, and then around behind the wagon.

I touched my ear to the aluminum shell.

Silence.

Modular trailers aren't built to be secure, and it didn't take me long to find a window that I could jimmy. I was just pulling myself up into the window when my cellular phone began its silent, vibrating alert.

I stopped, took it out of my pocket, checked the caller I.D., and saw that it was Harris.

I wasn't wearing the headset, so I held it to my ear and answered with a whispered, "Talk," hoping he'd understand that I could not talk.

He did. With no more prompting, he said, "We've driven back and forth over the Skyway Bridge about nine times. I think he was waiting for a break in traffic. Finally, he had us throw both cases off the bridge. It was from one of the lower sections, maybe sixty feet down to the water, but I never got a clear look at who was down there. But we did make delivery. When your pal Kong asked about *your* package, the guy on the other end said that we'd make the exchange in a week or so, and that he'd be in touch."

I doubted that Lourdes ever expected to release my son, but I didn't respond.

After a few long moments of silence, Harris said, "If you're in trouble, hit any key three times. The cavalry will be on its way."

I whispered, "I'm fine," then cleared the phone.

I PULLED myself through the window into a small room that had an elevated stage, and various show props stacked in the corners. I took out the tiny tactical aluminum penlight I'd brought, but didn't use it because there was enough peripheral light to see. The wall behind me was covered with a mural depicting a white dog wearing a professorial mortarboard and holding a microphone.

Hello, Dezi.

The trailer had a barnyard smell. Not dirty, but of livestock, straw, grain, and paint. Judging from the smell, the freak bear, apparently, was a real live animal. That meant there would be a cage.

Where better to keep an active, kidnapped boy locked away than a bear cage?

I moved across the room, toward the hall into which dim light filtered. Just as I was about to enter the hallway, my cellular phone began to vibrate once again. I stepped back into the shadows, took it from my pocket, expecting to see Harris's number. I saw, instead, that the caller's I.D. was blocked.

Only one person had done that before.

Dewey.

I fought the urge to put the phone to my ear just on the chance that I might hear her voice. Instead, I waited until the thing quit buzzing. Then I deactivated it and slipped it back into my pocket.

There was better light in the hall, which ran the length along the front of the trailer. There was another exhibitor's room to my left, plus a small vendor's kitchen with a two-burner gas stove and a soft drink station.

A greasy pan was on the stove. Someone had been cooking there recently.

I found where they'd kept my son, Lake, imprisoned just a little farther down the hall. It was a box that was walled and roofed with steel bars. The cage was about half the size of a small bedroom. Like the performing dog's theater, a mural of the bear was painted in bright colors on the wall behind the cage. The animal had a weird-looking Cyclops eye in the middle of its forehead. But there was no bear in the cage, and there was no boy.

There was, however, lots of young boy residue. Several things I saw were characteristic of what I knew and loved about my son.

In the far back corner was a cot, neatly made. The top sheet was pulled and tucked so tightly that you could have bounced a quarter on it.

It was the way I made my own bed each and every morning of my life.

There was a simple table and chair in the opposite corner, with a reading light plugged into an extension cord. On the table was a tin plate, a cup, fork and spoon, all overturned and neatly laid out atop a towel. There was also a magnifying glass, a blunt scissors, and a blank sketchpad. The table was dominated, though, by stacks of books.

I hadn't used my little flashlight, but I did now, turning my head sideways to read the book spines.

Most of the books were nonfiction: books about fish, fishing, biology, and the other natural sciences. There were a couple of the small Audubon guides that I had in my own library. I noted that there were also several standard physician's reference books, as well as one called *Studies in Abnormal Psychology*.

I wondered if Lake was reading that in an attempt to understand Lourdes. Or his mother?

It was a sad and touching question to consider.

They don't love anyone, Tomlinson had said. *They're not capable of the emotion.*

Could that possibly be true of Pilar when it came to her own son?

If accurate, it made Lake an emotional orphan of a sort—a description that I'd never applied to my own circumstances in life—and that possibility made me all the more desperate to find him.

I tested the cage door. It swung open.

I stepped inside, hoping that Lake had anticipated me coming and that he had left me one more clue; some kind of parting directive. As I did, though, I froze when a quivering voice, off to my right, said, "The boy, he gone, you know. They both gone. And they ain't comin' back no more."

Then the wagon's dim overhead fluorescent lights flickered on.

322

RANDY WAYNE WHITE

STARTLED, I jumped, turned, and found myself looking down into the face of a very old and thin, dwarf-sized black man. He was the color of a winter leaf, and so tiny that he looked as if a gust of wind might lift him skyward and float him away.

I suspected he'd bought the blue denim coveralls he wore in the children's section of some department store.

The man didn't have the oversized head and hands I associate with dwarfism, though. He appeared regularly proportioned in every way, and normal but for his eyes. Judging from the way he stood, with his head tilted back, and because of the blue film that covered his eyes, I suspected that the man was blind.

Even so, I immediately stepped to the cell's door so he couldn't slam the thing and lock me in. As I did, he said in what sounded to be a Cajun accent, "Are you him? You the one the boy call 'Doc'? Yeah, you must be. So I know it true, now. The boy said you'd come. I learn to never doubt that boy, Laken. He a good one, he is, jus' a good li'l boo-boy. When Laken leave, I pass a big ol' hug on him, I did. I'm gonna miss me that T-boy."

I said quickly, "That's my son. Is he O.K.? If anyone's hurt him for any reason—"

"Your boy fine," he interrupted. "He jus' fine. I took care of him myself. Made him eat good every day."

As the man spoke, I noticed that he backed away slightly just before I pushed the cage door open. So maybe he wasn't totally blind. Or maybe he just had the heightened sensory abilities that some say compensate for the loss of vision.

I said to him, "Where is he now? My son. Where did Lourdes take him?"

The old man's expression showed puzzlement. "Who that name you using? Lourdes?"

"Lourdes, the man who kidnapped Laken. Where are they?"

"Oh . . . that be Jimmy Gauer you talkin' about. *Mean* Jimmy Gauer. Jimmy, he used to live here when he jus' a squirt. We all thought the Gauers, that whole family, that they long dead till Mean Jimmy come back here two, three years ago, and buy him a little place."

I said, "The guy I'm talking about is a big man. Broad, with burn scars on his hands and face. Is that who you're calling Jimmy Gauer?"

"Oh yeah, he got scars," the old man said. "Mean Jimmy, that's what we called him as a boy. He got him lots of scars. More than jus' on his face, too. But me, I ain't never seen 'im. Not the way you and him sees things, anyway. Why you think he let me watch your boy, and not kill me before he go off? I be a blind man, you know."

There was a curious lilt of a smile in his voice, and on his face, when he said that. I wondered why.

I said, "That's the guy I know as Lourdes. If you *did* know where they've gone, would you tell me?"

"Yes indeedy, I would, sir! I'll help you any way I can. Ol' Baxter Glapion—which be me—I got no good things to say about Mean Jimmy. And I sure do like that li'l boo-boy of yours, Laken. So come in, come on in"—he was waving his arm as if to drag me behind, already walking down the hall—"maybe Jimmy, he forgot something back behind that'll tell you where they is. Believe me, that man didn't tell me *nothin'*."

I began to follow, then stopped. "Give me a second to look through my son's things first, O.K.?"

The old man waited patiently while I stripped the bed, looked through every book. I even got down on my hands and knees and looked under the table. Maybe something was written there.

Nothing.

As I was finishing, the old man said, "Laken, he left a book for me to give you. He knowed you was comin'. Called you 'Doc.' Didn't say you was his daddy. That one smart boy you got there, mister."

I stood quickly. "Show me the book."

Baxter Glapion moved with the gliding, sure-footed gait of a tightrope walker, or someone who navigates a room by memory. I followed him down the hall, past the main entrance, into a private living quarters. It was where the old man lived, apparently.

As we walked, I listened to him tell me that the wagon we were in had belonged to Lourdes' uncle, who'd died the previous year. Lourdes had inherited it. Lourdes' family, the Gauers, were old carney folk, he said, sideshow performers mostly, and Baxter had been an old friend of the family.

Lourdes had told the old man that he was keeping Lake locked up for his own safety, and as a favor to the boy's mother. There was a war going on down in Central America, he'd said, and Lake was a prime candidate for abduction. Trouble was, the boy refused to stay away from his mother. Kept finding a way to sneak across the border home each time she sent him away.

Partial truths always make the most convincing lies. But Baxter said he didn't believe the man anyway. Only pretended to.

We stopped inside the main living area. I turned on a light when he said he didn't mind. There was a couch that folded out into a bed. There was a worn chair, a table with stacks of books on tape, and books in Braille. A reader. There was a television, too, and the walls were covered with framed carnival posters. He motioned vaguely toward one of the posters and said that it was Prax Lourdes' mother.

I stepped to the wall and looked at a red, blue, and yellow print painting of a huge, muscle-bound woman with improbably large breasts. She had curly blond hair and wore a wrestling singlet. The poster read:

THE CANADIAN IRON WOMAN

THE GRAPPLING BOZARK

Remembering that Lourdes had used the strange word as his internet password, I asked Baxter, "What does it mean? 'Bozark'?"

"It an ol'-time carney bit. *Bozark,* that what we used to call a woman wrestler could beat a man. Edith Gauer, she could do that, too. She could beat most any man.

"Men she beat most often, though, was her husband, Benny, and her boy Jimmy. Benny, he were like me, a li'l peeshwank runt of a man. Had him a balancin' act. He used li'l Jimmy in the act until Jimmy fall and hit his head so bad. After that is when li'l Jimmy turn into *Mean* Jimmy."

"Because he fell. You're saying he wasn't always mean?"

The old man was shaking his head. "Nicest little boy you could meet even with his ma beatin' him. Until the wire they was on snapped, and he knocked his brain in so bad, the boy nearly passed over. After that was when he become *Mean* Jimmy."

That was a startling thing to hear.

Baxter had a drawer open, taking something from it, and now he handed me a book. "Your boy tell me to give you that."

It was the *Audubon Guide to Florida*, the same book I had at the lab.

"Is there anything else? Any message?"

"Oh Lord, you don't know how mean Jimmy can be if you think the boy dumb enough to risk slippin' a message to anyone; something dangerous as that. When Jimmy's head got all healed up, that when he start likin' to burn things. Cats and such. A chimp once, I'm pretty sure. He *crazy* mean. No, your boy woulda been riskin' ol' Baxter's life if he'd slipped me a message."

I leafed through the *Audubon Guide* more slowly than the other books, thinking that Lake may have, once again, used the animals noted in his e-mail as markers. It's what I would have done.

That's just what he did.

On page 307, under reddish egret, barely visible in pencil and written in miniature block letters, I read, "Lv Fl by ship, date X?"

It took me only a moment to understand that my son was telling me that he believed that he and Lourdes, or just Lourdes, would be leaving Florida by ship, departure date unknown.

As I looked up "bullfrog"—found nothing—then looked for "parrots"— not indigenous, so not listed—Baxter said with the same little prideful smile he'd had before, "When you look at the posters on the walls, anybody up there seem familiar?"

I was in a hurry, but I paused long enough to take a quick glance around the room. Something that immediately caught my attention, because they seemed odd and out of place, were a dozen or so photos that were tacked next to a mirror on the far wall. The photos were close-ups of men's faces— noses, cheeks, whole foreheads. They appeared to be from a medical journal, or a medical reference book. I realized that the photos were of male patients before and after they'd had various forms of plastic surgery.

The list of drugs Lourdes had demanded popped into my mind, and I thought, *What the hell is he up to?*

Baxter interrupted, pressing, "You don't see my posters no more? Them posters still up there, ain't they?"

Once again leafing through the *Audubon Guide,* now searching for page 296, the American alligator, I looked in the direction the old man was staring.

There was Baxter Glapion. His likeness was depicted on two posters that were mounted side by side.

In one, he was dressed in a straw skirt, gnawing on a human skull, and billed as Kiki, the Cannibal Dwarf. On the other, he was wearing a similar grass skirt. But he also had a turban on his head, and was holding a crystal ball and a magic wand. He was sitting on a cushion, head thrown back, arms outstretched as if in a trance. He was billed as Mystivo, the Pygmy Fortune Teller.

The smile still there, he said, "The fortune-teller bit, I can still do it. Let me think on you a moment now, and I'll tell you something about yourself. Somethin' nobody else ever knowed. It's not a lie, man, it *real*. I'm from the New Orleans Glapions—our family descendants of Priestess Marie Laveau. I've got the *voudon* blood in me."

Concentrating on the book, I said, "Voodoo, huh? I've got a sister you'd love. But unless you can tell me where my son is, I'm not interested."

The old man had his head back, arms out, palms up, just like the poster. I heard him tell me my correct age, a figure close to my weight, and the month in which I was born.

Still leafing through pages, I said, "You're good, Baxter. You really are. I've always wondered how you carnival people did that."

I'd found alligators in the reptile section and was squinting, searching hard for my son's tiny writing, as he said, "I only know how it is *I* do it, man. Back when my eyes was workin', they seen so much ugliness, all the light leaked outta me. My real vision, my good vision, didn't come back until I lost my sight."

He was silent for a moment before he added, "I see you had a bad time these last couple years. You and some a your friends, too. You were in the shadow time a your life. But better times here now. Your luck, and all the luck a those around you, done changed for the better. You got bright times ahead. Lots a laughin' and bed-happy-makin' love, and party times are ahead for you."

"Great," I said, absently. "Good to hear it."

On the page opposite two photographs of gators, I discovered that Lake had written something, but the letters were so tiny that it was very difficult to read. I stood and held the book next to the light, my face close to the page, as Baxter said in a more somber tone, "But you got you a little bit more trouble comin', too. I can see that. You got you some trouble comin' with somethin' that might happen to one of your two children. You maybe gonna lose one of them."

He moaned the next words very softly: "Ah Lordy, I sure hope that what I see ain't true."

Irritated, I said, "I don't have two children. I only have the one son, the boy you met. And a crazy man's got him, so, yeah, he's in trouble."

"No sir! I see two children!"

I said, "Well, you're wrong. Baxter—could you please be quiet for a while?"

Squinting at the book, I could now make out the words "LOURDES WANTS . . ." as Baxter ignored me and continued anyway, "I see only one more thing in your future that's bad, man. What I see is, I see that, one day . . . oh, this *is* a dark'un . . . I see that you gonna have to kill a man who's been a good friend to you. Whoo-whee—"

That moan again, but this time the sound contained pain and surprise.

"Ye-e-eah, oh Lord, I see this event very clearly. You be an unusual creature, Doc Ford! Yes, you are! That day gonna come. The day gonna come when you kill your friend, that be the darkest time of all."

I let him push on without comment—uneasy, though, with what I was hearing—and let him finish, saying, "But mostly . . . yes, I see . . . you got happy times and good feelin's ahead. You gonna be a smilin' man comin' up very soon—if you help that child of yours that's in so much trouble."

I looked at him sharply, wishing he'd shut up so I could concentrate. I said, "That's exactly what I'm trying to do," then turned away from him and hurried down the hall to the cage where they'd kept Lake.

From the desk, I took up the magnifying glass and found some decent light. The magnifying glass made his tiny block letters swell off the page.

When I read what he'd written, the photos of surgery patients tacked to the wall, and the drugs Lourdes had demanded now all gathered in my brain with terrible clarity, and I finally understood the intent of my son's abductor.

Lake had written: LOURDES WANTS MY FACE. HELP ME!

I dropped the magnifying glass and book, and jogged back to the living room, feeling the wagon tremble beneath my weight. I had to force myself to appear calm as I said to the old man, "Did Lourdes—the guy you call Mean Jimmy—did he ever mention a local plastic surgeon, a woman by the name of—"

I stopped because I was blanking on her name—probably because I was so scared, so adrenaline charged. Harris had said her name a couple of times. Finally, it came to me, and I continued, "Did Lourdes ever mention a Dr. Valerie Santos? Or did he show any interest in Tampa General Hospital? Particularly, the burn unit there?"

The old man was staring over my shoulder, not looking at me, but seeing me, shaking his head as he said, "No, Mean Jimmy never tell me nothing like that. But I heard what happened on the news. I know what you talkin' about. The pretty woman doctor who got stolen off the street. But he never say anything, and I don't know nothin' 'bout it.

"Understand—Mean Jimmy, he not like other people. His brain different. It never speak to my eyes. What he thinkin', his thoughts, they never did come into my head like your'n do, or other people's do. His thoughts is all scrambled. Inside Mean Jimmy's head, all my old eyes ever saw were gibberish. Lots of swearin', and a bright red anger. It like an outsider comin' to Gib'town and hearing our carney talk."

I stood for a moment, my lungs struggling against panic. Considering the drugs Lourdes had demanded, what were the odds that he was not involved with the abduction of the famous plastic surgeon?

Without speaking again to Baxter Glapion, I charged out the wagon's front door. I didn't slow until I reached my boat.

THIRTY
TWO

I TOUCHED a button on my plastic watch and saw that it was 9:40 P.M.

I also saw that my hands were trembling.

I'm supposed to be the icy one. The cold professional. I've been in so many tight spots, in so many places and circumstances in which my life or someone else's life was at risk, that I should know by now how my brain and body will react.

I've come to expect this response: The pressure to think and perform seems to banish emotion, and a kind of predatory chill moves in to fill that emotional void. My concentration becomes intense, as does my sensory awareness, although, oddly, color perception diminishes—as if color is an unnecessary frill.

This time, however, that's not how I reacted. Maybe it was because my son was involved. But I certainly didn't stay cool and collected. In fact, never in my life had I felt so frightened, so panic-stricken.

As I stood at the wheel of my skiff, steering at fast idle down Bullfrog Creek, I had to fight to keep from hyperventilating. My body trembled uncontrollably each time I exhaled. My hands shook when I took the cell phone and dialed Harris Lilly's number.

I've seldom used a cellular phone, but I discovered that, thanks to the little headphone unit, even while running a boat at speed, I could hear pretty well if I turned the ear containing the receiver into the wind.

When my friend answered, that's what I did.

Harris was alone, in his own vehicle now, he told me. Then he listened in stunned silence as I told him that I had reason to believe that Prax Lourdes, my son, and the abducted surgeon were aboard a commercial vessel somewhere in or around Tampa Bay.

When I was finished, he made a sneezing sound, then sputtered, "Jesus Christ, you're shittin' me! You think Dr. Santos is being held captive aboard a ship that checked out of our port? In that case, our agreement is off, Doc. Sorry, but I've got to call in the cops. It's not a private matter anymore."

I told him that I'd expected exactly that reaction. I understood that he had to do his duty, but added, "What scares the hell out of me is that local law enforcement is going to figure out which ship they're on, and then try to go storming in with choppers and SWAT teams and a fleet of boats. This guy Lourdes is a freak. He'll kill my son before they take him. That doctor, too. He'll set them both on fire just to watch them burn before they cart him off to the insane asylum. I know, because he's done it before."

"Then what do you want me to do, Doc?"

"I don't know. I don't *know*. I understand your position. I don't see any other alternatives. But you're right, we have to notify the professionals and get a search started."

I felt like sobbing.

Harris said, "O.K., O.K., we will. In the meantime, though, there's no reason you and I can't be sniffing around on our own. I can call our Tampa pilot dispatcher. There may not be a long list of night transits, and I can get the list of vessels that have been cleared to leave. We're figuring our bad guy's on a ship scheduled to spook out soon, right? I can get those names to you in five or ten minutes. But, Doc, we're not going to have a lot of time before the big search sweeps start. This woman is an internationally respected surgeon. She's *international* news."

If Harris could narrow the list of ships, then I might have a shot at finding my son. For the first time, I felt a slight surge of optimism. "We'll work with what we've got," I said. "I'm under way now—"

As I spoke, my phone began to make an odd chiming sound. It took me a moment to figure out that it was the Call Waiting option. I had another call coming in.

I said, "Hold it a second," and looked at the phone. The little face plate was flashing, showing caller I.D. information. I read: *Elmase Baretto.*

It was Jorge Balserio's thug, the husky little Nicaraguan, calling from the Miami area code.

I said, "Hey, this could be important. Do you mind checking on the names of those ships while I answer this? I'll call you right back."

I touched the Talk button, then said in Spanish, "You'd better not be calling to talk about clothes."

Elmase said, "Even when you not tryin' to be funny, you sound so very funny. I could teach you something about clothes. *Somebody* needs to."

Then he said, "Hey . . . what's all that noise, dude? You sound like you in a hurricane that's going on."

Trying to talk on the phone and navigate an unfamiliar creek, I was still traveling at fast idle. Because the boat was quieter on plane, traveling at much faster speed, I considered punching the throttle, but decided it was too risky while I was preoccupied.

I told him, "I'm in a boat, so you've got to speak loud. I don't have time to explain."

He said, "In a boat, man? That's perfect, man. 'Cause that's what I'm calling to tell you. General Balserio, he wants that crazy bastard stopped so bad. We want to help you, just like we say. The General, he's going to lose the Revolution 'cause of that crazy goat-fucker if he hurts your boy. So here's what we found out—you got something to write with?"

What Elmase told me, I didn't have to write down. Balserio, or his people, had discovered that Lourdes had some kind of connection with a tramp freighter that made regular runs from Nicaragua and Masagua to Havana, then on to Tampa and back. It often carried fertilizer, although the ship was such a wreck that the company was known to be willing to haul just about anything.

Balserio's people had it from a reliable source that Lourdes had made a cash deal with the captain and crew of this phosphate freighter to give him safe passage out of Florida, and that the boat would be leaving for Central America soon.

Elmase told me, "Here's the part you gotta write, dude, so you don't forget. If you find this boat, you gonna find the crazy Man-Burner aboard her. Maybe your son, too."

The name of the freighter was *Repatriate,* and it was registered out of Monrovia, Liberia.

It was the same decrepit ship, covered with rust and fertilizer dust, that I'd seen headed to sea, probably an hour or so outbound from the phosphate plant at Gibsonton as I was headed inbound.

I told Elmase, "I'm not going to forget."

I DIALED Harris immediately, but before I could speak, he said, "Hey, ol' buddy, I just noticed there's some old bastard in a cowboy hat tailing me in a white unmarked Ford. It's a damn old cop! If he was driving a Jag and wearing a beret, I'd still know he's a cop just because of the way he looks. What's the deal? Do you know anything about this?"

I told Harris to calm down, there was something I needed to ask him before I answered. I said, "Did you call your dispatcher and get the list of ships that are transiting tonight?"

"I haven't had time. When I figured out this was the third or fourth time I've seen Dick Tracy, I started a game of bumper tag just to make sure. The guy can drive for an old fart, I'll give him that much."

"Did you notify anyone that Dr. Santos, and my son, might be out here somewhere being held aboard a ship?"

"I told you I was. That's the first thing I did. I called Port Authority Security, and I told them to alert Coast Guard and the Hillsborough County Sheriff's Department. There should be an army of people scrambling right now."

"O.K., good. In that case, how far are you from the Sunshine Skyway Bridge? I need your help again. If you're willing. Or is there a better place to stop and pick you up?"

Harris said he was more than willing, and that he liked Blackthorn Park on the south end because of what it meant to him. But the little park on the St. Pete side of the Skyway was closer, so that would be better. Said he'd flash his car lights when he thought he saw me approaching.

I wrestled over the decision if I should tell him now or later about the tramp freighter, *Repatriate*. I finally decided to wait until he was aboard my skiff—but only after I'd asked him how long it took a freighter to steam from the bay into international waters.

I wanted to know because, if notified immediately, I wondered if it was possible for any of the state law enforcement agencies to intercept the Liberian freighter before it reached international waters. If not, they were powerless, because the ship would be out of their jurisdiction, and so the information would do them no good.

Only the U.S. Coast Guard, because of treaties with a variety of countries—usually related to anti-drug-trafficking agreements—has the legal right to stop and detain vessels on the high seas, and also to make arrests. No other law enforcement in the State of Florida does.

There wasn't time to stop them before they made it out of territorial waters. Not a chance, by my calculations. And the idea of a Coast Guard helicopter trying to intercept the vessel gave me the chills.

So instead of telling him about my conversation with Elmase, I asked him to call his dispatcher and get information on all ships transiting Tampa Bay that night. *Repatriate*'s data would be included.

I wanted a private, personal shot at the vessel before anyone in law enforcement did something stupid—like tip them off by contacting the *Repatriate*'s skipper by radio and demanding that he turn back to port.

If the ship's captain and crew were being paid by Lourdes, that would only put them on their guard and make it more dangerous for me, my son, and the surgeon—if they were both still alive.

Before hanging up, Harris asked me again, "But what about the old guy? The cop in the unmarked car. What should I do about him?"

I told my friend that once he got to our rendezvous point, pull over, stop, and introduce himself to Detective Merlin Starkey, who was probably now attached to the Florida Department of Law Enforcement.

"Let him know about Dr. Santos and my son. Tell him he's probably the first cop to know, and ask him to help. As a personal favor to me."

Harris said, "The way you're talking, it's like you're old friends or something."

I said, "He and my late uncle, they knew each other. But they weren't exactly friends."

I put the phone in my pocket, jumped the skiff onto plane, and concentrated on getting to the Sunshine Skyway as fast as I could. Because it was night, and because I didn't know the water, that didn't mean going as fast as my boat could go, unfortunately.

Not in the winding creek anyway.

I made myself take it easy. Run it safe.

There was a time when I seldom used the running lights required by law when boating at night. On a small boat, "running lights" consist of a red port light and green starboard light on the front of the vessel, and a white light on the back. All of the lights are bright enough to be seen one to two miles away.

On my Maverick, the bow lights are positioned so as not to be bothersome, but a white stern light can't help but impair night vision slightly. Which is why I once often made a practice of operating my vessels (illegally) blacked out.

Not anymore, and not on this night. There are nearly a million boats registered in Florida. It's starting to get busy, even after sunset. From what I witness daily around the marina, maybe a third of all boaters are competent during daylight, and the rest are a menace to themselves and everyone else day or night.

Which is why I now almost always use running lights. No telling what brand of idiot is out there, flying through the darkness.

So I had my lights on, running the serpentine river course as fast, but as safely, as I could. As my skiff's stern pivoted, the moon swung behind me as if on a pendulum with a kind of easy, skiing rhythm, and so my wake seemed to partition away as ridges of ice might, in rolling, congealed waves of silver.

I had a spotlight out, too—2 million candlepower handheld with a pistol grip switch, the unit plugged to the console, and lying on the bow seat, ready when I needed it. Which wasn't often. But when I did pick it up and touch the trigger, the little river seemed at once to explode with light but squeeze in closer, ablaze in a column of yellow—mangroves, roosting birds, oyster bars, and raccoons all frozen in the harsh beam.

At the mouth of the creek, I came around the final bend, and the horizon changed as if a curtain had dropped; changed from a black tree-wall to open sky, stars above, navigation markers flashing miles away, lights blinking as random as fireflies, and the night skylines of St. Pete and Tampa dimmed the moonlit clouds beyond.

The narrow creek seemed to hold less oxygen then the vast bay, and air came into my lungs easier. It seemed cooler, too, as I powered out onto the dark water, toward the four-second flashers that line the main channel.

When I was safely away from the creek's shoals, I increased my speed to a little over forty, banking southwest toward the high, carnival-bright lights of the Skyway Bridge. As I did, the phone in my pocket began to vibrate. I'd never owned one before, and now I was suddenly besieged by calls.

I took it out of my pocket, checked, and saw that the caller I.D. was blocked.

Dewey?

I couldn't seem to press the Talk button and answer fast enough.

I DIDN'T reduce speed; was still flying across Tampa Bay at 45 mph or so. Even so, because I was wearing the little headphone, I heard Dewey's voice just fine when she said, "Am I catching you at a bad time? I guess you were too busy to talk before."

I said, "Dew, are you O.K.? Is everything all right?"

"I'm doing better and better since I dumped a certain nerdy biologist. Why the hell did you hang up on me earlier?"

Had I? I thought I'd waited until it quit ringing, and then switched it off.

I said, "Sweetie, there's no person in the world I'd rather talk to. I can't wait to see you, and be together again. But there's a lot happening right now. *Listen*—I think I know where my son is. I'm in my boat. I'm in Tampa Bay. I'm going after him right now."

I explained the situation as briefly as I could, then listened to her say in a different tone, very concerned and serious now, "Oh my God, Doc, please be careful. Bring him home safe. And call me the instant you can, because I'm not going to sleep a wink tonight until I hear from you."

It was awkward having to remind her: "I don't have your number, Dew. You always block it. You don't want me to know where you are, remember?"

I felt a delicious surge of relief when she replied, "Hang up right now. I'll call back with the block off, then you can save my number. That way, you'll have it in your phone. Don't answer—concentrate on what you're doing. And stay safe, you big moron!"

I stared at the phone when the I.D. plate began to flash.

Where was area code 563?

THIRTY
THREE

AFTER what seemed like an eternity spent pacing, her mind checking and rechecking the information she had, Dr. Santos felt the boat slow, then something loud bang against the steel hull. After just a couple of minutes, though, the banging stopped, and the ship gained speed again.

That was around 10:30 P.M.

About an hour later, maybe 11:20, she heard slow, heavy footsteps outside, and the metal door clanked again, then swung open.

The surgeon expected to see the terrifying fat woman. Instead, it was the man who'd abducted her, face still wrapped in bandages.

From inside holes in the bandage, his, wild, wide eyes stared out at her. He seemed to be grinning, too. Showing big, bony teeth as he shook a bottle of capsules, and said, "Guess who just got his drugs delivered? So, if I start taking this anticonvulsion stuff, how long before my trig-eee-minal neur-al-gia says bye-bye?"

The woman was terrified, but she forced herself to sound calm; take her time, as if in control. "It depends on your own body chemistry, to a degree. It could be a day or a few days. It could be a couple of weeks. Do you want to discuss your dosage?"

She was thinking: *If I can make him dependent on me in some small way, he won't be able to rationalize hurting me.*

The man was wearing baggy pants and a nylon-looking Hawaiian shirt.

She watched him slide the medicine bottle into his pocket. Now he had his hands at his face, unwrapping the bandage as he walked toward her.

He looked even more gigantic than she remembered.

"No, Dr. Valerie, we can talk about pills later. Once you get done, I might not even need the fuckin' stuff."

She said, "You mean . . . because of your face transplant? Is that what you're talking about? I can do that for you. I really can—if you need it. But not here. Not like this. Take me back to my office, and I'll give you my full attention. I'll make you a personal project. You have my word."

Dr. Valerie could see patches of curly blond hair now as he unwrapped the bandage. The top of his head looked like a human skull over which melted wax had been globbed onto bleached skin, and there was dense scar tissue on his forehead.

He replied, almost as if flirting with her, "Come on now, famous lady. Never try to con a con man. We're not gonna talk about pills, and we're sure as hell not returning to the States. I'll send you back, though, all safe and sound. But only if you cooperate."

She could now see scar tissue on a crinkled ear, and then one wide, wild blue eye that, because it was lidless, looked as isolated from the rest of his face as a small blue planet.

She stared as he continued, "Nope. What I *want* you to do, is come see the little operating room I got fixed up. Then get ready to go to work. *Tonight.* Because our donor's about ready. And like you said in your e-mail, human skin goes bad real quick down here in the tropics."

THIRTY
FOUR

IT WAS ten-twenty when Harris swung aboard my skiff and I told him that I knew the name of the freighter we were after—*Repatriate*.

I backed away, turning toward the Gulf of Mexico. As I did, he took a piece of paper from his pocket on which he'd made some notes, and replied, "Good for you. You played it smart, keeping it to yourself for as long as you did. But now we need to get the Coast Guard involved. You've got an edge. If you can make it work, a little edge is all you'll need."

I said, "Fair enough." Then I added, "What happened to Merlin Starkey? Did you talk to him?"

Harris smiled. "Mostly, I just listened. He's a good cop, though. He says he looks forward to talking to you. But, man, he hates your uncle for some reason."

I said, "I'll tell you the story one day. It's kinda funny."

Harris was now holding the paper up to the stern light, reading. "O.K.— only four vessels were scheduled to transit, and I'm pretty sure I remember *Repatriate*'s destination . . ." He paused. "Yeah, here it is. Our dispatcher, Terri, said they're headed home to Bluefields, Nicaragua. That's an easy heading to calculate. They have to stay in international waters off the west of Cuba, the Yucatán Channel. So where's your GPS, and I'll figure out an intercept course."

I told him I didn't have a GPS. Only a compass.

"Suddenly," he said, "I don't think you're quite as smart anymore. So we'll have to guesstimate it. Figure it out in our heads. But we'll find 'em. Let me have the wheel—there are some tricky shoals in here. That'll gain us some time while we talk it out."

Then he said, "What about a VHF radio? Or is that too modern for you, too?"

"A radio, I've got."

"Good. Do you want to call the Coast Guard? Or should I?"

I STOOD beside Harris as he shot us expertly through channels and beneath bridges, past Pine Key, Passe-a-Grille Beach, and Mullet Key, into a black-domed star basin that was the open Gulf of Mexico.

Beneath us, the flat water of the bay began to undulate in long, slow swells as if something huge lay below, breathing. Harris found the rhythm of the swells quickly and ran at maximum speed.

I'd told him I'd crossed *Repatriate*'s stern at around 7:15 P.M. near the channel's intersection off Gibsonton. He broke the probabilities down for me. Told me how the process worked. He said an average freighter takes about two and a half hours to travel from the Gibsonton docks to the Skyway Bridge—with a Tampa pilot always in charge of the helm, of course.

He said, "Where you saw them, they were only forty minutes or so away. That would put them beneath the bridge around eight P.M. Right at sunset."

I could picture it. Ironically—or maybe not—Prax Lourdes had probably watched *Repatriate* steam past. Because I was certain that's how he had to work it. He'd been right there on the water in a smaller, faster boat, barking orders to Kong on the cell phone, working his extortion scheme, arranging the money drop. Probably chose that spot because he could visually confirm that his freighter was outward bound.

Once he had the money and drugs, he would then run offshore, meet the freighter, and board her.

But he couldn't do that until the American pilot had left the vessel. Harris said that on a standard freighter run, a pilot disembarked a foreign vessel approximately an hour or so after passing beneath the Skyway—probably around nine P.M. in this case.

"Our pilots disembark just past Palantine Shoals at sea buoys number nine and ten," he said. "That's six miles offshore."

Standard procedure, he explained, was for a freighter or tanker to slow to about ten knots as the pilot organization's 60-foot aluminum Brocraft transport, *Tampa*, approached from astern. With neither vessel stopping, the pilot then climbed down the outside hull of the freighter via a rope ladder like the one I'd seen hanging off *Repatriate*. Once aboard the transport vessel, *Tampa*, he'd be taken to the pilot quarters on Egmont Key, where there was plenty of hot coffee, food, plus a shower and his bunk waiting.

Harris pointed out that, because the transfer area is six miles offshore, there's only another six miles to go to international waters. Most freighters run at between twelve and fifteen knots. So add another half-hour, he said. Total time to exit U.S. boundaries: four hours. Plus, add another fifteen to thirty minutes for Lourdes and the freighter to rendezvous, and for him to board.

By our calculations, *Repatriate* may have crossed into international waters at around ten P.M.

"We're headed to the six-mile rendezvous point now," Harris told me. "The sea buoys. Who knows? Maybe they got delayed. Maybe the perpetrator—Lourdes is his name?—maybe he had trouble finding the freighter. It's a big ocean out here. Even if everything went perfectly for the asshole, we're not far behind, Doc. We'll find 'em."

I said, "What do you think the chances are that they left the pilot ladder hanging?"

Mentally, I was already considering options, moving through the freighter, imagining what it would be like, seeing the ship's layout, searching for my son.

Harris said, "Lourdes had to get aboard somehow, didn't he? If the ladder's not there, we can throw your anchor over her stern like a grappling hook, and you can climb aboard that way. But, Doc?" He said it like a question, then waited, wanting my full attention.

I could see only half of his face in the moonlight. His hair was combed back by the wind. "Yeah?"

"You're going to be dealing with a guy who just picked up a half-million in cash, and a shit-hole crew who'd cut a man's throat for a hundred bucks. We pilots *know* that vessel, and it's about as nasty as they come. Same with her female skipper. She's about the size of a middle guard, and she'd probably enjoy cutting you herself. You need to watch your six."

Watch your six: Watch your tail.

I said, "Did you say you were carrying a weapon?"

"I've got a Glock nine millimeter,"he said. "But I won't be carrying it once I give it to you."

WE LEFT the marker buoys 9 and 10 flashing astern, and continued planing hard west, straight out to sea, where stars seemed to be rising slowly out of the horizon as we left the mainland behind.

We saw the lights of several commercial vessels. Had I been alone, I would have had to I.D. them visually, one by one. But not with Harris aboard. He knew the designs too well, even by silhouette. There was a late moon burning.

Finally, at a little less than twenty miles offshore, we spotted three separate ships, all steaming in a direction that looked to be southwest, but separated by miles. They weren't running together.

Looking at them, Harris said, "The one most outward bound is a container ship—probably one of Evergreen's vessels. The next is a tanker, the kind that carries liquids. The closest one, though, that's a fertilizer freighter. That could be our boat."

I had the Glock in my hands, trying to familiarize myself with the minor differences between it and my old Sig Sauer.

I said, "Run me up close. If it's the one we're looking for, dump me. Then drop way back—way the hell out of small arms range. I'll use a light to signal you when I get things secured. Or I'll just turn the boat around."

He was looking at his Rolex: 11:35 P.M.

"You'd better make it fast. Unless I miss my guess, Coast Guard choppers are going to be on station out here fairly soon. They'll be making sweeps; shining big bright lights . . ."

He let the sentence trail off, his mind suddenly on something else, before bellowing, "Holy shittin' hell!"

He turned the wheel of my skiff so sharply, the gun nearly flew out of my hands.

Behind us, rocking in our wake, was the unmistakable profile of a Boston Whaler.

It was abandoned and adrift, its running lights off.

THIRTY
FIVE

HARRIS swept far astern of the freighter, then banked toward it so that we approached directly from behind. Our lights were switched off, and we were flying over low swells glazed in moonlight, running even faster than before.

He'd jotted down some data on all four vessels that were transiting that night, and he'd already told me what he knew about the phosphate freighter. She was many decades old, a Panama Canal–friendly commercial boat built in the yards of Boizenburg, Germany, but had had many owners. She was 375 feet long, with a beam of 50 feet—a small boat by industry standards.

As we neared the freighter, the big white letters on her stern grew larger and larger—*Repatriate*—and I could see her shape clearly.

The forward three-quarters of her deck showed no superstructure, and her lines curved gracefully upward toward the pitched bow. Far toward the back of the ship, though, there was an industrial-looking multistory building—probably five levels, all of them showing lighted windows. It was the ship's "house," in maritime terms.

The house was built so far back that the vessel looked out of balance. Looked as if it might tilt bow-upward and continue under way, headed for the stars. Because of the sweeping bow, with the house built as far aft as it was, it looked a little like the common depiction of an ark.

"Did you see it?" Harris yelled at me when we'd settled in behind the freighter. He had to yell. We were plowing at exactly her slow, diesel speed, directly astern, and only a couple of boat lengths away because we wanted to be hidden in her lee. Our data said that she was driven by a 1,000-horsepower Bergin diesel. The noise of her engine and prop was deafening.

I'd seen it. I knew what he was talking about. As we dolphined in over the ship's wash, I'd seen a ribbon of white hanging from the port side: a pilot's boarding ladder.

I told him, "Jump her wake and run me alongside, Harris. I'm cutting you loose."

I checked my watch: nearly midnight. I checked to make certain that my glasses were tied securely around my neck with fishing line. I checked the weapon's clip once again.

I was ready.

To have Harris at the wheel was such extraordinary good luck that it caused me to think of the tiny blind man at the trailer park who'd said that I had years of good luck ahead of me. But then . . . he'd also said that I might lose a child.

Hanging tight as Harris porpoised over the ship's rolling wash, I reminded myself that I don't believe in luck, good or bad, for the same reason that I don't believe in fortune-tellers.

THE pilot's ladder was portside. It was a heavy, commercial-weight ladder of rope and wood that hung down near the "27" on the ship's draft markings.

Running alongside the freighter in the moonlight, Harris put the bow of my skiff almost against the hull of *Repatriate,* matching her speed, nose right beneath the ladder, before he called to me, "Step up on the casting deck when you're ready!"

I was standing in front of the console, holding on to a mooring line for stability. I continued to hold the line as I reached high, took a ladder rung in my right hand, and then lifted myself free of the deck of the skiff. My feet found the rungs below, and I scampered halfway up the freighter's hull before turning to see Harris peel away in my skiff: dark hull throwing a silver wake.

I was on my own.

On my own—but not for long.

As I pulled myself up over the midship's railing, I could see a lifeboat stowed sideways against the railing, the ship's aft derrick, a trash can, a couple of what looked to be empty 50-gallon drums that weren't secured—odd. Or maybe not. Harris had said this was a dirty ship run by a nasty skipper.

Something else I could see was a tall man hurrying toward me, arms waving up and down for balance, as if he were brachiating, traveling from one invisible limb to another, and he called to me in a heavy Jamaican accent, "What de fuck you doin' climbin' aboard this vessel without my permission, man? I supposed to be in charge a this watch, and nobody done told me nothin'."

He was close enough for me to speak without raising my voice, but I still couldn't see him clearly because of the poor outboard lighting. He looked as if he might have tattoos on his face. Or unusually spaced birthmarks.

I stood there relaxed, my right hand feeling the grip of the Glock that I'd wedged between the small of my back and belt. If the guy gave me a hard time or tried to sound an alarm, I'd either club him with the gun or use it to force him into one of those 50-gallon cans. They'd make a handy makeshift lock-up.

I said, "I *have* permission. I'm with the guy who got aboard just a little while ago. My friend Jimmy. Didn't the captain tell you? She was supposed to."

The Jamaican flapped his hands at me, disgusted. "She don' tell me nothin,' man, that fat woman don't. She don' tell *nobody* nothin'. Never does post a schedule, just the duty list, so everything just random around here, man. Fuckin' random—you never know what she do next, man. This ain't no squared-away vessel, that much I can say for certain!"

In a ballooning gust of warm wind, I caught the heavy scent of marijuana that was on him. I said, "Where can I find Jimmy? Any idea?"

He was already walking away; seemed to be headed for the ship's house. It was brightly lighted, and towered five stories above us.

"Is that the big man that wear the face bandage? I never knowed his name, but I reckon they on D deck. I know they got some business going on, 'cause she tell me to keep that deck secure. Nobody allowed up there."

He waved to me, telling me to follow. "Come on, man. I point you the right way. I ain't standin' out here in the darkness no more. I goin' into the lounge with the resta the crew to spend my time. 'Cause if I ain't in charge of this watch, then *nobody* in charge. So fuck 'em."

I followed the Jamaican up steel steps to the first level, where, through thick storm glass, I could see men inside an open room. They were watching a television screen—a fishing trawler was battling mountainous seas—playing cards and smoking, bottles of beer on the stainless table. The seamen's lounge.

"You go up two more flights, that be D deck," the Jamaican said. "I'd take you myself, but that fat woman, she'll find somethin' new for me to do if she sees me. But if you don' find them, man, you come back, and I'll help."

I said, "I'll do that."

I waited until he'd disappeared into the lounge before sprinting up the stairs.

I entered D deck through a locking, watertight door, and stepped into a dimly lighted hall that smelled of paint and diesel. Almost every room on all commercial vessels is labeled, and I could see that D deck was the ship's specialty area because of the names stenciled on the doors that I passed: ELECTRICAL. AIR CONDITIONING/HEATING. LAUNDRY. STORAGE.

I moved from door to door, putting my ear against the cold metal, listening for voices inside.

Twice I stopped because I thought I'd heard a muted scream. It was a distant, feral sound that I seemed to hear with my spine, not my ears. It had a cat-whining pitch, something you'd expect to hear from the limbs of trees, high above.

I stood motionless, not breathing, my head moving experimentally for the best reception.

Then I heard a third, muted crying scream, and I was running again, gun out now.

THE door was marked INFIRMARY. Someone inside the room was crying, and there was a second person talking, very angry, but keeping the volume down.

I tested the handle to make sure it wasn't locked, then kicked the door wide and stepped into the room, sweeping the Glock at the same pace that I swept the room with my eyes.

I was disgusted by what I saw.

I've been in many infirmaries, aboard many ships, but I'd never seen one equipped like this. There was a surgical microscope on wheels positioned between two stainless-steel operating tables. Both were draped, ready to be used. Above both were also duplicate I.V. tubes, cages to hold bags of whole blood, and all the accompanying pumps, gauges, oxygen cylinders, and theater lights that any serious surgery requires.

But this room was equipped to handle two patients, not one. It was specially laid out to facilitate taking parts off one human being, and sewing them onto another.

Someone had paid to have this tramp freighter outfitted—Lourdes—and for his own sick purpose. Just as bad, in my mind, though, one or more people aboard the freighter had *allowed* him to do it.

I was fairly certain I was looking at one of the people responsible right now.

On the floor was a tiny woman with short black hair that was expensively styled. She was dressed as if ready to head out the door for a jog—shorts, knit shirt, running shoes. Instead, she was balled up in a corner of the room in a fetal position.

It was a defensive posture because a much larger woman was crouched over her, with a right hand drawn back as if to slap. The big woman wore jeans and a grease-stained red T-shirt, and her shoulders looked as wide as mine. In her left hand, I noted, she held a ball-peen hammer. There was no blood that I could see, so she'd only used it to threaten. So far.

Harris had said the master of the *Repatriate* was a nasty one. This woman looked about as nasty as any I'd ever seen.

Pointing the 9 mm Glock at her face, I said, "Hold it right there, skipper. Step up against the wall; drop the hammer. I've just taken control of your ship."

The last thing I expected was for her to scream, "Kiss my ass, you son-of-a-bitch!" and charge me with the hammer.

That's what she did.

I'd never touched or hit a woman in my life in anger, but I hit this one.

I ducked under the hammer's hatchetlike stroke and heard it *whap* against the bulkhead where my head had been. She whirled and tried to nail me a second time, but I caught her wrist just before she connected.

Still screaming at me, her piggish-wide face throbbed a violet red as she tried over and over to knee me in the groin. Sick of it, I held her away momentarily at arm's length, then let her lunge her chin toward me. That's when I hit her with a short left that numbed my elbow, but also dropped her to the deck as if she'd been shot.

The sound of her head hitting the steel floor didn't bother me a bit.

The tiny woman in the jogging shorts was on her feet now, breathing heavily and wiping at her face. Her eyes had a glazed look, as if she might be in shock.

She said, "Are you the police? Thank God you've finally come." Then, staring at the woman who lay groaning on the deck, she added, "She's just *awful*. Maybe the cruelest human being I've ever met in my life. Do you have any idea what she was asking me to do? Awful . . . disgusting things. And she *hit* me!"

The hysteria in her voice was the only clue I needed. I grabbed the lady before she could move toward the fallen woman, and then held her, hugging her as she began to cry, whispering into her left ear, "It's O.K., Dr. Santos. You're going to be all right. I'll get you out of here. But get hold of yourself. I *need* you."

Which seemed to do it. Made her shift emotional gears. People who are used to shouldering huge responsibility are the most likely to come through when the stakes are highest. These stakes were high.

I was almost afraid to ask. "Is there a boy aboard? A boy named Lake?"

She was nodding, but she'd buried her face again in my shoulder.

"Do you know where he is? Did they hurt him? The kidnappers?"

"The last time I saw him, he was in the same room where they locked me. It's the next floor down, and it says 'Visitors Quarters' on the door. He had a small third-degree burn on his arm when I examined him. But it was healing. You must be the police or you wouldn't be asking these questions."

I said, "No, not the police. I'm the boy's father. I've come to get my son."

Through the muscle tissue of my chest and shoulder, I heard her moan softly, "Oh dear God. And it's my fault. All my fault . . ."

I felt a sickening sense of helplessness. Sound communicates tragedy more powerfully than any combination of words. Yet, I continued to press on.

"Is he with the man who abducted you? If he is, I need to get to my son right away. The guy he's with is dangerous as hell. He's insane. I've got to go to him *now*."

Dr. Valerie Santos looked up at me through flooding eyes and whispered, "I can't let you do that. As a physician. Because of what you might find.

"That monster, that terrible monster, he told me he was going to kill your son nearly an hour ago, and he'll be bringing me his . . . bringing a *portion* of your son back here any minute. Even after I told him that nothing in the world could make me do his surgery!"

THIRTY
SIX

POINTING to the groggy woman on the floor, I yelled to Dr. Santos, "Use surgical tape. Tape her arms behind her; after that, her legs. If she fights, use the hammer on her!" Then I sprinted down the hall and out onto the midnight upper decks of the moving freighter.

To the west, the moon was about to set. It was partially submerged on the horizon's seascape and appeared as a golden island, fogged by low clouds. The ship's wake caught shards of the light, so that the ship seemed to excrete a boiling, crimson wedge astern. The wedge rolled away from *Repatriate* in the form of slow, expanding waves, moving across a black sea.

I had the Glock in my right hand, the guard rail in my left, and ran down the steps two at a time. From outside, the lighting appeared better on the lower deck. I assumed C deck would be laid out just like D deck. There would be a hallway with doors, and each door would be identified by a stenciled word or two. I was desperate to find VISITORS QUARTERS, the cabin where the doctor had last seen my son.

Perhaps she was wrong about Lake. She hadn't *personally* seen his body, so she couldn't be certain he was dead. She'd only been told that he was going to be killed. Perhaps the insane man, Praxcedes Lourdes, had lied to her. There was still a chance that I might arrive in time to save Lake. I'd saved other people under tough circumstances, so how could fate not allow me to save my own son?

I told myself that such an unfairness was contrary to . . . *something*. Momentum. Order. Reason, maybe.

I was hurrying. I felt rushed and clouded by panic. I certainly was. Because I was running far too fast as I approached the watertight entrance into the ship's house on C deck, and so was unprepared and vulnerable when the heavy steel door came flying open just as I tried to use it to stop my momentum.

I was lucky the impact didn't knock me unconscious. As it was, it sent the Glock flying, jammed both my wrists, and knocked a gash in my forehead. I felt and heard a couple of joints or small bones pop in my right hand.

Broken.

The collision had knocked me to the deck, so I was looking up into the house's bright lights when a huge man stepped out, paused, and then stepped over me. He looked to be wearing surgical scrubs that were wet in places, stained with some liquid—*blood?*—and he was carrying something by a handle. I realized it was a medium-sized Igloo cooler. The circular kind with a screw-on lid.

The big man said, "Watch where you're goin', you fuckin' asswipe. Fuckin' drunk merchant sailors are a pain in the ass." Then he pivoted, as if to proceed on his way.

Hearing the voice, I knew.

It was my son's abductor.

He wasn't wearing a mask.

THE moment Lourdes started to leave, I was on my feet, straightening my glasses. I lunged three long steps and grabbed him from behind. Grabbed him so violently that it nearly ripped the scrub shirt off him, and he dropped the cooler, which went banging down four or five steps to the next platform, slowed, then bounced down another flight.

He came whirling around in a rage, screaming, "Hands off, motherfucker!" and took a big, pawing swing at me that I caught with my forearms. "What is your problem, *asshole?*"

I ducked in close as he threw a couple more punches that missed, but he was so freakishly strong that they jarred me to the core. The shock of the punches made me unprepared for the bear hug that came next.

He was grunting, trying to squeeze the air out of my lungs, trying to crush my ribs, cursing into my ear with his sour breath, a terrible ether-stink about him, and I could feel vertebrae pop up my spine, and then maybe a rib or two.

I got my right hand free. It was already beginning to swell; had to be some broken bones in there. But it didn't matter. Not now.

As he continued to squeeze, I felt a racing, chemical chill move through me that I have come to recognize. It is the sensation that accompanies pure rage. Rage feels no pain, so I could feel no pain.

In the human brain is a tiny region called the "amygdala," a section of cerebral matter so ancient that scientists refer to it as our "lizard brain," or "reptilian core." It's here, in this ancient, isolated cellular place, that the killer that is in us all resides. It is from here that a million years of genetic memory encodes us with a horror of spiders, snakes, and tight, black places that might rob the air from our land-breathing lungs.

Rage resides in that dark area, as well.

Its presence is signaled in me by the physical chill, followed by a surf-like roaring in my ears . . . and then there is the illusion of a blooming redness behind my eyes that colors the world.

I rarely allow my rage to take control.

I did now.

THIRTY
SEVEN
────────────

WITH my free right hand, I grabbed him by the throat and dug my fingers into his carotid artery until he was woozy enough for me to pull my left hand free. Then, still holding Lourdes by the throat, I hit him across the bridge of the nose three times, as hard as I could, with the heel of my left hand.

The lighting here wasn't good, but I could see him clearly enough to know that his face wasn't as bad as the scorched teen I'd seen in the medical photographs. Lourdes had had a bunch of plastic surgery since then.

He would need another after what I did to his nose.

He screamed and dropped me, then bowed to put his face into his hands, yelling, "Don't hit me in the face!"

I grabbed him by his ripped shirt, turned him, then slammed him against the ship's house. I ducked through his arms, hit him with an undercut right, then held him up against the wall by the throat. "Where's my son? What have you done to Lake? Take me to him now!"

"No fucking way, asswipe! You'll hit me in the face again!"

"Tell me!"

"No."

His nose was bleeding. He was trying to use his hands to cover his face, but I could see in his eyes that he suddenly realized who I was. I was the biologist; the stubborn man on the phone. I was the father of the child he'd abducted.

His pale, lidless eyeball seemed to grow wider.

I yelled, "You don't want me to hit you? Then you better talk. Now! Because I'm going to *keep* hitting you until you take me to my son."

I did; hit him beneath the eye with my broken right hand, and I didn't feel it, so I hit him again.

He bowed his face into his hands once more, then shoved me away and sprinted down the stairs. For a man his size, he was an astonishing athlete. He'd apparently inherited the genes of his wrestler mother, the woman who could beat up men.

Even so, on the main deck I caught him from behind. I dragged him to a stop, then spun him against the ship's railing, yelling, "Tell me, damn it! What have you done to my boy?"

"Fuck you! Stop following me, asswipe! You're aboard *my* ship!"

This time, when I hit him, Lourdes went down in a heap, mouth wide, head bouncing on the deck, his lidless blue eye fluttering.

Unconscious.

WE WERE near the fantail, where I'd boarded. I left him lying, hurried across the deck, and grabbed one of the empty 50-gallon drums. Hurried because I could see a helicopter working far inland. It was umbilicaled to the night sea by the beam of a searchlight.

The Coast Guard would be here soon.

I laid the drum on its side at Lourdes' feet, using the guard rail as a stopper. Then I pushed and pulled until I had enough of his body inside the barrel to tip it upright again.

Breathing heavily, but not feeling the least bit spent, I hurried across the deck once more and returned with the drum's steel lid. Oddly, there were holes punched into the lid.

Breathing holes?

Perhaps.

It didn't matter. He wouldn't be able to benefit from the holes for long.

I shoved Lourdes fully into the barrel and started to seal the lid, but then stopped for a moment.

Because I had the drum braced beneath the outboard lights, I could see his face clearly for the first time. It was a mess. It was worse than I'd thought.

Along with the remaining burn scars, his face was a patchwork of skin colors and stitch scars. A patchwork doll—that's what he reminded me of. The man's cheeks, jaw, and lips were made up of strips of skin—rectangles and squares—all seemingly sewn together, but probably on different occasions, one small piece at a time. The skin color varied from place to place. There was brown skin, white skin, black skin, and a piece or two that had a jaundiced shade.

Did each piece represent a person that he'd murdered?

His nose had been hideous even before I smashed it. It was a discolored black flap, as if his body had rejected the thing. Now the cartilage that supported the dark skin was slowly peeling off his face.

I didn't feel sorry for him. Not a bit. He'd done damage to someone I loved. How much damage, I didn't yet know. I was still furious, and panicked, and it horrified me to think what I might find in that Igloo cooler.

I shoved his head down and banged the lid on tight. Then I dumped it on its side again, and was rolling it toward the ship's accommodation ladder, where I planned to depth-charge the monster known throughout Masagua as the Man-Burner into the open Gulf of Mexico.

He'd have been headed for the bottom within less than a minute, if I hadn't heard a voice behind me say, "Doc? Hey, Doc! What do you think you're *doing*?"

I stopped and looked around slowly, terrified that I was imagining the voice, and his words.

But no, there he was, dressed in shorts and a blue chambray shirt very similar to the one I was wearing—both of us stained with blood, it appeared.

It was Lake. It was my son.

THIRTY
EIGHT

─────────────

I RAN to him, tried to scoop him up in my arms, but realized he had grown too big for that: a lanky, rangy kid with a big jaw, big hands. So I hugged him to me instead, so weak in the knees that I felt my legs might buckle.

He stood very stiff, as if embarrassed, kept saying patiently, "O.K., Doc. That's enough, Doc. It's good to see you, too."

Then: "What in the hell took you so long? I sent you every damn hint I could think up, and you still took forever. You should have asked Tomlinson if you needed help figuring it out."

He wasn't smiling, but I found that funny and began to laugh, and he chuckled for a moment, too.

But then, looking at the 50-gallon drum, he grew serious. "Praxcedes is in there, isn't he?"

"That's right."

"What're you going to do with him?"

I could see now that there was a large, skin-colored bandage on my son's neck and another on his arm where Dr. Santos said he'd been burned.

I said, "I'm not sure," which was a lie.

I knew precisely what I was going to do—but I had to act quickly. A couple of miles away, I could see the helicopter's running lights now, broad white beam still scanning. It was getting closer.

I said, "It might depend on what the guy did to you. You can tell me. It's O.K. There's nothing you can't tell me."

My son shrugged, started to speak, but paused to listen to a banging that was now coming from inside the drum. Then a muffled howling, too.

As the pounding continued, he said, "The night he snatched me, he did this." Lake lifted his arm briefly, as if it were an exhibit. "But it's not bad. That's the only time he hurt me. Until tonight. Tonight, he knocked me out with ether. It made me puke. I guess he planned to kill me, but . . . I don't know what happened. I woke up, and had this—" He touched his neck. "It's a little cut about an inch long. I guess he started, but then stopped. There was blood on me, but he'd already stuck on the bandage. Or someone did."

He added, "I met a doctor he snatched, too. She's a nice lady, but really scared. So maybe she's the one who took care of me."

No—it couldn't have been Dr. Santos. She didn't know that Lake was still alive.

For some reason, the monster had spared my son.

It didn't matter. Not to me, it didn't. I was still going to take my revenge. The Gulf of Mexico awaited. But I had to get it done very soon. The Coast Guard helicopter had banked sharply, was now beginning to vector toward the lights of the freighter.

I said, "In that case, unless he gives me some trouble, I'll wait here with him until law enforcement shows up. You and I can talk later. But remember the lady doctor you mentioned? I'm worried about her. Would you mind running up to the fourth deck and checking on her? Maybe bring her down here to the main deck. So we're all together. With some luck, you'll be flying back to the mainland soon."

The boy didn't budge. He stood there staring at me, then began to shake his head. "You're lying, Doc. I know exactly what you're going to do the minute I'm gone. I've done a ton of research on you. It took me more than a year, but I found out *who* you are. What you did . . . and what you do. You're not going to do it again. Not with me here. I'm not going to let you kill him."

I was stunned. Was it possible? I said, *"You're* the one who found my files?"

"Yeah, me. And it wasn't easy. It took me fourteen or fifteen solid months to dig up the photos and piece it all together."

"Then showed it to your mother." I said this with unintended bitterness.

"No. I would never have done that. Not to either one of you. She . . . snoops through my things. It's the sort of thing she does. She has . . . some chemical problems. But I'm the one who found out that you assassinated my great-uncle, Don Blas Diego. You murdered him. Him and at least two other men who were fighting for my country. Our revolution."

Lake was walking toward me now as he talked. I realized, for the first time, that he'd found Harris Lilly's Glock 9 mm; that he was holding it near his leg so it wasn't easily seen. That's why he'd seemed so stiff when I hugged him.

Why would he feel it was necessary to hide a gun from me?

I said, "It's not murder if it's sanctioned. It's a *process.* You're studying biology, so you should understand the difference. Diego was a ruthless little psycho. That's the truth. We can talk about it. But later, not now."

Soon, I'd be able to hear the helicopter.

Lake said, *"Your* truth," as he continued to approach me. His attitude, his tone, the way he now carried himself, suddenly all seemed confrontational.

I said, "Lake? Why are you carrying that gun?"

I'd begun backing away, trying to maintain some space between us.

He seemed not to hear . . . or he chose to ignore me, because he said, "Praxcedes Lourdes was fighting for the Revolution, too. The man you have sealed in that can. He's crazy. He's a monster. But he was still part of the cause. *That's* why you want me to check on the doctor. It'll give you time to kill him. Because that's what you do, isn't it, Doc? Kill?"

Still backing, I said, "Do you have any idea how many people he's murdered? Look at his face—you'll see his trophies. He abducted you, for God's sake. My *son.* How do you expect me to react?"

His voice growing louder, Lake said, "But he's *insane.* His head was crushed in when he was a kid. He's sick. There's a medication out now that might change his entire behavior. Even if it doesn't, who are you to judge?"

I replied, "Someone *has* to," then watched, immobile, as my son began to lift the Glock toward my chest. He was letting me see it now, no longer hiding his intent.

"Nope. I'm not going to let you murder him, Doc. I can't. Your days of interfering with our country's politics are done. Same with the assassination bullshit. It's not *necessary.*"

My breath coming in shallow gulps, I held my hands up, palms out, wanting him to stop before I was forced to react—there was no way I could bring myself to hurt him.

But I had to act . . . had to do something. Still backing away, I asked him again: "Laken? What are you doing with that gun?"

I'd decided to dive toward him, to roll-block his legs from beneath him . . . when he suddenly flipped the pistol around in his hand.

The abrupt movement caused me to jump. I stiffened, expecting to hear a round explode.

Instead, he caught the handgun by the barrel, then held it out to me butt-first.

"I found this on the deck up there"—he glanced toward the ship's house—"when I first saw you knock Prax unconscious. I took the bullets out because I don't want you to use it. I don't want you to do that . . . *stuff* anymore. He's sick, Dad. People get sick and do crazy, terrible things. So let him out of the barrel, O.K.?"

Slowly, I reached and took the Glock from his hand, thinking that if it didn't belong to someone else, I'd have thrown it into the sea. Lake was facing me, standing close enough to put his hand on my shoulder, and he gave me a little shake.

"Hey—are you O.K.? You look all pale. Are you hurt? Your head's bleeding."

I leaned my weight against him, feeling weak-kneed again. "I'm fine. Just tired."

"Do you promise me that you're not going to kill the guy?"

I remembered saying to Tomlinson something about pathology; that when illness is involved, a person's behavior can't be judged as either moral or immoral.

Did I really believe that?

Sometimes. Maybe.

"*Promise* me, Dad?"

The pounding and howling from inside the drum were louder now, as I replied, "You know what, Lake? You're right. I promise. But . . . do you mind if we leave him locked in there? I really don't want to have to deal with the big bastard again."

My son looked at me, and then he grinned. "Sure. The guy did the same thing to me last night, you know—stuck me in one of those cans." He shook his head. "He really is an asshole."

The noise of the helicopter began to vibrate through the hull of the ship.

EPILOGUE

ON AN afternoon of dazzling, corn-belt blue in early June, my commercial flight touched down at Quad City International Airport, and I drove my rental car over a bridge that spanned the Mississippi River and carried me into the green, green land of area code 563.

I didn't realize how wide that ancient river is. I looked at it and thought of Mark Twain. I thought of paddle-wheelers and lazy summer afternoons, and of Huck Finn. The river did not, however, catalyze any association with the leggy, sailor-tongued, former international tennis star, Dewey Nye.

But she was here. She was living somewhere nearby.

I would have no trouble finding her, because the lady had kindly provided directions.

Even so, I missed a turn and ended up atop a city hill, parked outside a beautiful old brownstone behemoth, with a sign that said it was Central High School, home of the Blue Devils.

I wondered what experience the people here had with devils, blue or otherwise, in a city as pretty and peaceful as Davenport, Iowa.

As I thought about it, the face of Praxcedes Lourdes slipped into my mind and held me captive for a moment. The night that the Coast Guard boarded *Repatriate* and put the cuffs on him, Praxcedes and I had a brief visual exchange. Not a word was spoken, but the messages were unmistakable.

He glared at me with his wild, pale eyes, then looked to my son, who was standing nearby. He smiled—a leer—and nodded before looking into my eyes again.

The next time, I'll kill him!

That's what he was telling me.

My gaze unwavering, I stared back. As I did, I used a vague index finger to point to him, then at the 50-gallon drum that seemed to still echo with his screams. For emphasis, I patted at my heart.

Touch him, I'll bury you alive. Promise.

THE ROAD west followed the river toward Muscatine. It took me through Rockingham, Walnut Grove, and Montpelier, where I slowed and turned right onto Cemetery Road, which was little more than a shaded country lane. Then I took a left onto Wheelands, where corn grew on both sides of the road, so it was a little like driving through a tunnel. I had the windows down, and the car was flooded with the sweet, earthen smell of corn silk and clover.

I'd known that Dewey's maternal family had Midwestern roots. I didn't know that her great-grandmother had died recently and left her what remained of the family farm. It was to the farm that the lady had retreated to get perspective on her personal world; a world that seemed to be unraveling.

As one of the principal causes for the turmoil, I was eager to make amends.

After another mile or so, I found a road marked "Wagon Trail," and then the red mailbox she'd described. Her property was at the end of a long lane, in a valley of hardwoods and clover. There was a white clapboard house that looked a hundred years old, a broken-down barn, and several unpainted outbuildings that looked older.

I've noticed before that when I see old friends in new or unexpected surroundings, it takes the brain a microsecond to convert then reassemble their facial features from those of a stranger back into the face of the person I know so well. It is in that brief space of time that we see our friends as they really appear, unfiltered by personality quirks or our fondness for them.

As I parked, the door to the back porch swung open, and I saw a lanky, prairie-plain woman come striding out, jeans loose on her hips, plaid shirt bust-heavy, with sleeves rolled to the elbows. Her blond hair was cut boyishly short. She moved as if she were in a hurry to get chores done.

Dewey?

Yes. The short hair had thrown me. Then . . . there she was walking toward me, my old friend, my workout partner and love—the woman jock with the California beach girl face, the smile, the satirical eyes.

"Long time no see, sailor. Welcome to fly-over country."

By "fly-over," I took her to mean that part of the U.S. that most only see from a plane.

I said, "They don't know what they're missing. Now that you're here, anyway."

I was nervous, had a case of dry-mouth, but felt instantly better when she allowed me to hug her close, and then to kiss her lightly on the lips.

I said, "You smell great. I missed you."

"I missed you, too, Doc. And I'm so happy about your son."

"He's an amazing kid. You'll meet him. Soon."

She scared me a little when she replied, "I'd like that. No matter what happens between you and me. I'd like to meet your son."

On the phone, she had refused to tell me if she was pregnant. She said she didn't want it to influence discussions about our relationship. But just the possibility of being parents together had a huge effect on me. I wanted to *know.* So now I slid my hand to her flat belly, a brief touch . . . and felt her draw away.

"Put your bag in the guest bedroom. We have a lot to talk about."

I said, "Yeah, we do."

I SPENT two weeks with her there. Her family had leased out the tillable land, so it wasn't a working farm. But there was still a hell of a lot of work to do. I learned that it's always that way around a farm.

"Kinda like boats," I told her one night. "There's always something that needs fixing."

We were sitting outside on the porch swing, watching lightning bugs drift like time-lapse stars among the corn and black trees. Their cold strobing reminded me of navigational markers on Tampa Bay, and I felt a brief pang of homesickness.

When had I ever spent so much time away from saltwater?

That's what we did at night. Talk. We'd sit on the porch and talk. We'd go for long walks and talk. We'd drive into Davenport, have dinner at one of the great restaurants, then walk along the levee and talk.

The words she'd overheard me speak to Pilar had wounded her deeply, and so they had damaged us. Talking was part of what I hoped was a gentle reconstruction phase.

I told her just enough about my battle with Praxcedes Lourdes to explain the fresh scar on my forehead. Also told her about Tomlinson and me accompanying Laken back to Masagua, where the boy's mother was granting interviews and sharing the truth about Jorge Balserio's involvement with the kidnapping of her son.

"His political career is ruined," Pilar told me.

It was one of the few times that we spoke. When I gave her the nearly $200,000 I'd recovered from the ship, all she said was "Thanks." Which was fine with me. I was no longer even tempted to ask her about the e-mails I'd found, or about Tinman. She seemed equally uninterested in me. The woman no longer existed in my world, so perhaps I no longer existed in hers.

She seemed indifferent when I asked if Tomlinson and I could take Lake on a vacation tour of Central America's rain forests and jungle coastline.

"We deserve to celebrate," my friend said on my behalf.

Which was true. But I also wanted to spend enough time with Lake to be certain that he didn't show any delayed signs of post-traumatic-stress syndrome.

To be rescued does not necessarily mean that a victim is out of harm's way.

We had a great trip. The boy seemed to be recovering just fine. We laughed a lot, the three of us. We took tough hikes together, a couple of long swims in the Pacific, and we fished.

The only time we discussed the kidnapping or my son's abductor was when Lake brought up the subject. One night, as we sat at the campfire awaiting a dinner of snook fillets, freshly gathered clams, plus black beans and rice, he said, "Do you know why I think he didn't go through with it? Why Prax didn't kill me?"

I'd thought about it often, but I said, "No. Why?"

My son said, "At first, I thought it was because of some kind of Stockholm syndrome thing, except in reverse. I'd tried hard to make him see me as a person—just like the advice in that e-mail you sent me. I did things for him. I talked to him like I cared. I could tell I was getting under his skin a little. So in the end, he couldn't do it. Or at least that's what I thought originally."

I said, "But not now?"

He was shaking his head, gazing into the fire. There was no hint of emotion in his voice, only a scholastic curiosity as he said, "No. I think it may have played a small role. Subconsciously, *maybe*. But I think the real reason he didn't . . . didn't go ahead and cut my throat was something else." He looked right at me. "It wasn't *fun*. He started to kill me, but realized he wasn't getting the emotional charge out of it that he usually got."

Quietly, I'd come to the same conclusion.

I listened as Lake said, "The guy *burns* people. That's his pathology. That's his sickness. There was probably some sexual component keyed only by fire. So he had to do it *that* way.

"I think Prax still planned to kill me, but he wanted to enjoy it. He always carried this little blowtorch with him. So he left my room to search for something that would protect my face so it wouldn't be damaged. Then, when he came back, I think he would've waited until I was awake. Then he would've set me on fire. It's the only way he could *enjoy* it."

Tomlinson and I had exchanged glances, both of us thinking, *Smart kid*.

The highlight of our getaway, though, was being "captured" by a little band of guerrilla troops who were under the command of my old friend General Juan Rivera. They took us to his secret mountain baseball diamond, where Tomlinson played centerfield. Lake and I alternated innings catching the bearded, revolutionary pitcher.

When my son and I said goodbye at the Masaguan airport, he'd looked into my eyes and said, "Relax, Dad. You get so damn emotional. We'll be together again in August—when I come to the lab to visit."

IT TOOK took some convincing to get Dewey to agree to allow me to visit her in Iowa, so I spent the last week of May working with scientists from the University of Florida on our tarpon-spawning project.

I also entertained a surprise visitor: Detective Merlin Starkey. One afternoon, he came ambling up the boardwalk, cowboy hat tilted at a jaunty angle, carrying something heavy in a brown paper sack.

Tomlinson happened to be with me. The guides had finally gotten the police boat to stay under, and we were discussing a good time to fish it.

Starkey stopped at the bottom of the steps to my lab, touched the brim of his hat in greeting, and we listened to him say, "When I'm wrong, I admit I'm wrong. And I was wrong about you, Mister Ford. I come to congratulate you on getting your boy back. Plus, I brought you a little make-friends present. You don't seem to be the slimy little snake that Tucker Gatrell was."

I said, "Thanks. In that case, come on aboard," and accepted the sack when he handed it to me.

The "present" was as unexpected as the ending of the story that I asked him to repeat for Tomlinson's sake: why he still hated my uncle.

This time, the man actually seemed to get a kick out of it himself. He didn't sound so bitter. Maybe it was because of the pleasant coolness that comes to Dinkin's Bay at sunset. Or maybe it was the tall El Dorado rum drink that Tomlinson got down him.

Sitting in one of the deck rockers, Starkey told Tomlinson, "The way it happened was, I was runnin' for sheriff of Collier County, my first election, and ev'body knew I was gonna win. It was all set. Mr. Ford's uncle come to me with a problem—I already had a lot of power, and I was soon gonna have a lot more."

Tucker Gatrell's problem, Starkey told us, was that the drug investigation branch of the county sheriff's department suspected that my uncle had somehow hijacked a stash of marijuana. They also suspected that he had it hidden somewhere on his property. The department was seeking a search warrant.

Tucker told soon-to-be-Sheriff Starkey that he didn't have the marijuana. But he did have a moonshine still that he'd prefer not to disassemble. Could he pull some strings and have the search called off?

Starkey continued, "Tucker was a Freemason. I'm a Freemason. You may have heard of it. If so, you know that's a secret and sacred brotherhood that dates back to the time of the Crusades. He asked for my help using a certain word I won't tell you. Because he used that word, I was immediately obligated. But Tucker Gatrell was just as obligated to tell me the whole godly truth when I said to him, I says, 'Tucker, I don't care if you stole the dang drugs or not. Jus' swear to me it ain't on your property, and I'll see what I can do.'"

Starkey said that Tucker's exact words to him were, "Brother Merlin, I don't got any more of that stolen marijuana hidden on my property than you got hidden away on yours—on my oath. I swear it's true."

The old man stopped rocking in his chair, took a big sip of his rum, and said, "So I talked to the right people and got the search called off to help my brother Freemason. I had the power—I was gonna be sheriff of Collier County for a long, long time. That's what ev'body thought, me included.

"But then one of our helicopters spotted something odd hidden away on the back section of a little hunting camp I owned near Mango, not far from your uncle's ranch."

Two tons of marijuana had been stolen. Approximately a ton of it—or half—was found on Starkey's property.

"Tucker had swore to me that he didn't have any more of that marijuana on his place than I did on mine," Starkey said. "I reckon that was accurate, but it still ain't the way to treat a brother Freemason. That was the end of my run for sheriff."

We talked for a little longer before the old detective gave us a farewell salute and disappeared down the boardwalk into the mangroves. Because he'd asked me to put off looking into the paper sack until he was gone, I did.

Inside, I found my old 9 mm SIG-Sauer, the handgun I'd planted in Balserio's car.

There was also a note:

> *My lawyer has an envelope addressed to you. Inside is the name of the person I think was responsible for the fire that killed your folks. You'll get it when I pass into a better world than this one. Don't ever ask me about it again. You'll understand when the time's right.*

A few hours later, working in the lab, I received another emotional jolt when Tomlinson tuned in an oldies radio station, WAXY 106, and turned the volume up, saying over the music, "Hey, remember the great band I told you about? The band that hired me as a roadie before I lost my memory? America, right? This is one of their best songs."

Then he blasted the volume even louder, and I listened to the rock group who'd inspired Tomlinson sing:

> *. . . Some are quick to take the bait*
> *And catch the perfect prize that waits among the shelves.*
> *But Oz never did give nothing to the Tin Man*
> *That he didn't, didn't already have*
> *And cause never was the reason for the evening*
> *Or the tropic of Sir Galahad*
> *So please believe in me . . .*

Tin Man?

Tin Man!

In reply to my fierce, quizzical expression, Tomlinson shrugged his shoulders, took a long drink from his fifth or sixth rum, Adam's apple bobbing, before he said, "It's always been a race between alcohol and my memory. So far, the alcohol's winning. Thank God."

We listened to America sing, *"No, Oz never did give nothing to the Tin Man . . . that he didn't, didn't already have . . . ,"* before Tomlinson locked his eyes into mine, and then asked softly, "Does it really matter?"

I thought about Lake, replayed the inflection when he called me "Dad," before I replied.

"No. Not between us."

THE next morning, to fullfill his "moral mandate" as a spiritual warrior, Tomlinson wrote a letter confessing that he was responsible for the long-ago bombing of a San Diego naval base. He addressed it to the federal courthouse in Fort Myers and put it inside the mailbox that sits outside the marina office, flag up.

"They'd have treated me like I'm a kook if I went there in person," he said.

I told him, "Yeah, they would. Those samurai robes take some getting used to."

When he was safely away in his dinghy, puttering back to *No Mas* to say goodbye to his beloved boat, I removed the letter from the marina's mailbox and closed the lid, flag down.

I would later touch a match to the letter and use it to light my propane stove before cooking a dinner of bay shrimp steamed in coconut water, lime, and cilantro.

That wasn't the end of it, though—as only I knew. A week earlier, upon my return from Central America, I'd found Hal Harrington waiting on me at my lab—Hal Harrington, head of the organization of which I was a member, and would never be allowed to leave.

I wasn't surprised.

Quid pro quo, he always said. *Quid pro quo.*

But I hadn't been cooperating lately, Hal told me.

"With the exception of the executive action you took against Omar

Mohammed, former head of Abu Nidal, you haven't done anything for us, Doc. I offered you three assignments. You turned them all down."

I remembered Lake telling me that he wanted me to stop the assassination bullshit. That it wasn't *necessary*.

I said, "I keep telling you, Hal. I'm done. No more assignments. Not those kind of assignments, anyway. Not for me."

"Doc, there are certain countries where you've operated that would love to extradite you. After a few months in one of their prisons, you'd be begging for the firing squad."

I said, "Go ahead. I'll risk it."

"Are you absolutely certain?"

"I'm absolutely certain," I told him.

He said, "I expected as much. But I'm afraid it's not that easy. You owe us one more. At least one more. And you know it."

Harrington is not the sort of man who engages in debate. He threw an envelope sealed with wax onto my stainless-steel dissecting table as he said, "Here's the name. Your last assignment—if that's your decision. I have no choice, Doc. If you don't do it—I'll find someone who will."

I waited until Hal left before I opened the envelope and took out the small, familiar duty card.

The name was familiar, too, as familiar as my own. I'd read it on a similar card long, long ago . . .

Later, I thought. I'll deal with this later.

SO I had a lot of things to share with Dewey during our long talks, though, of course, Hal's visit wasn't one of them. My next-to-last night in Iowa, she said she had something to share with me, too.

I'd moved from the guest room into her bedroom, and over the last several days, we'd been sharing a lot more than just words.

She asked me, "Remember the night I came to your house and told you about the little ceremony I wanted to have? With those pregnancy test strips I bought at Bailey's General Store?"

We were in the kitchen, had just finished cleaning up after dinner. I watched her hold up a little box. It was similar to the one I'd found in her bathroom on Captiva.

I said, "Oh yeah. I remember *that* night."

She wagged her finger at me, a fun, familiar look in her eyes telling me to follow her to the bedroom. "Well, it's about time you found out if you're going to be a dad again."

Later, as we made love, windows open, the smell of hardwood, clover, and corn moving through my girl's bedroom, she spoke into my ear, "Are you sure?"

I was thinking of Lake, and Dewey, and of friends who had become more than friends. Key elements came to mind, then key words: family . . . heredity . . . genetics . . . *blood.*

I leaned and kissed her, then kissed her again, feeling her hands on me, searching; felt the imperceptible shifting of her legs as she made a wider space and began to guide me.

"I'm sure," I said.